Mighty Rahiem

A note to the reader.

There comes a time in every author's life when they must chose between editing their work and maintaining their sanity.

I have chosen the former.

Henceforth all errors of spelling, grammar and continuity must be intentional, so as to appease the god of soup and pistachio haircut.

The Old Guard of Zerth

by Mighty Rahiem

ISBN: 978-0-9998398-0-5

Cover and illustrations by Righty Mahiem

Mighty Rahiem

This weird bullshit is dedicated to the aimless cynic.

You aren't alone.

And you suck.

The Old Guard of Zerth

Another note from the Auguh

From the beginning, music has played an integral roll in Zerth's development. For this reason, you will find the names of songs and their respective artists in bold as they appear throughout the story. I would encourage you to indulge in the mood as you read. It's a gimmick admittedly, but not intentionally so. I would argue that none of these stories would exist without them, so how could I leave them out? Soup without crackers? Preposterous. Coffee without cigarettes? Unthinkable. Zerth without music? You get the idea. So, I invite you to throw some soup on, pour yourself a cup and light one up while you take in some truly heady tunes.

Also, please don't sue me.

Mighty Rahiem

I've watched you, dead man.

Bitter and harnessed by burdensome time.

What sense in suffering when the goal proves sour?

What better reprieve than to escape from laborious care?

For care is poison to men without direction, and sour objective
is unmet by those who seek no end.

So, no end will you find, dead man. No bitter fruit and no cold.

For you – Everlight. For you – Forever Morning.

To the travelers far from home, I sing to thee.

This world is yours and here you are free.

-Arguthaerie

The Old Guard of Zerth

THE OLD GUARD OF Zerth

By
Mighty Rahiem

The Old Guard of Zerth

Chapter 1

Gustav D. Gustav

On Earth, Gustav was a chinless Bob Ross with coke-bottle glasses and no lips. On Zerth, he was a sleek, pink skinned giant with impeccable rhythm. Modeling his style after Hair Bear, he wore a loud, pineapple print button-down with the collar popped. He left the top four buttons open to frame a bronzed, sunken chest and necktie that he wore like an ascot. His pants were khaki cut-offs and his boots were snakeskin buckaroos which wobbled freely around knee-high tangerine argyles. Around his waist was a drooping holster and matching fanny pack, stuffed tight with an assortment of vodka shooters, chewing gum and loose bullets. His fingers gripped a HART brand ratchet with 3/8" socket. Walmart import circa 2011, slick with sweat in the rising suns.

Roldolph endured with labored breath, hands above his head, holding the speaker cabinet in place while the Human finished his wrenching. He was great bulge of a Morouni.

The Old Guard of Zerth

If Gustav was double-sized the average Zertian, Roldolph was triple – sideways. Nearly seven feet tall and five feet wide. An absolute unit. He was a Corbinal breed, making him the odd man out in any family photo. The great oaf was a lop-eared, snaggle-toothed behemoth with a wet nose and a bowl haircut. His rippling pec-fat was stuffed into a dingy yellow t-shirt, flooded with sweat. It spilled over a man-sized bandoleer that doubled as a belt. Below that, some smart Tommy Hilfiger cutoffs in beige, then a mass of fur stuffed into a pair of checkered Converse. He didn't lumber as much as he wobbled, but the hairy trunks that were his arms did the job of hoisting speaker cabinets perfectly well – and when he leaned over, his irregular shape made for a functional staircase. At least, that's what Gustav said.

Gustav gave the ratchet one last yank and it slipped from his hand, bouncing across the dobistone rooftop. He tried to follow its trajectory but was blinded by sunlight, stumbling over his toolbox and kicking a pipe clamp over the edge.

"Did we have to put it on the roof?" Roldolph said. His arms were beginning to shake from fatigue.

Gustav blinked the stars from his eyes as the sunlight crept behind the great tarp above. "Hey, I didn't pick the spot, this was your idea. Besides, the sound carries better up here. We can light up the whole town now". He admired the work with his hands on his hips.

"It wasn't my idea to put it on the roof," Roldolph huffed. He had plenty more to say but his energy was spent. "You about done?"

The Human lingered for a moment, turning his back to survey the town below. "Oh, sure. All done."

Roldolph dropped his arms and immediately went for a rag in his back pocket. "Should'a done this one first. Got me all worn out." He dabbed the fur over his forehead and plopped down.

Gustav chuckled, slapping Roldolph on the shoulder. "If we did the roof first, you would have keeled over before I was done with you. Then what would I do?"

Roldolph held his chest. "You Humans and your dying. The rest of us only have one go-around. Keep that in mind the next time you put me to work in the suns."

"Everybody's got a hobby," Gustav winked. He strolled over to the steel post sprouting from the roof where his work now hung. Snug and pristine. He admired the craftsmanship of the cabinet with its chestnut finish, and wondered why he never built one on Earth. It didn't seem worth it. He turned to Roldolph with a silly grin, then flicked the toggle switch. "Let's see what's on the radio."

Beborn Beton – Another World. Right in the middle of the goddamned chorus.

Gustav caught himself reaching for his wrist. It was an instinct meant for privacy. Not that it mattered, Roldolph's head was bobbing. "I guess that's it, then."

Roldolph clearly dug it, as did everyone within earshot. The lack of gunfire was a good indicator that the Human hadn't fucked up. The Morouni wobbled to his feet, stuffing the rag into his back pocket and reaching for his tools. "And now, I believe you owe me lunch," he snickered while consciously sidestepping the rays of sun. They were creeping across the rooftop once more. It was a delicate dance that neither of the men could afford while occupied. Not worth the trouble. On Zerth, the rising of a Sun was like a gust of wind. Too fleeting to predict and too frequent to note.

11

The Old Guard of Zerth

The two let gravity deposit them atop a dumpster behind the diner, then down to the street. One with an awkward leap, followed by an embarrassing courtesy that spilled the contents of his toolbox – and the other with a casual collision only a Corbinal could perform without onlookers calling for aid. After a brief period of self-reflection, they made their way inside for a well-earned meal.

The diner was a crunchy little nub of a hut made for midgets. Half-staffed and lazy, with a dozen patrons not so occupied with the bustle of city life. The smell of too much sugar hung in the air, like a cotton candy machine with stucco walls. Though the blinking sign above the door advertised *Fresh Humen Food from Erth*, Barry Bickel's Whiskey-Waffle Emporium wasn't made for Gustav's size. Upon ducking through the entrance, the ceiling fan assaulted his afro, forcing him to retreat to the nearest available booth. More draped than sitting, he found a good balance and took the snickering of the locals in stride.

Roldolph seemed more attentive to his own giant's plight, skillfully dodging the blades as if it were second nature, though the booth was another story. He twisted into it with great difficulty. Gustav almost expected the man to end up sideways with back-fat momentarily swallowing the table as he corkscrewed his way in. Despite engulfing the seat, the Morouni hunkered down quite adequately in a stuck ball form, then went for a menu.

Off in the corner, embarrassing butt-goth pounded through two speaker cabinets. They were newly installed just an hour earlier. Nobody complained, but Gustav was getting antsy. The waitress hobbled to the table and leaned in. She was plump for her height but did well stuffing herself into the bubblegum pink uniform. A plastic badge with the name *'Ketchup'* was strategically placed to draw the eye to exposed cleavage. Furry cleavage, but cleavage nonetheless. She fluttered a foot-long pair of false eyelashes. "Earth must be a pretty great place, huh boys? Thanks for puttin' up them speakers. Them's some good tunes," She said, sliding a hairy arm across her belly and giving it a good scratch.

Roldolph nodded to Gustav. "Don't thank me, babygirl. He's the man with the plan."

"Oh, I know," Ketchup said, giving Gustav a sensual purr, "he's got prime-rib written all over him." She licked her muzzle with a giggle.

Gustav's face dropped. "Well, you know what? I'd like to order something now. Whiskey Waffles. Whiskey Waffles for both of us. Double whiskey sauce all around." He could swear the girl was inching closer. The smell was just weird and she smiled like a tuna can. He tossed the menu away to punctuate the conversation.

"That's a lotta' whiskey sauce. Yer really rackin' up the bill, aren't ya?" Ketchup said with a flutter.

"It's what I do," Gustav replied, attempting to recline away. His arm invaded the booth behind, dipping generously into another man's cup. He shuffled around, casually awkward.

The waitress leaned in, eye-ball height to the recumbent Human. Her whiskers came dangerously close to invading his space. "Suit yerself, big man," Ketchup winked. She turned to the kitchen and howled, "Garry, two coffee, four stacks of waffles for the big boys. Make it good, one of em's a real Human!" She turned back to Gustav with a proud look on her snoot. "Extra special for Humans. We like ta' make ya feel at home, ya know?"

Gustav answered with a tight smile, attempting to end the conversation at all cost, but Ketchup maintained. He squirmed around, sliding deeper into the booth, finally settling on a position that ruffled his shirt but allowed his elbow to rest on the sill of the open-air window. It didn't work. She was gawking – eyeballing his exposed shoulder and tattooed skin. A purple tongue flicked across a fang.

"Shame on you, Guz," Roldolph said, erupting into a breathy snicker, "teasing the girl like that. Have some self control." He turned to Ketchup. "Go on, babygirl, get us your best. We're hungry."

Ketchup cocked her head with a broad grin. She shuffled off to the kitchen, her bare feet squeaking against the tile. Gustav raised his eyes to Roldolph who was trapped in a private chuckle-fit. He shook his head and joined in the laughter, finding himself agreeing with the tilted sounds of something moody from his speakers. Not his favorite, but he could do worse. "Speakers sound good," he said. "Good tone."

"Damned good tone," Roldolph said. "We did good today. My compliments to the DJ."

Gustav sucked air through his teeth. "Yeah, to the DJ... I wonder who he is. Must be a hell of a guy, you know. Play music for the whole world to hear. Lucky, nobody complains."

"Yeah, I don't know about that. Just wait until the Elders hear it. They'll bust a seam and boil. They'll go butt-hurt and bleed out the ears." Roldolph said with a chortle. "And if they find out who's putting up the speakers? Koplin's justice – they'll pull your eyes out through yer ass."

Gustav laughed, "Something tells me you'd enjoy watching that."

"Maybe I would," Roldolph said. "Rubin Walter, that guys' got the right idea. If yer gonna kick it, might as well make a show of it."

Mighty Rahiem

"Yeah, but what about you," Gustav said, leaning forward. "You aren't the slightest bit worried that somebody's gonna rat you out to the elders for helping me?"

Roldolph lowered his eyes and nodded. "Nah, the old farts don't hang out in this part of town. Too many mutts. Too many Dirgs like me."

"Yeah, I suppose you don't need any more attention than you already get," Gustav said with a smirk. "I know you big types get all sorts of shit from your own kind. I got a buddy like you. Big guy. Marinal breed. He's got all kinds of horror stories."

Roldolph shook his head. "Old habits die hard, as you pinkies say. Sure, guys my size were a burden back in the day, but we got plenty of food now. Plenty of room to grow. You'd think that would change things, but for the Elders, tradition is tradition. Live by it and die by it... preferably just die by it."

The sentiment tickled Gustav's anger-bone. He couldn't help but sympathize as he could tell the big guy had some fire in him. The thought elevated his spirits for a moment, but floated away at the notion that it could end all too easily.

"Anyway," Roldolph said, dropping a brick on the mood, "I've got some business to take care of here. Got somebody to talk to." Gustav was somewhat caught off guard as the great oaf relieved himself of his seat with ease. The Morouni gave a nod and headed up the aisle towards the kitchen, taking care to keep his girth away from dangling obstacles.

For a moment, Gustav had a brush with loneliness, but he quickly found his private demeanor. The solitude gave him a chance to right the wrongs that had been done in the absence of his better judgment. He took the opportunity to enlighten all the goddamned weirdos with some glorious head-rock.

The Old Guard of Zerth

His Talkman was the key. It was Gustav's lifeline, as it was for most everyone on Zerth. It was Both decades ahead and behind his old Samsung Galaxy S4 back on Earth, and only half the size. He didn't mind that he couldn't play games on it. Who needed games? He couldn't store money on his Samsung, nor could he triangulate the position of the nearest satellite. The latter of which was most important to his peace of mind. Despite the electric wonder that was the Talkman, it wasn't built for storage. He kept all that on Earth in the year two-thousand... whatever year it was back there. He couldn't remember.

With an innocent stretch, Gustav slipped his wrist under the table and tapped at the screen of his Talkman. A quick poke – CONNECT TO LOCAL SOURCE – then shuffled through his playlist to find something suitable. It would be an abrupt end to the bullshit he never intended others to hear, and the anticipation of the shift in mood sent a quiver up his spine. Would it be received well? Would somebody die today? Who's to say? **Gonn – Blackout of Gretely.** The speakers above the kitchen let loose with a twang, followed by garbled Human nonsense.

Gustav's heart skipped a beat as heads began to bob throughout the diner. No weapons were drawn. Success. Gustav was in heaven. Something about the intro dug into his mind and he had to stop himself from replaying the song from the beginning. He was warned against doing that.

As far as music was concerned, he had planted his seed in most major hubs of Zerth. From Southtown to Calibur, Ghong to Tarqus and dozens in between. He would even plop his speakers down in the wilderness if he happened across a particularly inspiring vista, but the city of Ortega was untested territory. It was home to a great deal of the older generation of Morouni who weren't accustomed to auricular, harmonic expression, let alone Human auricular expression. If he could dig in here, he could dig in anywhere. The great experiment continued.

Mighty Rahiem

To maintain confidentiality, Gustav played the part of a sort of musical Clark Kent. A simple supplier of speakers and audio cables which allowed the denizens of Zerth to get an earful of the sweet beats of his planet of origin. He was an importer, nothing more – just like every other Human. Nobody had to know it was *his* selection of tunes. In fact, it was crucial that no one found out at all.

It started as an innocent joke. Where is that music coming from? Oh my, how strange. So curious! I wonder who could be making that sound? Nothing more – just a joke. But it didn't take long for Gustav to learn the power his jams had over the virgin eardrums of the average citizen, for it's the same energy that propels a toddler to shake its diaper that can drive a mild-mannered Zertian to hysterics. Not all of them, of course, but it only takes two to start a knife fight. The rest jump in for the fun of it. Violence begets violence, and on Zerth, so does music. The thought terrified him, but also filled him with a sense of power he never had on Earth, and so he kept it hidden from all but those closest to him.

With his chills settling, Gustav sat back to take it in. Outside, the courtyard was busy with foot traffic. Morouni mostly, with a sprinkle of Legomi, and the occasional Human poking above the crowd. He could see the toll booth of the dusty lot where his ride was parked against a shoulder-height red brick wall. Blue skies peered over, with a gust of sand. A group of Legomi sprouts were playing foot-butt in the empty spaces. A roaming vendor with a cart of jingling bells skittered across the cobblestone. The scene was lit in rose shade from the great tarps covering the whole city. They kept the heat of the suns at bay, hanging loosely like slow rolling sails in the wind. They were propped up by great steel masts that sprouted through buildings and alleyways – one of which now claimed by a hand-made speaker cabinet, beating away to the rhythm of his heart.

The Old Guard of Zerth

Ketchup arrived with a rattling cart of plates. She swung it around wildly, parking it at the end of the booth. Her claws scratched against the stoneware as She slid the dishes across the pint-sized table. "Here ya go, sweety-poo," she whistled. "The best of the best. Real Humin food for the real Humin."

Gustav didn't want a slice of home, he wanted bug-juice and xeno-cooch. He wanted something wrong, something unique. It was the absurdity of the dish that attracted him to it in the first place. But what did she know? He couldn't blame her for not being a mind reader. As for the dish itself, it looked somewhat wet, even under all the whiskey sauce. Despite Gustav's better judgment, it felt right to compliment. "Real slice of home. I bet those old folks of yours would blow a gasket if they saw you serving this."

Ketchup groaned and dropped her shoulders. "You wouldn't believe them assholes. Some o' them came in here the other day and started up a hissy-fit. They got all kinds of angry. *The Fist don't like Morouni abandoning their heritage. Thinning the culture,* they says. *Morouni should sell Morouni food. None of that mutt food.* Want's to make an example of the place. Scare em all straight. Bring back the old ways."

"What is Morouni food anyway?" Gustav said, nabbing a toothpick-sized fork from the cart.

"It's like some wooden stuff. I dunno," Ketchup said, making a face. "Fiber bars and stuff like that. It's so boring but those assholes insist we sell it. But, whatever , Human food is *so* much better, don't ya think?"

"Well, whiskey waffles aren't *really* Human food," Gustav said, twirling the fork in his fingers. "I mean, it kind of is. We've got whiskey and we've got waffles, but not usually at the same time."

"Really?" Ketchup said with a frown.

"Yeah, we mostly stick to tiger meat, sometimes with waffles, though."

"What's tiger?"

"It's a huge flying beast with a machine gun for a dick. It pees bullets. We catch em with our bare hands and eat em raw." Gustav said with a nod.

"That is so sexy," Ketchup growled. She leaned in, "I bet it's *so much* better than fiber bars."

"There's no accounting for taste," Gustav said, doing his best to keep the waitress out of his booth. He straightened his shirt and adjusted his tie. Ketchup grinned, beaming at the pink giant before skipping off down the aisle.

Gustav shifted upright to better feed himself but his ankles knocked against Roldolph's bag beneath the table. He casually propped his legs atop the heap and turned to his breakfast; two golden waffles with a sprig of dandelion garnish and a hefty ramekin of whiskey sauce with dribbles down the side. His coffee was equally thick. It steamed with the scent of maple. Maybe he ordered too much sugar. Across the table was a duplicate of his plate. It started to feel weird. He fished the dandelion from the mess and held it up, twisting it in his fingers before flicking it out the window.

The Song ended and Gustav had to catch himself. Dropping his fork into the syrup, he fumbled with his Talkman under the table, keeping his playlist in check. Garage rock with a hint of proto-punk. **The Wimple Winch – Save My Soul.** Too good to skip. He settled down to absorb the sound as a rubber baseline filled his head in tandem with the sweet-acid ping of the lead – then that knuckle-punch snare. He scanned the diner for other kindred spirits as taken in as he was. It never got old.

The Old Guard of Zerth

Roldolph emerged from the back, making his way through the aisle. He paused at the table, not wanting to sit. "Gotta split," he said. "Business ain't goin' so well. Kinda short on cash."

Gustav pulled back. "It's my wallet. Have a seat, grab a bite. You gotta be starving. Gotta fill that gut."

"Nah," Roldolph said, leaning his palms on the table. "Got more stuff to do. Box my stuff up for yourself. You earned it."

Gustav could tell Roldolph's attention was elsewhere. "What, you didn't work up an appetite?"

"It was only three speakers," Roldolph replied with a grin. He snapped his fingers in a gun gesture, then gave the Human a beefy pat on the shoulder. "Next time, buddy. Gimme a call. You'll be around."

Gustav gave his friend a nod and watched the oaf lumber down the aisle, then out the front flap that served as a door. He rubbed the back of his neck and looked around, wondering why he was still there.

Ketchup returned with bill in hand, doing an awkward curtsy as she placed it on the table. "Take yer time, honey. No rush. You can stay as loooong as you like."

Gustav stopped her with a finger. "Naw, that's okay," he said, pulling his credcard from his wallet. He handed it over without checking the charge. "I think I'll just cash out right now. Could I get a box for these? I guess I'm not as hungry as I thought."

"Well yer an indecisive boy, aren't you?" Ketchup squeaked. She slid the plastic card through her Talkman. "You got places to be instead of with me?"

Gustav didn't want to say anything so he let a minor chuckle escape.

Ketchup's eyes darted to the empty seat. "Hey, did your guy leave too? I couldn't help but notice."

"Uh, yeah. I guess so," Gustav said. "He seemed like he was in a hurry. I don't think he paid."

"Son of Captain Andy!" Ketchup groaned. "And you let him? What an asshole. Don't people know I got seventeen kids to feed. That shit come's out of my paycheck, you know."

"Hey, hey," Gustav said, waving his credcard, "I'll take care of it. How much did he owe you?"

Ketchup perked up. "Really?"

"Yeah, of course, I really don't mind. What's the damage? What can I give you?"

"The bill's for a buck-fifty. Same as yours. Can you afford both of em?"

"Yeah, no problem," Gustav smiled.

"Wow, mister. You make a lotta money or somthin'?" Ketchup said, wagging her eyelashes. She drew closer.

"No," Gustav said with his hands. "I just don't like seeing people get put out by jerks."

Ketchup leaned into the booth, taking Gustav's thumb in her paw. "Yer a terrible liar," she winked, then hopped back to the floor, her mustache pulled back to reveal a genuine dog-smile. Lhasa Apso mixed with Pug, maybe. Possibly Pit-bull, Gustav thought. She swiped the card again and went right back to gazing at the Human with loving eyes. Gustav started to panic. "What's that tattoo mean?" She said.

Gustav paused. He looked down to see his shoulder exposed once again. He cursed his fashion sense for keeping so many buttons undone, but decided to give in. He pulled his shirt

21

open to reveal a newly minted tattoo across his shoulder. A circular crosshair with a slash through it. No aim. The universal sign of the wanderer. "It's the mark of the wanderer," he said. "It's kinda personal. It means stuff, and things."

"Is it personal to your buddy, too? I seen it on the back of his shirt. Looks a lot better on you, though. It's super sexy," Ketchup whistled.

Despite the fact that a dog was hitting on him, Gustav's moral was boosted. He couldn't help but bask in the glow of admiration. The feeling died when he caught the girl's eyes drifting towards his holster. He hoped she was starting at his holster.

"Jeez, mister, that's a pretty shiny gun you got. And you say you don't make lots of money."

"I don't," Gustav said with a dumb smile. He left his meal and made a hasty exit.

Gustav ducked through the curtain, entering into the shade of the courtyard. His Talkman blipped, signaling the change in temperature. **98° - Relative Humidity: 0.5% - wind speed: 2mph – travel speed: 3.3mph.** Leaving the diner felt like walking on to a stage. Four suns beat through the roiling tarp, casting awkward shadows. He made his way across the cobblestone to the parking lot where he knocked on the wall of the booth, rousing the attendant from his slumber.

It was a top-heavy Legomi with rough, speckled skin and tired eyes. Probably derived from some kind of onion or leek, as far as Gustav could tell. He had a distinct top-knot of greenery flaring out of his skull which was kept in place with a faded bandanna. The Legomi scrambled awake and wiped his eyes with a leafy forearm. "Hey buddy, what's up? Don't I remember you?"

"Yeah, I'm parked over here," Gustav said. "Yer name is Bingus, right?"

"Hey, that's pretty cool, you remember my name! Yer that guy who gave me money before."

"Yes I did." Gustav smiled, "I paid you to let me park here."

"Yeah..." Bingus said, searching for his bearings. They weren't around.

Gustav turned to the group of sprouts roughhousing in the lot. "Are those your sprouts?"

Bingus squinted a bit. "I dunno," He said, "maybe."

"Well, why don't ya get em something nice. My treat," Gustav said, flicking out his credcard again.

"What's wrong with you?" Bingus scowled. "You just giving away money or something?"

"Yes I am." Gustav replied, with a wide smile.

"Wow, you gonna die soon, or what?"

"Maybe. It's not unusual."

"Dam, that sucks. Well, I guess if ya can't take it with you-"

"That's an obsolete axiom," Gustav interrupted.

"The fuck is an axiom?" Bingus said, scratching the roots on his head.

"Don't worry about it," Gustav said, swiping his card. He transferred a hundred bucks to the Legomi's Talkman.

It chirped and Bingus's eyes popped. He leaped to his feet. "A hundred bucks? Dam dude, I don't have to work for a month now!" He swung open the door of the booth and took off running down the cobblestone, whooping.

The Old Guard of Zerth

Gustav watched the plantman scamper away, then turned to the sprouts who were now mulling around in the dirt, counting their toes. He turned back to the empty booth and thought It would be pretty crappy to leave it that way without telling anyone. The owner wouldn't be too happy if he knew his lot was unattended and people were parking for free. Maybe he would spend the day being a parking lot attendant?

The mood died as the radio switched to something awful. It was like nails on a chalkboard. He dashed into the shade of the booth, then ducked beneath the window. He swiped the screen of his Talkman in a fury, desperate to kill it before the chorus. Success. Checking his flank, Gustav stealthily emerged to the tune of **I'm Not Like Everybody Else, by the Kinks**. No witnesses.

Kicking through the dirt, Gustav circled around the sprouts to the driver's side of the van. He smacked the front quarter-panel and the gull-wing hissed open.

"Hey mister," a sprout spoke up. "Gotta buck we can borrow?"

Gustav paused with one foot in the bus. "Ya see that booth over there?" He said, pointing.

"Yeah," the sprout replied.

"Well, that's a money booth. If you sit in there and someone comes to park, you can swipe their card and you'll get free money.

The sprouts exchanged a look and turned back to Gustav. "Then why don't *you* sit in the money booth and get free money?"

"I already did. I got lots of money now."

"How much money do ya got?" The spout asked.

Mighty Rahiem

"I got all the money in the world," Gustav smiled, then pulled himself into the bus. He watched the sprouts beat the tar out of each other as they raced to the booth. It was always a treat to watch prepubescent plants kick the shit out of each-other. He chuckled while fishing his sun-goggles from his neck, then cupped them around his glasses, yanking the strap tight. He shoved the key in the ignition, and with an electric flutter, the bus lurched off the ground. The fans kicked up a steady cloud of dust as the machine came about in a tight spin.

The bus was a modified Aerian troop transport outfitted with the latest in modular UPP-port technology. With a suggested passenger capacity of 14, the interior boasted leather-fab seating, a vaulted ceiling for comfortable range of motion, and a top of the line Bummhauser 550 climate control suite. Burgundy interior complimented the tobacco-stained air filter in the ceiling, and the rear hatch could be dropped for easy departure. A gun mount was also available under the rear seat cushion. Under every other seat cushion was a refrigerated compartment stocked with all kinds of beer.

The exterior was a hardened plasteel nanofiber weave, adequately bulletproof and painted sandy beige with gloss burgundy accents. The topper was honey yellow with black louvered vents and speakers set within. The repulsors were 'Blinkbottom eights' - an industry standard in flying bus technology, capable of a comfortable cruising altitude of about 8ft at a speed of up to 140mph.

Pulling out of the parking lot, Gustav found himself squared up with the frontage of the diner. Something caught his eye that he hadn't seen on his way in. Across the dobistone wall by the door was some wet blue paint in the shape of a fist. New graffiti. Then came Ketchup through the front flap. She was hauling something heavy behind her. From the looks of it, it weighed more than she did. The girl stood in the doorway and started shouting. "Hey, somebody forgot their-"

The Old Guard of Zerth

The diner erupted in a flash of heat. Shards of glass cut across Gustav's face as the bus spun sideways, rolling from the blaze with a whine of bent turbines and scattered carbon fiber. Gustav was heaved from his seat and tossed aside, then pulled through the window and thrown to the ground as the bus continued to tumble over his legs, grinding him to a paste.

As the smoke cleared, the shock set in. Gustav wheezed. One of his feet was pushed across the charred cobblestone like a soft crayon. Bits thrown here and there with streaks of gore leading to the parts he could no longer feel. His left arm was lose but the right felt stiff. It didn't feel like his arm anymore. It was in the wrong place. His breath stuttered as he craned his neck towards the site of the blast.

Amidst the smoking rubble of Barry Bickle's Whiskey-Waffle Emporium stood a steel post, atop which sat an untarnished speaker cabinet eulogizing the destruction. **Optical Sound, by the Human Expression.** It all seemed too fitting for Gustav. He was often the last man standing at a party and the cabinet did a pretty good job of reflecting his feelings on the matter. He glanced toward the bus which was laying sideways, clear across the courtyard. Still in one piece. Thank god, he thought, Wad would kill him if he wrecked his bus.

Gustav had to focus on his right hand to get it to move. It felt weightless, even difficult to control with how it freely it wagged around. He managed to tap at his Talkman to signal for a wrecking crew. He then reached across his crushed hip for his pistol which he unbuttoned from the holster with a shiver. Smith and Wesson .44 magnum, just like Dirty Harry. With a jerk, he pulled it free let it wave about for a moment before pushing it against his temple. He exhaled, then pulled the trigger and put one in. The music stopped and all went black.

The next thing he saw was his divorce attorney.

"Did you fall asleep?" Devin said with an awful look.

"Yeah, no," Gustav said, standing up. He tried to wave off the shock.

"This is serious, you know."

"Yeah, I... yeah. I think?" Gustav fumbled, "You know, I'm really busy right now. I really need to do something." He stumbled down the hall in search of his office. He couldn't remember where it was.

"Gustav!" Devin yelled, as his client threw himself into a darkened room. Gustav plopped into his swivel chair and wiggled the mouse. The windows background snapped into view and he had to shield his eyes. "Gustav, what are you doing?" Devin said again, as Gustav flipped through his MP3 files, mass deleting the Beatles folders.

"The Goth shit was bad enough, but the Beatles is too much. They already dominated one planet, I can't let them take another. I need something deeper. Deeper with more grit. I need more Lunesta!"

"More Lunesta?" Devin said, "You just took three Lunesta ten minutes ago!"

"Oh really? That's great!" Gustav said, staggering to his feet. "It should kick in any minute then, huh?"

"Gustav, we're trying to have a talk about your situation. You remember? Your wife."

"Wife? What wife... er, yep. yep, we can do that. Let's... let's do that right now. Let's go talk in the living room. I'll just lay down on the couch and you can talk to me about anything you want – but I need salt! Let me get some salt. I always forget the salt."

"Gustav, what in the hell are you talking about?"

27

"Everything is okay," Gustav replied with an ugly smile. "I just need the salt. It'll help with my headache. Trust me."

Gustav ran to the kitchen with his lawyer hot on his heels, babbling about alimony and child support payments. He threw open the spice cabinet, tossing a box of crushed red pepper to the floor, then snatched the container of Morton's Salt. He held it close to his chest. "I think I've got everything I need," Gustav said. "Wait, I almost forgot, Wad wants to see what condoms look like. I need some condoms!" Dashing back through the hall, Gustav emerged from his bedroom with a hand full of flavored Durex condoms.

"What the hell has gotten into you, Gustav?" Devon yelled, but Gustav didn't answer.

"My gun!" Gustav said in a panic, reaching through his bathrobe. "Ahh, there it is!" He pulled the Magnum .44 from the liner. His lawyer shrieked. He popped the cylinder to check his viability. Six shots, all full, all viable. "I'm ready to talk now," He said, slapping the cylinder shut, "lets go sit on the couch and get comfortable."

With his lawyer in a sweat, Gustav got comfy on the couch with his salt, his condoms and his gun – and no more Beatles. All was right with the world as the Lunesta took hold and brought him home.

Chapter 2

Mayors of Southtown

Wadley Saxo stood atop the conference room table surrounded by stabbing glares. His P:9-G4 Plasma pistol was pressed against the Mayor's temple. The Mayor did his best to keep the plastic mustache from falling from his upper lip, further complicating the situation. Wad's Talkman chirped and the room stuttered. He dropped his weapon and flicked his finger across the screen. "Ah, shit," He said. "The Whiskey Waffle Emporium just blew up."

"What!?" Mayor Digby said, dropping his pistol from Mayor Meecrob's forehead. "Are you serious!? Who would do such a thing? What happened?"

"Bombed," Wadley said, "Sounds like another terrorist attack. No more Whiskey Waffles."

The Old Guard of Zerth

The room drooped with a collective whine and all the Mayors dropped their pistols. They shuffled around and found their seats, holstering their weapons and consoling each other. Wad scratched his leafy scalp, trying to make sense of it all.

"Wadley, what actions do you suggest the Mayor's office take regarding this bombing?" Said Mayor Studdwanker.

As an adviser to the Mayor's office, Wadley had a hell of a job determining who he was advising. There were seven acting Mayors at the moment, and over a dozen interim Mayors. That didn't include those like Mayor Meecrob, who had just showed up, declaring the position for himself. Shootouts were common, and it wasn't a big surprise when two or three Mayors were gunned down in the street by others looking to take the position by force. Not that it was any more desirable than another job, but it did come with a top hat, sash and fake mustache that suggested a bit more swank than the standard public service.

"I guess we should see if anyone claimed responsibility," Wadley said. "It could be the Blue Fist again. They've been gaining ground in Ortega so it could be indicative of a larger problem. But who knows, maybe somebody just hates waffles."

"Waffle-bombing is the most despicable act one can commit," Mayor Meecrob spit. "A public condemnation is in order. As Mayor, I pledge to put an end to the practice."

"That's ridiculous," Mayor McBean said, reaching for his pistol. "You aren't campaigning for anything. And besides, everyone knows bombings are detrimental. As Mayor of Southtown, you shouldn't be afraid of taking a strong stance against these kinds of threats. I take a strong stand against these threats, for I am Mayor of Southtown, and the safety of the people is my number one priority."

"As the Mayor of Southtown, I think bombings are pretty cool," Said Mayor Steve. Mayor Steve was 8 years old.

Mighty Rahiem

Wad took a step back to wipe his brow and clear his head. There were too many Mayors and it was clear that most of them were only in it for the sash and top hat. He was starting to regret flyering for the position the year prior. He didn't understand why so many people would seek out such a tough job just to squander it. Wad sighed, "Why can't we be more like the city of Ender? They all get along just fine with nothing but a city council. They don't even have a mayor, let alone dozens of them."

"There you go with Ender again," Mayor Digby scoffed. "Ender's population is only a third of Southtown's, and most of them are Sectoid. Order comes naturally to them."

"Which is why *I* should be the one making decisions," Mayor Locus said, whipping out his pistol and revealing an Aerie Empire tattoo across his forehead.

"Buglover!" Mayor Meecrob snapped. He jumped from his chair and pressed his finger into Wadley's face. "Why don't you just move to Ender if you love it so much. That's all you ever talk about. Ender this, Ender that. Your love for that meme town of thieves and fanatics has clouded your judgment as of late."

"Hold on, I'm no fan of Ender" Wad said with his hands up. "And besides, you've only been here for 10 minutes."

"That's right," Mayor Steve shouted. "Meecrob is a traitor! Let's kill him!"

"Gadzooks! I've been outed!" Meecrob cried. Pistols flew from their holsters and shots lit up the room.

Wad slipped out the door and slammed it shut. Aside from muffled gunfire, the hallway was quiet, with a dusty red runner spanning the length. Framed pictures of past Mayors lined the walls, at least those that survived long enough to have their picture taken. There were over 100 of them in total for a span of time less than a year. He found a spot and dug through his vest for a smoke, nailing the tip with an electric lighter and pulling in a drag.

Wad was small for a Legomi, Four foot, five inches. His parentage was assumed to be a brussels sprout, which the Humans told him was related to lettuce. They insisted the resemblance was uncanny. He had a rough cover of foliage across his head and shoulders which gave way to a slight frame. He wore a standard beater with necktie hung loose and a tweed vest and trousers in blue. His holster was taut around his waist, with easy access to his P:9, which was a key element in negotiations. To him, the ensemble was a smart pick. The tightness in the armpits gave enough weight to feel legitimate, yet restricting enough to feel at home when he removed it all. His face was unremarkable for a Legomi, though his eyes, sunstruck and colorless, said he had weathered the harsh wilderness and lived to tell the tale.

The coffee boy emerged from an open door at the end of the hall, pushing his cart in Wad's direction. Eyes met and the boy took on a submissive posture. The kid pointed at the Mayor's office without speaking and Wad shook his head. "Is that the coffee boy?" Amelia said, poking into the hallway. The boy spun the cart around and pulled up to the door. "I need all the coffee I can get. These donation logs are killing me. What's wrong, Mayors not cooperating again?" She asked, pumping brew into a plastifoam cup.

"Oh no, everything is fine," Wad said. "Hopefully we'll have a few less Mayors in a minute."

"So, I have to ask," Amelia said. "Did they come to a conclusion about the gun on the roof? The construction crew has been sitting idle for three days and the budget is getting thin. One more day and we'll have to go out to collect more donations."

"We didn't even get that far," Wad sighed. "We couldn't make it passed roll call. Mayor Studdwanker claimed a doppelganger stole his identity and was making bad policy, so he wants to change his name to 'The Real Studdwanker' and backtrack on all his positions. He thinks it will boost his popularity."

"You think it will work?"

"Who knows. He wants to flier the town with attack adds on his former identity. When his name came up for roll call, he went off on a rant and tried to shoot himself."

"Yikes," Amelia said, setting her coffee down. She pulled out of her chair and straightened her skirt, then found a spot to lean on the coffee cart. Amelia was a Human in her mid 30s. She was tightly built with a mousy face and matching haircut. A pair of thick-rimmed glasses drew any attention away from her fashion sense. She wore a lumpy green sweater and black pleated skirt with a run in her stockings, and heels that made sitting a priority. Her eyes were too large to be taken seriously, but her demeanor made up for it. Though often soft spoken, and generally difficult to hear, her speech had a way of cutting through walls when she had a point to make. "So, did you hear about the bombing in Ortega?" She said.

"Yeah," Wad said with a puzzled look. "Not sure what to make of it. Blue Fist, maybe? They've claimed responsibility for three of the last four bombings that made the feed."

Amelia crossed her arms. "You don't seem too bothered by it. What if it happens here?"

"It hasn't," Wad said, matching the girl's posture. "And if it does, then we'll have problems, but for now, we've got more important things to worry about."

"Like your gun on the roof."

"I already told you, the target reticle should be arriving today. When it gets here, we can put the men back to work."

"You were supposed to get the Mayor's signatures for the project, Wad. That's what we agreed on. You told me the whole thing would be fully funded by tax donations but I can't allocate anything until those signatures are on the proposal. The crew downstairs has been idle for *three days* collecting hourly wages paid for by a proposal that doesn't exist, and that's on you, Wad. Petty Cash is gone and the only reason those workers have received anything at all is because I funneled Mayor Succulent's insurance policy into the accounting department. That should be illegal, Wad."

"That's fine," Wad said. Mayor Succulent has been dead for over a month and his main beneficiary was his top hat... we have an accounting department?"

"Wad."

"Tell you what. Once that reticle shows up, we'll get it to the crew right away and they can finish up. A day or two, tops. We'll send the order of completion off to the mayors and somebody will be dumb enough to sign it. I promise."

"Oh, I see how it is. Anything to avoid a difficult situation, is that it?" Amelia said. "And that's why you didn't take the Mayor's position for yourself."

"Or maybe I don't feel like getting shot today," Wad stabbed back.

"Oh, please, Wadley. We both know you'd gladly take a bullet if it meant you could push off your responsibilities for another day."

Wad buttoned up, hiding behind a puff of smoke. Amelia reached for a stack of manila folders and shuffled through as Wad rubbed his temple. She produced a printed scan of some hastily scrawled graffiti, then pushed it into the Legomi's hands. "Blue Fist," She said. "That picture was snapped about ten minutes before the Poori-Poori lounge in Tempeg exploded. That graffiti wasn't there an hour prior. Someone is marking these businesses for demolition."

Wad planted the cigarette between his lips and took a closer look. It was a quickscan from a Talkman camera. A snapshot of the entryway to some kind of boutique selling Human imports in the coastal town. To the left of the doorway was a scrawled fist in blue paint. "This isn't news," Wad said. "They claimed responsibility, didn't they?" Without warning, another print was shoved into his arms.

"Don Sanders," Amelia said. "Ever heard of him?"

Wad looked over the print without a word, then took a drag of his cigarette. It was a snap of an elderly Human, as far as he could tell. Like a ball of dough with lips and wild hair. Frazzled, behind thick-rimmed glasses.

"He used to be an engineer for Bumhauzer a few years back. Quite a talented mind, in fact – up until the Kaggwerks absorbed their munitions department and gave him the boot."

"He's not a Morouni," Wad said.

"You are correct. Only Morouni allowed at Kaggwerks," Amelia said with a nod. "And wouldn't you know it, a few weeks after they let him go, bombs started going off at Kaggwerks subsidiary plants. Magenite bombs, to be exact. What was Sanders' primary contribution to munitions? Magenite starting caps. He was one of the only people with access to enough refined Magenite, and the only one with a motive."

"So, he blew up some factories," Wad said with a shrug. "Ancient history, right?"

"Sure, but his revenue stream dried up and he dropped off the radar a few years back. Nobody knows where he went. Here's the kicker. Right around the time he vanished, the Blue Fist showed up."

"So you're saying this old ball of skin is working for a Morouni Supremacy group?" Wad said with a stink-eye.

"I don't know," Amelia said with a solid look. "But I do know every one of the recent bombings fits a theme. They're all Morouni owned businesses. The Whitewatch in Calibur, the Cordovan Republic in Ghong, the Poori Poori in Tempeg and now the Whiskey Waffle Emporium in Ortega. All Morouni owned – and like you said, Sanders is most definitely not a Morouni. The last piece I have yet to put together are reports from witnesses from a few of the bombing sites. They all mention a character seen milling around each of the targets just prior to the act. We don't have a name, but my sources say he's a big guy. Really big. They say he's got an accomplice, too, but we don't have a description beyond 'about five feet tall'. Anyway, the big guy was spotted fleeing Ortega just minutes before the explosion."

"Well, okay then," Wad said. "So what do you want me to do about it?"

"I want you to know that I'm handling it. What I want *you* to do is take care of that dang gun on the roof. It's what you're *supposed* to do and it's what I *need* you to do. And I'm going to need those prints back," she said, snatching the files from his grip. "They're archive copies and you aren't going to do anything with them anyway."

Wad shrank back feeling somewhat belittled. Here, his aid was cracking an intercontinental bombing plot and he couldn't even get a signature on a piece of paper from one of a dozen idiots. It was also the first he heard that his office had an archive. He turned to find the coffee boy still standing by his side, gazing at him with wide eyes. Wad lost hold of his cigarette and it hit the floor. He had to think quickly if he was going to make it out of the office without an earful, and in truth, he wasn't too happy with his own bullshit either. It was time to turn things around.

Wad slapped his hands together. "Alright, then. I've got a plan. We'll write up a writ of extension citing extraordinary circumstances and have the building crew sign as witnesses. Once we get that reticle, and they get back to work, their signatures protect them from non-compensation as long as we both sign off as procrastination for absent mayors."

"You mean procuration."

Wad snapped his fingers "That's why you're my aid." He turned down the hall with his head held high. The coffee boy followed close behind.

"Oh no you don't," Amelia said, pushing past the cart. "That means we need documented proof that the mayors aren't available."

Wad pointed to the door of the conference room. There was smoke rising from the bottom. "If you want a signature, you can get one yourself. Be my guest."

"That's not fair, Wad. I don't want to get shot either. I've got too much work to do."

"Tell ya what," Wad said, spinning on his heel. He poked his temple. "Put Mayor Studdwanker's name on there. Maybe we can get him to believe he actually *does* have a doppelganger. Make it look legit."

"Wadley..."

Wad grinned and continued down the hall with Amelia fumbling behind. The coffee boy followed with the clattering cart, hollering for payment.

The Old Guard of Zerth

"You know what, why don't we head over to Mackey's for lunch. I'll have him fix up some fish sandwiches. Never work on an empty stomach! He's got those cozy booths with the little lights over 'em. Perfect for paperwork." Wad said, as Amelia scrambled through her purse for her credcard.

"I didn't know you ate fish. I thought you ate..." Amelia trailed off, pulling out her card and spilling a bag of tampons across the floor, followed by lip gloss which rolled under the door of a nearby office. "Dammit!"

"Sure, anything," Wad said with a wave of his hand, "Mackey knows me. He busts out the cheap plates whenever I come around cos he knows he wont get em back."

"Way to kill my appetite," Amelia groaned. "If I could digest anything, I still wouldn't eat a plate." She dropped to her knees and went fishing for her lip gloss.

"You know what?" Wad sad. "Why don't you bring the donations log. Might as well get that done at the same time."

"But that would take hours, Wad."

"Not between the two of us," Wad said. "Come on, we'll make a day of it. Knock out all those pesky logs together. It'll be a nice, quiet lunch date."

Amelia leered up at Wad. She let out a huff and crawled to her feet, giving him a worried look. "You'd really do that for me?"

Wad nodded with a distant smile. Amelia scurried back to her office, returning with a large stack of papers that she held against her chest. She struggled for the coffee boy's payment, blindly handing over a tampon, then scrambled to catch up as Wadley pushed through the door at the end of the hallway.

Mighty Rahiem

A lingering heat settled in the shade of the cobblestone alley as the two exited through the side door of city hall. Wad held the flap open for Amelia as she nearly tumbled out, clutching her paperwork to her chest. He let the drape fall and idled for a moment, taking in the misty scent of sea-breeze and munda. Amelia caught herself fixed on the foliage of Wad's shoulders as they seemed to unfurl to the moisture in the air. She turned away, slightly embarrassed to have been staring. There was nothing to look at, so she planted her eyes firmly on the munda-duct overhead.

Despite being the first and only city planner, Wad didn't plan shit, but he loved his alleys. They were fashioned with more care than the streets. After all, that's where the shade was. Dirt roads were dug out where it seemed to make sense, but the empty plots were a free-for-all. Buildings were often plopped down wherever there was room, by whoever cared to build. The result was a maze of channels and passages that Wadley loved to tinker with. For that reason, the narrows of the city were often the main thoroughfares. They were usually decorated more lavishly than storefronts. All neatly tiled, sanded and kept up by Wad's free time, which was something he often found an abundance of.

Potted vegetation filled every possible nook. Set against peach-colored dobistone walls, they gave life to the otherwise monotone scenery. No mater where you were in town, the trickle of running water was ever-present, and along with it came the sweet scent of munda. Each and every building was outfitted with a crown of water ducts, out of which sprouted a great jumble of munda vines. They kept the water pure and looked pretty nifty to Wad. The vines weren't his invention, but the plumbing was. That much he was proud to take credit for, if anyone remembered.

The Old Guard of Zerth

Out to the street where the heat danced across every surface. Just up the road was a gathering of Morouni steel workers waving signs at the steps of City Hall. Big yellow coroplast flaps with the Kaggwerks logo painted across each one. They chanted demands at the windows of the Mayor's office above, occasionally hurling a bottle or two through the open shutters. Wad could hear Mayor Studdwanker's shrill cries for an end to the chaos, followed by a gunshot. Amelia's wide eyes seemed to be tuning it all out.

Wad could see the frustration in the girl's posture. He gently brushed her wrist, which popped her out of the trance. "You said on Earth, they only have one mayor, right?"

"No, there are a lot... I mean, there's only one mayor per town," Amelia stumbled. "But things are different here. They have to be different. We made it different and we have to accept that."

"But we can change that at any time, can't we?" Wad said. "What's stopping us from getting rid of all the mayors and just going back to how things used to be?"

"Total chaos?" Amelia laughed with frustration.

"It doesn't have to be chaos," Wad said. "Look at everyone else. Ghong is Ancap and so is Calibur. They don't have these bureaucratic hangups. Hell, look at Ortega. Total Anarchy and they don't have any problems."

"No problems?" Amelia scoffed. "Except your Anarchist town just had a bombing an hour ago. Very organized. Let's be more like them. We'll see how well that works."

"Yeah, but Ender..."

"Ender is filled with Sectoids, Wad. They couldn't go crazy if they tried. That's the thing, your town is only as stable as the people in it. Nobody blows up anything in Ender

40

because there aren't any crazy people there. This place, on the other hand..." Amelia paused, seeing Wad look away. She pursed her lips and shut up.

Wad turned with a solemn look. "It's not the easiest thing for people like me," he said. "Where I come from, you're either very stupid or very angry. I don't like either of those, so I try my best to get passed it all. I know I'm not perfect, but that's why I'm not a mayor. I don't want that kind of responsibility." Wad's tone shifted and he perked up. "But enough of that. Let's get this work done."

Amelia nodded and let it slide.

The street was mildly active with foot traffic moving along at a steady pace. Across the way, Dingus Mackey's fish market was hopping with customers. There was a line that stretched around the corner and into the alley. The rooftop mezzanine was bunched-up with standing room only as crowds shuffled beneath red and white parasols. They mingled in contrast to the floating hydro-condensers tethered to rooftops throughout the city. A deep beat pounded through a wooden speaker atop a street sign, proudly proclaiming the direction of Saxo Street.

"Oh hell," Wad said, stepping into the dirt road. "It's free fish day. This won't be quick at all. Can we skip lunch?"

"Skip lunch?" Amelia frowned, "What about the gun on the roof?"

"Yeah, I mean afterwards. Skip lunch and go for drinks," Wad shrugged. "Come on, we'll just hit up the Leaf. It'll be great."

"Oh, that's just like you, Wad. You're always trying to get me into your bar. Look, I know it's a point of pride and I know that you take it seriously, but I'm not a drinker. You know that."

"But you could be," Wad said with a dumb smile.

"Wad, I don't want anything to do with that kind of stuff. And besides, I still don't think it's the best image for you to portray. The Mayor's adviser running a shady establishment filled with... undesirables." Amelia paused to gauge Wad's reaction. It didn't go well so she backed away. Wad followed up with a disingenuous shrug.

The two walked south, arriving at the open bay doors of Herman Wibble's Exploding Erotica. Herman specialized in retrofitting large caliber firearms to vehicles, but also carried an assortment of mortars, RPGs and landmines. *'The one-stop-shop for boner-inducing booms'*. It was his business that held the contract to build the cannon on the roof of City Hall, and the workers were lounging in the bay. Koenig, one of the crew, cupped his hands around his mouth and shouted, "Hey, Bigman, we gonna sit around forever?"

The sound of the name 'Bigman' always caused Wad to turn on instinct. It came less often those days, but it always brightened his mood when he heard it. It filled him with a sense of authority and purpose. "We're here to get you guys on track," Wad said, pushing out his chest.

"Thank the suns," Koenig said. "You got that reticle? We can't do anything without it. It's tied into the guidance system."

"Soon," Wad said. "Gimme an hour or so. It'll be here. And you'll get your pay, too. I'll make it happen with or without the mayors." Wad paused, noticing the evil glare coming from the woman. "I mean, yeah, we'll get the signatures. Everything is in order."

"It's about fuckin' time," Koenig said, scratching his roots.

"So, in the meantime, Wadley and I are going to draft a writ that lets you get to work." Amelia said, stepping in.

"Later," Koenig said. "We're on break."

Mighty Rahiem

"They're on break," Wad said, pointing to the crew, but something in the shade caught his eye. It was a dangerous looking contraption on a work cart. "Hey, what's that?" He said, as he strolled into the darkness of the garage. He approached the crew with a friendly nod and they responded in kind. It was a standard pit-style shop which Wadley was all too familiar with. Greasy air mixed with shadows and hot concrete. The ever-present thrum of dangerous equipment. Chewing tobacco stains. The memories kept him comfortable as he hovered over the strange machine and rubbed his chin. It looked like some kind of motorized hair-dryer with a roll cage.

"That there is the facefucker 5000," Koenig said, grabbing the thing and holding it to his chest. "Eight round capacity, high profile, low resonance grenade launcher. Seventy bucks."

"Dam, that's steep," Wad said, eyeing the contraption. "How's it work?"

Koenig handed the chunk of steel to Wad, who nearly lost his balance to the weight of the thing. It was a beast of a machine. He slid his arm through the roll-cage and wrapped his fingers around the handle.

"Ya gotta get it started first," Koenig said, pointing at the pullcord on the side. "Give it a yank and hear that baby purr."

Wad exchanged a look with Amelia. She wasn't smiling but he didn't care. He reached down and yanked the pullcord and the contraption bucked, then steadied to a lazy bumble in his hands. "Is there a safety?" Wad said gazing at the machine with wide eyes.

"Sure. When ya run out of ammo it don't shoot no more," Koenig laughed.

"Very nice," Wad said. He ducked out the bay door to the sidewalk where he waved the thing around in the open. A mother and child ran screaming.

The Old Guard of Zerth

Koenig cupped a hand around his mouth and shouted. "Gotta make sure ya stand back when ya shoot it. It's got a real short timer."

"Wadya mean 'stand back', I'm attached to it," Wad said.

"I'm just sayin"

Wad shrugged and took aim at a sign post. With a squint, he squeezed the trigger. The gun jumped with a brilliant flash. Amelia dove for cover and the workers busted into laughter. Wad shook the stars from his eyes. The signpost was still there. He turned to the girl who was hiding under a workbench; his face was blackened with soot. "Who's face is this supposed to fuck?" He said.

"Everyone's!" Koenig laughed.

"Awesome!" Wad cackled. He squinted and held his arm out, keeping his bicep steady with his other hand. Again, he pulled the trigger as a blast of heat erupted from the barrel, singing his skin and blackening the tips of his leaves. The motorized turret whizzed and deposited another shell into the chamber, ready for another go. Wad squealed with delight. "You should put a scope in the front," he laughed. "Make 'em get *real* close, then POW!"

"Hah!" Koenig popped, "serious trolling!"

Wadley wiped the glee from his face and composed himself. "What kinda rounds?" He asked, looking the thing over.

"30mm HE-6260 grain," Koenig said. "Expensive stuff."

"I know all about it," Wad said. "Does it fire slugs?"

"Ten Feet," Koenig replied.

"Ten Feet what?" Wad said.

"It'll fire a slug ten feet. It's not designed for distance, as you can see. It don't do much without high-explosive rounds, so it's gotta be the HE-6260."

"That is pricey," Wad said, pulling his arm from the roll-cage. He thanked the men with a nod and lazily tossed the machine to the workbench. The crew leaped up and rolled to the floor as the gun whined and jumbled on the table. "What's the big deal?" Wad said. "It's not like-"

-Foom-

The workbench fired across the room, crashing against a toolbox, ripping it apart with a horrid clang. It fell to the concrete and rocked. Wad pulled his head from between his shoulders, then gave Amelia a look. Without warning, all men burst into laughter. Amelia was petrified.

"Special feature," Koenig said, pushing himself to his feet. "It's real touchy."

"I have *got* to get me one of those," Wad laughed. "Who sells em?"

"Kaggwerks special. Factory direct, if you can get through the door. Yer shit outa' luck if you ain't a Morouni, though. And not just any Morouni. Ya gotta be in good standing with Mr. Ammison Kagg himself. Pure-bloods only. No mongrels allowed. The only reason we got it here is because it's in for repairs. They say it's broken, I say it's full of surprises."

"Goddam that's tough," Wad said. "What's wrong with it?"

"It ain't loud enough!" Koenig said, slapping his knee. The men fell apart with laughter while Wad shot them a 'peace sign'. He fished Amelia out of her hole and pulled her through the bay door.

The Old Guard of Zerth

Back out to Saxo Street where Wad was having a hell of a good time entertaining memories of thirty seconds ago. Amelia was crushed. "I can't believe you encourage them," she said. "Here we are, trying to build some kind of order and the Mayor's Adviser is trying to blow up the town."

"It's just a bit of fun," Wad said, but the girl wasn't having it.

Amelia pulled away with a scowl. Wad got the hint. "How would you like it if someone blew up your bar," She said. "How would you like it if someone shot up the place. You have to *think*, Wad. It's not just about you and your fun. The people don't want explosions and bullets and chaos, they want peace. Peace and quiet so they can live their lives. Isn't that what you want, too?"

Wad sighed and dropped his shoulders. The music of the speakers petered out, bumping into **Remind Me, by Röyksopp**, which didn't seem right at all. He was compelled to stew on it. Something about the tune in tandem with Amelia's worrying brought back memories of his former life. Before all the brickwork and politics, before Humans and before all the responsibility. There was something else there. Something hiding deep below his skin. A burnt wound that forgot to heal. Maybe he wasn't the cool and collected person he wanted to be, but he tried every day to make it right. At least he wanted to try, when there wasn't anything else going on.

"Wad, get out of the street," Amelia yelled, as a bus zipped by.

Wad shook himself back to reality. He gave Amelia a genuine grin and gripped her hand. "I'm sorry," he said. "I don't mean to cause problems. It's not easy for me... I didn't want to be put in this position, but I'm here now and I'm trying to make the best of it." He looked down at the smooth, pink skin in his calloused palm. It was so soft to the touch. He rubbed his thumb over the back of her hand, it seemed so delicate and out of place. It was something that needed to be protected. Needed to be maintained. He raised his eyes to meet hers. "You're right, I'll work on it."

Amelia looked as if she were about to tear up. She held Wad's leathery palm like a prize. Cradling her stack of documents, she nodded across the street to the bar on the corner. "The Leaf Bar and Grill," She said. "If you can learn to straighten yourself out, maybe I can learn to loosen up."

Wad's smile was as wide as a boat. He led the way with an open hand as the two walked side-by-side across the street.

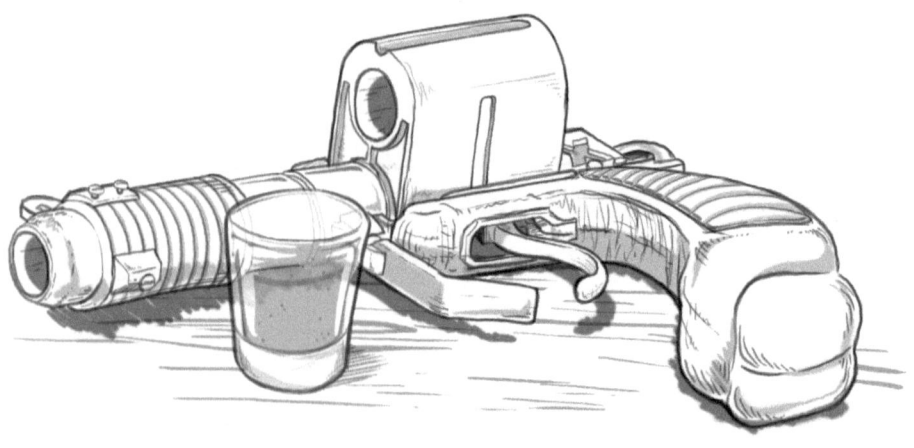

Chapter 3

The Leaf

"Smite the awkward and wring the impurity from those who deviate from the old ways! Let us flutter to bits in the winds of change as we struggle to muster a mere thought of progress. Let us cast out all good things, simply because they are new, and hold fast to the detriments of our heritage, simply because they are old."

Meri's voice vibrated through the speakers above the stage, mixing with an odd assortment of head-rock. Rich tobacco smoke wafted through the sun-shafts of the tavern, tickling his chin-whiskers as he continued.

"This is what they wish to return to. This is their goal. A rigid defense of a tradition steeped in ignorance and fear. Their cowardice is blinding and they have no retort when called to sense. If our progress as a society were as a ladder, Mr. Kagg and his precious Kaggwerks would have us lighting ablaze the rungs and praising the ashes."

Meri squeezed the last words, letting the venom drip. As he spoke, he reached over his audience, testing the elasticity of his suspenders. The crowd responded in kind, pushing to the stage, eager for more of the eloquence for which the speaker was known.

Meri was a beast of a Morouni, roughly six-foot-five, prematurely balding and carrying the weight of several men in his gut. He kept it in place beneath a pair of hiked-up blunderhose, with the waistband snug below his sternum. A pair of suspenders looped over a mound of flesh that was his shoulders. His face bared the weight of twice its age and his eyes were drooping and tired. His lips were small, framed by a heavy jawline and upturned snout, but when he spoke, everyone could hear. Meri elevated his volume as all eyes were fixed upon him. All eyes but one.

Potato's eye was heavy with boredom. Leaning over the bar, he nursed a dying cigarette, glaring at the near-empty bottle of Jim Beam on the shelf. Straddling the bottle were two virgin specimens of something local that he wanted nothing to do with. The urge to hop the bar for one last gulp was stronger than his loyalty to inventory management, but Wadley warned him of the consequences of drinking all their stock. Human booze kept them in business, but as far as the Legomi was concerned, he would be drinking it as soon as he got paid.

Potato was tall, about five feet, with a shape like an elongated light bulb. His neck was his head, with shoulders sprouting through a pair of PISS packs, where his ears might be, if he wasn't Legomi. Chiseled arms spanned the height of his body, with his wrists dangling around his calves. His waist was slim, supporting a pair of reed-like legs which ended in size 18 wafflestompers. A matching garb of green leather covered an otherwise russet colored body, weathered with lumps and knots of calloused skin. His great, dinner plate-sized eye blinked as he returned to his cigarette, which had dumped its ash and left a gray smudge across the woodwork. He rubbed it away with a meaty palm and pressed the cigarette between his lips, sucking on nothing but stale air before flicking the butt behind the bar.

The stereo had drifted from a well kept string of garage rock to a jumble of genre-skipping beats with no direction. **The Cramps – Green Fuz.** Meri was struggling with the constant shift in tone as he spoke. Potato caught a cringe in the Morouni's speech when the song took over, but the gaggle of patrons huddled around the stage didn't seem to mind. Gustav must be occupied, Potato thought. It wasn't like him to allow that kind of mess. The Human was warned to stay on point. His particular brand of audible expression was well adopted by the locals, but any strong deviation had a tendency to set them off. Music-induced riots were something to be cognizant of. Not that Potato minded much, but he had become accustomed to Gustav's micromanagement, and to hear such variation wasn't normal.

The front curtain pulled aside as a trio of Humans shuffled in with a gust of dirt at their heels. A rough looking crew. The lead Human eyed the room, noting dozens of occupied patrons around the stage in the rear. He then turned to the lethargic Legomi with a smirk. He nodded to his comrades.

The Human was tall and thin, sporting a dry-turd-white Stetson, Ray Bans and a sprig of wheat anchored between his lips. His shirt was a loosely tucked floral thing, and his jeans – faded and beyond hope - were far too tight. Faux-leather kickers of bad size seemed held in place with hope, and a forced twang in his breath twittered through patchy, try-hard stubble over rosy cheeks. He moseyed, even when standing still.

His companions were equally offset, though perfectly mirrored on the flanks. They wore a scuffed duster that might have been black from a distance, but not quite hiding a greasy ponch. Dual mustaches twirled with palm-sweat and faces hiding behind the cracked plastic of Oakley Shields. Top it off with a charcoal 20-gallon hat hiding something undesirable. They sweat in perfect tandem.

Potato pushed to his feet and approached the group to check for weapons, waving a blunt finger at their dusters. "You trying to shoot yourself in the foot with that?" he said, pointing at the nested revolver at the man's hip.

"What in the hell are you talking about?" the man spit. His cohorts chuckled.

"The safety is off. Turn it on."

"That ain't no safety. That's single-action. What the hell do you know about guns, weed?" the man laughed, letting the hammer down with his thumb. He followed with an exagerated shrug that untucked his shirt, revealing a soft underbelly.

Potato pulled his vest aside to reveal a barrel-sized holstered sidearm. "I know a lot about this one," he said.

"The fuck is that?" the man scoffed. "That some kinda flintlock or something? The grip looks like a cock."

"This is Paulina. She makes everything better," Potato said, pulling the beast of a pistol from its holster. He waved it loosely.

"Paulina?" The man laughed. "Well you can tell *Paulina* that Carbon Dale and the Dollar Bills are in town. I'm Carbon Dale, and that there is Bill. The other one is also Bill. They're the Dollar Bills. So what the hell do you got to drink in this place? Me and the posse is thirsty."

"We got booze." Potato said, turning to the bar. "You keep those pistols where they belong and yer welcome to drink here."

Dale gave an aggressive nod. He lead his men to a table, kicking his feet up and demanding service. Potato ducked behind the bar and shuffled through the cupboard for clean glasses. "What'cha wanna drink?" He said.

"Bourbon," Dale shouted. "I need me some Jim Beam."

Potato turned to the dwindling bottle and panicked. That was his booze. "We got a special on Granite Hill Bourbon, made right here in Southtown. Half-off. It's the best you can find."

"Neah, I want me some Jim Beam."

"It's the last we got," Potato said, "Double price. It don't come easy. And really, it ain't half as good as the local stuff."

"Look at me," Dale said. "Do I look like a local? I ain't no talkin' broccoli or a friggin' fish, or whatever. I'm a Human and I want Human booze."

"It's gonna cost ya," Potato said, reaching for another bottle. "Supply and demand, ya know."

"Okay then, I *demand* some Jim Beam, and I'll *supply* you with money. T'ain't no problem. I got money out the ass," Dale said, snickering with his posse.

Potato was floored. The bastard wasn't giving up. He had to think quick. "You know, ten bucks is a lot of money," He said. "It's really not worth it. You can get a lot more of the other stuff for that."

Dale kicked his boot atop a bar stool. He posed with pride. "Y'all see these babies? Genuine Bork-skin boots. Had em delivered yesterday. MᵃFuggin direct. You think these things are cheap? Do I look cheap to you? Anyway, what the hell kinda business are you running here, spud?" Dale said.

"It's a bar. Don't call me Spud," Potato said.

"Tell you what, son," Dale said with a toothy grin. He hovered his hand over his revolver. "You get me that Beam and I'll play nice. Otherwise, we might have a problem. I came here to drink, not argue, but if you wanna argue, we can do that too." He patted his firearm gently.

The urge to turn the bar into a war zone crossed Potato's mind but the buzz of Meri's voice forced him to bite his lip. The last thing he wanted was to interrupt yet another speech. He sharpened his gaze and ripped the bottle from the wall, tossing the cork aside and splashing the last of it across three shot glasses. He invited the men to retrieve their drinks with a gunshot glare.

"That wasn't hard, was it?" Dale sneered, waltzing up to the bar. He pulled out his credcard. "Three drinks, thirty bucks."

Potato thought for a moment. He could charge anything he wanted for the last of his bourbon, but he pulled away. His battle was lost and any more hostility would only drive the nail of defeat deeper into his brain. "No," He said, "I was wrong. It's only a buck. Three bucks for three." He shuffled the glasses forward with his knuckles.

"Oh, now yer just bein' a sore looser," Dale heckled, "You said thirty bucks, that's what I'm gonna pay you."

"I ain't taking thirty bucks for three shots," Potato scowled.

"Yer gonna be mighty angry when that's what you get," Dale smiled, wiggling his card. "Come on, boy. I'm gonna pay for my booze."

"Thirty bucks for Jim Beam? That's a steal!" said Meri, barging into the scene. He snatched a shot off the bar and tossed it down his throat. "Bleagh, that stuff is nasty. Absolute swill!" he said, wiping his lips with the back of his hand.

"The fuck is this!?" Dale shouted, as the Morouni hovered over the remaining glasses.

"It's an acquired taste, isn't that right? Bourbon? This, my friend, is me acquiring the taste," Meri said. "It's a shame I don't enjoy it yet. Allow me try another." To the panic of the company, Meri snatched the second shot off the table and quaffed it. "Gahh, no good, but I can feel it growing on me. A third should do it, don't you agree, my man?"

Potato swiped the glass and held it to his chest as Dale began to sweat. "That ain't right," Dale squeaked, "That's my Beam."

Mighty Rahiem

Meri stared into the air with a satisfied grin. He licked his lips. "You know, I'm really craving some *Jim Beam* right now. It's called Jim Beam, correct? Bartender, one more shot of Jim Beam."

"Fuck no," Potato said.

"Bullshit," Dale cried. "That Beam belongs to me."

Meri leaned in and widened his eyes at the shrinking Human. "So it's war, is it?" the Morouni growled.

"No, sir," Dale said, shaking. "I wouldn't dream of it."

"Hah!" Meri chortled. "He called me 'sir'. I do believe this man takes me for a ruffian."

"Yer – yer not?" Dale squeaked.

"Hah, I'm just the entertainment. The muscle is right there behind the bar," Meri said, pointing at a deadpan Potato. "That one keeps things in line. That one you *should* be afraid of."

Dale turned to the stone-faced Legomi and let loose with laughter. "That little turd-bucket? Hell, he ain't even fit to carry my bags. He's the best you got to offer?"

Meri gave Potato a nod and returned to the Human. "Tell you what, my man. Seeing as how we three have the same goal in mind, how about we play for it? A gentleman's game? You seem eager enough, and you're quite obviously not afraid of our champion. How about a game of Little Icarus. I trust you carry a set of dice?"

"Of course," Dale scoffed.

"Exquisite," Meri said.

The Old Guard of Zerth

The ashwood table creaked as the party gathered around. They took their places, sliding chairs across the hardwood floor and getting comfortable. Potato set the final shot of Jim Beam at the center. **Straight Ahead – Tube & Berger** began to pound through the speakers, eliciting a sour look from Dale. He muttered something to himself and pulled a set of dice from his pocket. The two Bills flanked him, sharing chipmunk smiles beneath bushy goatees. Potato fidgeted in place while Meri produced an opaque plastic cup, taking Dale's dice and dropping them inside. He shook the cup and slammed it down, keeping the roll obscured.

"We all know the rules," Meri said. "Whomever comes closest to guessing the roll, without going over, wins the shot." He shoved the cup to the center of the table next to the prize. "I'll go first. I'm guessing thirty," Meri declared without hesitation. "On to you," he said, pointing to Bill.

The two Bills leaned forward, their eyes hidden behind mirrored Oakleys. They gripped their jaws, stroking their beards in unison. They both tilted their heads, but only one spoke. "Nine," he said, with a nasal drawl. They both turned to their left and nodded.

Dale shot an eye at Meri, then followed up with a grin. "Thirty," he said. "That's a big bet. I'm guessing yer the optimist of the group."

Meri offered a nod. "Maybe," he said. "Or maybe I'm testing the waters. Given the situation, and the stakes as high as they are, one might be favoring a more adventurous strategy. Wouldn't you agree?"

"See, that's just it," Dale said, sitting back, "yer not playing the game at all. Yer trin' to play *me*. I know yer type. I know what yer trin' to do and it ain't gonna work."

"Fortune favors the bold," Meri said.

"Fortune favors the winner," Dale replied with a finger.

Meri shrugged and pulled back as Dale studied the cup. The Morouni began tapping his foot to the beat of the music, then followed with his thumb. His claw clicked to the rhythm of Dale's frustration as the Human wiped the back of his neck with a restless palm. "Who puts this shit music on, anyway?" Dale said.

"A friend," Potato replied.

"Yer *friend* don't know shit about proper atmosphere. I'm trin' to be a cowboy here, and what do I get? Club music. Fuckin' club music. Where's the old-time western stuff? Where's the good, bad and ugly... oh wait, we got that right here!" he said, motioning to the company.

Bill sort-of chuckled.

"Yeah," Dale mumbled, "good bad and ugly."

"So, my guess was thirty," Meri said.

"Okay, okay fine. Thirty-one," Dale spat, slapping the table.

"On to you, my man." Meri nodded at Bill#2.

"Oh, he doesn't talk. He's not playing," Bill said.

"Yeah, he's not playing," Dale added, then turned to Potato. "So it's all you. What's yer name, anyway?"

"Potato," Potato replied.

The Humans froze in place. They quickly mashed together in a private huddle, whispering frantically before returning to the table with ugly smiles. They studied the Legomi. Potato shrugged it off and leaned forward, blasting the cup with a single-eye'd stare. He lingered for a moment before drawing back and crossing his arms. "Eighteen," he said.

"So... *Potato*," Dale interrupted.

"Yeah," Potato replied with a cautious squint.

"*The* Potato?"

"The only one I know," Potato said, maintaining eye contact.

"Yeah, yer the cyclops, alright. Not much meat on ya," Dale said, then shifted. "So, tell me about that gun you got there."

"What of it?" Potato said, sharing a look with Meri.

"Wha'cha call it, again? *Paulina*?"

"Yeah, I do." Potato replied, pulling the cannon from his belt. He slapped it down to the table, spilling a bit of Jim Beam down the side of the shot glass.

"Goddam, spud. That is a hell of a thing."

"Double-round 30mm slugshot. And don't call me Spud."

"You trying to shoot airplanes or sumthin?"

"If hairplains mess with my bar, damn straight I'll shoot hairplains."

"So, this is *your* place, huh?"

Potato pulled back and gave Meri a look. "It's mine enough," he said.

"The *great* Potato," Dale continued. He pulled his chair back licked his lips before catching himself. "So, before we get going, I have to know one thing. How come that gun looks like a penis?"

"What's a peenits?"

Dale was taken aback. He shuffled forward in his chair. "You... you know, a big shlong. Big johnson."

"I don't know what that is. It's shaped that way so I can hit people with it," Potato said, waving his finger around the butt of the handle.

"You don't know what a johnson is? What the hell do you got between your legs?"

"A nerve sack?" Potato said, confused. Meri buried his face in his hands and muttered something.

"And yer the bouncer? Kinda makes ya lose respect for a guy that don't have any equipment down there," Dale said. Beneath the table, he casually slid his hand to his holster.

Meri turned to Potato with a breath, rubbing his knees.

Potato cocked his head and loosened his knuckles. "You know it's my job to make people afraid of me," he said.

"What's yer point?" Dale laughed.

"I think it's time I get back to work," Potato snarled.

"Is that a threat?" Dale shot back.

Remind Me, by Röyksopp took over and the bar froze. All eyes shot to the speakers. A chair hit the wall and the bar went sideways with bedlam. Meri dove for the Jim Beam and the Humans jumped from their seats to avoid the whale of a man sliding towards them. Dale was caught unaware as Potato dashed in from the side, flattening him to the ground. The two Bills howled in unison and promptly collapsed. Meri rolled to the floor with the booze in his fist. He flipped the table and crawled behind it, waving for Potato who was straddling Dale, mashing him into the floor.

Dale reached for his shooter, drawing it awkwardly and depositing the barrel directly into Potato's fist. The Legomi twisted the pistol from Dale's palm and grasped it with both hands, bent the barrel tightly, then assaulted him with the maimed steel.

"Are you enjoying yourself, my man?" Meri shouted as bullets pelted his cover.

The Old Guard of Zerth

A hot pain struck Potato's arm and he turned to Meri with clenched teeth. "What the hell is Gustav thinking!?" He shouted, before a second bullet struck him in the jaw and sent him upright. The Human broke free and scurried off like an animal. Potato slid behind the table and bumped against Meri as bullets whizzed overhead. He rubbed the seeping wound with the side of his fist. "Where the hell is Gustav? This music is gonna get us killed." Meri returned with a crazed smile and downed the shot of Bourbon. "Hey!" Potato yelled, "I was gonna pay for that!"

"Fortune favors the bold," Meri said, smacking his lips.

Half a chair flipped overhead and landed in Potato's lap as a chandelier crashed to the ground beside them, followed by an unconscious body skidding across the floor. Potato spotted his gun beneath a heap of debris and lunged for it as a steel-toe connected with his face.

Dale stood over the Legomi, beaming, then took a bullet to the knee and crumbled. As he lay prone, he spotted Potato's rogue weapon within reach. The cowboy dragged himself across the floor, and grasping the weapon, propped against the footrail of the bar. He took aim at his target, gripping the beast of a pistol with all his strength. Potato stared down the barrel of the cannon. He thought quick, snatching the broken chair and flinging it towards Dale, who pulled back, shielding himself from the incoming furniture.

With a click and a boom, Paulina went off in Dale's hand, twisting his arm like a rag-doll. A sizable chunk of wall collapsed across the ground, filling the bar with dust.

The room went silent but for the tiny beat of the speakers. All patrons stared like guilty toddlers as the smoke cleared. Through the gaping wound in the wall, a silhouette stepped through the daylight. It kicked through the rubble before pausing. Its eyes met Meri and Potato, then turned to the crowd of paralyzed patrons. It then turned its attention to the impish beat of the radio. The room was frozen.

"Gunfight!" Wadley yelled, dashing across the floor. He slid behind the table alongside his comrades. His pistol went to work, blasting at everything and nothing. The bar took flight once again.

"Wadley!" Amelia shouted, darting into the fray. "What did you just say about-" A bullet pierced her neck and she fell to the floor, papers scattering in a wave, fluttering in every direction. Shots zipped above her as she struggled to breathe. The blood flowed across the floor as she pawed the wound with a quivering hand, unable to speak. With her final breath she reached out to Wad as he plugged away with his P:9, eyes wide with glee.

"Yer girlfriend died," Potato said.

"She's not my girlfriend," Wad yelled back. "She's the Mayor's aid. Are you sure she's dead?"

"Pretty sure," Potato replied, spotting the growing pool of gore.

"Here," Wad said, handing Meri his pistol. "Take over. I've got to make a call." Wad sank behind the table and tapped at his Talkman. 'AMELIA DEAD, AZURA 10 MIN', then motioned for Meri to return his gun – which he didn't.

"I respectfully refuse," Meri shouted, taking pot-shots at the crowd. "This is too much damned fun."

Wad huffed and pulled a second P:9 from his liner, fishing a battery from his back pocket. The galloping bass of **Aerosmith's Back in the Saddle Again** pumped in and the exchange of bullets became less personal. Friendly even. "That song," Meri shouted, "I do believe our man Gustav is back. He must have gotten himself eradicated again."

"Well that explains a lot," Wad said, slapping the battery into the grip of his pistol. "I wonder what killed him this time?"

"I'm sure we'll hear all about it," Potato grunted, just as a bottle exploded across the side of his head.

"Gotcha, Spud!" Dale laughed, then ducked behind the bar.

"It's a deadly pincer attack!" Meri cried. "Cover the rear!"

Potato jumped to his feet and dashed towards the bar as Dale assaulted his advance with bottles of booze. Potato weaved and dodged, performing a flying leap over the bar and crashed into the backboard. He recovered quickly, hopping to his feet as Dale came at him with a bottle of Galliano, brandishing it like a sword. The Human took the position of a fencer, cradling a clearly broken arm to his chest and hobbling on one foot. "Have at you, knave!" He shouted with a twisted southern twang.

Potato lost his urgency as Dale hopped around with an unhealthy grin, prodding the air with the elongated bottle. He took an unassuming swipe as Dale parried the attack, then jabbed the Legomi's forehead. Potato repeated the swing as Dale pulled back, lifting for an overhead bash as the bottle broke in two, dousing the man in herbal liqueur. Potato's boot pounded into Dale's chest and the man sank to the floor, gasping for breath.

The Legomi stood over the Human with an eye for vengeance. He locked his fist around Dale's collar and dragged him to his knees, putting his knuckles to work on the man's face. The speakers cracked and Meri's voice intruded. Potato turned to see the entirety of the tavern huddled together on the stage. Everyone was whooping and laughing, cradling wounded limbs and broken jaws.

Mighty Rahiem

"Well, that was a good gunfight," Meri said. "The owner has informed me that if you stick around and assist with the clean-up, your tab will be graciously covered by the house. Thank you all. We will have to do this again some time." The crowd groaned and applauded as Meri stepped off the stage. Potato turned to the pile of Human in his hands. It blinked and gurgled a bit, looking strangely satisfied.

Chapter 4

Twosday Morning

Wanned: Ded or Aliv.

5,000 bucks.

Ansers to the name 'Potato'.

Identifehngeng Marks: Big hed One Eye.

The wanted poster looked nothing like Potato. It was a hand-drawn sketch of a balding Human with an eye erased. Meri studded the picture with a smirk as Potato paced around the room. "They certainly captured your good side with this one," Meri laughed as Potato shot him a sneer. "The real question is, who would want your head – and why? Not to disparage your dashing good looks," Meri continued, rubbing Potato's scalp as he passed by. Potato batted at Meri and continued pacing around the office as Wad entered from the back, fidgeting with his Talkman.

Wadley's office was a tight nook above the boutique next door to the Leaf. He owned both buildings, but was renting out the space below to a friend. Without intruding, the only access was an impromptu plasteel catwalk from the roof of his bar. Wad preferred it that way as it kept unannounced visitors to a minimum.

As for the decor, Earthly curiosities and geological tidbits littered the abundant shelf space. Between which, the walls were plastered with maps of all sizes, some framed and others hastily tacked to the dobiestone walls. Three couches and an armchair, of varying styles encircled a large grathskin rug. The head of the beast was mounted on a plaque between two bay windows which looked westward over Saxo Street. Wad called it his office but it was more of a second home. With quick access to City Hall, he could retreat to comfort between summons and disputes. He would doze on the couch and eat meals wherever was convenient, as he believe dining rooms were waste of space. For a Legomi, everywhere you stood was a buffet, so every room was for eating – in more ways than one.

The ceiling fan fumbled along, beating an air of dust around the ceiling. A pair of hobbywood speakers, courtesy of Gustav himself, gave forth a soothing tune – **Amon Tobin – Hey Blondie.**

"The guests are comfortably secure," Wad said. "and Gustavs' just getting back in town. He should be here any minute. Apparently he was killed in that bombing in Ortega. I wonder if he ran into Amelia."

"The timing would be impeccable, though the logistics of their meeting would be ever so fortunate," Meri said, sinking into an armchair and lighting up his pipe.

"What's yer deal with that girl, anyway?" Potato grumbled, leaning against a file cabinet. "Ever since you two met, she's all you talk about."

"That's not true," Wad said, whipping out a cigarette from his vest. "She's the Mayor's assistant, she assists the Mayor. I just happen to be the adviser to the Mayor. We work together and that's all there is." He nailed the tip with his lighter and took a deep drag before giving Potato a smirk. "Am I detecting a hint of jealousy?"

"Hah," Meri bellowed, "She's not his type. Any woman sufficiently inferior to his own stature just isn't worth his time. Isn't that right, my man?"

"I like tall women," Potato said.

Wad shook his head and fell into the couch. He nabbed the bottle of Glencaviar off the end table and poured himself a drink, then chucked the bottle to Potato, who swiped it from the air. He poured himself a glass and flung it to Meri who did the same.

"So who are these guys I've got locked up in my storage room?" Wad said, taking a sip.

"Headhunters," Potato said.

"Care to elaborate?"

"From the looks of it, they weren't specifically on the job," Meri said, setting his glass down and licking his lips. "They seemed genuinely surprised to meet their target."

"They didn't need the money," Potato said. "The dude was gonna give me thirty bucks for the last of the Jim Beam."

"Are we out of Jim Beam?" Wad said.

"Greed is a powerful motivator," Meri said through his rumbling pipe. "How much *more* bourbon could a man afford with a cool five grand on his card?"

"Hey, at least yer worth five grand," Wad said. "I just wanna know what you did to deserve it. Ya kill anyone important that we don't know about?"

"Probably," Potato said.

"I Live Again!" Gustav yelled, ducking the curtain and hurling through the door. His bathrobe blew out behind him, revealing a patterned pajama bottom and slippers.

"There you are," Meri said, tossing the bottle of Glencaviar to the Human. "Potato was beginning to get worried about you."

"That's not true," Potato grunted.

The Old Guard of Zerth

"Wow, man," Wad said, pointing at Gustav's bare chest. The bottle shattered against the wall. "What's wrong with your skin?"

"Yeah, I don't get much sun on Earth," Gustav said, poking at his doughy form. "So how bout' some scotch!"

"Lick it up," Potato said.

"Man, somebody's grumpy," Gustav teased.

"Oh, he's just pissy because he's got a price on his head," Wad said.

"No," Potato interrupted. "I'm pissy because your music nearly got us all killed. Remember what we talked about? Remember yer responsibility? If yer gonna force tunes on people, you gotta be responsible with it. People don't take that shit lightly."

"Ahh," Gustav nodded, "so the mess downstairs is-"

"Yeah," Potato shot back.

"Oh Surely, Wad doesn't mind one bit, do you, Wad?" Meri said, giving Potato the stink-eye. "Don't forget who owns the place."

Potato sat back with a grumble. Gustav plopped down next to him, throwing his arm around the Legomi and kicking his foot over his knee. "So, let me guess – The Beatles, right?"

"No," Potato said, "it was that tiny crap. Whatever it's called. That mushroom band."

"Röyksopp," Meri said. "The cowboys hate it. Personally I find it to be quite the welcome change of pace."

"Shit," Gustav said, thumbing through his Talkman. "I thought I deleted that a long time ago. I'm sorry about that. It's a personal thing, okay? It's not meant for mass distribution. I'll have to remember to get rid of it the next time I go... dammit!"

"What is it now?" Potato sighed.

"I'm on lunesta!" Gustav said, slapping his forehead. "I took a bunch of sleeping pills before I came back. I didn't want to have to struggle to pass out. Besides, my lawyer is there and I don't even remember why. I think I was getting divorced or something, but I don't remember. That was like, six years ago. Either way, If I go back, I probably wont be waking up."

"Ahh, to be Human," Meri recited. "What sense do you find in suffering? What sour destiny met? What better reprieve than-"

"-than escape from care itself" Gustav finished with a smile. "I love that poem."

"Arguthaerie; three-through-four," Meri nodded, then handed his glass to Gustav who downed it quickly and winced.

"So, I have to ask," Wad said. "My bus?"

"It's on the way," Gustav said, dismissing it with a waving hand. "I called a wrecker."

"What!?" Wad popped, jumping from his seat as Potato started to snicker.

"It's all cool, man," Gustav said. "It's just got some broken windows. I think. And the right side front suspenser is off."

"What do you mean, off? How far off?"

"All the way off. It's not attached. I saw it fly away."

Potato slapped his knee and let loose.

Wad threw his hands up. "I don't understand why you don't just buy your own bus. You always say you've got so much money. So use it, why don't you."

"What fun is that?" Gustav said. "If I buy my own bus it gets all familiar and boring and I don't appreciate it. I'm an American, Wad. I'm a consumer, it's what I do. I consume things... *your* things. Tell ya what, lemme play you a little song to make you feel better."

"No, I don't want that," Wad said.

"No, no, it's okay. You'll love it. It's a song for you," Gustav said, messing with his Talkman.

"Guz," Potato said with a finger.

"It's okay," Gustav said, nodding. "It's a segue. It will blend naturally, I promise."

"It better," Potato said.

Gustav punched at the Talkman and the warble of **Thumb, by Kyuss** crept in. He nodded along to the guitar with a sideways glance at the Legomi, who glared at the Human with a suspicious eye. The drums kicked and heaved into a heavy chug. Gustav's afro whipped out of control as he spread his legs and head-banged in the middle of the office.

"Okay, that works," Potato said, sitting back and following the beat with a tapping boot. Meri fished through the end table for another bottle. He poured himself a drink and Wad fell back into the dent in the couch, content do take it in.

"Is that the son of a bitch responsible for the goddamned musical catastrophe?" A voice cried from behind the wall.

Gustav turned to Wadley. "I think there's someone in the storage room," He said.

"Yeah," Wad said. "That's the guy that tried to kill Potato."

"The headhunter? He's here?" Gustav said. "What did you do, put him in the cage?"

"Yep," Wad said with a smile.

"Hah! That's crazy," Gustav said, straightening up. "So what did Potato do this time?"

"Hell if I know," Potato said.

"It's a bona fide mystery," Meri added.

Gustav paused with a scrunched lip. "Did you ask *him*?" he said, motioning to the storage room.

"Yeah, lets do that," Wad said, pulling himself out of the couch. He stopped by Meri to nab the second bottle of scotch, taking a swig and passing it around as they ducked beneath the curtain.

The rear of the storage area was caged off with thick carbon fiber bars spanning the length of the room. All around were awkwardly stacked crates of liquor and tobacco. In the cage was Dale, cradling a mangled arm close to his chest. The two Bills were hunkered on the floor among chipped cardboard bedding and dried grath scat.

"Who the fuck keeps a goddamned cage in their goddamned office?" Dale shouted as the crew entered.

"If it makes you feel any better, I didn't build it for you," Wad said.

"No, it doesn't make me feel any better. And you owe me a new gun," He yelled, with a finger at Potato. He aimed at Gustav and spit. "What the fuck are you wearing? You think yer Hugh Hefner or sumthin'? Yer pathetic."

"He's a rowdy one, isn't he?" Gustav said, tossing back a swig. He handed the bottle to Meri, who downed some himself, approaching the cage.

The Old Guard of Zerth

"So," Meri began. "We have a dilemma. It seems someone has put a price on my brother's head and you know who it is. Seeing as how we have you at a disadvantage, you have two choices. Relinquish the name of the man who hired you, or become a rug like the previous occupant."

"You ain't gonna scare me, Morouni. I know yer type. Yer all talk and no action. And yer spud there don't scare me neither. He just got lucky, that's all," Dale mugged.

"That may be," Meri conceded, putting his hand on Gustav's shoulder. "But my friend here talks far less than I do, and he's certifiably crazy. He's the worst one by far."

"That's right!" Gustav cried, as he flung open his bathrobe, but his thumb caught the drawstring of his underwear and they dropped to the floor. He lingered for a second, taking note of his sudden nudity, then let out a primal scream while shuffling towards the cage. Dale shrieked and kicked to the back of the wall as the bare genitals approached, wagging. Gustav waved his junk around through the bars before spotting the two men in the corner. "Bill? Is that you?" He said.

"Hello Gustav," Bill #1 said. Both Bills waved.

Gustav yanked his boxers up and hastily tightened the drawstring. "Holy shit, it is you," He said. "I know this guy. It's Bill, from HR. He worked with me at LINTECH back on Earth. He's a mess – watch this!" Gustav whipped the revolver from his bathrobe and pointed in Bill's direction. Both Bills made a sound like a hiccup and seized, freezing in place and tilting over. The Human's head slapped against the ground and his oversized hat rolled to the side, revealing a strange mechanical contraption around his cranium.

"You killed my posse!" Dale shouted.

"He's not dead," Gustav laughed. "He's just sleeping. He's got cataplexy. He passes out when he gets excited. We used to screw with him so much at work."

"And sleep apnea," Dale yelled. "He can die in his sleep. That's why there's two of them, the other one is a corpse."

"Oh, shit," Gustav said. "Sorry, Bill."

"You nitwit, you just did me a huge favor," Dale laughed. Now my posse can come back and get me outa this cage, and then I'll have *three* Dollar Bills. Y'all see that there brain-cage on his head? That's how he does it. That's how he controls his doubles. I'll be outta here in no time."

"Yer not going anywhere," Wad said. "Not until you tell us who put the hit on Potato."

"Ain't gonna happen," Dale laughed. "Yer boy is in the network now. Every headhunter is gonna be after him."

"Just a thought," Gustav interrupted. "Where exactly does Bill spawn in?"

"Bonzo beach," Dale said. "He can be back here in a few hours to spring my ass."

"Than we'd simply kill him again?" Meri said.

"Be my guest," Dale replied, "The more you kill him, the stronger he gets. He'll have more bodies under his control and you'll be dealing with an army of Dollar Bills."

"So, to get to the point," Wad stepped in, "you're not gonna tell us what we wanna know?"

"Eat yerself, weed," Dale sneered.

Wad turned to Meri. "I think the rug option is the best way to go. We could put it in the bar."

The Old Guard of Zerth

"Oh, I'm not quite sure," Meri said. "He's a bit small for a rug. He might make a better throw pillow."

"Throw pillow it is," Potato said, pulling Paulina from her holster. He drew aim at Dale's cranium.

"Throw pillow, not soup," Gustav said, grabbing Potato's wrist. "There won't be anything left of him."

"Make it clean," Meri said. "The skin must be intact."

"Yeah, I don't want *another* hole in my wall," Wad sighed.

"Pfft," Dale scoffed, "Y'all are doin' a shit job. You ain't gonna scare me. Go ahead and try again. I'll wait."

"Okay, I got a better idea," Potato said, sliding Paulina back into the holster. "Wad, open the cage."

"You're the boss," Wad said, producing the key. He handed it to Potato with a smile. "I think you got this covered. Call me if you need anything."

Potato nodded, loosening his knuckles. "Got everything I need, right here."

The crew shuffled back into the office, leaving Potato in the storage room. They got comfortable and popped the cork on another bottle of Glencaviar, then shared small talk to sound of muffled screams and **North Eastern, by Sun Dial**. Gustav tinkered with his playlist and Wad swept up the broken glass in the entryway. Meri was content to nurse a rumbling pipe on the couch.

A moment later, Potato emerged from the storage room with Dale's bloody head. He juggled it between hands as he studied the shape of it with a bit of confusion. The Legomi made his way across the office and held it above the stuffed Grath head.

"A little higher," Wad said, rubbing his chin. "That looks good. We should call the taxidermist."

"I'm on it," Gustav said, tapping his Talkman.

"How's the rest of the body?" Meri asked Potato.

"It's good," Potato replied. "Kinda scrawny, though. He's gonna be a real small throw pillow."

"We'll see what the taxidermist can put together," Wad said. "I'm sure he can come up with something nice."

"Taxidermist is booked solid for the next two days," Gustav said, reading off his Talkman. "We're gonna have to preserve him till then."

"The whole thing?" Wad said. "How are we gonna do that?"

"Put him in booze," Gustav laughed. "It might pickle him a bit, but he should be good."

"That's a lot of booze to waste for a throw pillow," Wad said. "Maybe we'll just keep the head. It'll fit in one of those big two-gallon jugs of Granite Hill."

"Bourbon?" Meri laughed. "I'm hearing the rhythm of poetic justice."

"Serves the bastard right," Potato said, tossing the head to Wadley, who turned it side to side, looking it over. Potato moved back to the storage room, returning with a large glass cask of Granite Hill bourbon. He set it down on the end table and examined it, flipping it upside down and unscrewing the copper base. "Whole lotta bourbon gonna go to waste if we put the head in there."

"We could just drink it." Wad said, plopping the head next to the cask.

The Old Guard of Zerth

"That's no small feat," Meri said, quaffing his scotch. "But where there is a will, there is a way. What's the damage, my man? How much are we looking at?"

Gustav poked at his fingers with his eyes darting around the ceiling. "Roughly a gallon, I would assume," he said. "Thirty or forty shots for each of us. Is that even possible?

"We can make it possible," Wad said.

Chapter 5

Twosday Afternoon

An hour passed. **Death in Vegas – Scorpio Rising** thrummed through the office. The grath head was bobbing in the cask of bourbon. Gustav's Talkman chirped. He yelped and fell off the file cabinet, rolled to the ground, then leapt to his feet like a ballerina. He held the screen to his face, tripping sideways into the wall. "Yer bus is on its way!"

"That's the ticket!" Meri cried, tossing the couch aside.

"Lets get in the bus!" Wad shouted as he gripped a half-eaten Human head.

"The bus is fun!" Potato yelled, lunging off the desk and in to the ceiling fan. The blades exploded.

The crew pushed through the door and into the light. They piled up on the catwalk and looked around. Eight suns blasted the alleyways crisscrossing below and the heat of the day made it wrong to linger. Behind the office was the community garden, nestled in an embankment beneath a tarp. Wad cradled Dale's head under his arm and sneered at the greenery. "Look," he burbled. "Radishes!" He gripped the head and flung it into the garden. It bounced and vanished beneath the tarp.

"The radish is nature's fury food!" Meri agreed.

"Fuck radishes!" Gustav howled.

"Get em!" Wad cried, as he dove over the railing. He hit the ground and slid down the concrete embankment, tumbling into the soil. The crew followed, dropping from the second story. They hurled themselves into the muck and ripped at the leaves with angry fingers. Potato spotted the head and attacked it, punting it over the fence. It landed in a bin of fish behind Mackey's Fish Market.

Potato chortled at the sound and stared at the sky with a wobble. His focus floated down to the head and his eye widened. "Fish!" He said.

"Fuck Fish! Gustav howled. The four men scrambled up the embankment and over the chain-linked fence.

Dingus Mackey was hard at work, gutting and skinning his catch before tossing the meat to the skillet. He reached into the barrel and pulled the last of the cod, slapping it to the cutting board and putting his knife to work. "More fish!" He said, turning to the counter where his sprout, Mingus, handed out fillet sandwiches to eager customers. Mingus nodded. He hopped the counter and squeezed through the cluster of patrons, then rushed down the hall and out the back door.

Free Fish Day was a great success. Customers from all over town lined up for a free meal, provided they accompany it with a full priced lager. The beer itself was a tough sell; a mulled brew sans carbonation that left most critics shaking their heads. But when paired with free food, the barrels emptied themselves. He kept it stored in a two-story vat that required a hole in the ceiling, and would eagerly blast out pints at a time through a large hose in the base. Customers were treated to a raucous blitz of a fill, often getting soaked in the process. No one complained about Mackey's antics, as his demeanor made it clear that it was all part of the fun.

Mackey flipped the last fillet and tossed it to a bun, adding a blob of horseradish sauce and topping it with a clod of lettuce. He nabbed the beer-hose and glass, holding it at arm's length, then let loose, injecting a splash to the excitement of the crowd. He wiped his hands on his apron and looked around. "Give us a minute, everybody," he said. "We're just waiting for more fish. Shouldn't be more than a minute." He leaned over the counter to see what was holding up the line.

Just then, Mingus came dashing through the dining area clutching a barrel of fish. He barged through the line of customers and kept on running, right out the front door. A second later, a bloody head followed. It flipped through the air and slid across the tile leaving a streak of gore. It came to rest against a woman's shoe. A moment later, Wadley bounded in with a heap of greenery in his arms and a hellish smile. He paused at the head, then turned to the woman. "Radish Attack!" he yelled, as he spiked a vegetable in her face.

The assault was followed by a barrage of fish from down the hall; a salmon storm and tilapia torrent, pelting the crowd with perch. "Free fish day!" Gustav hollered, as he gave them some more. Meri followed close behind with a barrel in his arms, supplying ammunition for the attack.

Mackey hunkered down as the patrons scattered. Some rushed for the door while others were caught in the storm sliding under tables for cover. Potato gave the head a running punt. It bounced off a wall and landed on the skillet, then sizzled and ignited. He let out a whoop and jumped after it.

"It's free fish day!" Wad yelled, as a fillet smacked him in the mouth. A gang of customers were returning fire from behind a table. They had headgear and everything. Wad leaped for safety behind the counter as Mackey peered over. "They're berserk!" Wad shouted, spitting a huck of phlem into Mackey's eye. "They gonna take your life. We'll protect you!"

"What did *I* do?" Mackey said, wiping the booze-spittle from his face.

"You gave them food!" Wad cried, as he dumped his radishes across the floor, then reached for the bucket of fish guts. Mackey started to say something, but a carp dashed him in the jaw. He fell to the floor in a heap. Wad turned to see Mingus supplying the enemy with fresh munitions. He motioned for Meri to come to his aid. The burly Morouni came lumbering through the dining area, but took a sturgeon to the hip and went down. The barrel crashed to the floor sending a wave of seafood in every direction.

"Victory!" Gustav yelled with his hands in the air, before receiving a sockeye to the groin. He hit the tile and went still.

"Man down!" Wad shouted, flinging guts at the attackers. Blobs of parts splashed across the enemy's cover but they didn't let up.

"Grenade!" Potato yelled, lobbing the flaming head into the enemy's entrenchment. They scattered into the open as Wad picked them off, one by one, before a blast of beer flattened him to the ground. Mackey stood over him, hose in hand.

"Why'd ya doing that?" Wad sputtered, "Yer on our side!"

"I am?" Mackey said.

Mighty Rahiem

"Yeah!" Wad yelled, yanking the hose from Mackey's hand. He pointed angrily. "That's the enemy!"

Mackey poked over the counter as a wave of walleye crashed against the side. He ducked back to find Wadley with his lips around the hose, firing beer into his belly. He snatched it away and turned on his customers, spraying down the dining area with a golden wash. The clientele slipped and skid across the tile as they scurried for the door. Mackey advanced, leaping over the counter with hose in fist. He chased the last of the patrons out the front and into the street where he let out a bleating war-cry, blasting the air.

Beer rained down and Dingus Mackey had won the fight. He let out a heavy breath, wiping the beer from his face while nodding at passersby with a triumphant smile. He lingered for a moment, shuffling around to gather himself before turning to find that his comrades had abandoned him.

"It's free fish day!" Gustav hollered, as the crew chugged down the alley, pockets stuffed with all kinds of seafood. Potato booted Dale's charred head and again, they chased after it, rounding a corner and breaking into the street.

Wad looked around with foam dripping from his teeth. The suns blasted his eyes. He pointed north with determination. "Go!" he shouted, and the crew followed, scurrying up the sidewalk, heaving fish at onlookers. They arrived at the corner of Saxo and Main, but paused as a shining point of illumination broke their minds.

It rumbled over the street like a fellow drunkard with a fresh coat of paint – warbling cleanly with a factory-new set of Blinkbottom 9's. The sound of balanced head-fans chopped the air. The windows were clean and bright and a glint of suns shot off the chromed bumper. Heads turned as it ambled passed, bouncing up the hill. The bus was back.

"The -**HIC**- caravan of contentment," Meri muttered.

"The bus is fun!" Potato said.

"Lets get it!" Wad cried. The crew took flight down the street, pushing through pedestrians and bowling over the elderly. Their target, a mere half-block away. Dingus Mackey didn't know what to think as the men who rushed his store charged passed without even a nod.

Sunlight peered through the alleyways, flashing through the windshield. The heat rested across the Sectoid's face as he casually piloted the machine down the street with a smile. Hesh looked no different from thousands of Sectoids. His face was plain; earless, noseless and hairless. His eyes were gloss black bulbs and his lips were flat and unremarkable. As an Etheros breed of Sectoid, Hesh was spindly up top and ploddy at the base. His torso was the bulk of his figure, and his legs were prominently bowed, only about 20 inches long in total. It gave him, as well as all Etheros Sectoids, a distinct penguin-like shape. His skin was dusty teal, and he wore a standard sleeveless beater, accented by a worn bandoleer holster.

His pants were tan plunderhose and his boots were scuffed Aerie Nation 12 hole stompers, which came up to his knees. They worked the acceleration pedal with calm control. At his side, he carried a brown leather man-bag, snug between his hip and the burnt red armrest of the pilot seat. In it he kept his tools and personal grooming products, as well as any curious scraps of electronics he might have come across. Hands at ten and two, he sat behind the wheel with a proud posture, letting the rays of sunlight flicker across his face as he floated the machine down Saxo Street.

Mighty Rahiem

Rounding the corner of the two-hundred block of Saxo Street, an alarming scene forced Hesh's foot to the break pedal. A sizable chunk of Wadley's bar was laying in the road in pieces. It was like a bomb went off, and children were playing in it. Muffled conversations among the patronage of the bar continued, unphased by the lack of privacy. As Hesh slowed to a halt, he parsed the information into the category of things that should not be – yet are – and due to their frequency, no longer cause alarm.

The gull-wing hissed open and Hesh stepped into the wreckage, lifting his feet to avoid scuffing his boots on the debris. The face of the tavern was a wreck, with a great hole blasted in the wall next to the entrance. Through the wound, Hesh could see customers casually sipping their drinks to the tune of odd music. He sighed and poked at his Talkman, typing out his notice of arrival, but halted at the sound of a voice crying out. It was a desperate howl from around the corner. He couldn't quite tell if someone was in need of help. The syllables were slurred and truncated. It sounded like someone yelling 'free fish day'.

Out of the corner of his eye came a mackerel. It slapped to the concrete and laid still. Then, a walleye, followed by a haughty pile of men crashing around the corner. The Sectoid dove for cover as the mob trampled his position. They slapped at the windows of the machine, wailing with glee.

"Gimme the keys," Wad said, turning to Meri with foaming jaws.

"I have no keys!" Meri bellowed, clawing at his scalp. "I have nothing! It's -HIC- it's a Calamity!"

"Who has the keys?" Wad panicked.

"I have the key," Potato said, whipping out Paulina. He aimed at the driver's side hatch.

83

The Old Guard of Zerth

"That's the ticket," Gustav said with a nod. His glasses were fogged over with sweat.

"We don't need the ticket, we need the key!" Wad shouted, flapping his hands in the air.

Hesh appeared with the key hanging between his fingers.

"The bug stole the keys!" Gustav said, pointing an angry finger at Hesh. "Get him!"

Hesh shrieked and dove into the bar, dropping the keys to the ground. The crew dogpiled the sidewalk, kicking and biting and throwing elbows. Wad emerged from the cluster with his fist full of metal. He clamored to the bus and jammed the key into the lock, then swung the hatch open and hurled himself head-first through the door. He popped the key into the ignition and twisted. The machine bucked up and hovered with the sound of spinning head-fans and the rest of the crew piled in. "Go!" Wad shouted, as he stomped the accelerator. The bus took off down Koplin Street, swerving and dodging pedestrians.

"Where are we -HIC- going, my man?" Meri said, doing his best to keep his head upright.

"That way," Wad said, pointing forward.

"Well, let's do it, then," Meri trumpeted excitedly.

"I'm trying!" Wad said, with a scowl. He swiped at Meri, pushing him into the passenger seat. Meri howled and rolled the window down, leaning into the wind.

"Guys, guys guys," Gustav said. "I'm gonna put on some music. Yer gonna love it." He tapped his Talkman and **The Moody Blues – Tuesday Afternoon** took over. The bus swooped north and took off up Billion Boulevard, passing through the city gates, leaving Southtown behind. They raced across the terrain, through fields and pastures and over rocky hills. The suns beat across their faces as a great wind rushed through the cabin.

"That," Potato said, pointing at the music. "Gently swaying through the fairyland of love!"

"Yes!" Meri agreed, "We have to find the -**HIC**- fairyland of love. We must go a-swaying!"

"Where is it?" Wad said, gripping the wheel.

"That way," Potato gestured.

Wad cranked the wheel and the bus shot left. Meri pulled himself out the window and vomited into the wind. Gustav went hunting for a beer. He snagged something mysterious and shuffled the music.

"What the fuck, Guz!" Potato said, giving him the eye.

"What?" Gustav said with his hands up.

"Put it back on, asshole. We need to go swaying through-."

The bus shuddered and bucked, then hit the dirt. Wad dropped the wheel. "I'm not doing this!" He yelled.

"Don't tell me you've -**HIC**- lost faith in the fairyland," Meri said, wiping his lips and downing a swig of scotch.

"No," Wad said, "I'm not driving!"

"I'll take over," Gustav said, popping his head between the front seats.

The bus jerked and came about, tossing everyone from their places. It aimed south and accelerated back toward Southtown.

"See," Wad said. "It's driving without me!"

Meri's window slid shut and he panicked. "Where am I -HIC- supposed to vomit?!"

The Old Guard of Zerth

"Haunted bus!" Gustav yelled. He heaved into his seat and yanked at the window but it wouldn't budge. "We're locked in!"

Meri pounded at the glass while Wad attempted to squeeze into the vents in the ceiling. Potato whipped out Paulina and took aim at the passenger hatch. He steadied his arm, then pulled the trigger – but nothing happened. Potato turned the safety off and aimed again. Just then, a familiar voice came over the stereo. "I thought I would let you boys enjoy the moment before roping you back in. I don't work for free, you know," the voice teased.

"It's the ghost of Hesh!" Gustav said. "We stole from him and now he wants revenge!"

The bus carried the crew back through the city gates and down Koplin Street. It hung a left at Billion Boulevard. and merged with light traffic. Then traveled east and came to a halt outside the Leaf, where Hesh was waiting patiently. Amelia was standing with him, clothed in a nightgown and bare feet. She was clutching a jumbled mess of paperwork.

Wad popped the hatch open as Meri tumbled to the ground, followed by Potato, who chose to not fight gravity.

Gustav stepped over the pile and approached Hesh with a finger. "Where do you get off dragging us back to-" he spotted Amelia and froze. "Why, hello," he said, swaying. "And what name might your be?"

Amelia was terrified.

"No, don't you answer, it will ruin the surprise," Gustav continued. "I see you share my enthusiasm for sleepwear. That's admirable. Mind if I admire you some more?"

"She's married," Wad groaned, stumbling out of the bus. His heel caught the top step and he slid his way into the pile of bodies at the door.

"I'm not married," Amelia said, then slapped her hands over her mouth.

"Oh, that's so super interesting," Gustav shmoozed.

"Why did the bus move on its own?" Potato yelled, pushing to his feet. "Why did it do that?"

"Why does my heart move at the lovely maiden?" Gustav said, attempting to curtsy, but stumbled over himself, tripping through the door of the bar. The curtain swung shut behind him.

"Wad," Amelia said. "You're all drunk."

"He's drunk!" Wad said, pointing at Meri, who was passed out on the curb.

"I don't think you listened to me," Potato said. He came at the Sectoid with a deadly finger. "Why the bus moved?" His eye was looking at nothing.

Hesh backed up with open palms. "Allow me to explain myself," He said, producing a Talkman from his pocket. He tapped at the screen and the bus started up again, lifting off the ground and nudging Meri to the sidewalk. Meri grumbled and rolled to his back.

"Why is it doing that?" Potato said with a squint.

Hesh moved to the front of the bus and pulled open the louvered nose-panel. Alongside the radiator was a little black box with a red flickering light. "You see that light?" He said, speaking deliberately. "That's a remote receiver. When you hit *this* button on *this* Talkman, the manual controls shut down and the auto pilot engages. The bus will do *what ever it needs to do* to get back to this Talkman. It's called a FETCH system."

Potato scratched his scalp with a dumb look.

"I can tell you aren't receiving me," Hesh said. "It's okay. We aren't all blessed with the gift of rational thought."

Potato snatched the Talkman from Hesh's hand and hopped into the street. He moved to the rear of the bus and fastened the strap around the bumper, yanking it tight. He then tapped the Talkman and stepped back as the machine began to spin. Potato gave the Sectoid a smirk. Hesh stared back through his palm. The bus spun faster, prompting Potato to back up. It kicked up a cloud of dust, and the sound it made was like a ceiling fan. They could only gaze at the scene.

"Great job, idiot," Hesh said. "How are we supposed to stop it now?"

Potato was fixed to the mechanical whirlwind with a drunkards stare. He reached into his holster and gripped Paulina, but was slapped down by Wad.

Meri groaned and sat up. The tufts on the side of his skull were fluttering in the wind. He gave the bus a look before digging through his pocket for his pipe. He lit up, puffing away, never talking his eyes off the horror.

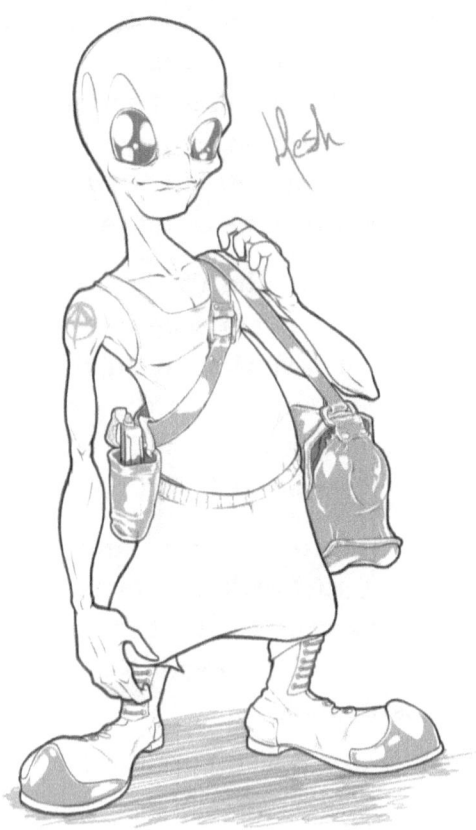

Chapter 6

Hesh the Bugman

Brian Jonestown Massacre – Infinite Wisdom Tooth.
Hesh fancied himself a picador of drunks. Through his
efforts, he managed to poke and bleed the typhoon of
inebriation until it had sufficiently petered out in Wadley's
office, at which point he felt safe to indulge in a beer. He
quietly sipped a bottle of Bubblin' Brown against the file

cabinet with an Osharoot Cigarette in the chamber. Despite his jovial nature, he made frequent jabs at the crew regarding their lack of control. Not so much as to criticize – more so to gauge the reaction. Though their folly kept them in good spirits, Hesh could see the seed of regret just below the surface. He knew why – he could read their minds.

As a Sectoid, it was Hesh's job to set an example of moderation. He did it well. Between pint-sized sips of ale, he kept tabs on each man's spirits, and if they showed signs of rising too quickly, he would douse the fire with a verbal jab. This lead to a quiet scene around the coffee table with no clear direction, but at least the booze had run its course.

Hesh took a drag of osharoot and winked at Amelia, who was struggling to break the miasma. "Wad, are you listening to me?" She said, as the Legomi was busy flicking the leaves on the back of his head. No reaction. She turned to Hesh with a hostile look.

"Wad, old buddy," Hesh said and Wad turned. "Amelia would very much like to stab you. She wishes you dead."

"What?" Amelia said. "That's not true!"

"Never argue with a Sectoid," Potato stammered. "They never lie. Hesh couldn't lie if he wanted to."

Hesh's teal cheeks turned red. "That's not entirely true, though I will say, as a matter of course it is highly discouraged. And I do mean *Highly* discouraged."

"Pfff," Gustav spit, leaning out of his seat. "That's lame."

"I'll put it this way," Hesh said, giving the Human the stink-eye. "Just as *Gustav* is perfectly capable of shitting in his own pants, his own conditioning would make it quite uncomfortable to do so – and it would require some effort. And just like shitting one's pants, the practice of lying is quite embarrassing for a Sectoid, as the aftermath tends to be equally fowl. A liar in a room full of mind-readers is quite the sore thumb – therefore the practice denotes somewhat of an infantile quality. Babies shit themselves – small minds lie."

"Yeah, but not everybody is a Sectoid," Gustav said, tapping his temple. "So you can like, lie to anyone else."

"Sure," Hesh said, without missing a beat. "But there's no pride in it. Nothing to celebrate. It's like winning a rigged game. Walking away victorious, pants heavy with excrement."

"That's delusional," Gustav laughed, then held back a spell of vomit.

"And it's annoying as hell," Wad said, holding his head.

"Speaking of annoying as hell," Hesh quipped, "our collective inebriation has been quite the distraction. I suggest we give the floor to Amelia. My dear, I can see you have a lot on your mind. Care to speak about it?"

"He's right," Gustav slurred, tossing his arm around the girl. "You hear that, Amelela. We're gonna listen to you now. Whisper sweet nothings into my ear."

Amelia skillfully slid from Gustav and moved to the wall where she aimed a scowl at Hesh. "Oh, I've got plenty on my mind right now," She growled.

Hesh blinked and turned to Wad. "Wadley, I no longer care to spend time inside of this woman's head. It doesn't reflect well on you."

Wad's forehead was buried in his palm. He seemed to be talking to himself.

"Wadley, my man," Meri said. He reached to comfort the Legomi before the contents of his own stomach went off. The Morouni leaped to his feet and made a hasty shuffle to the restroom, managing to glance the door frame and spin, letting loose with a guttural spray that missed its target by a full 45 degrees. He continued speaking as it came. "I'm -**HIC**- okay," he promised, even as the door frame came back around and put him on his ass. Having done the deed, he crawled back to his seat to stew on it. The front of his shirt resembled a pit-stain with chunks, but the coolness of it brought him some relief.

"Look at you people," Amelia said. "You're a mess. One big fat mess." She turned to Wad who was counting his fingers. "Wad, what about the gun on the roof? What about the writ of extension you promised? What about my logs?"

Wadley did his best to tune it all out. He knew he fucked up and he didn't need anyone to tell him that. The more the angry voices piled up the more hostile he grew. He replied with an intense look of something confused and angry. There was no way for the girl to interpret it.

Amelia reacted with a shrug. "What is it with you people?" she huffed. "I just don't get it. How can so many people be so irresponsible with their lives. I don't even know how you manage. How do do that? What drives you to this place?"

"The bus," Potato said.

"What is it that makes you think this is a good way to live? What do you have to live for? What do you aim for? What's the end goal? Do I have to bribe you to get things done?"

"No good, girl-baby," Gustav schmoozed. "I literally can't be bribed... by money."

Meri was poking at the chunks on his shirt.

"Booze," Amelia shouted. "Is that all you want?"

"We already have more booze than we want," Potato said with a burp.

"This is insane," Amelia popped. "What happened to personal responsibility? What about civic duty and care for your fellow man? Do you not have that? Is that not a thing on this dang planet? Wad, you are the advisor to the Mayor's office. You have a duty to this town and its people. You have a duty to this world."

"No," Wad said, emerging from his safe-spot with a scowl, "I have a duty to the office of the Mayor, and I do that just fine."

"Wadley, Wadley, Wadley," Hesh said. He brushed some dust off his shoulder then leaned against the window. "How far you have come and how far you could go. You built this town, didn't you? It belongs to you. The people here know you. They know what you've done and they love you for it. That's why you're the Mayor's adviser. They trust what you have to say. What happened to the Wadley I remember? Where is the hero of the Pit – the savior of the Legomi? Where's the man who lead the greatest exodus in history? These things happened, Wad. You made them happen. Now that you've accomplished your goals, you rest on your laurels? Where's the fire, Wadley? Where's the sense of purpose you once had?"

"I accomplished it," Wad said, pushing to his feet and stomping to the window. He threw open the shades, blinding the room with sunlight. "I did what I had to do and I finished it. Everything you see in Southtown is here because I wanted it to happen. I wanted peace and freedom. The freedom to do what I want, when I want. I wanted that for *everyone* and now they have it. I'm finished."

"No, Wadley, you didn't fight for freedom for freedom's sake, did you? Wasn't it *your own* destiny you wanted to plot? The freedom to take on your own responsibilities? Isn't that what you've afforded yourself? And now that destiny finally comes calling and you turn away?"

The Old Guard of Zerth

"I'm not turning away from anything," Wad said, waving his arms out the window. "There are six-thousand people out there that have taken what I gave them freely. Do I do their dishes? Do I brush their teeth? Are they incapable of managing their own problems?"

"You gave them a foundation, Wad, now you have to maintain it."

"It's *their* foundation," Wad shot back. "It's *their* job to maintain it. If they can't keep it up, then they don't deserve it."

"Now there's the Wad I remember."

"What are you smiling at?" Wad scoffed. He turned to Amelia who was echoing the pressure with pursed lips. It was too much. He searched the room for some kind of escape but all he could find was the door. He broke from the conversation and stomped towards the exit, turning for a final remark. "Have fun in *my* office." He threw the door flap aside and vanished.

"Wadley," Amelia shouted. She started after him.

"Let him go," Hesh said. "He's not the type to be forced into anything. It's best to leave him alone. He's already come around, he just doesn't realize it yet."

Amelia withdrew with a huff. "I hope you're right," she said. "I just wish I could get through to him."

"You do get through to him," Hesh said with a smile. "Believe me, without you he'd be much worse off. You give him the ground he needs to stand. He may never admit it – hell, he may not even know it, but the truth is plain to see. At least it is for myself. I can't speak for the rest of these hooligans," he jabbed with a wink, eliciting a spirited chuckle from the men.

Mighty Rahiem

Potato reached for a beer. "Wad's not as bad as you think, lady. He drinks because he remembers the time before all of this. What we got now is a reason to celebrate. I dunno when you showed up, but it was well after the shitshow we use'ta have. Otherwise, you'd be drinking, too."

Hesh caught himself before speaking. Something about the simplicity of the Legomi's speech cast a fog over his intentions and he found the Legomi was impossible to read. Hesh had spent time with Potato before, but never in such a confidential manor. It was off putting, but not unwelcome – regardless, the Legomi's point was well taken. "Potato isn't wrong. Not that I condone the recklessness of it all, but my girl, you may be taking the situation for granted. To you, it seems as if the whole world is collapsing in on itself. Chaos in all directions, but I assure you, this is a paradise compared to the old world. I myself was a refugee of that horrible experience, so I assure you with all confidence that you are living in a time of prosperity and peace."

"Peace," Amelia said with wide eyes. "You call this peace? People are dying in the streets. I got shot in the neck a few hours ago. I died! I was killed because Wadley wanted to have fun shooting things with his gun." She spun on her heel and whipped a finger in Gustav's face. "You know better than anybody, don't you? Tell me how many people you saw killed today. Tell me how peaceful that bombing was."

Gustav was happy to receive any attention from the girl, regardless of her mood. "Bombing? What bombing?"

"The bombing that killed you, you doof," Amelia said, swatting at Gustav's shoulder. She immediately regretted her decisions to engage in what might be perceived as flirtatious behavior, so she backed up and covered herself. "My point still stands. Just because we can come right back from death, doesn't mean we can go around acting like morons."

The Old Guard of Zerth

"Says the Human," Meri said bluntly. His eyes were sharp as they met Amelia's. "Care to speak so plainly to a mere mortal?"

Amelia retracted.

Meri pushed himself to his seat. The wreck of a Morouni, vomit-stained and dripping, drilling a hole in her with a hurt scowl. "In all your haste to cast judgment on we, the wretched, has it once occurred to you that you are standing in a room surrounded by living beings, un-killed and still drawing breath enough to muster another drink of sweet life. I most certainly have never been killed, as if I had, I would clearly not be speaking to you – neither would my brothers Sectoid and Legomi. I'm sorry, my girl, but you have no authority to speak of mortality. I advise you to cast any remaining criticism to the closest mirror."

"But I'm not the-"

"To the mirror," Meri barked. He calmed himself with a breath and continued. "With no ill judgment towards you and your kind, it is clear to see that your species has lost its sense of self preservation on this world. The effects of it have bent your mind. *Your* mind. Blame guilt, if you like, but do not blame others."

"Bullshit," Potato said. He swigged his beer and popped it down to the table. He pulled a cigarette from his pocket and moved toward Amelia. The look in the Legomi's eye sparked panic in the girl and she instinctively backed away. He held the smoke to her hands. "Smoke this," He said, flatly.

"No," She said.

"Why not?"

"It's... it's bad for you."

"See," Potato said, turning to Meri. "She don't wanna smoke. It's bad for her. Stop bullying her. I don't like bullies."

Mighty Rahiem

Hesh held his forehead in his fingers, wincing.

Potato turned to Amelia. "You don't let them gang up on you like that. You say you're scared of living, I believe you. Nobody should be scared to live, especially not a friend of Wadley's. You say we're too rough, then we need to calm down. That's all there is to it." He turned to the rest of the men. "You hear that? When the lady is around, we calm down."

"But it's not just when I'm around. It should be all the time," Amelia said. "If you want a better world, you need to act that way regardless of who you're with."

Potato paused for a moment, looking towards the floor. He shrugged, abandoning his tirade. "We already made a better world. You don't like it, go make your own."

Amelia felt pushed to a corner. There was no convincing these men. She teetered on the edge of despair before Hesh pulled her back.

"That's what she's doing," Hesh said. He turned his glossy black eyes to Amelia. "Despite the opposition, Wad needs you. You are what makes him better."

The girl lowered her head with a labored breath, then backed out through the curtain with a nod.

Out on the roof, the wind blew casually across the dusted dobistone. Wad perched at the ledge overlooking Billion Boulevard. Beyond the skyline he could see the rocky shore. The waters bobbed, waveless and stagnant, only disturbed for moments at a time as freighters glided through the strait. To the east, about twenty miles out, fishing trolleys from Tempeg skimmed in slow circles before returning home over the horizon.

The Old Guard of Zerth

Down below, the bus continued spinning. A small crowd had gathered, taking pictures with their Talkmans and laughing. The rubble of the bar was spread out into the road and children were hucking bits of debris at each other. That was his bar they were playing with. That was his wall with a big hole in it. That was his bus spinning like a top. At that moment it felt like his escape to the roof didn't take him far enough away. He wanted to put as much distance between himself and all the bullshit he created, but every thought of running only soured with the feeling of moving backwards.

A figure entered his peripheral vision and he turned to see Amelia standing at the western edge of the roof. She leaned against the raw dobistone that that would have been the walls of a second floor, had he managed to finish it. She looked through the crude opening of a window, out over Saxo street, towards Town Hall, keeping quiet but speaking volumes with her posture. Wad looked back to the rubble in the street, finding that it was boring a spot in his chest. Swallowing his pride, he stuffed his hands in his pockets and approached the girl. He rested against the rough stone by her side, leaning out the hole in the wall for a look. Down below he found another scene of disorder. The protesters were gathered around a small bonfire which he recognized to be the podium Amelia had ordered a few days earlier. She went to great lengths to have it built and delivered for a press conference that never happened. She wanted the Mayors to address the grievances of the people. Democracy in action, she said, but none of the Mayors cared. Wad didn't care. He didn't understand what she was so happy about when it arrived, but after seeing her hard work in flames, it struck a nerve.

"Isn't that your podium," he said.

Amelia didn't answer.

Wad took a breath. "I'm sorry-"

Amelia preempted him. "No, I'm sorry." She hesitated. "Sometimes, I forget where I am. The world I come from wasn't that great, either. I understand the urge to act out – I really do. But I don't let that get in the way of who I want to be. Is this who you want to be, Wad?"

The question hit Wad in the gut. He thought of apologizing, but the last time he tried that it only worked for a few minutes. It wouldn't last at all if he tried it again. Not that he didn't mean it, it was a genuine regret. He just wished it would last longer before it fluttered away, replaced by the next bottle, or bowl of tobacco, or gunfight. He searched for some way to express it genuinely, which didn't go unnoticed.

"You're afraid, aren't you?" Amelia said.

Wad didn't know how to answer. It wasn't fear, it was something deeper. Something under his skin that he couldn't place. She looked at him with an odd smile, like a tense embrace or a handshake held too long. Wad could see the pain behind her eyes and he struggled to find an equal in his own memory. The only time in his life he felt stress of that kind, he went all gung-ho and broke the damned thing out of pure spite. He thought back so many years ago and found the same thing in the woman standing before him – only she was unable to let it break – desperate to hold it together. He wanted her to let it go. Let it spin lose and go all shitty. Let the pieces fly and revel in the chaos. It worked just fine for him.

"What is it that drives you, Wadley?" She said.

The question deflated Wad's expectations and he found himself elated with the ease in which the girl spoke. It was refreshing to hear, and for a moment he felt proud of her. There was a strength there that he didn't have. He looked up to see the pain had given way to a natural simper, so he replied with a ducked head and a light laugh. "I honestly don't know," he said. "But I suppose until I find out, I can at least try to make people happy."

Amelia smiled. "Lets work on duty first, then we can work on happiness, okay?"

Wad nodded and the two began to make their way back across the catwalk towards the office. The street-level discord faded away as they walked beneath the gentile bumble of the floating condenser atop the roof. It swayed a bit with the calm breeze which blew across the crimson drape of the office doorway, revealing a tiny yellow square pinned to the cloth. Wad curiously plucked the note from the drape, giving Amelia a shrug. Upon closer inspection, Wad's face dropped.

M^aFUGGIN DELIVERY SERVICE

FAILURE TO RECEIVE:

JARUS 9, 112

22:18:39

Sorry we missed you. Per your request your package

will be delivered to the next available recipient

within your provided contact list.

COD amount: ₴450.00

"What the fuck?" Wad barked. Twenty-two Eighteen? Where was I at twenty-two Eighteen?

"What is it, Wad?" Amelia said, looking over his shoulder.

"The asshole delivery guy didn't deliver my reticle." He waved the note in her face.

Amelia snatched the paper and examined it. "Twenty-two O'clock?"

"That was like, two hours ago. What the hell?"

Amelia dropped the note to her side and buried her face in her hand. "You were drunk, Wad."

"What?"

"You were terrorizing the town, Wad. You and your friends were out drinking and you missed the delivery. Now it's going somewhere else."

"Where is it going?"

"I have no idea, Wad. Why don't you call them and find out."

Wad shot his attention to his Talkman. He poked at the screen but nothing happened. It didn't even turn on. He tried again, jamming his finger harder into the plasteel casing. Blank screen. A chill ran up his spine. He turned to Amelia with a look of dread.

The Old Guard of Zerth

Empty Page Cock

Chapter 7

Gone

"What do you mean you've never backed up your Talkman," Gustav said, laughing. "That's like, rule number one. I back mine up every ten minutes."

dEUS – Fell off the floor, man

"I didn't know you could back it up," Wad said, pacing through the office. The crew gave him ample space. "Why would I have to back it up anyway?"

"Well, in my case I tend to die a lot," Gustav said. "It's what I do. It's what we all do, don't we honey?" He made a kissy-face at Amelia but she ignored him. Gustav recovered gracefully. "You think I take the time to search for my corpse to get all my stuff back? Fuck that. Just get a new Talkman from the fishers and upload my data that I *backed up* before I died."

"Yeah well, I don't die all the time. If I did, I wouldn't need a Talkman at all. I got one and that's the only one I've ever needed," Wad said.

The suns were low in the sky and the shadows stretched unevenly throughout the office. A light breeze passed from window to window and Meri was passed the fuck out behind the armchair. Amelia kept to herself in the corner while Hesh sat at the desk, leaned over Wadley's disassembled Talkman. He wasn't sure how to tell Wad that the circuits had blown due to interference by foreign materials, most notably, beer and fish guts. He opted to keep his mouth shut for the time being until the emotions of the concerned party had leveled out.

Potato reached out to Wad as he passed by, holding out his wrist. "Here, lemme show you how to back it up."

Wad waved him off. "So, theoretically, what did I lose?" He wasn't addressing anyone in particular but he was prepared to explode at whoever answered.

"It's not theoretical, Wad," Hesh said. "And you need to calm down so you can better understand the situation."

"What did I lose?" Wad growled.

"Everything," Hesh said. "Your money, your proof of property, your contact list. Technically, you've even lost your position in the Mayor's office, given that you have no verifiable identity, though I don't think anyone would mind."

Amelia winced.

"Shit, I hope this doesn't mean you're going to start borrowing stuff from me," Gustav said. He was only half joking.

"None of this makes any sense. How does that even work?" Wad said. "You can back up your money? What's to stop you from reloading it after you spent it?"

"Hashcode in the blockchain," Gustav said, sitting up. He spotted the Sectoid giving him attention and he shrunk back, catching himself before he revealed too much. Too many mind readers in the room, he thought.

Hesh cocked his head. A flicker of ill-possessed knowledge and wanton excess was read, followed by a flash of fear, but faded to images of boobs and baseball. "Gustav is right," he said, eyeing the Human. "While your money is stored in your Talkman, it carries with it a unique ID. When that ID is found to have made a transaction, it generates a hashcode in the metanet blockchain which contains the amount before and after the transaction. Its checked against previous transactions to verify the amount – and I hear what you're thinking. No, that hashcode can't be translated into currency. It's only a snapshot of your wallet at that time."

"What about contacts?" Potato said.

"Same thing," Hesh replied. "But there's nothing to encrypt so the data is stored clearly. He paused for a moment, picking up on Wad's thoughts. "You recently gave a courier full access to your Talkman data. Three days ago, in fact."

Amelia stepped forward. "Of course he did. There's nothing wrong with that. You have to give them access to your data so they can find you."

"Maybe it's not all gone," Hesh mused to himself, then perked up. "The courier service. You allowed them access to your data, but you opted for a deferred delivery to the next available contact in your list, therefore some of your data still exists. Your contacts, at least.

"Great, so everything is gone but at least I don't have to reprogram my contact list. That's not making things any better, Hesh." Wad said, loosing patience.

"No, you misunderstand," Hesh said, waving his hands. "You gave the courier service access to your Talkman – period. They are using the data taken from your Talkman – period. When you did that, a false backup was created in the form of a hashcode.

"But I didn't back-"

"You didn't have to." Hesh interrupted. "That hashcode is just a shadow-copy of your Talkman data.

"So, you're saying it automatically backed itself up?" Gustav said.

"You're missing the point, my ugly pink friend," Hesh said. "At some critical juncture, Wadley was required to upload either part or all of his data to MªFuggin courier service in the form of a hash. Now, I can't speak to the principals of the MªFuggin operation, as I've never had the pleasure of dealing with them personally, but if luck is on our side, they're absolute criminals and have robbed Wadley of his Identity.

"And why would that be a good thing?" Amelia said.

Hesh poked his temple repeatedly. "Think, woman. It's binary. Either Wadley's data is lost completely or it was stolen. Those are the only two possibilities."

"Again," Amelia said, raising her voice. "I don't understand how that could be a good thing."

"You Humans and your lack of perspective," Hesh said, as kindly as he could. "If his data was stolen, that means it exists in its entirety. It's merely in the wrong hands, which is something we can fix. We have moved from total confusion to two potential absolutes. We are making progress and I'd appreciate it if you suppress your opinions long enough to understand the situation."

Meri snorted and sat up, blurry-eyed. He poked at the dried crust on his shirt. "My lord. Someone has put vomit on me."

Wad dug his fingers into his scalp. "Alright, everyone shut up. Assuming MªFuggin are crooks, what we need to do is track down one of their delivery guys and steal their Talkman. That will give us a rout to the block they store their network in. Then we can just can steal my data back."

"Don't gotta track anybody down. They'll come to us." Potato said, waving the yellow slip.

"And how do you figure that?" Wad said.

"Cos you told them to," Potato said. "Says here they're gonna deliver the package to the next closest contact. That's us."

"You'd think they would have done that by now," Gustav said. "It's been a few hours. How long does it take... unless."

"Unless what?" Wad said.

Gustav leaned back defensively with his hands up. "Wad, you know I love hanging out with you. We're friends, right. It's all copacetic. I do for you, you do for me, but... they might be looking for someone with a fixed address.

Meri spoke up. "I would assume my address is the bar... or this office. It's more than accommodating." He crawled into the armchair and kicked his feet up on the coffee table.

Wad was speechless. It hadn't occurred to him before, but he realized that his friends might be homeless. "Wait," he said. "You guys don't live anywhere, do you? I mean, we've been hanging out for what, six years?"

"Nine, my man," Meri said without missing a beat. "Though I was just a dot-of-a-lad. My memory may be lying to me." He light up his pipe and bumbled away.

Gustav knew better than to answer. He tried to hide by staying very still and avoiding eye contact.

"I have a home," Potato mumbled, then realized he had suddenly become the center of attention.

"You do?" Wad said. "Where?"

"I'm not telling you assholes where I live," Potato barked.

"Ahem," Hesh grunted. "It seems clear to me that we can solve all of this one step at a time. Seeing as how organization isn't one of Wadley's strong suits, it's safe to assume he hasn't prioritized his list of contacts on his Talkman in any meaningful way."

The Old Guard of Zerth

"I..."

"I don't need you to confirm that, Wad, I already know it. Therefore, your list of contacts defaults to those in closest proximity to you. Not that it matters as the terms of delivery were to demand payment upon receipt. Cash on demand, correct? Nobody is going to pay for a package they didn't order so it's more or less destined to wander the planet until you stop it... but if you ask me, the easiest way out of this mess is to simply track the package."

Potato clapped his hands together and jumped to his feet, quickly vanishing into the back room.

There was a hush throughout the office. "Did we make him angry?" Meri said. He tried to tap his pipe out but the stem snapped in his fingers.

Amelia made a sad cooing noise.

Gustav burst out laughing. He rocked in the couch, holding his knees, then went for his Talkman and a beer. **Wire – Men 2nd**. "What the fuck is going on?" He continued laughing. Hesh thought seriously about walking out of the office.

A moment later, Potato returned, wiping his hands on his pants. He produced a tarnished Talkman and hucked it to the coffee table. "There, track your guy. That fucker Dale said he did work with the Delivery guys. Gave him his boots. MªFuggin direct. I heard him say it."

Hesh was speechless.

Potato didn't know what to do with the silence. He started to feel a bit defensive so he raised his voice. "Bug says we can track the delivery guy. This Talkman gotta hatch-mode right to em."

Hesh shook his head. "The owner of that device has most certainly already respawned and loaded his backup to another Talkman. It's probably already empty."

Potato poked at it. His silence indicated Hesh was correct. "Yeah, but it's got the hatch-mode."

"Where did you get that?" Amelia said.

"From the corpse in the back," Potato replied. He seemed hurt by an assumed accusation.

"Wad has a corpse in his office?" Amelia shouted.

"There used to be three, but two of em' took off, I guess," Potato replied.

"What? Why? How?!" Amelia moaned.

"They got legs. They can walk," Potato answered.

Amelia shook the nonsense from her mind. "No, I mean why are there corpses in your office, Wad?"

"They tried to kill me. Got a price on my head and all that," Potato said.

Wad nodded, pointing at Potato.

"Oh, that's just fabulous," Amelia huffed. "Hanging out with criminals, now." She approached Potato with a scowl. "Look, I don't know who you are, but it's obvious to me-"

"I'm Potato. Headhunters' trying to kill me but we killed him first. What's the big deal?"

Amelia whimpered with her face in her palm. "Wonderful friends you have, Wad."

"Is it still a Headhunter if he's missing his head? Does the identity remain or is it wiped clean? Does he cobble together a new identity of Hunter of Head? Hunter of his own head?" Meri mused philosophically to himself.

"I'm a hunter of head," Gustav chuckled, then tried to shoot a sexy wink at Amelia, but missed and hit the file cabinet.

"Back on track, boys," Hesh said loudly.

"In the words of Phineas P Derigible – Make Me," Meri said, attempting to suckle his broken pipe with great difficulty.

"Damn, Meri, What crawled up your ass?" Gustav chuckled.

"He gets cranky when he pukes on himself," Potato said.

"As I should," Meri nodded with authority.

Hesh thought quickly. The Morouni's mood was in danger of compromising the crew's stability, and there was clearly little that could be done to elevate Meri's spirits. He needed a detour he could control. No more booze... but maybe? It wasn't the most ideal option – if others existed – but given the circumstances, it might be just the trick needed to dam up the negativity. Hesh went for his manbag. He scrounged around, producing a gunmetal-gray spherical bauble. He spun the top open and handed it to the Morouni. He didn't say a word, but shifted his eyes to direct Meri's attention.

"Cocaine," Meri said. He turned to the crew. "The benefits of a mind reader in one's company is truly astounding. When we of the hairy persuasion find ourselves on the wobble, a little boost is always appropriate." He took a modest pinch and put it to work.

Amelia threw her hands up and left the room.

"Cocaine!" Gustav shouted, barging in.

"Cocaine," Meri sang deeply to himself, shuffling in a circle.

Wad looked on as the two with noses indulged. He turned to Hesh. "Got anything for me?"

"Some advice," Hesh said. "This whole ordeal is your fault. I suggest you take ownership of it. I've fulfilled my duty as a friend by clearing your path of obstacles. Now, it's your turn."

Wad sat down, half defeated. He look to the two men to his side as they hurled rhyming epithets at each-other in some kind of game – then to Potato, who seemed out of place.

"Strudel," Potato said.

"What?"

"Strudel's got an address. She's downstairs. Maybe she got the package."

Hesh held his head. "We don't need the package, we need the delivery boy and his Talkman."

"If she scanned the package, she's got a hatch-mode to the delivery guy's Talkman. We can track him."

Hesh didn't have anything bad to say, but it was starting to bother him that he couldn't read Potato.

"Strudel?" Wad said. "The Boutique downstairs?"

"Shopping!" Gustav hollered, jumping in. "Look at this filthy robe. I can't go out in public wearing this!" He yanked the green fuzz from his body and chucked it out the window, leaving him bare naked. He stood proudly for a moment before making finger-guns and ducking behind the couch.

"New attire would do me wonders, I say." Meri bellowed. He slapped his belly with open palms.

"Okay, then," Wad said, finding a bit of energy. He turned to Potato. "We'll go see Strudel. You coming?"

"Nope," Potato said. "Gonna go to the Mayor's office and find the files on MᵃFuggin Delivery.

"Oh no you're not," Amelia hollered, as she stormed in through the curtain. "No public allowed – especially not a criminal. I'm not letting you anywhere near the Mayor's office." She turned to Wad. "Wadley, tell this hooligan he's not allowed in the office."

Potato stepped forward with a sneer. "I'm gonna help Wad. Try to stop me and I'll break your fuckin' arm."

Amelia snapped back. She looked to Wad for backup but he only shook his head at Potato, indicating he wasn't allowed to mangle the girl. Potato continued to stare, challenging her to press the issue. She hesitated, noting a glint of something in the brute-Legomi's eye. It was a familiar look she had seen on occasion with Wadley. Something fiery and wild, yet familiar and loyal. Like a pit-bull. She hesitated, running some things through her head while sucking on her lower lip. Dropping her eyes, she made her way to the corner of the office, gathering her papers which were dry-stained with her own blood. She packed them neatly against her chest and gave Wad a look. "I'm doing this for you, Wad. Don't forget that."

Wad looked up at the girl from the couch. "I know," he said.

Amelia meant to be stern but couldn't muster the anger. There was a look of desperation about Wad that deflated the tension. In her dealings with the Mayor's Advisor, she had seen many different sides of the man in a professional setting, and it was his total lack of professionalism that nearly sent her running for the hills. After her first month on the job, she discovered Wadley's method within the madness, not that there was a method, rather, he was profoundly adept at dealing with the madness. For that time she was blind to his means of coping, but now it was laid out naked for her to examine every unpleasant little bit.

Mighty Rahiem

"Shopping!" Meri hollered.

"Flopping!" Naked Gustav harmonized. The two men bounded after each-other in a circle. Gustav hit the couch and bounced, throwing himself through the curtain. He promised he wasn't hurt.

Potato snatched a beer and shot a look at Amelia. "You stay outa' my way, you hear?" He took a man-sized swig and started out the door.

"Not without me, you're not," Amelia hollered. She followed close behind with fists balled, hollering G-rated obscenities.

Hesh joined from behind, shaking his head at Meri. He shouldered his man-bag and tossed a cigarette to the ground. "There's something about that Potato that I just cannot read. I'm glad someone can control him."

"Who, Potato? Oh, you don't control him," Meri laughed. "You wind him up and point him in the desired direction. A machine he is, with battery charged by the suns themselves." Meri then bent over and vomited across his knees. "I'll be needing some new pants now." He righted himself and swaggered out the door with his thumbs in his suspenders. "Wadley, my man, will you join us? We're off to shower my loving self with gifts of adoration in the form of a new suit."

"Shopping!" Gustav could be heard from outside.

Hesh turned to Wadley with a shrug and a smile. "Well, I can't think of any place I'd rather *not* be than the Mayor's Office. Shopping it is." Wad bit his lip and shook his head as the two made their way out the door and into the bar.

Chapter 8

Strudel's Closet

Imported Humin sherts 50% off

"Fifty percent off what? There's no price tag on any of these," Naked Gustav said, rubbing his hair. He flipped through the rack of loud shirts in the 'SHERTS' aisle of Strudel's Closet.

"Double whatever you offer," Meri teased with an unusual amount of snark. The cocaine did him well.

Strudel's Closet was one of the few Morouni establishments in South Town that specialized in Human goods, but it added to the flare of the place. Tiki torches, watermelon prints and lawn flamingos dominated the decor. Caribbean inspired clothing was the special, as was a bounty of Earth-imported dried dog food, which was piled on steel-framed racks along the walls. The ceiling was dotted with "Real Humin stars", recognized by Naked Gustav to be several knotted up strings of Christmas lights. It gave the place a sickly, festive glow that made it difficult for the him to place the color of clothing in the racks. Not that it mattered in the least.

Naked Gustav pushed passed Hesh and moved on towards the aisle marked 'SHARTS,' where he assumed the shorts were located. He wasn't wrong. He snatched up something bad and placed it over his hips, wagging about. Hesh gave him a thumbs-up, primarily to encourage an end to the nakedness. On to the hats.

The Old Guard of Zerth

Meri strolled by with a fantastically large pair of blunderhose over his arm. Pink and yellow striped with a four-inch belt loop. Altogether they stood taller than the Sectoid. He scrounged the shelves for a belt buckle that could handle the girth, finding a stylish imported clock – numberless with exaggerated hands. It was useless for keeping Zerth time, but would make an excellent belt buckle. He picked out a pea-green polo to compliment the pants, and bring out the same in his eyes.

Wad approached the counter where the owner of the establishment was perched. Strudel was a pint-sized Morouni girl with dyed pink pigtails and a penchant for plugging her nose-holes with one or many fingers. She bared a close resemblance to a marmot with a finger up its nose. She sat atop the counter behind the register, happily munching away at a bag of dog food under her arm. She noticed Wad and wiped her hand on her pants. "Well, if it ain't the big man himself. What can I do for you? Buying, selling or whatever?" she squeaked.

"Neither," Wad said. "I'm looking for a package that might have shown up here. Anybody drop anything off?"

"Maybe," Strudel winked playfully. "What's it to ya?"

Wad sighed. "Look, I don't wanna play any games. I just want to know if anyone tried to drop off a package. It would have been in my name.

"Maybe they did, maybe they didn't. All's I know is that I got customers, so if you ain't buying nothing, I got better things to do." She sat back and jammed her paw into the bag of dog food.

Wad held his head. "Fine," he said. He quickly scanned the front desk for something cheap, finding a cardboard display filled with what looked like rocks. The tag on the front advertised 'Real Humin Teeth.' It was a box of teeth. He nabbed a handful. "Here, how much are these?"

"Two bucks," Strudel said, poking the number into her Talkman. She held out her wrist to accept Wad's card.

Wad instinctively retrieved his credcard and swiped it.

>*KEEK*<

Strudel frowned. She glared at her Talkman and shook her head, then held it in Wad's face. "What's this say?"

>NO ACCOUNT FOUND<

Wad planted his face in his hands and groaned. "Look, Strudel, I just need to know if somebody came-"

"Ya got changing rooms?" Gustav called out from over a shelf.

Strudel dropped the bag. "It's in the corner, honey. Take yer time." She turned back to Wad with an impatient look. "What, you got no money, or something? How come you got no money?"

"Fuck it," Wad mumbled. He dropped the teeth and marched off to find Hesh.

Gustav threw open the door of the changing room. He was decked out with an open collar pool-shirt with trilobite print and white khaki shorts. A pair of rustic, 17 hole linesman's boots shot up to his knees and he had a swastika armband looped around his afro. He smiled like he never had before.

Meri pushed Gustav aside and slammed the door shut, emerging moments later in something clean and regal, yet stylish and compelling. The lines extenuated his mass – a daring ensemble.

"You look like a blind Ed Grimley," Gustav laughed.

"Well," Meri shot back. "You look like a-"

"Don't start," Gustav interrupted. This is traditional Human attire. In fact, *not wearing* this stuff gets you thrown out of churches. Tell me I'm wrong."

"One moment there, my man. What's this?" Meri said, scratching at Gustav's lips. "If my eyes don't deceive me, I do believe you've got some bullshit coming through your lips."

"Oh, really?" Gustav said. "Tell me about your travels to Earth, my friend. What did you see? Tell me all about what *we humans* are supposed to wear."

Meri shook his head and walked to the counter with Gustav close behind. Strudel looked the two men up and down and punched a series of numbers into her Talkman. "Two-oh-five bucks," She snapped.

"Two hundred and–" Meri burst, but Gustav stepped in.

"You see this headband," Gustav said, pointing at the swastika. "This thing ain't worth the cotton it's printed on. In fact, I would probably get shot if I wore this thing on Earth. And I'd deserve it, too. You'd be lucky to give this thing away."

"And here you are about to buy it," Strudel pushed back.

Gustav looked at Meri with wide eyes. "Goddam, she's smarter than we thought. Somehow she knew the headband was valuable!" He turned to Strudel with a grave look. "You're a sharp cookie, my friend. You're in the right business, for sure. I can tell you've got your knowledge of Earthly junk down pat. Take this shirt, for example. You'd probably be selling this for about two bucks, but the truth is, on Earth, yer probably paying about fifty. Honest to God truth. And these boots? Well over two hundred alone."

"Yer a grade-A bullshitter," Strudel schmoozed. "Ain't nuthin' worth what yer sayin'."

"A liar doesn't get far when faced with a bugman, does he?" Gustav said. He whistled to Hesh in the rear of the shop. "Excuse me, sir. We would be most grateful if you could bless us with your talents."

Hesh cocked his head and approached the counter with Wad in tow. "What the hell are you on about?"

Gustav leaned into the bug with a shit eating grin. He laid it on thick and hammed it up to the roof. "This shirt would cost me fifty bucks on Earth... this headband would cost hundreds, if not thousands. Tell me I'm lying."

Hesh looked Gustav over with a sour eye. He turned to Strudel. "He's telling the truth," He said. "These are very valuable items. The man isn't lying."

"Thank you," Gustav said, shooing Hesh away. "So you can see, I actually do know what I'm taking about. I am, in fact, a Human."

"No way," Strudel said, stunned. "You mean I can sell that there headband for a thousand bucks?"

"If you were on Earth, sure. But here on Zerth, things are much different. Everything is naturally cheaper here. It's just the way things work. I could go on and on and explain the reasons, but I know you don't have time for that kind of crap. Neither do I. You wanna know something else? A full plate of waffles is what, a buck here? On Earth, yer lookin' at about fifteen."

"No way." Strudel's mouth was agape.

"He's not lying," Hesh shouted from the corner.

Gustav drew closer to Strudel and lowered his voice. "So when I tell you that this whole pile of junk is only worth about twenty bucks, you know I'm telling the truth."

Strudel nodded with wide eyes. She deleted the '5' and rang up the charges as 20 bucks.

"And the deal is done," Gustav smiled.

"Jeez, mister," Strudel drooped. "If everything is as worthless as you say it is, I dunno how I'm gonna make rent."

"What the hell are you talking about?" Wad said, stepping in. "I don't charge you rent."

"Yeah," Strudel sighed. "But the taxman shows up and says I gotta give him money. Says the store is gonna go bye-bye if I don't pay. Boom-bucks, he calls it. And speakin' of waffles, my second-half-sister worked at the Whiskey Waffle place over there in Ortega. Boss didn't pay and now she's a goner."

Gustav chuckled, reminiscing over his death.

"That's unimaginably fucked up," Meri said, slapping his hands on the counter. "Who is doing this to you?"

"I don't know," Strudel said. "He shows up and wants money. That's all I know and that's all I'm gonna say."

Wad threw his hands up. "That's what I was trying to tell you. Somebody showed up and wanted you to pay for my package. It's a COD, not a bomb threat. Nobody's gonna blow you up. They just wanted to deliver my stuff. What did he look like?"

"Big guy," Strudel said. "Corbinall. Big n' hairy. And no joke. He said he's gonna blow my butt up. I didn't make that up."

"An aggressive Corbinall?" Meri said, squinting.

"That's what I said," Strudel whispered. "It's really creepy."

Gustav pushed in, flapping his hands around. "What the hell are you two babbling about?"

Mighty Rahiem

Meri turned to Gustav with a shake of the head. "I'd be quite happy to regale the nature of my brethren to you some other time. Now just seems improper, wouldn't you agree? I'd say it's more important to worry about why this man would be demanding money from our sweet Strudel."

"Sounds like extortion to me," Gustav said, rubbing his chin. "An extortion ring disguised as a delivery service. Ingenious! That's like, straight-up like Mafioso shit."

"What does that mean?" Wad said.

Gustav leaned down to Wad. "All right, check out this crazy shit. Back on Earth, we got these guys that run around and do all kinds of horrible junk, but their smart about it. Organized criminals with a hierarchy and everything. They do stuff like this, threatening business and shit like that. The guy at the top is call the Don. He's the head of the snake."

Wad paused Gustav with a finger. "Wait. Amelia said something about a guy called Don. Don Sanders. She said he was the guy blowing up all the Morouni businesses."

"There ya go!" Gustav said, excitedly. "MᵃFuggin Mafia! We gotta take out the big guy at the top – the big boss. This delivery guy is probably just a goon. I'd betcha anything this Don Sanders is the big kahuna targeting Morouni businesses. And here we are in a Morouni business he wants to blow up. Case closed!"

"That's it, then," Wad said. "Meri, send a message to Potato. We got the guy. It's Don Sanders. He's the boss of the Blue Fist. Amelia's got a whole file on him."

Meri nodded. He tapped away at his Talkman, then mused aloud. "Why Morouni businesses? I don't see the angle. How could a Human be connected to the Blue Fist?"

The Old Guard of Zerth

"Why don't ya just ask the Tax Man when he shows up?" Strudel said. "He said he's coming soon, then I gotta pay out the ass."

"Is that so?" Meri said with a grin. "Tell me, sister, what does he charge?"

"Four-hundred and fifty bucks," Wad said with a nod. "That's the COD for the reticle."

"Naw, he wanted more than that," Strudel said, waving her hand. "He said five hundred or me and my stuff go bye-bye."

"I suppose that makes sense," Wad said, rubbing his chin. "He's probably skimming off the top for himself."

"Idea," Gustav said with a finger in the air. He whipped out his credcard and tossed it across the counter. "Go ahead and charge six hundred bucks. That'll pay the COD and a little extra for your troubles."

The two Morouni were stunned. They glared at the Human who beamed with satisfaction – hands on his hips and teeth in the air. Gustav turned to Strudel who wasn't touching his card, then to Meri, who's expression rivaled a train-wreck. "What?" He said.

"After all that haggling?" Meri boomed. "And to allow this poor woman to drown in her plight is clearly unconscionable. What happens if he returns a second time?"

"First off," Gustav started, "nobody tells me what I *have* to pay. I pay what I *want* to pay, and that's the end of it. Secondly, logic dictates the path of least resistance is the best option. Are you going to fight the mob? Am I? If we fail, things become so much worse for this poor girl."

"But, the principle of the thing," Meri hollered. "It's just not right."

Mighty Rahiem

"When principle clashes with logic, historically, everyone loses... except in some cases. Some really extraordinary cases," Gustav scratched his head in thought. "Really extraordinary people would be required to do it right and I'm not vain enough to claim that descriptor."

"Oh, you most certainly are," Meri gasped.

"Ahh, I see how it is," Gustav winked. He held his hand to his chest and heaved the other to the ceiling. "Some are born great, some achieve greatness, and some have greatness thrust upon them."

"William Shakespeare's Malvolio," Meri growled reluctantly.

"Are you thrusting *something* upon me, dear Meri? Dare I say, greatness? Am I now an agent of the righteous calling? Must I bare the weight of this great expectation you've so selfishly plopped in my lap? The hero is tired. How bout' you do your own heavy lifting."

"You struggle only with the weight of your delusions. Tell me, my man, how much do you bench?" Meri cracked a smile.

"Not nearly as much as the people deserve!" Gustav feigned. "Alas, with a humble heart, I am spent with the tears of the common folk – so tired. The people will perish as I lament my impotence. Farewell, plebeians, your hero sucks."

The two men descended into a fit of laughter as Strudel stood by with a frown. Wad interrupted with a clearing of the throat.

"What's the deal?" Gustav said, poking at Wad. "No one gets hurt. The guy gets his money and you get your Talkman back. It's a win-win."

"Oh, right," Strudel spit. "You just gonna pay the guy every time he shows up?"

The Old Guard of Zerth

"Hey, no problem," Gustav said. "Really, I'm just upstairs. Just a few steps away. Call me whenever. It'll be fun!"

"Yeah? What happens when *you* run outa money?" Strudel added. She was tapping her claw on the counter.

"Not in the cards, honey," Gustav said. "It's so much easier this way. It's so trivial it's not even worth mentioning. Like a mosquito, you know, a mosquito? Takes more calories to swat than he can suck outa me. Not worth the effort."

"So, what are ya, some kinda millionaire or sumthin?" Strudel said through a sour look. "You can't be that loaded."

Gustav scoffed. "I got all they money in the world."

Wad pushed between the two men. "Good, so it's settled." He leaned into the desk and pointed at Strudel. "When our guy shows up, shoot me a mess-" He stopped cold at the sight of his empty wrist. He pointed at Gustav with his thumb. "Send him a message. Same ID he used to pay you with. We'll come running. We aren't far away."

Meri's Talkman blipped. "Speaking of messages." He scrolled through the text on his screen. "Hah! Do your own dirty work, you silly lug." He typed away at the screen with a bent claw.

"Who is it?" Wad said.

"The lump of joy himself, our man Potato. He's offering me ten whole bucks to stop our bus from spinning. The nerve!"

"You mean *my* bus?" Wad said, with more than a hint of frustration.

"Pssh," Gustav spit, spinning on his heel. "Tell him we'll give him *twenty bucks* if he can stop it himself." He laughed. "It's his fault it's spinning anyway, isn't it?"

Mighty Rahiem

Wad dismissed it as an embarrassing reminder. He gave Strudel a point and a thumbs-up, then turned to join the two men as they made their way out the door. Gustav threw open the curtain with a flourish and a loud grunt, heaving himself into the light of the day.

As soon as they were out of sight, Hesh approached the counter to inquire about the price of teeth in the display.

Amelia kept a mental eye on Potato as he paced tirelessly at the mouth of her cubicle. His hand occasionally brushed at the hilt of the giant gun in its holster, which gave the girl reason to find the file quickly. Her fingers flipped across hundreds of manila folders but she had no luck tracking down the contact information for MᵃFuggin Delivery Service. She was certain it was filed in her stack of purchasing orders, but it just wasn't there.

The place was an open floor plan with room for another thirty or so cubicles, yet Amelia was the only one there. She holed up next to the door for easy access to the coffee boy when he came through on his rounds. The rest of the space was barren. Nothing but ashwood floor and dobistone walls with the occasional potted succulent in westward facing windows.

Her cubicle was a cheap recreation of something pleasant. A few vinyl flower stickers adorned the lining, then a mass of post-it notes organized by color and size. Atop a small shelf was a copy of James Cameron's Titanic: the novelization, followed by a framed picture of a fairy sitting on a leaf. The desk was bare, save for a stack of files and a box of tissue with a floral pattern. It smelled like hand sanitizer and rubber bands.

The Old Guard of Zerth

Potato let out a huff and sat down on the floor to keep from fidgeting. He could hear the Mayors babbling loudly down the hall. It sound like barking. The thought had occurred to him more than once to insert himself. He had to hold himself back from kicking down the door and instituting his own brand of broken-arm-negotiation, so he turned back to the cubicle to get lost in the post-it notes.

10:00 am: Mayor Digby conference call; 10:25 am: Mayor Locus sponge bath; 10:45 am: Mayor Steve nap time.

"You do all those things?" Potato said.

Amelia spun her chair around with wide eyes. "Huh?"

"You do all those things on those notes?" Potato said again.

"No," she said. After a brief pause she turned around and checked her Talkman for the time. She then pulled a few notes off the wall and threw them into a wicker basket under her desk.

Potato took a peak, finding the basket nearly overflowing with the little colored paper. "So why do ya write em all down?" he asked.

Amelia spun around again, looking a bit flustered. "I'm just keeping track of the Mayors routine. It's important stuff for me to work around. I am the Mayor's assistant," she chuckled with a hint of distress. "If I don't keep track of it, nobody will."

"Where do you spawn in?" Potato asked.

Amelia buckled a bit. "Why do you ask?" she said, then tried to go back to her files.

"Azura, I bet," Potato nodded.

"Why... why does that matter?" she said, thumbing through the files more quickly.

"Yer outta control."

"I'm not out of control," she said with her back to the Legomi.

"That's where Humans go when they're out of control. I seen it myself. People get all screwed up in the head and they end up in Azura."

"That's not true," Amelia mumbled, with her back still turned.

"That's why Guz spawns there. He's a fuckin' nutcase. The only difference is, he knows it. He knows it and he likes it."

"I am not out of control!" Amelia said, swinging around and knocking the stack of papers off her desk. They rained down atop the Legomi but he didn't react.

Amelia made a whimpering noise and leaned over, gathering up as much as she could, bundling them together and tapping them on her knees to straighten them out.

"What's that?" Potato said.

"What's what?" Amelia said, defensively.

Potato leaped up and fished a file out of the girl's lap, causing her to jump and squirm. "Excuse me!" she shouted. "Can't you ask nicely? That's extremely rude."

Potato carried on, unfazed. He yanked a file out and flipped it open.

"That's city property, mister," Amelia shouted.

She lunged for the folder but Potato yanked it away. He pulled a picture out, showing it to Amelia. "Who's this?"

"None of your business," she barked.

"Gotta be important," Potato said, flipping it around and looking it over. It was an elderly Human with wild white hair. "Ya got all that other stuff stored away but this one ain't.

The Old Guard of Zerth

She swiped at the file again but Potato dodged. "Okay, fine. It's important, but not right now. Can I please have my file back?"

Potato held the picture, spinning on his butt and turning his back to the girl. "Guy looks mean. How much you wanna bet he's in on all this? Maybe he's the guy that put the price on my head."

Amelia groaned. "Highly unlikely. He's a bombing suspect, not a delivery man. And chances are, you've got a price on your head for being a jerk."

"I gotta feeling about this guy," Potato said to himself.

Amelia reached over his head and grabbed hold of the file. She tried to wrench it from his hands but failed. It felt like it was cemented in place. Potato turned slowly and looked her in the eye, then released his vice-grip. She let out a huff and organized the file, then placed it back on her desk with a scowl. "Now, if you don't mind, we have work to do."

Potato turned away, restless. He fidgeted in place, picking at the ashwood texture in the floor. The coffee boy rolled by in the hall and kept going. There was a loud thump heard from the Mayor's office, then some muffled yelling. His Talkman bleeped and he slapped it quickly. It was a message from Meri.

MERI: GOT NAME – DON SANDERS – FIND HIM AND YO FIN WADS TALKMNA

Potato nodded to himself and stood up. "Told ya."

"Told me what?" Amelia said, still bent over her files.

"Found the guy that took Wad's hatch-mode."

"Really," she said, turning around. "Who is it?"

Mighty Rahiem

Potato snatched the file off the desk and threw it in her lap. "That guy." He pushed his Talkman into her face. "Meri said so. Meri ain't a liar."

Amelia thought for a moment, trying to parse the information. It didn't add up. "I don't believe that," she said, shaking her head.

"Don't care. I didn't say it, Meri said it. Bet he put a price on my head, too. Let's go get him."

Amelia conceded with her palms up. "Okay, okay, fine. But he didn't say anything about putting a price on your head, so you've got no reason to-"

"-he looks like somebody that wants me dead."

Amelia rolled her eyes. "I know a lot of people that look like that," she groaned.

"Really? Who? I'll give em' a boot party." Potato sneered.

"Never mind," Amelia said, wagging her hands. "So, let's say it really is Don Sanders. How do you expect to track him down?"

"Look at the picture paper," Potato said, poking the file in her hands.

"There's nothing like that in here," she said. "The only thing in here are pictures and a brief – *brief* history of his actions. He dropped off the map a long time ago. He's vanished. Nobody knows where he is, so how do you think *you're* going to find him?"

Potato seemed genuinely confused by the question. "We'll just get in the bus and drive around. That's what we usually do. It'll work."

"Oh, really?" Amelia said, sarcastically. "The bus?"

The Old Guard of Zerth

A look of dismay crept across Potato's face. He looked down at his boots. "The bus is spinning."

"You're right. It is."

"How we gonna stop it?"

"*We* aren't going to do anything except remove you from this office. You can do whatever you want outside, but as far as I'm concerned, we're done here."

Potato looked a bit frazzled. "I got an idea," he said, then carefully poked at his Talkman with an over-sized finger. "I'm gonna pay Meri to fix it. I bet ten bucks will get his ass in gear."

The coffee boy darted passed with a rattling cart. "Mayor Purcell is dead," he yelled into the door. He kept running, leaving a trail of plastiform cups across the hallway.

Amelia winced a bit and dropped her shoulders. She reached up and started nabbing post-it notes off the backboard.

Potato's Talkman blipped again. "Meri says he'll give me twenty bucks if I can get in the bus. I gotta go!" Potato dashed out of the office. A moment later, a crash and yelp of a tiny coffee boy.

Chapter 9

Sober At Last

"Hey Sam," Wad said.

"Yeah, what?" Potato replied, downing a swig of Granite Hill from behind the bar.

"Why is the bus in the bar?"

Plexi – Dayglow.

"Cause that's where it ended up. Fuck you and your questions."

Given the state of the bar, the bus didn't seem out of place. It sat neatly atop two crushed tables, front fender kissing the north wall. Wad took a seat at the bar and Potato poured him a glass of Granite Hill. He slapped the bar and nodded at the bus with a smile. "That right there is twenty bucks in my pocket."

Wad downed the drink and wiped his lips. "How do ya figure?"

"Meri said he'd give me twenty bucks if I could get it to stop spinning. Well, there ya have it. The shit don't spin no more."

"Easy money," Wad said, calling for another drink with a tapping glass. He sucked it down as quickly as it arrived.

Potato rested his elbow on the bar and leaned forward. He shifted the mood with a grunt. "Hey buddy. Straight talk. Whadya gonna do when all the booze is gone?"

The Old Guard of Zerth

Wad thought for a moment, wondering if the question were a metaphorical one. It dawned on him that he didn't have a bank account to order a replacement bottle if they finished it off. Not that they could do it so easily. There were hundreds of replacements in his office, so it wasn't an immediate threat. "We'll worry about that when the time comes," he said, then tapped the bar for another.

Potato didn't immediately follow through. "Wad, old buddy," he said. "You don't look like ya don't care too much about bein' broke. I mean, sure, you still got all this great stuff, but-"

The two Legomi looked around the bar. It didn't even look like a bar any more. It looked like wreckage. Wad had done plenty of repairs in the past, replacing smashed tables, patching bullet holes in the wall, scrubbing plasma burns off the floor, but it was never this bad. And now he couldn't pay anyone to fix it. Hell, there was a bus in there, now. It was taking up a lot of space.

"Goddam," Potato said. "Really looks like a bomb went off in here."

Wad lowered his head. He didn't want to think about it. He just wanted his money back so he could pay someone to make it all go away, just like he always did. He thought maybe he could just take over one of a dozen other properties he owned and start over. He'd have to evict the current occupant, presumably by force. His mind wandered to Strudel and her boutique. He pictured what it would look like if a bomb went off in there. Probably wouldn't be much different from what his bar looked like currently. It would probably end up the same if he took over. He groaned and buried his head, mumbling. "I just want my damned money back."

"We'll get it," Potato said. He poured his buddy another drink and slid it his way.

"Oh, this is much better," Gustav yelled, stepping over the rubble. Meri and Hesh followed, with the Sectoid having a bit of difficulty scaling a larger chunk of wall. Gustav smacked the back of the bus with an open palm. "I don't know how you did it, but you did it." The Human skirted around and threw himself into a bar stool, then slapped the wood and received a drink. Hesh examined the thing, attempting to buff out a scuff on the rear suspenser with his breath and his shirt.

Meri took a stool and aimed a wide grin at the bartender. Potato replied with smug lips of his own. "Twenty bucks," the Legomi said. "or you don't drink."

Meri leaned forward. "My man, I do believe the deal involved you getting *into* the bus. I'd be glad to settle up if you wouldn't mind serving me that bourbon from the front seat."

Potato's eye darted to Wad, "You got the keys?"

Wad threw his arms up.

Hesh cleared his throat. "Ahem. Regarding the information gleaned from the visit to the boutique-" He began.

"-I deepened my concern regarding Gustav's moral bankruptcy," Meri finished. He called for a drink with a double slap on the bar.

"I, on the other hand, am quite proud of the man," Hesh Smiled. "He got us all the answers we were looking for, whether he intended to or not. The truth of the matter I don't care to say."

"Damn right," Gustav said, fist pounding the bar. "Extortion all the way. They got a whole racket going and Don Sanders is at the center of it. She doesn't pay, she explodes. That weird fucking girl says our guy is showing up soon. The question is, how would we like to approach this one?" He pounded his bourbon and tapped for another.

The Old Guard of Zerth

"Don Sanders," Potato rumbled low. "You say the delivery guy is connected, I say we take the bastard to pound-town and beat him 'till he tells us where Sanders is. That way, we don't gotta drive around looking for him. Right, Wad?" He gave Wadley a nod.

"Bad approach," Hesh said. "We want to keep it smooth and non-violent."

Potato ignored the Sectoid. "Right, Wad?"

Wad was off in his own world, swirling his finger in an empty glass.

"What's with the sour-puss?" Gustav said, leaning around Meri.

"He's worried about bein' broke," Potato said.

"No," Hesh interrupted. "He's thinking about something else." He leaned over the bar to catch eye-contact with Wad. "Thank you for doing that. I really appreciate it."

"A drink for Wadley!" Meri bellowed, hoping to intercept it for himself.

"We all need drinks," Gustav said, wrapping his arm around Hesh's neck.

The bugman shrank back and found another seat. "I disagree. Given the situation, I suggest the subtle approach. Listen and learn – information gathering – Recon. We know this contact is expected to show up some time in the near future and we don't want to-"

"Hesh is right," Wad said. "Don't forget, Strudel's place is right under the office. No guns blazing. We get in and hang back. We don't need to interrogate him if we can get his Talkman."

"I'm out," Potato said, throwing his hands up. He turned back to Wad. "Now, gimme those keys."

"I got a better idea," Gustav said, pointing at Potato. "You're going to be my distraction. You get the fucker's attention and I'll pull the old switcharoo with Dale's dead Talkman." He reached into his pocket and dangled the tarnished Talkman in the air.

"Masterful plan," Meri said. Even Hesh nodded with approval.

"How am I supposed to do that?" Potato said.

"Just blink at him a lot," Gustav replied. "It's creepy as shit when you do that. One big eye." Gustav framed his hands around Potato's eye as the Legomi swatted him away.

"And me?" Meri asked with building excitement.

"Stand in the door," Gustav said. Don't let the guy leave until I give you the signal that it's all clear. Wad, you're the lookout. You go in first – alone. You make like everything is peachy and just keep watch. If shit goes sideways, you know what to do."

"Pretty sure I do," Wad nodded.

Hesh hopped from the bar stool, clapping his hands. "You boys are actually starting to impress me. I am genuinely pleased. I thought for sure I'd have to step back in as the voice of reason and restraint, but here you are, traversing the path quite naturally."

"Discipline is key in matters of espionage," Meri said, going for the bourbon.

Wad cupped his hand over Meri's glass and gave him a knowing look. "We do this quiet or we don't do it at all."

Meri's lips slid to a smirk and he set the glass down gently, pushing it away with a claw. "Discipline indeed, my man, though my sobriety comes at a price. The keys, please,"

The Old Guard of Zerth

"Hey," Potato shouted. "I'll be sober, too."

Wad chuckled with his head in his hands. He did his best to retreat from the situation.

Hesh smiled and backed away. "You boys take care. I'm turning in for some much needed rest." He squeezed through the gap between the bus and the stairwell as his shadow vanished into the light above. Potato capped the booze and joined the crew as they went over their plan in the privacy of the darkened bar.

Chapter 10

Boot Party

The door flap lifted and the giant entered, ducking beneath the dobistone archway. His shadow stretched across the floor and mingled with confused lighting. Deep grunts and heavy breathing grabbed Strudel's attention as she looked up to meet the visitor. She jumped to her feet in a panic, furiously dialing on her Talkman.

The Old Guard of Zerth

The mammoth of a man walked slowly across the tile floor, beads of blue and green and yellow flashed across a crooked fang jutting from a distended lower jaw. His eyes were obscured, deep-set beneath a thick, drooping brow. As he approached, nostrils flared and he bared his teeth with a stilted smile. He rose over the woman behind the counter, saying nothing but demanding everything. He stood motionless, blocking any resistance Strudel could offer. A glint of light across a dusky eye was all that told him apart from a statue. Strudel was helpless.

The speakers cracked and the beast spun around.

Desert Sessions – Goin to a Hangin.

The flap flew aside and Wadley entered at a frantic pace, barefoot, with his boots gripped tightly against his chest. He let out a primal hoot, going airborne and pounding the footwear into the flesh of the beast. The Legomi recovered from his attack, striking a victory pose. Three more bodies entered, gnashing and snarling and hurling insults.

"-**HIC**- Justice!" Meri cried, with a finger, more or less, in the direction of his target. He barreled forward, missing the giant by feet, then gut punching through the front desk. Splinters of wood fired in every direction. Strudel was sent flying. Her head cracked against the backboard and she was out. Meri lost his balance and went down, vanishing behind the wreckage of the counter.

Gustav slid across the floor and swept the legs of the enemy to no effect, then lay still. Wad burst into laughter, dropping his boots. Potato came in from behind, wrapping a meaty elbow around Wad's neck and dragged him to the tile. Wadley choked for breath as Potato invaded his pockets with a quick hand, yanking the keys to the bus from Wad's jacket. Potato eased up, then jumped to his feet, jingling the keys in the air. "You owe me twenty bucks, motherfucker!" He took off out the door. Meri emerged from the rubble with a look of distress.

Mighty Rahiem

Wad caught his breath and pointed to the target. "Guys, we're supposed to beat that guy up and take his stuff." He patted himself down, producing a bottle of Vodka, then took a hearty swig and assumed battle stance.

The beast looked on.

"Fiend!" Meri shouted. "Thou hast -HIC- incurred the wrath of vengeance. Prepare -HIC- yourself for mortal combat!" Meri put up his dukes and began reciting Hamlet – from the beginning.

Gustav performed a limp, defensive roll and sprang to his feet, hurling backwards into a tie rack. He shook it off, trying to steady himself on his knees, breathing deliberately, holding back the vomit.

Wad sprang, lunging forward with a blinding jab to the knee cap, then a left hook to the hip. An uppercut to the balls doubled the beast over. Wad was knocked silly by an unintentional headbutt atop his skull as the mountain of a man came down on top of him. Gustav jumped in, bear-hugging the giant's ass. He pounded his knee into the man's jewels like a jackhammer. The oaf tightened up, catching Gustav's leg between two powerfully squeezed thighs. The two went down.

In came Meri. "Stay! Speak, -HIC- speak! I charge thee, speak! EXIT GHOST!" The Morouni hurled himself into the fray with a flying elbow atop a massive midsection. The structure of bodies pancaked and the struggle began. Four men rolled down the aisle in a tight ball, bashing through racks, dragging articles of clothing into the skirmish. A furry arm broke loose and Wad was fired through the air, crashing into a rack of dog food. The supports gave way and the Legomi rode a wave of Alpo as the bags spilled to the floor.

The Old Guard of Zerth

A muscular elbow came down, pinning Gustav at the sternum. He lost his breath and seized. Meri was nabbed by the nape of the neck then thrown sideways. He slid across the tile without loosing momentum, right into the changing room. Wad stumbled to his feet, readying a charge –

"Gustav?"

"Gugh – Roldolph?"

"Oh, shit. I'm sorry, Guz." Roldolph nabbed Gustav by the his collar bone, lifting him to his feet, then dusted off his shoulders. "I thought you were bandits."

"Hah," Gustav laughed, swaying. He gave his big buddy a slap on the shoulder. "It's okay everybody, it's Just Roldolph. He's cool. Nothing to worry about."

Wad staggered over barefoot. "You know this guy?"

"Of course I do, Wad. Me and this big galoot go back years," Gustav said. "Holy shit, I'm so sorry, man."

The great pile of a man leaned down to match Wad's height. He offered a bear-claw hand to shake. "It's a pleasure, Mr. Wadley Saxo. Guz has told me a lot about you. That's quite a left-hook you've got there."

Wad beamed, swaying.

"A friendly? -HIC- Can it be?" Meri sang, sitting up. "And a Corbinall at that. My friend, this poor woman -HIC- believed you to be a threat." He pointed blindly at the girl's body under the wreckage.

"Lots of people think I'm a threat," Roldolph said. "I mean, look at me." He slapped at his belly and broke into his trademark snicker.

"So, to be clear," Wad said with a suspicious squint. "You don't know anything about Don Sanders?"

140

Mighty Rahiem

"Don Sanders? Of course I know about Don Sanders," Roldolph said nodding. "Terrible man. Crazy man. You have a beef with him too?"

"Indeedarino," Gustav said.

"Well, I think we should sit down and have a chat. Exchange notes and whatnot," Roldolph said.

"That too calls for celebration," Gustav cried. "Anything for a drink. What's say we head back to the Leaf."

"Sounds like a goddamned plan," Wad said.

The crew made their way down Saxo Street like a headless entourage. The suns blasted down and pedestrians dove for cover. Each man experiencing their own vision of a perfect high. They rounded the corner of Billion Boulevard as Wad could only brag about the Roldolph-sized door he had recently installed. It fit the Morouni perfectly.

Upon entering, Potato swung his head out the driver's side of the bus. "Twenty bucks, motherfucker. Wait, who is that?"

"It was all a big mix-up," Wad said. He nabbed a couple of tables and yanked them together, forming a lop-sided surface around which a group might comfortably sit around.

"He's a MERC," Potato shouted, swinging the gullwing open. It bounced against the ceiling causing a cloud of dust to rain down. He hopped from the seat and approached the hulk of a man. "Yer Roldolph Rimbaud. Yer a MERC," he said, with a finger in the gut.

"Yep," Roldolph said with a smile. "And you're Potato."

Potato ignored the pleasantries and went right into it. "You got a two-thousand buck bounty on yer head for Robbery. I know the guys you run with. I know guys who want yer head."

The Old Guard of Zerth

Gustav pushed between the two men, not having much luck moving either of them. "Calm down, assholes. You got a bounty on you too, remember? It's okay. He's a friend."

Potato didn't let up until Wad gave him the okay, at which point the Legomi backed up and gave Gustav room to breathe. The Legomi glared into the tiny little dot-eyes, finding nothing threatening, but he was still cautious. He reluctantly raised a meaty hand. Roldolph responded with his own. "If yer a friend of Wad's, yer a friend of mine," Potato mumbled.

The five men took seats around the catastrophe of a table, Potato opting to wait until Roldolph sat so he could take the seat opposite the beast. Meri did the same, hoping to engage in some Morouni-to-Morouni antics. Wad noted the absence of booze so he quickly excused himself to prepare drinks. "Music," Potato hollered.

Gustav went for his Talkman, but paused, giving Roldolph a look. "Fuck it, whatever." The Human tapped away and the song shuffled. **Eagles of Death Metal – The ballad of queen bee and baby duck.**

"Now, how did you manage to do that?" Roldolph said.

"Some friend," Potato muttered.

"Fuck it," Gustav said aloud. "It's all me. Everything you hear is mine. I control it all. Now you know my secret. If you tell anyone, we'll kill you. No hard feelings."

Potato leaned across the table and gave Roldolph the eye. "We'll really kill you."

Meri slapped Potato's shoulder with the back of his hand. "Pay no attention to the angry sprite, my man. He's a bundle of rockets, but he's worth your time."

Potato slapped back. "Twenty bucks, asshole."

Mighty Rahiem

Wad returned with a tray of drinks on a rickety cart. He spun it around for all to see. Four pitchers of Gnarlwood Pecker, two bottles of McVeigh McVino, ten Lemmy highballs and five tops of Dingus Mackie's famous *Get-the-fuck-off-me* Lemmonbomb Schnapps. He distributed them evenly across the rocking tables, then threw himself into his seat. "So," he started, "tell me what you know about Don Sanders."

Roldolph reached for the Gnarlwood and quaffed the pitcher too quickly. He wiped his lips with his arm. "He's a wooly old freak," Roldolph said, breaking into his breathy chortle. "He used to give us MERCS all kinds of trouble. We shut him down pretty quick and put him on his ass. He went quiet for a few cycles, but I've heard he's got a new posse these days. His operation is pretty small. Somewhere off-grid up north."

"Can you be more specific?" Wad said. We don't want to drive around looking for him. He reached for a Lemmy and dove in.

"Not much beyond that," Roldolph said, slurping down the last of the pitcher with a second gulp. "I can tell you about his posse. Three guys. Two are brothers, the third might as well be an army. He can copy himself like a Slugg."

"Dollar Bill," Gustav said, reaching for the McVino. "He's just one guy, but each time he dies, he comes back and somehow resurrects his old body. I knew him back on Earth. He's a total choad."

"The brain-cage," Roldolph said. "Aerie-tech meant for the bugs, but it works for Humans too, just not as well. Some of the bugmen I run with told me all about it."

"Technomancers," Wad said. "Aerie had these guys that would wear crazy headgear that let them control other people with their minds."

The Old Guard of Zerth

Roldolph nodded. "They'd use the headgear to amplify their own neural signals, then project them to another body."

"So that's how the bastard does it," Gustav said, slapping his knees. "All the duplicate Bills recognize the neural signals as their own. I guess that means they aren't corpses at all, just comatose."

Roldolph gave a novel smirk. "So, why are you so interested in the old gas bag?"

An awkward silence came over the bar. Wad wasn't too keen on exposing the wound, so he let it sit. He then noticed every eye was on him. The look he gave in reply was enough for his friends to understand.

Potato took a deep breath and spoke up, "He put a bounty on my head." He rubbed the back of his neck, then went for the booze, not sure which to start with. He nabbed a pitcher and drew it close. "He's got something against me so we're gonna end his ass."

The great Morouni erupted into a wheezing snicker-fit. He looked like he was about to choke. "That's right, I caught that. How much are you worth, my friend."

"Five thousand," Potato said with a bit of embarrassment.

Roldolph let out a whistle.

"Tell me, my man," Meri said, shifting the conversation. He slid a shot of Lemmonbomb to Roldolph, then nabbed his own. The two Morouni lifted the glasses and drank. Meri licked his lips. "what of these bombings? Word has it they're targeting Morouni businesses. Our brothers and sisters. To compound the issue, my own Brother Guz was killed by these beasts and his death will not go un-avenged."

"Hell yeah," Gustav said. I want to avenge my death too!"

Roldolph swallowed the drink. "We were under the impression that the bombings were the doing of Kagg and his Kaggwerks. The Blue Fist is just a cover. Those men you see out front of the Town Hall. Any one of them could be the culprit as far as I'm concerned. Keep the bloodline pure and all that Elder nonsense. Especially with the anniversary of the Great Arrival coming up soon."

"Indeed," Meri said, "There is to be a rally right here in Southtown."

"Hey, that's right," Wad said, wiping his face. "You plan on doing anything for that?"

"Oh, uncertain," Meri said. "I haven't put my name in the hat or anything of the like."

"You should," Roldolph said. "Guz tells me you're quite the public speaker. He says you speak for the Mongrels, so I should thank you for that."

"Indeed I do," Meri said with chin raised high.

"I've got a guy for that," Roldolph said with a wink. "I'll set something up for you. Put you to work. Come on by Ortega tomorrow late. Meet my associate. We'll be bumming around a little grill called Fairaday's Faith in the south-east quad. Bring the whole crew. We'll hook you up with a guy who can track Sanders for you. Get the job done."

Potato was starting to feel left out. His distrust for the man he knew to be a criminal was getting in the way of a good time. He gave it a good thought and came to the conclusion that if he were caught for half the things he had done, he might be in the same boat... scratch that, he *was* in the same boat. The revelation lightened his mood and he felt more free to open up. He snatched his pitcher and threw it back, then nabbed Roldolphs attention with knocking knuckles on the table. "Meri tells me the big ones had lots of trouble before the Great Arrival."

The Old Guard of Zerth

"Hell yeah, they did-" Gustav started, but was cut off by the blunt Legomi.

"Shut it," Potato said. "I wanna hear it from this guy."

"It's true," Roldolph said. "I was bound as a pup. Thankfully, it wasn't too long after when the Great Arrival happened. They didn't care much for the practice after that."

"What do you mean, Bound?"

Meri stepped in. "If you haven't noticed, we Corbinall, and Merinall alike, are quite large. Much larger than the rest. If you could picture where our kind comes from – a cavernous, condensed space not much larger than Southtown."

"Well, that doesn't seem so bad," Wad said with a burp.

"There were forty-thousand of us," Meri said, lowering his eyes. The room grew quiet. "Forty-thousand of us in a space meant for a few thousand. Five thousand would be too many, and yet there we were. And so we lived like maggots in the walls, feeding on scraps left by those above us. It was never meant to be a home. In truth, the home of my people was nothing more than ventilation shafts and ductways.

Now, for the most of us, we were able to live relatively well in those conditions, but you can imagine the horror in a mother's eyes when she finds that she has given birth to a Merinall – or worse, a Corbinall. While the Cabrio, Darlin and Bendo infants could survive on a ration a day, we larger breeds would starve on it. And with limited supply of food, a method was proposed to deal with us."

"Binding," Roldolph said.

"Binding," Meri echoed. "From birth, we were wrapped tightly in linen, preventing us from reaching our natural size. Each cycle, a new wrap of cloth. Over time, our bones warped and forms retarded until we were nothing more than a living husk, unable to move about on our own and cursed to starve every hour of our wretched existence." Meri pounded his fist into the table, stopping the hearts of the company and sending liquor to the floor. "This is what they want to return to. This is what the Elders see fit for us and our kind. And I will not stand for it."

The Leaf was quiet. Nobody cared to retrieve their drinks from the floor. Meri sat back with a terrible tremble and drew in a breath.

Wad ignored the beer in his lap and looked up to Meri. "Meri, you never told me you went through this. I had no idea."

Meri cleared his throat. His eyes moved to the side. "I didn't," he said. "I was born after the Arrival... but that doesn't change a thing. Does it, my brother?"

Roldolph sat quietly in his seat. Deep within his misty eyes, a look of fear was plain for all to see. He lowered his great head and shuddered. "I was there," he said. "I remember it all. Given what I was, what I am – they took me aside one day. Put me in a chair. They made a spectacle of it, like it was some kind of blessing. There was a party and a feast as it happened. At the time, I thought I was so special for being born with such a gift. And then they ate and sang. They said it was a celebration of my passing into adulthood, but in reality, it was a feast to recognize all the meals I would be denied that would allow them to flourish. It wasn't but a few months later that the Great Arrival came to be. Still, the damage had been done. I didn't walk again until I was two years old."

"Well, that doesn't sound too bad. Two years old?" Gustav said.

"I learned to walk at three weeks," Meri said. "All Morouni walk at three weeks."

The Old Guard of Zerth

"I walked just fine before they put me in that chair," Roldolph said. "I suppose we Morouni do mature quite a bit faster than the rest of you folks. For context, imagine having your back broken as you reached sexual maturity – as a matter of tradition."

Potato nodded with a stern look. He gave Wad the same. The two Legomi understood it all too well. "People go through tough shit," Potato said. "We all go through tough shit, don't we, Wad?"

Wad sat back in his chair. His eyes drifted as the memories welled up like a growing tide. The darkness and the fear. A sickening loss of self. A longing for death. The agony of a tortured spirit, whipped, flattened and maimed to a pulp of living waste. The spark ignited and he found himself breathing heavy, feeding the hate that lay starved within him for so many years. The adrenaline blasted through him and he pushed from his chair, hovering over the battered table. He felt like he could move the sky. The crew fed on his rage, egging him on with their stares. Wad's pin-point eyes darted across the floor for some release, something to lay waste to, something to alter irrevocably... but there was nothing there. Nothing worth burning. Nothing worth a goddamned thing.

The doused fire in his gut made it clear that there was no fuel. He didn't care about anything. He looked around the Leaf to find a crumbling vision of a half-hearted attempt to give a shit. A paper-thin facade of a luke-warm dream. Worst of all, there was no more anger. He was impotent. Wad's scowl fell away, replaced with a blank frown. He looked at his friends as though he had betrayed their trust. In their eyes he saw their lust for a fire that had burned out so many years before. It was excruciating.

"You okay, old buddy?" Potato said.

Mighty Rahiem

The fear in the cyclops' eye was just more weight. It was as if old bandages had been removed to find the wound now gangrenous.

"What's wrong?" Gustav said, standing slowly.

Wad shook his head and let out a fake breath. "Yikes, that really got to me," he said, then reached for the floored McVino. Nobody stopped him as he popped the cork and upended the bottle into his stomach. In fact, they encouraged it. Wad felt as if he were flogging himself in public – to the cheer of the crowd no less. With each glub of wine that he took in, he felt more empty. In a former life, he ruined himself to spite the powers that be, but now there was nothing left to spite. There was nothing left but the ruin. He didn't know what else to do, so he fed it.

"Ya almost got me worried, buddy," Potato said with an elated breath. He turned to the crew and raised his drink. "For Wad!" he shouted and the men gave a cheer.

The five drunks got on with their bullshit, testing what remained of the structural integrity of the bar via kinetic energy. Bullets, empty bottles and damaged furniture. Two hours later, Roldolph took his leave, citing a long awaited fishing trip that couldn't be missed. It was around happy hour that other patrons began to show up, finding the owner passed out in the corner and the bartender in a deep slumber under the bar. A few more bodies scattered here and there, and not a single piece of functional seating.

Chapter 11

All Clean

J-Walk – French Letter. The thing was on random. The rising of the seventh sun blasted through the hole in the wall as Hesh made his way down the stairs and into the shit. Every ounce of optimism that had helped him sleep was thwarted by the sight of living wreckage. He pondered the next step to take in reliving what he anticipated to be a great headache. He gave it a real good thought. After running through a few angry scenarios in his head, the Sectoid decided his patience had stretched to the point of breaking – but a thread still remained. He cursed that thread as he methodically roused each shell of a man from their stupor.

It wasn't until Hesh found Wadley in the corner that he managed to lighten up – if just a bit. His friend wasn't passed out at all, at least not fully. He was sitting still, face in the corner, cradling what looked like an empty picture frame. Upon further inspection, Hesh found the blazed Legomi was wrapped around the leaf that would have hung above the bar, immortalized within a glass frame. The namesake of the establishment. It was the only glass in sight that wasn't shattered, leaving Hesh to conclude that the dense fucker was trying to keep the thing safe.

The Sectoid leaned down and wrapped his fingers around the frame, finding that it came loose without a fight. Wad turned to Hesh with glazed eyes. "Take it," he mumbled. "Take it and run." The Legomi then smiled and made a cooing sound, then lumped over and began to snore through his mouth. A cursory glance at the drunk's mind revealed serenity and a feeling of accomplishment, having relinquished the prized leaf to a trusted ally. It was safe and he could die in peace.

The Old Guard of Zerth

Hesh chuckled. Same old Wad. Same as he always was. Despite the cloud of inebriation that had settled over the last ten years, Wad still showed signs of himself from time to time, though it pained him that it was so seldom that he had to be reminded that way. It was that kind of twisted tenacity about the dumb bastard that kept Hesh rooting for the guy.

"Would you look at this," a voice rang out.

Hesh knew it was Amelia, though the cadence of her voice made it hard to tell right away.

"Just look at this place. I should have known this would happen if I left him alone."

Hesh didn't want to argue. He didn't like the outcome much either, but he wasn't about to rub it in with an avalanche of bitching. That wasn't going to help anybody. In the moment, he actually felt a bit defensive and so he took the route of any Sectoid when confronted with an impending verbal assault – stay one step ahead. And so he did. He moved to the bar where he gently hung the framed vegetation back in its place, then turned without warning. "Can you change the wind, Amelia, or does it anger you that water runs down hill?"

The girl scoffed as if she felt the question was posed unfairly. "You act like all of this is totally acceptable. You're okay with this?"

Hesh shook his head. "I accept that when I stumble and drop my belongings, they will hit the ground. Given the natural order of things, these men are on their way down and there's no stopping them. Is it desirable? No. Is it natural? Yes. Like it or not, the men in this room have a trajectory and a motive. They will reach their goal. Suns willing, they bounce."

"So you're telling me to accept it?"

"Yes," Hesh said bluntly.

"Oh... my god. You're so... hot." Gustav ambled roughly in Amelia's direction with what looked like a clump of hair in his hand. He seemed to be trying to gift it to her.

"Down, beast," Hesh spit, waving the man away.

"Restroom... restroom," Meri said, before emptying his guts. It was clear he was cognizant enough to avoid getting any on his new blunderhose. "Nevermind," he said, slurping a bit of dangle from his lip. He stood and attempted to join the conversation naturally, tipping his crushed hat to the lady.

Potato wasn't doing well. He stood like a statue, blank as a rock with his hand on his belly. He was focusing with great intent on something internal. "Uh," he mumbled, then turned to Hesh looking a bit worried.

The Sectoid took a moment to think. "Come," he said, grabbing Meri by the elbow. He pulled the lout towards the stairs, then instructed Gustav to fetch Wadley from his corner. Potato shuddered and shook, then returned to his stoic self and followed. The group made their way up the stairs and into the sun with a squawking Amelia in tow.

The weather on the roof was just fine for the sober ones – terribly uncomfortable for the rest. They shrank from the heat like wilting flowers, cursing the light and formulating plans to escape back to the darkness of the bar. Gustav stared at the sky with his mouth hung open. His face contorted to a sort of open-faced grin as he shuffled to the ledge, arms dangling at his side. "What day is it?" he said.

"It's Foursday," Hesh said. "Foursday morning."

"What happened to Threesday?" Gustav said, searching the sky for an explanation.

"You spent the whole day drunk and stupid," Amelia said, approaching the man with balled fists.

Before the girl could continue, Gustav turned with a dumb grin. "Was it good for you?" He laughed at himself and started to tip over.

Hesh stepped in, grabbing everyone's attention with a finger in the air. "I'm organizing a day-trip and you're all invited. In fact, attendance is mandatory. Any attempt to flee will fail. We're taking a flight."

"I can fly," Potato said.

"You are a terrible pilot," Hesh said. "I'm calling us a cab. Gustav, give me your credcard."

"Fuck you!" Gustav mumbled.

"Fine," Hesh said, clearing his throat. "This one is on me, but I won't be forgetting it." With tight lips, the Sectoid tapped at his Talkman.

"Where are we going?" Wad said stumbling across the rooftop.

"Ender," Hesh said with the same amount of spite. He ignored Wad's bitching. "Pickup in thirty seconds," he said, reading off his Talkman. He moved to the ledge and nodded up the street.

Just up Koplin Street was Carton's Famous Flightpad, well within sight of the rooftop. It was a two-story concrete building resembling an Earthly parking structure covered in colorful banners and advertisements. Graffiti as well. Atop the flightpad, a small aircraft lifted off and hovered. It headed north before turning in their direction, bobbing casually through the air, skimming the rooftop of City Hall. The mob in the streets below hurled bottles and rocks at the passing craft, shouting obscenities and making rude gestures. It approached the bar with a blast of dust from the repulsers. The whine of the head-fans filled the air as it passed overhead. There was a cartoon image of a Morouni giving a thumbs up painted across the hull, and a word bubble proclaiming *"OFF AND AWAY"*.

Mighty Rahiem

The crew backed up, allowing the craft to safely land on the roof. It hit the dobistone with a thump and the rear hatch fell open. From inside the darkened cabin, the captain emerged. A stump-sized Morouni with a mustache that reached down to his boots. He waddled down the steel plank and waved. Everyone waved back. He jabbered something and took Hesh's credcard.

The Sectoid nodded with respect. "My friends, I'm sure you're familiar with the famous Captain Carton, of the Off and Away.

Carton lifted his leg and let out a toot, then charged a modest twenty bucks to the card. He handed it back and invited the group to enter.

"Off and away, indeed," Hesh smiled.

The journey to Ender was a melancholy affair. Headaches abound as the four men did their best to stave off hangovers. Much to the ire of Hesh, he did what he could to keep Carton from offering them more booze. The cabin was comfortably available with room to spare. The playlist worked on its own, following a string of post-punk specials. **Wire – Used To.** Amelia shuffled out of her seat and made her way up the aisle.

As the men slumbered, Hesh peered out the porthole, watching the cliffs of Redrock pass below. Amelia plopped down next to him with a sigh. Hesh turned and gave her a smile. She returned with a tired nod. "I don't know how you put up with these guys," She said.

"It's not all bad," Hesh replied. "The nature of the brilliant mind is one that is often mired in excess. It's like staring into the sun."

Amelia shook her head. "I just don't see it," She said. "You've known Wadley for a long time now, haven't you?"

"About seventeen years," Hesh said.

"Has he always been this way?" She asked. "Has he always been so scatterbrained and mindless?"

"No," Hesh replied. "He only does that when he's comfortable – but if you give him reason to care, he will turn the world upside-down to make it right. Not always to the greatest effect, but that's the strength of the company he keeps. He relies on us to keep the ball from falling off the pedestal."

"But they're all as crazy as he is," Amelia frowned.

"What is it about Wad that keeps *you* so tied up?" Hesh said.

Amelia lifted her eyes to meet the black pools of inquisition. She turned away. "When someone has that kind of reputation, you tend to put a lot of faith in them. And from a distance you can see it. But you get closer and you see that they are really no different than anyone else. So I started thinking, couldn't anyone do what Wad does? Couldn't anyone be the hero?"

"Sperm," Hesh said.

"What?" Amelia shot back.

"Every sperm carries the same DNA. Every one is identical in that way, but they all have their own unique bits that sets them apart. They are all put forward with the same potential, yet only one will manage to break through to the egg. Why is that?"

"This is making me uncomfortable," Amelia said.

"And when you find yourself feeling that way, you retreat?" Hesh asked with a smile.

Amelia nodded.

Hesh laughed. "You don't *have* to pull away, you know," he said with a wink.

"Are you coming on to me?"

"No, no," Hesh said. "I mean the act of pulling away is what separates you from Wadley. You don't *have* to run when you feel uncomfortable, but you do. Wadley runs the opposite direction. He runs *towards* the fire. Combined with his natural Legomi advantages, he can be quite the force to be reckoned with.

"What natural Legomi advantages?" Amelia asked.

Hesh leaned in with a twinkle in his black eye. "Did you know that a Legomi has no cognitive blink?"

"I don't know what that is."

Hesh chuckled. "Cognitive blink is the brief pause that all other sentient races experience when posed with a potential threat. It only lasts a second or so, but it's often overlooked. It's the moment that allows for the psyche to determine fight, flight or freeze. Legomi don't have that. After all, what kind of threat would a vegetable feel? That lack of stimuli was passed on to them in their birthing, and so they are free from it entirely. It may not be so visible to the casual observer, but we Sectoids see it plainly.

And so that combined with Wadley's chosen values allows him to play the roll of the hero quite effectively. It also helps that he has a certain self-destructive streak. Sure, he may flail about and make a mess of things. He may make things worse for all he knows. The point is, he doesn't back down, and that's why I feel the need to goad him from time to time. Otherwise he looses momentum and that's just not good for anyone."

Amelia agreed and sat back. "I never knew that." She turned to the window and ducked her head for a better view. Out over the basin, she watched as several bubbly clouds pass through the rainbelt, then disperse with the change in pressure.

"More on your mind" Hesh said.

The Old Guard of Zerth

Amelia laughed through her nose while shaking her head. "So, why exactly are we flying to Ender?"

"Ender is famous for a few things. Number one, our aesthetics, and second to that is our coffee."

"Ah," Amelia said. "So you fly him all the way out here for a cup of coffee?"

"Sure, why not?" Hesh said. "But more importantly, I needed to get Wadley out of his comfort zone to challenge him with new ideas. He needs a reminder to kick his ass into gear. Something to push his buttons. In all the years I've known him, the one thing that I've seen consistent is his competitive edge. Show him something amazing – something to tap into his imagination and get the wheels grinding – and he will do what ever he can to trump the competition. If Wad's ever going to get his data back, best he start in a place that doesn't belong to him."

"That seems so childish," Amelia said.

"It is," Hesh replied. "But that doesn't make it a bad thing. That childlike nature is what drives innovation. It's the foundation of wonder and enthusiasm that makes change possible. If I can bring Wadley back to that feeling, there's no telling where he will go with it."

"So you really aren't concerned about this whole stolen identity thing?" Amelia said. "You seem kind of disinterested."

"Mildly disinterested," Hesh said. "Wad is right about one thing. It's not his job to care about the world. It is, however, his job to keep his own things in order. I can't just let him sit around and rot away, so I feel a bit obligated to help him regain what was lost."

"So you're perfectly satisfied if we go completely off the rails again as long as Wad gets his money back?" Amelia scoffed.

Mighty Rahiem

Hesh took a breath. "Amelia, all change is good. There are an infinite number of facets to life, most of which we will never see the end of. When was the last time you influenced somebody? Was it direct, or perhaps a young child caught a glimpse of you walking down the street, at just the right time in their life, that that memory of you will stay with them forever. You see, it isn't important that we push so hard that the future hinges on our actions. Rather, we collectively carry on in the way most conducive to our good nature. My goal isn't to push Wad to a specific outcome, it's to push him to be himself fully once again."

Well, I suppose whatever the outcome, I appreciate the help," Amelia sighed.

"I could see you needed it," Hesh said.

Chapter 12

Thieves and Fanatics

An hour passed. The caution light of the cabin snapped on filling the space with a red glow. Amelia pushed through the aisle, then knelt down next to Wad's seat. She gently shook his shoulder, rattling him from his dozing. His eyes popped open and he shot to his feet with balled fists. "Okay now, let's go!" He shrieked, then staggered backwards, holding his head in pain.

"It's okay, Wad, we're here," Amelia said.

Meri propped himself up and straightened his back with a hurt look on his face. Gustav wiped his eyes with a yawn. Potato didn't budge.

Wad looked around through a squint. "Wow," he said, "my bus looks really different."

"This isn't the bus," Amelia said, coaxing him out of his seat. "We took a flight."

"What?" Wad said, rubbing his scalp. "Where are we?"

"We're in Ender," Gustav said, peering out the porthole. "I haven't been here in years."

"Ender?" Wad sighed, turning to Hesh. "Why Ender?"

Hesh gave the weary Legomi a look. "Given the circumstances, I don't really care to explain myself."

"Who do I know in Ender?" Wad said, rubbing his leaves.

"You know me," Hesh said, "and you know Chelli."

The Old Guard of Zerth

"Chelli?" Wad said, shaking his head. "No, no, no. She's gonna jump all over me for that damned bike again. She never lets it go. That was like, ten years ago. Come on, Hesh, My head is pounding."

"Seventeen years," Said Hesh.

"Who's Chelli?" Gustav said, perking up.

Hesh winked. "She's a smokin' hot babe. They say she can kill a man with her thighs,"

"Oh hell yeah," Gustav said, pumping his fist. He jumped from his seat, then regretted it.

The cabin went weightless for a moment as the craft made a sudden dip in altitude. It stabilized gracefully, then began a steady corkscrew groundward. The sky shifted through the portholes and the shadows of red sandstone took its place. The temperature change was noticeable. Hesh gathered his things and made his way toward the cockpit door. He waited there with his manbag slung over one arm, the other leaning on the carbon-fiber hatch.

The decent slowed considerably, then a gentile bump and shudder. They had arrived. Carton slid open the cockpit door to do a quick sanity-check to make sure his living cargo had survived the journey. Hesh offered his card, which Carton slid eagerly, then thanked the Sectoid with many bows and curtsies. The mustachioed Morouni gave everyone a thumbs-up as they fumbled out of their seats and drifted into the aisle.

Amelia's Talkman chirped, causing her to drop back into her seat. "Well guys, this is where I have to leave you. The Mayors have apparently tried to stage a coup against themselves. We've got a dozen bodies to clean up. Sorry I can't stick around. You guys mind if I take this ride home?"

Hesh shook his head. "Not at all. I'll get em home safely."

"You can keep them," Amelia said, half joking.

Mighty Rahiem

A steady wind blew through the rocky channel leading into town. The crew stumbled along, dragging their feet as Hesh guided them away from the landing dock. They did their best to avoid scattered patches of light that broke through the craggs above, causing them to Meander from shadow to shadow, hiding their eyes from the pain. The crew moved down the hill where quiet crowds lingered in the sandstone shade. Ender was aglow with color. The air was sweet and cool and Gustav was compelled to swap the music out for something less head-bursty. **South – Sight of Me.** The townsfolk responded well.

For Wad, the return to Ender was a sour reminder of everything he should be doing. Like a coincidental crossing-of-paths with a former lover. He didn't want to take it all in, it was embarrassing. He felt the need to puff out his chest and dominate the town with his demeanor, but he couldn't shake the hangover. It pushed him to the ground and kept its foot on his neck.

They continued through the canyon where townsfolk idled on their balconies overlooking the street. Stunted trees sprouted through cracks in the rock walls, ablaze with red berries. The air was permanently snared with the grit of fresh-brewed coffee. Gustav nearly lost himself as they passed by a cafe. He broke from the group and flopped down on a bench, folding his hands over his head.

"Get up," Wad said as he kept moving, but Gustav didn't budge. "We can get coffee back home. I don't wanna be here any longer than we need to."

"Oh, settle down," Hesh said. "Maybe a good cup of coffee is just what we need."

Meri dashed to a planter and emptied his guts. He wiped his lips and composed himself, then snapped his suspenders. "Coffee does sound quite enticing," he said with a burp.

The Old Guard of Zerth

The sign above the door read '*Amber Hollow*' in floral lettering. The doorway was flanked by bar-style seating, looking out to the cobblestone. Planters with the same bushy trees underlined the windows. "Not my usual haunt, but it should do just fine," Hesh said, as he dragged Wad through the door by his wrist.

The group separated, taking two tables. Wad and Hesh found a table for two, while Meri and Gustav took another. Potato flopped down next to Meri, then promptly passed out. The barista came around with a pot for each group. Gustav flipped out his credcard. "Keep it coming," he said with his hand glued to his forehead. "Like, seriously. Give me *all* of your coffee. I'll buy it all. I got all the... money."

Hesh summoned the barista with a wagging hand. He pointed pointed at the carafe. "Might I request something a bit stronger?"

The barista hurried back to the counter, returning with two white carafes. "Not that strong," Hesh laughed. "We would like to survive the day." The barista then brought two yellow carafes and took Gustav's card. He looked it over.

"Charge whatever you want," Gustav said. "Just don't stop until I say so."

Wad slumped down in his chair. He hid a scowl as Hesh splashed some brew into a stoneware mug. The Sectoid slid it across the table. "No hard feelings, man," He said as Wadley avoided eye contact. Hesh took a child-sized sip of his coffee. His pinky was extended while he shot a sideways smirk at the Legomi. Wad peered through his scowl, letting a snicker break his mood. He threw his arms back and rocked in his chair, soaking up the decor.

Mighty Rahiem

The cafe was a comfy hole in the wall, as were all structures in Ender. The decoration was a tasteful flare of sepia-toned everything. There were hanging pots of dried beans around the ceiling, and a dim amber glow flickered through checkered block-glass in the sandstone walls. Carbon fiber girders served as molding. The beams were wrapped in munda vines that spiraled off in their own direction, creeping down the walls and out the window. The furnishing was a gaggle of re-purposed scraps of machinery. The chairs were bent fanblades and the tables were fashioned from old armor shielding. All sanded, stained and finished with a bright resin to lock in the state of inorganic decay. The general ambiance brought a flood of memories to Wadley's mind.

"There it is," Hesh said, prodding into Wad's thoughts. "That's the Wad I know."

Wad pulled back, realizing his thoughts were on full display. He rolled his eyes.

"There's no use hiding it," Hesh smiled. "I see all."

"Why did you bring me here?" Wad said. "To rub this all in my face? Don't tell me this is about Don Sanders."

"I thought you needed a wake-up call," Hesh said.

"So you *are* rubbing it in my face."

"I suppose you could say that," Hesh smiled. "It isn't a lack on Amelia's part. She just doesn't know how to flip your 'on-switch'. That's where I come in, and that's what Ender is best at."

"And what exactly is it that you are trying to do?" Wad said rubbing his temple.

Hesh sat back and rubbed his hand over his scalp. "Wad, for the better part of ten years now, I've watched you settling in to something that may not be as healthy as the world demands. You've still got the energy in you to be a force for

165

change and I don't want to see that energy wasted on booze-fights and bashing."

"We've been through this," Wad sighed. "The world needs to do better without me. I don't need to hold everyone's hand. If you think the whole planet is going to fall into chaos without my input, then I'd say there's a bigger problem."

"It's not the world falling into chaos, Wad, it's you."

Wad sneered. It wasn't the fight he was looking for but he knew he couldn't steer a conversation in the presence of a mind reader. Damned Sectoids, always a step ahead, he thought. Hesh laughed, catching the tail end of the Legomi's mental griping. He motioned for Wad to focus on the coffee, which Wad did with a huff.

"Slowly," Hesh said. "It's strong."

The Legomi lifted the mug to his mouth. Roasted steam filled his senses as he took a sip. The hot brew trickled down his throat, causing the leaves on his shoulders to unfurl. He sat back and let out a breath.

"That's the feeling I was looking for," Hesh said. "Capitulation. You don't have to fight it. Ender isn't going to run you over, but she does miss you. Why not let her in?"

Wad turned to Hesh with a foggy look.

"You don't think you deserve her, do you?" Hesh said.

Wad lowered his eyes.

"It's okay," Hesh continued. "It's your decision. I can't force you to be inspired. If Ender doesn't do it for you, something else will. The question is, what?"

"No," Wad said, "it's not that I don't appreciate it, because I do. It's just – it's hard to focus with so much going on. My Talkman, my bar, my money. I don't know what to say, but I just can't seem to feel anything about it. I mean, I'm not happy, and I know that, but that's just where it ends. It doesn't make me feel one way or another. Its like a bullet without a primer... or smoking a broken cigarette. It's just getting lost somewhere inside."

The Sectoid took Wad's hands and went quiet. He crept deeper into the Legomi's thoughts, finding a memory of the drunken romp from the day before. It was a sharp recall. Painful to experience. A feeling of total loss, total regret, followed by a tangible wave of self-disgust. Hesh pulled away on instinct. Not what he was expecting to find. It wasn't as revealing as it was traumatic. He gathered himself, folding his hands and drawing a breath to clear his head. "You feel there's no more fire in you," he said.

Wadley lowered his eyes. "It's just not there, I don't feel anything anymore. I can't even feel angry about it. This place isn't helping, either. Ender is just too much right now – too big of a leap. I feel like a sprout staring up at some kind of kingly force. It's so far out of reach. If anything, I feel more helpless here."

"Fair enough, man," Hesh said. "I'll lay off for the time being. At least we can sober up and get our bearings. Do we have a deal?"

Wad nodded and went for a sip.

"...and while we're at it, we can go see Obie. He might get a bump from seeing Uncle Wad."

Wadley squinted. He dropped the mug to the table. "Hesh, please. Not in this state."

Hesh looked Wad over. "I get it. I won't push it. He turned to his own mug and took a sip, but was interrupted by the Legomi's heavy hand on the table.

"How is he?" Wad asked.

Hesh hesitated. "He's got some work to do, I think. He's not like you at all. I gave him his space and that seems to be all he needs..." he trailed off, hoping to retreat from the topic, but Wad relented.

"You didn't tell him I've been a drunk all these years, did you?" Wad said with a defeated chuckle.

"He knows," Hesh said flatly. "I've told him."

"Goddam, Hesh," Wad said, scraping together a smile. "You know sometimes it wouldn't hurt to be dishonest."

"I've often thought that myself," Hesh said with a forced grin. "And while it's true that our bag of tricks didn't include that little bonus, it seems entirely called for in some situations."

"What are you talking about?" Wad said.

"Lying," Hesh replied.

Wad raised a skeptical eye, laughing under his breath.

Hesh continued. "I can't deny the benefit, at least in some situations. It works fine in a bubble, but when new factors are thrown into the mix, it becomes quite troublesome. At least, it *can* become quite troublesome. I sometimes find myself wondering: Whilst in our bubble, have we truly drifted so far from a core part of our being that we've lost touch with the connecting tissue that allows us to empathize with-"

"This is really good coffee," Wad said, gazing into his cup.

"-with those around us that make us who we are. After all, what is an empathizing creature if he has no one to empathize with? It's a wasted quality." Hesh paused. He was drifting and Wadley was tapping at the table in a circular motion, following his finger.

"I think that'll about do it," Hesh said.

Mighty Rahiem

"Woo! That'll do it!" Gustav shouted, slapping the table. He was twirling his head. "That's some dam good coffee. Waiter, add another zero onto whatever I'm paying you. This stuff is great."

Meri pushed from his seat. He straightened his tie, then bucked up his chin. "I do believe this magical garbage has imbued us with the fighting spirit – though our comrade here is still on the downs." Potato was still face-down on the table. Meri slapped the Legomi's back. He didn't move.

"Idea!" Gustav said. "First, some appropriate music." **Slayer and Atari Teenage Riot – No Remorse(I wanna Die)** He bounced to the beat with a toothy smile, wagging his hair. He unlatched the harness connecting Potato's PISS pack and slid the pads off the Legomi's shoulders.

"Gustav, I don't believe that's the best idea," Meri warned.

"Nonsense," Gustav said. "It's just what he needs."

"He's not going to like it, nor should he," Meri scowled.

Gustav waved the Morouni off and continued. He danced behind the counter to the protest of the barista, who swatted at the intruder. "Fuck off, I just gave you money," Gustav yelled, as he snatched a white carafe from the counter and dumped it into the leather reservoirs. He filled them to the point of bursting, then returned to the table and gently slid them over Potato's shoulders. The Legomi wobbled as he yanked the strap tight.

"Are you sure that's a good idea," Hesh said. "That's pumping directly into his bloodstream."

"Hell yeah, it is," Gustav smiled. "Just give it a second."

"You have no right," Meri growled. "He's not going to like that one bit."

"Have some faith, big guy," Gustav said, slapping the Morouni's belly with the back of his hand. "It's just a little pick-me-up."

"Have it your way," Meri said. "But I won't be defending this kind of nonsense."

In an instant, Potato's meaty fingers shot to a fist. His head jerked across the table as he pulled in a gasp of air. He slowly lifted his head to reveal an impossibly dilated eye. The crew shrank in awe as the Legomi gradually rose to his feet, then craned his head towards Wadley with a frightening grimace. He spoke too casually through clenched teeth. "We should go now before I kill every-single-one of you."

"Right away," Wad said with a fearful nod.

The crew gathered their things, returning their cups to the counter, but Potato wasn't having it. His foot began to shake violently, then his heel slammed the floor like a hammer press. Everyone froze. "Right now," Potato said, calm as could be. He looked like he could eat the table.

"Maybe the music was a bit much," Gustav said, tapping his Talkman.

"No!" Potato exploded, then returned to a monotone buzz. "If you even think of changing the music, I will take your arm off and put it in your mouth. Do you understand me?

Gustav nodded.

"Thank you, Guz. I can see god." Potato slapped his hand on Gustav's shoulder. The man shriveled. The Legomi then floated from the table on bent knees, hands locked in a grasping position. The barista ran to return the credcard, but Potato slapped his hand to the kid's forehead. He eased the barista to the floor with his eye on something distant. "Get out of the way," he mumbled. Gustav's credcard ended up in his hand through sheer force of anger. He flicked it at Gustav and the corner stuck in the man's chest. Gustav winced. A trail of blood ran down his belly while he whispered an apology. The Legomi crept towards the door and the crew sheepishly followed.

Out into the street, Potato led the way with his eye as wide as a dinner plate. It was looking at nothing. He moved slowly, splitting crowds as they entered into the town square. The crew followed like hurt puppies. "Where are we going?" Wad said, but Hesh quieted him with a furious head-shake while he rummaged around in his manbag.

"I'm going shopping," Potato droned. "I wanna buy-" he slammed his boot into the cobblestone and it burst into dust. "A SHIRT!" He switched off and looked to the sky. All eyes were fixed on the foam dripping from his lips. "It's Foursday. Foursday is payday," He said, creaking towards Wadley. "I'm gonna get paid now." He extended a vibrating arm towards his employer. "Pay-me."

Wad became a puddle. He didn't know how to respond.

Potato craned his face towards Wad. "Pay. Me."

Out of the blue, Hesh leaped into action, jabbing a large syringe into the back of Potato's head. Potato seized as the Sectoid jammed down on the plunger. Hesh then dove for cover. The Legomi froze for a moment, then bucked up. "Whew!" He huffed, twirling his shoulders. "That's a hell of a kick." He waved his massive arms in a circle. The crowd trembled.

"What did you give him?" Wad whispered to Hesh.

"Dunebat tranquilizer," Hesh said.

"And he's still standing?" Wad gasped.

"Like you said, it's really good coffee."

The Old Guard of Zerth

"So how bout' that goddamned shirt," Potato said, bouncing on his toes. "And how bout' this fucking music?" He began boxing the air.

"How long is it gonna last?" Wad said, carefully.

"About four hours," Hesh replied. "We've gotta get that PISS pack off of him before that."

"Shirts will do it." Gustav said. "He wants a shirt, he's gonna have to take his PISS pack off to try it on."

"If we take it off too soon, he'll melt," Hesh said, shaking his head. "We've got to time it right."

"Group huddle!" Potato said, barging into the conversation. "What are we talking about?"

"Should we tell him?" Gustav said.

"Tell me what?" Potato said, bouncing with glee.

"Allow me," Meri stepped in. He placed a hand on Potato's shoulder and spoke clearly. "My man, your friends have poisoned you."

"No!" Gustav shouted.

Potato looked over the crew with a confused grin. "That's some good poison," He said.

Meri turned to the group and shrugged. "If he likes it, I can't see the harm. Our man wants to shop, so shopping it is."

"Well, okay then," Wad said. Should we split up? I need batteries for the P:9 and the armory is on the other end of... dammit!" He turned to Hesh with a look.

Hesh nodded. "Sure, this will be my treat. But don't think for a minute that I'm not going to forget this. I've lost count of how many favors you owe me."

"I need clothes," Gustav said, ripping the swastika out of his hair. "Nazi paraphernalia is so ten minutes ago. Besides, these old rags are starting to get a bit ripe."

"I would love to pick up one of those P:9s. They're quite the hoot. Hesh my man, I'll gladly pay you Twosday for a P:9 today."

"Not in the cards," Hesh said. "Unless you want to organize a raid on Aerie Tower, your P:9 will have to wait. Those pistols are quite the rarity, you know."

Meri scratched at his chin. "Well, I suppose any old thing will do. Don't disappoint," He smiled.

"Not to come across as unwelcoming, but I don't run a charity," Hesh said. "Hospitality is one thing, but I don't believe supplying firearms to alcoholics qualifies as anything of the sort."

"My man," Meri said, stepping forward, "If you find yourself in a tight spot, 'tis better to have a capable ally than to fight the battle on two fronts."

Hesh cocked his head. He looked deep into Meri's mind to find a block obscuring something unexpected. He realized the Morouni wouldn't take no for an answer. On top of that there was quite an intellect hiding beneath all of that gusto. Rather than descend into a battle of wits he may not be able to win, he conceded. "Fine," he said. "Any *old thing*, I suppose."

"Good deal," Wad said. "We'll meet back here around-"

"-four hours," Hesh interrupted. "Very important that we are back here in four hours." He nodded towards a jittery Potato.

"Good point," Gustav said. He checked the time on his Talkman. Foursday – 09:12 – 89°. "Let's meet back here at thirteen thirty. That should give us plenty of buffer to figure this thing out."

The Old Guard of Zerth

As the group began to part, a deafening clap ripped through the square. The crowd ducked for cover as the stone walls shook with the echo of a proximate explosion. Loose pebbles rained down the canyon, bouncing across the cobblestone, kicking up a thick cloud of silt. Through the rays of dust, Wad could see the silver smoke of the detonation curling above the roof of the canyon. He could swear he recognized the pattern.

Chapter 13

Dale Walinski

You won't believe you eyes when you see what Molly Ringwald look like in 2014 Like and Subscribe.

Dale tapped the 'like' button on his iPhone 6. Nothing happened. He tapped it again and his phone popped with an add for an online dating site. He had ignored the call from his parole officer who left a message demanding he get in touch before Wednesday evening. Dale didn't give a rat's ass. He didn't even remember his Parole officer's name. The only call he cared about was from Clint, who was supposed to have called back thirty minutes ago. He was desperate to get his hands on a waterproof lawnmower battery before he passed out, and his car had been impounded by the state. There was no way he was going to walk to Walmart in that weather. He didn't even remember where Walmart was.

Dale dropped his phone to the pillow before scooting across the mattress to the end of the bed. His boots were there on the floor beneath a bundled blanket. They were warm to the touch in the path of the space heater, which was set to swivel across the hardwood floor. Everything else in the room was frigid. Gotta remember to put those on, he thought to himself. Don't want to be showing up barefoot again.

It was snowing in Greely, Colorado and the room stank of cow shit. His mattress stank of cow shit. Even the snowflakes, he assumed, stank of cow shit. From the time he was accepted to UNC, to the time he dropped out and became a manager at Black Jack Pizza, to the time he quit his job and started dating 17 year-olds, Dale never got used to the smell. Even for a cowboy, it was too much. It didn't bother him when he was drinking, so he did that a lot. At least, he remembered doing that a lot. It had been a while since he had spent time in Greely.

His phone chirped and he instinctively tapped at the Talkman on his wrist, only to find bare skin. Wise up, Dale. You're on Earth, now. He found his bearings and snatched up the phone.

"Where win you last night bro????"

It was a message from Clint.

Dale set the phone down on his thigh to think for a moment. When the hell was last night? That was too long ago to remember. He turned to the Call of Duty: Advanced Warfare calendar on the wall, but it just made him angry. The days didn't mean anything to him. He tapped at the digital keyboard on the screen.

Mighty Rahiem

"Srry busy," then waited a few seconds.

"WTF Bro. Emily wish all in PLUMBER!!1"

Dale chucked his phone to the floor.

He pushed to his feet and moved to the window, finding a glaze of condensation dripping down the glass. It was obscuring his view of a dead bush. Outside, a Ford Explorer bumbled down 8th Avenue in low gear. The tail lights flashed while the driver pumped the breaks around the corner as it slid out of view. Walmart is out of the question, he thought. A real cowboy wouldn't be begging for a ride anyway.

Dale wrapped his mind around autonomy, scolding himself for drifting. He began humming the theme from The Good, The Bad and The Ugly. He didn't need Clint. He didn't need anything but the sun in his eyes, the wind at his back and a trusty six-shooter. And a battery. A waterproof lawnmower battery. He snatched his Stetson hat off the floor, plopping it on his skull, then turned to the mirror on the closet door. He gave it a wink.

Dale was a ratty looking twenty-something with week-old stubble and sunken cheeks. His hair was a greasy mop of clutter tied back in a ponytail which he used to draw the attention of younger girls. Meth gave his face the edge he was looking for, but even that had come and gone. Back then, the after parties and cast meet-ups went on too long, and almost always ended with him leaving before someone brought up his arrest. But none of that mattered anymore. He found a way out.

He spent the last of his savings on a wet suit, rebreather and waterproof backpack. Only later did he discover the backpack wasn't actually waterproof. Despite the claims, there actually wasn't such a thing as a waterproof backpack. At least, not in the way he wanted. Regardless, it all sat in a bundle in the corner of a room devoid of purpose. It wasn't where he lived anymore, it was just where he was at the moment. His earthly obligations sat right below relationships on his list of priorities, somewhere around earthquake insurance and brushing his teeth.

A chirp broke the silence prompting Dale to mosey on over to the smartphone.

"SRRY AUTOCORRECT!!! FIND YOU'RE OWN RIDE! LOL"

Just as he expected. Gotta go it alone. Dale didn't want to do it, but he snatched the ratchet set from the pile of gear on the floor. With a nod to himself in the mirror, he hurried down the hall, into the kitchen and through the garage door. The scent of rotting cardboard filled his nostrils, and the temperature gave him a shock. It was dark, damp and freezing, a rough combo for Dale in his socks and boxer shorts. He hopped across the icy concrete to the hood of his roommate's 1999 Jeep Wrangler and popped the latches.

Dale fished around for the safety release and threw the hood open, blindly jamming the prop-rod into place. He got to work with his ratchet, loosening the connections from the battery posts, then tossing them aside. He reached in and yanked the thing from the base, pinching his fingers between the wiring harness. Dale shot upright, letting out a silent yelp – at the same time, bashing his head into the hood. The boom echoed through the garage. His Stetson was crushed!

With hands shaking, Dale pawed around, squeezing the wiring harness from its place. He lifted the battery out, then retrieved his ratchet before tip-toeing back to the warmth of the kitchen, shutting the garage door with a foot. He rushed to the bedroom where he chucked his haul to the mattress, then scurried around looking for his wet suit. He found it laying somewhere messy on the floor so he did his best to shake it off before returning to the mirror. He uncrinkled his Stetson, then gave himself a sexy wink. It's cowboy time.

Mighty Rahiem

Dale slipped into the neoprene bodysuit and zipped up, taking a spare second to waddle around and loosen up. It always wanted to mash his balls, which is something he wished he was aware of before he bought it. It also had a problem riding up his ass, but that much he didn't mind. He plopped to the mattress and got comfy, then forced his feet into the snakeskin boots. He went for his backpack, fumbling through and taking a mental inventory of the contents: Waterproof Ball jar with salt shaker – Check, Hunting knife – Check, Party-sized Bag of Chex-Mix – Check, Ratchet set... Dale reached for the ratchet set and threw it in the bag. Ratchet set – Check. The battery wouldn't fit without smashing the salt, so he kept it aside.

He reached for the bottle of Ambien at the edge of the bed and fumbled with the child-proof lid. It popped off with a bit of effort. He downed a handful of the little pink pills, chasing it with the last of his Jim Beam, which he capped and rolled across the floor with a defiant smile. He didn't want to wake up again. This was his moment.

Dale threw his arms through the straps of the rebreather, then slid the mask on tight. He topped it all off with his trusty Stetson. He hobbled to the mirror on the door for a look. To his horror, his reflection didn't look nearly as badass as he thought it would. In fact, it looked kinda dumpy. And the boots didn't match at all. Dale hesitated. Maybe it wasn't such a good idea. He fidgeted a bit, trying to justify the silly getup, but the chalky taste in his throat reminded him of his situation. There was no turning back, Dale. Better strap in. He calmed himself with the notion that he would be removing the suit exactly when he was finished with it and not a moment later... long before anyone saw him, for sure.

Laying down on his mattress was more difficult than he thought it would be. He was just kinda draped over his backpack with his crotch in the air. It felt really weird in combination with the tightness around his jewels. He kept wanting to adjust himself, but no amount of shifting seemed to help. Maybe it didn't matter, Dale thought. Once the pills kicked in, he wouldn't feel a thing. He clutched the battery tightly in his hands, prepared to tense up as soon as he felt the rush. He knew how easy it was to loose one's grip when it happened. Just a moment later he felt the wave kick in and all was right with the world.

Mister Walinski's roommate didn't know what to say when she found her battery in the hands of the cowboy diver in her guest bedroom. She dialed the police, but Dale was gone.

Through the void came a flash, followed by a pressure and release, then the shock of a trillion gallons of water in every direction. Dale opened his eyes and peered into the darkness through his dive mask. It worked. He was home. He waved about in the murky blue, sucking oxygen through the mouthpiece as he felt himself dropping. He clutched the battery tightly, kicking his legs to right himself. As he flailed around, he found the suns piercing through the surface. That was up. Gotta go that way.

Dale pushed upward, but the awkward scramble only sank him further. The snakeskin boots didn't help one bit. In fact, they seemed to be making things worse! For an instant, he almost thought about which item he had to ditch if he was going to survive. That's what happened last time, and last time, he didn't even have the boots. There was no way he was letting them go. All at once, a hand broke through the surface. It grasped the dive harness by the shoulder and jerked him around. He was yanked upward as the glisten of a half-dozen suns blasted the glass of the dive mask, blinding him completely as he felt himself tossed into a lump.

Mighty Rahiem

Dale blinked the spots from his eyes. He pulled the mask to his forehead to meet two sets of glossy black bug-eyes glaring at him. They weren't friendly. One scowled at the other. "This guys' a respawn," then turned to Dale. "Got trade? We don't got much."

Dale struggled to find his vision. He nodded. "I'll give you the suit and the oxygen for a set of clothes, but I need this battery. I need bluejeans, a button-down shirt – plaid – and a leather duster – black. I got salt for a pistol and a ride to Southtown."

The fishers exchanged a look, then burst into laughter. "Wadaya' think we are, merchants? We're just fishers, buddy. We got dry pants and Talkmans. That's it. You gonna trade or you wanna go walking around in that sweat-suit?"

Dale remembered his mission. He had to escape from the suit as quickly as possible. He looked like a total retard. Thankfully, he remembered to put on the accent. "Whatcha got for britches?" he said. "Gimme something tight. I need me some Levi 501s."

"We got butt-pants!" the Sectoid laughed, holding up a stained pair of extra large sweat pants. The fishers burst into laughter. Carbon Dale was screwed.

Having been thoroughly dismantled by the fishers, Dale was forced to wade to shore where he suffered the indignity of haggling in his wet-suit in front of dozens of laughing beach-goers. He didn't look anything like a cowboy. An hour of back-and-forth bullshit and he finally got his sweatpants and a Talkman in trade for nearly everything in his bag. Not that he had a choice in the matter. Once the deed was done, he immediately snapped his Talkman on and typed in his account number to lock out the old device. The screen popped.

TWOSDAY – 33:16

The Old Guard of Zerth

Dale had no idea how long he had been dead, but his Talkman account hadn't been tampered with. All his money was still there. Clearly, his murderers were idiots. He had the upper hand. Now, to find a ride back to his corpse to resume the hunt for the Potato. It was a two hour drive from the beach to Ghong, and if he was lucky, he could catch a flight to Southtown with the next air-a-van. He could be back in business by Threesday morning. He bet his life on it.

Foursday Morning – 06:72. Dale was rustled from his turbulence-induced stupor. Thirty-plus hours of bouncing and bumping in the back of a flying pickup with no shade. The right half of his body was red with blisters. His ass felt like a washing machine had its way with him until he passed out. He didn't feel so good.

The driver pulled over and idled next to the sidewalk where Dale could see the street sign with the speaker on top. Saxo Street, two-hundred block. Right back where he started. The cowboy gently lifted his tortured rear-end over the side of the bed, causing a terrible sting across his right side. The burn was pretty bad. It felt like his skin was about to pop open. He stumbled to the sidewalk where his driver was waiting with open hands.

Dale grumbled. He went for his bag, leaving his over-sized sweatpants unattended. They hit the ground, giving everyone a clear view of his rocket ship. The Driver was choked up laughing as Dale handed over the last of his Chex-Mix, leaving the cowboy with nothing but his battery and a battered ass. The driver rubbed it in, tossing him a bungee cord for the trouble, which the cowboy sheepishly wrapped around his waist to keep the pants where they belonged. His ride sped off unceremoniously, leaving the half-toasted Human alone on the sidewalk.

Saxo Street was packed with energy. A general hustle was felt on the wind as People were dashing around in a hurry. Dale stepped onto the sidewalk where a dried mackerel lay at his feet. A few yards up, a gang of sprouts were poking at one another with sticks. The dawn sun beat down on his freshly burnt skin, causing him to walk with an awkward slant, lest he cause further irritation to his right side. No matter, sunburns were distinctly cowboyesque. His sunburn was the best sunburn and he was prepared to fight about it.

Carbon Dale shaded his eyes to scan the corner, finding a trail of dead fish along the sidewalk leading to the storefront of the local fish market. The shop keeper was sweeping the carcasses into the street with a push-broom. The next door over was a small boutique, and next to that was the Leaf – the focus of his ire. Shitty music blooped and beeped through the stereo, bringing Dale's blood to a boil. It wasn't cowboy music at all. Those assholes had no idea what they were doing. It was up to him to set them straight. A *real* cowboy from the *real* wild west was there to show em how it was done.

Just then, Dale spotted something. Just up Koplin street, on top of that crappy bar, there was a woman and a Sectoid and that degenerate frizzy-headed pervert who didn't know a damned thing about western music. Then he caught his target. The one-eyed menace. The bastard Potato. Dale ducked into the shade of a nearby garage to avoid being spotted. It was comfortably abandoned so he was able to keep a close eye on his pray from the safety of the shadows. Too bad he didn't have his gun, he could pick the bastard off from hiding and get away with it scott-free.

Dale got comfortable, studying the Legomi with a squint. He wished he had thought to bring a toothpick to chew on. That would have been badass. Carbon Dale the cowboy, chewing on a toothpick, contemplating murder. Epic. He leaned over a workbench, finding a dirty rag atop some jumbled machinery. That rag would look badass hanging from his back pocket. It was covered in carbon. He needed it. Dale snatched it up to find it was concealing something incredible.

The Old Guard of Zerth

It looked like some kind of robo-cannon. It had motor and a roll cage and everything. It even had a big scope. It was everything Dale wanted in a gun, and there it was, free for the taking. He checked over his shoulder to make sure there were no witnesses. Luckily, there was no one around to stop him from connecting with his dream weapon. It was confirmed, God wanted Dale to be a cowboy. He whispered a prayer of thanks and snatched the machine off the bench, then slid his arm through the cage and took aim at the bar. He found it odd that there was such a distance between his eye and the scope. He had to choke up and rest his chin directly above the barrel to get a good target.

Just then, the whine of head-fans buzzed through the air. A cloud of dust kicked up, flooding the bay with grit as a carrier passed overhead. Dale peered out, seeing the craft come about above him, then watched as it descended to the roof, blocking his target entirely. He dropped the gun with a sneer as his prey boarded the ship and lifted off. A stupid cartoon painting of a Morouni mocked him as the craft headed northbound, darting over the rooftops. The hunt was on. But first, his clothes.

Dale skirted around the corner of the bar, finding a crowd gathered among a pile of strewn debris. They were all laughing and chuckling and snapping pictures with their Talkmans. Through the hole in the wall, he found a bus parked on top of a few tables. If he didn't know better, he would have assumed the thing had plowed through the side of the bar. The cowboy shook his head in disgust. The office should be empty now, he thought. Nobody saw Dale as he slipped in through the hole in the wall and dashed up the stairs.

Inside the storage room, Dale found the cage with his decapitated body laying across the floor. The door was open and dried blood was crusted across the bars. The two Dollar Bills were missing. Must have come back around to collect the bodies already. No worries, that meant his posse was still out there somewhere. Probably busy making duplicates he could use for the hunt. Good man.

Dale got to work. He leaned over his corpse and unbuckled the holster. He tossed it aside and unbuttoned the shirt, then the jeans. He yanked the trousers down around the waist but was knocked back by an awful stench. Apparently his body had shit the pants. Dale staggered backwards with deadman poo smeared across his knuckle. It was his own deadman poo! He waved it around in a panic before rubbing it across his sweatpants with a cringe.

Dale weighed his options. Poo-jeans or poo-sweatpants. Poo-jeans it is. He kicked off the sweatpants and hucked them across the room, then slid his legs into the jeans. His seat was moist with the foul waste, forcing him to hop around with an icky grimace, flapping his palms. He calmed himself with a deep breath. Stay focused, Dale, you're a cowboy now. Cowboys aren't afraid of shit. Now, to get his bike.

Just down Koplin Street was Carton's Famous Flight Pad. Dale had stored his bike in the lower lot after the battery died. His posse helped him drag it into the shade, but he didn't need to drag it around any more. The jeep battery was more than adequate. As he entered the shade of the lot, a familiar image caught his eye. There was a sandwich board in front of the entrance with that damned cartoon Morouni. It was Carton himself. He must be the pilot that helped his target escape.

He ran inside and found the flight schedule drawn up on a chalkboard next to an empty office with the glass broken out. *Ender – Arrival: Foursday – 8:05.* Boom. His target was going to Ender. What a place for an ambush. God smiles on the cowboy again.

Dale found his bike and hucked his backpack to the concrete. The nylon strap scraped against his burnt skin causing him to seize in pain. He had to assure himself that a cowboy would never do that. Deep breath, Dale. He fished his tools out and cranked the bolts off the top of the battery housing, then lifted the dead weight and tossed it to the ground. The jeep battery was a bit large for the housing, but as fortune had it, he had been blessed with a bungee cord. Destiny was calling.

As the bike shot across Koplin Street, Dale was in heaven. He raced through the city gates, leaving that god-awful music behind. It was replaced by the buzz of the head-fan and the wind in his hair. A cowboy and his mechanical steed trekking across the desert with a mind set on revenge. He popped the display on his Talkman to calculate a stealthy route to Ender. With any luck, he could slip above the northern shears unnoticed. From there, he would have a perfect shot at anyone in the city. ETA 3 hours. He might even get there before his prey.

Foursday – 9:08 – 101°. Dale kicked across the plateau with his cannon over his shoulder. Bullhoppers leaped from his path while the suns blasted the cracked terrain like a million stage lights. Somewhere on the wind was music. He pushed through a grove of hobby trees and shuffled towards a veiled drop in the dirt. To an outsider, Ender was entirely invisible, but hidden in the cracks of a slot canyon were hundreds of carved-out structures concealed within the rock face. Mesa Verde on steroids. He had been there once before, but only as a tourist. This time, he was there on business. *Yeah, business.* He repeated the words in his mind, thinking again how cool it would be to chew on a toothpick.

Below him was a great circular courtyard amass with townsfolk of all shapes and sizes. He dropped to his belly and dug in, finding a comfortable position to lay so as to not excite the burn. There's got to be some kind of skin cream for cowboys, he thought. Something hardcore like maybe some kind of charcoal-cream. Yeah, charcoal-cream. That would be badass.

Some casual music drifted up the canyon, spiking his ears. *Not-Cowboy-Music.* He scoffed, drawing back an ugly grin. No more music for you, Potato. He propped his cannon up and rested his chin atop the barrel, spying through the scope. It was a good scope. It even had the little green lines and everything. It just made Dale feel even more hardcore. Those lines meant he was a professional. A professional carrying out his duty as a cowboy.

He zoomed around through the scope making a buzzing sound with his cheeks. There were a lot of people down there. There was a great black statue in the center of the courtyard. Off to the right was a wooden sign painted with the words *'Gregor's Gall Bar and Grill'*. Maybe he would get himself a drink after the deed was done. Yeah, that would be *so* western. You shoot a man, then you down one for the dead.

The music shifted to something unexpected – heavy and so hardcore. He found his head bouncing. It was awesome. He wanted more to fuel his blood-rage. Dale began to drift with thoughts of the electric cowboy struggling through hardship to win the day. Win the day with technology! He deserved that damned Jim Beam.

Just then, Dale spotted him. The Potato. There he was, walking slowly through the courtyard with his posse of poseurs. Now was his chance. He shifted his position and drew aim. That big, bulbous head in his cross-hairs. Dale pulled in a breath and held – finger on the trigger – Wait! The Sectoid attacked the Potato – no? Okay, he's fine. False alarm.

Dale calmed his thumping chest as he wondered how big the boom would be. How much firepower was the cannon capable of? Maybe he could take out the whole group? What a show that would be. Again he drew in, holding his breath like in Call of Duty. That's how it was done and he was doing it expertly. 360° no-scope. Maximum Pwnage. Chin on the barrel and finger on the trigger. No escape. Carbon Dale squeezed the grip and pulled the trigger.

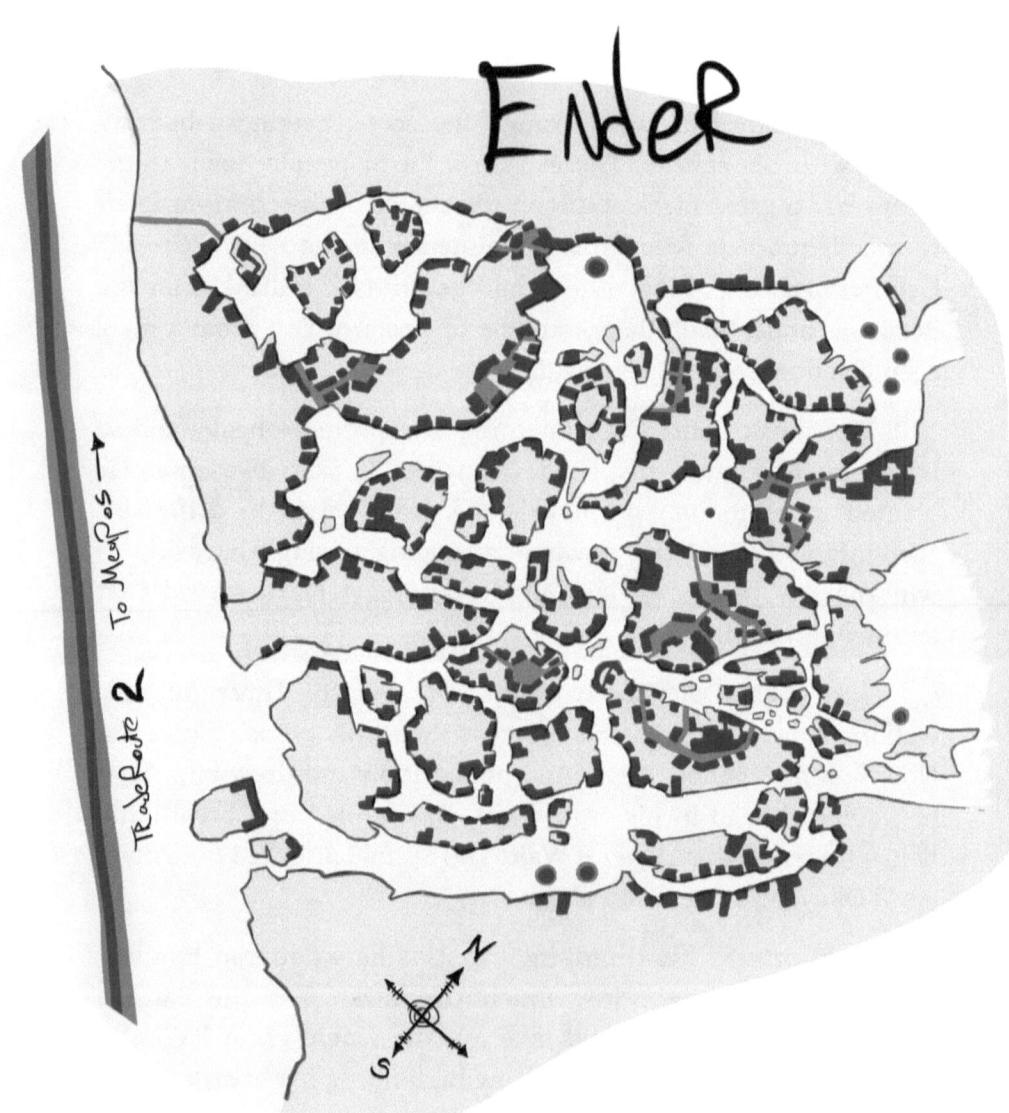

Chapter 14

Memetown

"Is this who I think it is?" Gustav said, rubbing his chin.

"Ironically, he's easier to identify *without* a head," Meri joked.

The crew mulled around the corpse in the heat of the northern shears. It was dug into a crop of wheatgrass that sprang from the soil like a patchy beard. The buzz of bullhoppers joined with something melodic, courtesy of Gustav, while Ender carried on dispassionate, hidden in the canyons below. The townsfolk seemed eager to ignore the explosion that had just rocked the canyon walls moments earlier. Wad couldn't tell if it were a testament to their resilience or their smugness.

The body was splayed face-down, sans face, with a black satchel off to the side. Bits of skull fragments and gray matter were splashed across the dirt, and a large tuft of smoldering wheatgrass was fanned out around where the head should be. It looked like a singed halo. About a yard back, a Stetson hat was flipped backwards with a sizable chunk of cranium packed within.

Potato hovered over the rear of the figure. "Looks like he shit himself – twice. How'd he manage that?"

"No idea," Hesh said, kicking at the body. It lumped to the side, revealing the cannon wedged into the dirt. He curiously leaned down, dusting it off, then held it up for all to see.

"Looks like someone got their face fucked," Wad said, grabbing the thing. "Anyone wanna big stupid gun?"

"It seems fortune favors the patient as well," Meri said, snatching the weapon. "It looks to be about my size anyhow." He fiddled with the leather-fab sling, then swung it over his shoulder. It fit quite comfortably.

"Well, this is failure number two," Potato said with his fists on his hips. "The dumb fucker isn't giving up. That pisses me off." He tapped his boot nervously before losing interest in anger. He found a new focus in Dale's boots, then leaned down, following the tracks in the dirt with his finger until they vanished over a lump in the terrain. He pointed off in the distance. "Dibs on the hyperbike!" The Legomi trotted away, vanishing down an embankment. A moment later, the whir of a head-fan carried across the plain. Potato bumbled up the hill on the rickety machine, pulling to a halt at Wad's boots. "It's got shit on the seat. He shit on his bike," he said, pointing to his butt.

"Not a bad haul," Hesh said. I could clean that thing up for you in trade for that battery, there."

"Sold," Potato said with an uncharacteristic thumbs-up. He was smiling, too. His teeth were exceptionally white.

Gustav cackled. "Well, I suppose we've grieved the dead long enough that we can move on to the looting phase. Dibs on the Talkman." He lifted the wrist, then yanked the device free, tapping through the screens for the account details. "Fifteen hundred bucks – not bad."

Potato's fist clamped around Gustav's fingers, wrenching the Talkman from the Human's grip. "We got the fucker's Talkman now. It's still active." He threw it to Hesh and tapped his temple. "Now we can do the hatch-mode thing and find the asshole that got's Wad's data. We can track him now! Go on, do the thing."

Mighty Rahiem

"Hell yeah," Wad cried, clapping his hands in a ball. "We gotta get that thing decrypted before the asshole comes back again. My guess is we've got a few hours before the data gets wiped." He turned to Hesh. "Who do we know with a data-ripper?"

"Well..." Hesh said, trailing off.

Meri stepped in with his chin in the air. "Wadley, my man. Let's not waste our efforts on the small fry. We'd do better holding back until our man Roldolph can supply us with the whereabouts of the fiend Sanders. Best cut the head off the snake, isn't that right, Mr. Hesh?"

"Not exactly what I had in mind," Hesh said with a grimace. "But I suppose the choice is Wad's." He turned to the Legomi, beaming. "I do happened to know someone with a data-ripper. Someone very close by who can rip, clone and emulate that Talkman without breaking a sweat. And she's very interested in seeing you again."

Wad's palm hit his forehead. "Not Chelli! I told you–"

Gustav pushed between the two, nursing his crushed fingers. "The super sexy ultra-babe? Fuck yeah, what are we waiting for?"

Wad grit his teeth. He ran through the options in his head. On one hand, he could sit back and let a MERC do the work for him – track down Sanders, put a bullet in his head and get Meri a gig at the Great Arrival festival. On the other hand, he could hack a Talkman at the expense of many hours of ridicule from a woman with very large breasts, potentially tracking down the man who stole his identity, pinpoint the jack-hole who put a price on Potato's head, and undoubtedly give Gustav a boner for an hour. He checked his Talkman, which wasn't there. "What time is it?" he mumbled.

The Old Guard of Zerth

"Nine Twenty-two," Hesh said, then lingered with an eye on Gustav. "She does have fantastic breasts."

"Super sexy ultra-babe!" Gustav cried.

Wad nodded. "We'll do both. We've got time before we have to be in Ortega. We'll drop the Talkman off with Chelli, say hello *briefly,* Gustav can get his boner, and we'll leave for Ortega. If Chelli picks up anything, she can call us from very far away."

Hesh grinned. "I'll have her to go easy on you." He pocketed the Talkman and turned to the rest of the crew. "It'll take a few hours for your bus to get here, so I suppose you've got some time to bum around town. We can spare Wad the indecency of being mocked in front of his friends, so I won't ask you to be present for the hacking."

Wad signed with relief. "Wait, what's that about the bus?"

"We'll, I'm not driving you to Ortega. I've done enough travel for one day," Hesh said. "I installed the FETCH system for this reason, you know. I suggest you use it now if you're in a hurry."

"Oh, shit," Potato said, reaching into his pocket. He pulled out the Talkman he had retrieved from the spinning bus. "I guess this does kinda belong to you." He handed it to Wad with a big smile. "Guess now you got a Talkman again. At least we can send you messages and stuff."

Wad took the device and looked it over. It was practically new. Never used for anything but bus-retrieval. He turned to Hesh. "This thing empty?"

Hesh nodded. "You can enter your old ID number if you want, but it'll clear every hash of your data from the blockchain. Since you didn't back anything up, it's got nothing to retrieve. In short, if you use that Talkman as your own, you'd better be absolutely certain that your data was stolen. Otherwise, you'd have to start from scratch."

Mighty Rahiem

"I thought we *were* sure it was unrecoverable," Wad said.

"I'm a telepath, not omniscient, Wad," Hesh said. "I may be wrong, I may be right. Though I do appreciate the trust you put in my analysis. I just can't say one-hundred percent."

"Just hold off, my man," Meri said. "There's no zerthly reason to be hasty. What if he's wrong? Your own hand would be erasing everything. That's you're whole life, man."

Wad looked over the Talkman, rubbing his thumb across the screen. The oil from his finger left a residue that evaporated in the morning heat, leaving only a blank, black screen. "Not my whole life," he said, looking to Potato. Potato wasn't paying attention. He was busy twiddling his fingers.

Wad twisted the leather-fab strap around his wrist, fastening the clasp tight. It felt rigid and clean against his skin. Nothing familiar about it, yet it seemed so necessary. So important. He tapped the screen and a green box appeared with two options. ENTER ID and CALL BUS. He tapped the second option and Meri gasped. "I'm calling the bus, you weirdo," he scolded. Meri wiped his brow and sat back with a deep breath.

A notification appeared on the screen. *ESTIMATED TIME OF ARRIVAL: 3:18:84.*

Wad tapped the screen again. *ENTER ID*. He hesitated, then looked to Hesh. "No reason to get ahead of ourselves, right?"

Hesh replied with a short hum.

"Ahem... good call," Gustav said, butting in. "Sooo, the bus should be here right about the time Potato explodes. Hey, Hesh, why don't ya give yer sexy lady a call and we'll all meet back at your place. That'll give ya some time to crack the Talkmans and figure out the next step."

"What's this about me exploding?" Potato perked up.

The Old Guard of Zerth

Hesh cleared his throat. "My strange friend, in about four hours the tranquilizer I injected you with is going to wear off and your body will again be inundated with a mix of cocaine and strong coffee. You'll then become a wrecking ball the likes of which the world could never face. You wont feel pain, pleasure, fear or remorse as the blood in your veins will be overtaken by pure, unfiltered murder-juice. I don't want to live in a world with that kind of beast running around, especially when it's someone I'm assuming I would have to share a great deal of time with."

"There was cocaine in that coffee?" Gustav said. "Score!"

Potato blinked. With a rock-like furrow in his brow, he reached an arm under his other, unlatching the harness of his PISS pack. He pulled his arms out of the leather-fab sleeves, then squeezed the juice from the reservoirs into the dirt.

"That's right, my buddy. Get it all out," Meri said, patting the Legomi on the back.

Gustav dashed to Potato's side and ran his hands through the stream of coffee. He rubbed his fingers into his gums. "Dam, there *is* cocaine in there," he said, smacking his lips and wagging his tongue.

"Wait," Wad said. "Won't he just pass out without–"

Potato's eye drooped. He swayed a bit, then mumbled something before collapsing in the dirt.

"Oh that's just great," Wad yelled, "He's gonna be out for the next four hours. You just stood there and let that happen?"

"It takes care of our problem, doesn't it?" Hesh said.

"I'm taking this," Gustav announced, snatching the PISS pack from the ground. "Never know when ya might need a little bump."

Mighty Rahiem

"That's about enough from you," Meri said with a growl. First you poison the man, then you swipe his belongings. Have some respect."

"Have some cocaine," Gustav said. He squeezed the PISS pack into Meri's face.

The Morouni spit and gurgled a bit, then willingly took it in. He pulled away and howled. "That's the ticket," he said, wiping his lips. "I'm up for some shopping. Who's with me?"

"Not I," Hesh said. "Give me the brute and I'll let him crash on my couch. I'll give you a call when Chelli is ready." Hesh leaned down and wrapped his hands round the beef that was Potato's arms. It wasn't as easy as he expected, but he managed to hoist the lug over the back end of the Hyperbike, taking care to lift his legs into the cargo straps. The Sectoid mounted up, fumbling with some loose wiring and squeaky joints before firing up the head-fan. It bumbled and bucked, causing him to make a face. He gave a timid thumbs-up to the crew while the bike shuttered down the hill and out of sight.

Gustav gave a nod and thumbs-up. He turned to the remaining men. "And now, we shop!"

The trio worked their way through the market, amassing a modest pile of junk and drawing more than a bit of attention from the locals. The townsfolk of Ender were Sectoids and Legomi mostly, with a light peppering of Human and Morouni filling in the gaps. Meri made a successful trade of his Facefucker for something less invasive, and Gustav emerged from a corner boutique sporting a lightweight bathrobe, which he delighted in throwing open to blind passersby with his pale skin. He maintained his footwear and even picked up a matching holster for his peacemaker. Good trades all around.

The Old Guard of Zerth

Wad abstained on account of lost identity, though he did take interest in a few knickknacks that he was too embarrassed to ask his friends to pay for. He filed them away in the part of his memory reserved for bad jokes and drunken bucket-list shenanigans. The act of non-participation shook something lose in his brain, revealing a tender nerve. There was no good reason he was being left out. He felt like he had been sucker-punched, but his friends carried on while he was left in the dirt with a black eye.

The sore spot grew as the day went on, as did the flavor of Ender. He couldn't shake it. It had crept in unnoticed and made itself at home within his mind. With every storefront he passed, memories came creeping back. They mixed with his emotional black eye, leaving a bitter taste. The rot of isolation, the willing retreat of capable men in the face of adversity, and now his friends were doing it, too. Nothing had changed... or had it? There was nothing left to fight against, yet the people of Ender were the same, as if the Aerie Empire never even fell. Wadley felt the urge to break from the group and find a spot for himself.

Through the golden shade of a narrow passage, Wad strolled passed the alley-dwellers of Ender as they carried on with their daily routine. An old Morouni woman was sifting through some garbage and a pair of Legomi took turns strumming on a makeshift guitar in an alcove behind a furniture store. Nameless peoples of a town outside his influence, he was just another passerby. It was a humbling notion, but one that freed him from the burden of conversation.

Out from the alley and up the hill, beneath the shade of latticed munda on a dead-end street. It bumped against a low rock wall holding back the eastern wind. A lone dobi stood at the corner with potted flours in the windowsill. A small barrel-cactus roosted in a tin bucket at the front door. A condenser buzzed lazily above, trickling moisture down a rubber hose and into a trough that followed the contour of the cobblestone. The lattice ended there with a distinct line of demarcation before the suns of the desert took over.

Wad propped himself against the wall and rested his arms in the heat of the sunlight. Gazing out across the plains, he found himself thankful for the moment of peace. He counted scattered hobby trees and followed the occasional northbound pubber as they bobbed through the rainbelt, hauling their cargo above the waves of dry wheatgrass.

He heard they were building a city up there, just north of Ortega, on the other side of the Braskey Mounds. Rumor had it, a natural spring had been discovered in the downlands. Half-way to Muscan, all the way to the end of Traderoute 7. He wondered who would take credit. Who would name the city and what would it be called? Southtown was his, but who would this new city belong to? Would anyone care? Did anyone care about Southtown?

Back home everyone knew his name but no one ever mentioned why. In the early days, he felt the need to highlight his deeds and rope them around the necks of the younger generation. Really drive the point home that he had suffered for their prosperity. Though as the years passed and the city grew, the foundation he laid was overshadowed by the accomplishments of a thousand others. It was a strange feeling that only turned rough when he didn't get out for a few days. Like the world was leaving him behind. On occasion, he felt compelled to keep relevant by making public appearances.

Public appearances, Wad thought. Was he still relevant? Maybe Hesh was right. His bar was still in ruins and he just took off and left it that way. That's what he was leaving behind. A trashed vision of what could have been a decent idea. Trashed visions of other people's decent ideas as well. Under normal circumstances, an ample wallet would brush it all under the rug.

The Old Guard of Zerth

Make it go away with the swipe of a credcard. Now, his credcard was useless. Just a strip of code on a plasteel slab pointing to empty pockets. He wasn't even allowed to fix his mistakes.

His friends weren't helping much either. Meri was a bag of sand with too much momentum, and he was pretty sure Gustav wasn't capable of understanding hardship in the least. Hesh was up to his usual tricks and only seemed interested in pushing buttons. Potato was... well, Potato was himself. Probably the only one who cared to help, if only with moral support. The only one he had left from his former life. Wad looked down to the virgin Talkman on his wrist. Of all his friends, Potato's ID number was the only one he had committed to memory. The rest were saved electronically so he didn't have to remember.

Wad scolded himself for his lack of conviction. All the drinking, all the bashing, all the shutting out. All the avoidance. He didn't want to pretend it didn't bother him anymore. It was too big. Too much to hide from. He had nothing and no amount of bullshit would change that. It wasn't a sense of duty that propelled his finger to the Talkman. Rather, it was a familiar feeling in his gut. Something he hadn't felt in a lifetime. A lick of flame in his chest. An inward twisting of rage, spiced with regret and garnished with disgust.

He tapped the screen. A familiar keypad appeared, wreathed in a green glow. He let out a quivering breath as the old hate chewed at him from the inside. Painful and angry, filled with spite those who had wronged him. Spite for the man he had become. Spite for everything that kept him docile for so many years. Spite for every cardinal direction. He wanted to see it all burn. Wanted to see it all go to shit beneath his feet as he danced on it with a beer in one hand and a stiff middle finger in the other. He wanted to poke his own eyes out with them. Keep em' there as a trophy of everything he had lost and everything that couldn't be recovered. Everything he conquered with his anger.

Mighty Rahiem

He began to type, quickly entering his ID into the device on his wrist. It peeped. And like that, it was gone. Gone by his own hand – if it even existed to begin with. He dropped his hands to his sides, looking out over the stone wall. The expanse of grass seemed bigger. More wild. More that needed taming and he was the man to tame it. And now he had a reason to fight for it. That delivery boy was gonna pay.

His wrist chirped. He looked down as if the last three days hadn't happened. It was Hesh, inviting him to his contact list. He poked the *'accept'* button and a message appeared.

WELCOME BACK TO YOUR LIFE, WADLEY. I'M PROUD OF YOU. STOP BY FOR A CHAT. SHE'S READY TO SEE YOU.

-HESH

The Old Guard of Zerth

Chapter 15

Sexy-Hot Super Babe

Gustav ducked under the curtain and entered into Hesh's living room. Meri's wide eyes followed close behind. "Holy Christ on a stick, this place is-" Gustav pulled back and cupped his mouth.

The sandstone interior was alive with the scent of curling munda vines. The south wall was a series of recessed waterfalls that drained into a trough. It bubbled into a network of garden plots within the floor. The garden was bright with tobacco leaves and chili peppers growing out of control, giving the room a musty, living scent. The north wall was open to the elements of a shear cliff-side, making the whole room feel more like a covered balcony rather than the standard arrangement. Carved balustrades, chiseled and polished from the natural stone, were the only thing between Gustav and the belly of the ravine about sixty feet below. The street was layered with cobblestone and brick with a decorative pattern. The odd carbon-fiber beam jut out from the rock, holding directional signs that swung lightly in the breeze that blew through the canyon walls.

A cut beam of sunlight split the room, highlighting cotton tapestries along the walls. They depicted foreign symbols of status with an otherworldly pride. Carved alcoves in the natural stone were home to a modest collection of dishes, glasses and utensils, all glistening with a light coat of dew.

The Old Guard of Zerth

Gustav moved away from the balcony in a daze, bumping a well loved dining table and nearing stumbling over a chair. He followed the channel of water down the hall. It passed a series of plasteel doors, then into the library, a second balcony-style room, lined with book shelves and upholstered seating.

Gustav walked slowly through the library as a free wind blew across his face. He didn't feel indoors at all, but somehow still removed from the elements. He moved passed the couch where a snoozing Potato was mushed into the cushions, then up to the stone rails. He leaned out, gazing across the expanse. A high horizon shimmered in the heatwaves and he then realized he was gazing into the interior of the Gorgio Gorge. It was enormous. It must have been three-hundred feet across. All carved out and smooth like a borehole. Bits of greenery here and there from the cracks. It reminded him of Christmas.

The base of the gorge was paved flat from overuse. Nearly polished under the pressure of the repulser lifts of hyperbikes and mid-sized haulers. It was the closest thing to an interstate Zerth had to offer. They called it Traderoute 2 and it was packed with traffic going to or from the Meapos Peninsula. Gustav was too impressed by the sight. All those people making things work on their own. There were no speed limits, no traffic laws, no interstate police, yet nothing was exploding. Nothing was going to shit. Hundreds of vehicles passed by, all going where they needed to go in peace. He tapped his Talkman and looked out in silence. **Assemble Head In Sunburst Sound – The Chocolate Maiden's Misty Summer Morning.** Meri approached the Human but was waved off with a quick hand.

Hesh entered the room with a smile but was met by Meri's shaking head. He pointed at the Human with a 'shush' motion. Hesh nodded, then waved for Meri to follow him. They moved into the living room where The Sectoid pulled a chair from the well-loved wooden table, inviting the Morouni to sit.

Mighty Rahiem

The surface was scribbled with carved wanderings and etched profanities. Not an inch was untouched. The chairs were equally loved, but much less hearty. They wobbled a bit more than they should.

As Meri studied the table with childish curiosity, the curtain of the door brushed open. Wadley entered with a look of resolve on his face. He took a deep breath, then tried to hid a smile. The leaves atop his shoulders unfurled at the scent of running water. Hesh met him with a genuine grin. "Welcome. Come grab a seat. Coffee's going on in a moment."

Wad greeted Meri and looked around. "Where's Guz?"

Meri thumbed over his shoulder with a snarky look. "Our man is enjoying a moment to himself."

The jangle of the guitar caught Wad's ear. "Ah," he said, taking a seat at the table. He locked his fingers together and leaned forward, eyeing Hesh. He prefaced his question with a deep breath. "What have we found out?"

"So," Hesh started. "Mr. Potato is resting well. I'm sure you can appreciate that. Chelli is down in the workshop and we can join her as soon as you are ready. Concerning what we've found so far, the Human's Talkman is quite old. It seems to have belonged to at least one other individual throughout its lifetime. It's not uncommon for them to be reused, but it makes deciphering them a bit rough. As for recent activity, well, that's where you come in. Without reference, it's just a jumble of names and statistics. Can I get either of you some coffee?"

"Sans cocaine, please," Meri said.

"Take it or leave it," Wad replied, waving his hand.

Hesh chuckled. He spun around and grabbed a hotpot from the shelf in the wall, then moved to the waterfall where he dipped it into the cascade. He returned it to the table, tapping a switch in the base. "Give it just a minute," He said, then rummaged around the shelf, producing three stoneware mugs and a glass jar of coffee grounds. He scooped a spoonful into three mesh baggies, then dropped them into the cups. The hotpot jumbled with a bit of steam and he splashed a good amount in each mug, then slid them across the table. They rattled over the numerous grooves in the wood, spilling a bit on their way. The music ended and started back up again. The song was on repeat.

Hesh swirled his mug, eyeing the speakers. "So, I see the pink one is having some difficulty?"

"We don't bother him when he gets like that," Wad said. "At least we try not to. He can wander sometimes. It's best to let it happen. He gets cranky if we don't."

"A man needs time to think," Hesh agreed. "Any clue on the subject?"

Wad looked passed Hesh and nodded to the hallway where Gustav stood with a helpless posture. His glasses were all fogged up.

"You okay, Guz?" Wad said.

Gustav lifted a shaking hand to his glasses and pulled them off. Tears were streaming down his cheeks. He pressed his thumb and finger into the bridge of his nose with a squint. The Human let out a deep breath and moved to the table, drawing a chair and throwing himself in. He leaned forward and cupped his hand over his mouth, raising his eyes to meet Wad.

"You cool?" Wad said again.

Gustav forced a smile. Without warning, he jumped from his chair and leaned over the stone balustrade. "Ya know," he said, with a quiver in his voice. "The first time I heard this song, I was coming back from lunch break at LINTECH. I was walking across the street and I had my-" he stuttered and laughed through the tears. "I had my headphones on. And I saw this guy on the sidewalk – this homeless guy. He was all done up in rags and shitty clothes and everything. And he was just sitting there along the wall, shivering to death in the cold.

I kept walking and someone came up to the guy and gave him a sandwich or something, some kind of food or something. And the look on the guys face... I could never smile that much in my life. It wasn't even a smile, but it was so real and so genuine, and he sat there and he started crying. And as I watching him, this song came on. I'd never heard it before but it came on and it was playing as I watched this man bawling his eyes out over a sandwich.

I couldn't help but think that this guy had it so much better than me. All he needed was that sandwich and I'm there with all sorts of dumb problems. I was the one in the rut. I couldn't smile that hard if I tried, and here was this old codger, showing me how to do it. He ate that sandwich and he was crying, and I could tell he was so far away with everything that mattered that I couldn't begin to understand that kind of love and gratitude and freedom. All it took was a damned sandwich and the bastard was in heaven.

From that moment on, I wanted to be that guy-" Gustav choked up. "- and now I am. This whole place... you have no idea what this place means to someone like me. To anyone like me. Every man or woman who has been stuck under the boot-heel of that godawful planet. It's a curse, a real curse. But this song comes on and shows me that it doesn't have to be. We can go far away to any place we want and make it ours. Places like this or anywhere else."

Hesh pulled away with buckets pouring down his face. "Oh my," he said, "that was a lot to feel."

Gustav turned to the Sectoid with a smile. "You didn't have to see it – but thank you for seeing it. It's good to know that someone else sees it too. I have to be honest. The minute I walked in I wanted to buy this place. I was prepared to offer you anything and you know I would pay it. Millions I would have paid. Billions, even."

"My lord," Hesh said, seeing Gustav's thoughts. He turned to Wad with a frozen expression.

"Guz, my man," Meri piped up. "It's not uncommon for you to brag about your income, but exactly how much money do you have?"

"I got all the money in the world," Gustav said, clawing back to his usual snark. He sniffled and smiled.

Hesh turned to Meri with a dead look. "He's not lying."

"What do ya mean, he's not lying? How is that possible?" Wad said. "How does that make any sense?"

Hesh leaned towards the Human and probed deep. Gustav let him in freely, holding his finger to his temple with a wince of pain. The Sectoid pulled back with a disturbed look, then creeped out of his seat. He tapped his Talkman. "You boys will have to excuse me," he said. "This is a bit more startling a revelation than I had expected. I need to make a call." He turned and hurried down the hall. The two men looked to Gustav who was hiding an embarrassed smirk.

"So?" Wad said, throwing up his hands. "What's the story? What the hell's the deal?"

"You really wanna know?" Gustav said through a laugh.

"Out with it, man," Meri said impatiently.

"Okay," Gustav said. He took a breath and made sure the song was still on repeat, then sat back. "So, this was a while back.

Mighty Rahiem

I caught the little fucker out behind the Dove. You know, the Reaver Dove? That little bar up Saxo Street. He liked to run his mouth. He kept going on about how he was hot shit and he was gonna ruin me. *Do you know who I am? I know Gregor!* That kind of thing... so I killed him. Shot him in the face. Mind you, this is before I found out that Sectoids didn't just come back to life like I did. I mean, hell, by that time I had died like, ten or eleven times already. Ya can't blame me for that, I didn't know any better.

Anyway, I go to loot the dude and he didn't have a Talkman, but he did have a credcard. What the hell, I say. I swipe it to see if I can transfer anything to my account. That's when I realized what I had found. The little shit had well over 400 trillion bucks on that card. That's like, four times all money on Zerth. So I did some research and found out the dude was some guy named Leggis Asinus. He's the dude that invented the currency! He had gamed the system and given himself sole access to Zerth's reserves. It was supposed to be set aside as a hedge against deflation, but now I have it."

"My word, Guz. I don't think anyone would ever believe that," Meri said.

"Why do you think I joke about it? The truth is so far beyond belief that I don't mind saying it. As long as Sectoids aren't around."

Wad was puzzled. "So, all this time you've been borrowing my shit, living in my office-"

"I think what our man Wadley is trying to say is that he is respectfully requesting that you share the wealth," Meri said with a stink-eye. "Given his current predicament, it's only right."

"No," Wad said. "That's not what I'm saying. My money is my money and I'm going to get it back. I don't want anyone else's. I just wanna know why you never pay for your own stuff?"

The Old Guard of Zerth

Gustav pushed from his seat. "Well, that wouldn't be any fun, would it? Come on, Wad, Humans are predators. We like to hunt for our material possessions, remember? *Your* material possessions." He leaned into the Legomi. "So yes, I'm still going to borrow your stuff." He jumped back and did a little jig.

Wad buried his face in his hands, but something piqued his attention. "Wait," he said. "You said a name. The guy you killed mentioned a name."

"Yeah, sure," Gustav said. "Gregor, or something."

"Gregor? Are you absolutely sure you heard that right?" Wad said.

"Hundred percent," Gustav said. "I've been looking around for this Gregor dude ever since that day. I wanted to rub it in his face."

"No!" Wad said, pushing forward. "No, you don't do that."

"Why not? What's the big deal?" Gustav said, loosing his edge.

"It's not just Gregor, its *a Gregor*. Gregor-"

"Gregor Garab," A gruff voice said, joining the conversation. A groggy Potato leaned against the corner. "Where did you hear that name?"

"Yeah," Gustav said, turning his seat. "Garab. That name kept popping up in my research, too. Who is he?"

"Same Guy. Gregor Garab. He's a Gregor. Gregors are no good," Potato said, taking a seat at the table. He reached for Gustav's cup and tossed it down, then went for the pot of water. Down it went. He then turned to Gustav. "Music," he said.

Gustav scrambled for his Talkman. The music stopped. He turned back to the conversation. "What were we talking about?"

"Gods," Wadley said plainly. "Evil gods."

208

"Just a moment," Meri interrupted. "I can handle this nonsense. The Morouni people have dealt with this issue for generations, even after the great arrival. Gods most certainly do *not* exist. Koplin, Billion, all of that tripe – they are a figment. A sham. It is a blight in our history that many of us work very hard to erase. The old ways, the elders, they live by these so-called gods. It is *the* reason I do public speeches. If any of you had bothered to listen to anything I say, you would see it quite clearly."

"I listen," Potato said.

"No," Wad said. "These aren't heroic figures that developed a cult following, these are *real* gods with *real* power."

"Nonsense," Meri scoffed.

Potato slapped the table. "They are real. At least, they were. We thought they were all dead but there is still one left no one can find. They say he's in hiding, pulling strings and making things happen. Hesh knows, ask him. They made all the Sectoids and they made all us Legomi. They're the creators and they ain't good guys. They kill you with their brains. That's all they gotta do, just think at you and you die."

"So what happened to em all?" Gustav said.

"Ask Wad. He's the hero," Potato said, nodding to his friend.

"You killed the gods?" Gustav said. "Way to go, buddy!" He slapped the Legomi on the back but Wad didn't respond. "Well, okay then."

"No, you don't kill em, they kill each other. That's the only way you can take em down. They're too strong for mortals."

Potato fuddled a bit. "Well, that ain't all true. They're only flesh and blood, but that don't mean shit. They can still turn yer face upside-down."

The Old Guard of Zerth

"Your tone suggest you have first hand knowledge of this?" Meri said with a grimace. "And you are to believe that one is still at large?"

Potato nodded and turned to the Human. "Guz, what did you read about Garab?"

Gustav thought for a moment. "That island just off the coast of Southtown. Hollice Island, I think they call it. I saw a shitload of money moving around there, all with this Gregor guy's name on it. I did some more digging and I found that he had a matching reserve fund. It's tied to mine but in a separate account. Same thing, trillions of bucks being shuffled around to different things. Construction, mostly. I figured he was building something."

"Whatever he's doing, it's no good. I promise you that," Potato said. "They don't do nuthin' good at all."

"I suppose, in time, we will see," Meri said.

Hesh returned to the living room with a determined look. He moved to the head of the table and wrapped his fingers around the back of the empty chair. "My friends, I apologize for the secrecy but there are some things that are just beyond our control at the moment. I can see you've been discussing the same issue that concerns me and I need to stress the level of danger involved. This is not something that can be handled by us alone so I've taken steps to pass the word along to some powerful allies. With any luck, the menace will be located and eliminated. Again, I cannot understate the danger. It would be wise of all of you to put this issue out of your minds as greater powers are at work, and the last thing we want is to be meddling in the affairs of a Gregor." Hesh punctuated his statement with a vague smile and looked away. "So," he said, "shall we all get on with our business? Something a bit more tuned to our specialty?"

Mighty Rahiem

The group pulled from the table. They followed Hesh down the hall and through the library. Embedded within the southern wall was a galvanized steel door with an access panel alongside. The Sectoid tapped the panel and the door slid open with a buzz, revealing a well lit elevator car.

"Maybe I do wanna buy this place," Gustav said.

"If you like it so much, the rock next door is available for development. This one's not for sale," Hesh said with a wink.

The crew piled in as Hesh tapped the inside panel. The door slid shut and bare limestone took the place of steel walls as the car began its descent. A moment later the crew hit ground level with a thump. The door chimed and slid open to a raw stone hallway, dimly lit with strategically placed orblights. Electrical conduits and pipes lined the walls running the length of the hallway which curved out of sight about thirty feet down. The floor was a steel grate covering a channel of tubes and cables set within the rock. They blooped and bleeped with yellow and green lights of random function.

"Hesh," Gustav said, "I really *really* wanna buy this place. I'll give ya ten million... make it ten billion."

Hesh chuckled and led them down the hall to one of many plasteel doors. "I hear the doors are lacking a bit in flavor. That may diminish the resale value," he said with a sly wink to Wad, who huffed. "Inside joke," Hesh said, as he tapped an access panel. The door slid upward with a hydraulic hiss and the crew were met with a warm wave of burtmoss scent.

The room was dark and moist. Scattered around were chirping electronics and glowing growboxes filled with moss and vines. The ceiling was bare stone with dangling wiring, all leading to the rear of the room where a digital display emanated with an ambient green readout. An odd looking silhouette flickered in the light. It turned and stood.

The Old Guard of Zerth

Gustav squinted in the darkness, making out the shape of child-baring hips swaying eagerly in his direction. The man's jaw dropped as he lost himself in the view.

"Keep it in your pants," A voice called out. Chelli emerged from the shadows. She shot a wide grin at the Human, resting her hand on her hip. She was tall, much taller than Hesh. 6'2" when standing with a proud posture, which she did to the delight of every man in the room. Beneath a shear ensemble of white lace and denim shorts, her form was on full display. Teal skin and a slender 'S' curve of the back gave her motions an entirely suggestive thrust.

She was completely hairless, save for the arc of her eyebrows, which drew downward to a pair of onyx eyes set deep within smooth cheekbones. Nose-less, ear-less, but her lips moved like a wave, and a playful tongue teased behind chicklet teeth. An over-sized lace top hid nothing, draping over her shoulders and loosely down her arms, her hands were hidden within the massive cuffs. A pencil-thin waist widened to low cut denim, which abruptly halted at the top of her thighs. From there, skin down to her shins, where a dusky pair of combat boots were neatly secure. Not a goddess, that would be too regal. More a girl born aware of everything she was and with total mastery of her form. It was only a kind of innocence about her that allowed one to look and not be blinded.

She pointed at Wad. "There you are, you little shit. You finally bring back my bike?"

"Eghm," Wad replied, dropping his mood like a brick.

Chelli lumped to her knees and dove for the Legomi. She wrapped the lace around him, pulling him in for a hug. Wad pretended to struggle against bare breasts as they mooshed against his face.

"I am also here," Meri announced.

212

Chelli ignored everything and popped back to her feet. She cocked her head at Potato. "I know you, don't I?" She bounced her hip to the side.

"Yep," Potato said.

"You're Samuel Tuber, aren't you? I know someone who knows you. Ancient history, right?"

"Yep," Potato said.

"Sam what?" Gustav burst. "I didn't know you had a real name." He turned to Chelli. "He has a real name?"

"My name is Potato. She can call me Sam. And so can Wad."

"I don't wanna call you Sam," Wad said. "You told me to call you Potato."

Potato turned from the group and found a wall to lean against. He pulled a cigarette from his vest and lit up. The glow of the flame exposed the avoidance in his eye.

"Sammys' a Cool cat," Chelli said, mimicking Potato's baritone. She turned her focus to the group. "So, we've got work to do." She bounced across the room and threw herself in to the pilot seat. It spun fully around while she raised her hands like a conductor, then blasted away at the keypad.

"This is your hacker girl?" Meri said. Hesh nodded.

Chelli began. Her words gushed like a fire-hose. "So, this is the data I pulled off Mr. *Dale Walinski's* Talkman. That was his name, if you were wondering. It's all safe and secure in my personal emulation drive. Interesting stuff, if you're a voyeur maybe, but otherwise meaningless. We've got location drops, points of access, money transfers, travel calculations – the usual. What I think *you* guys would be interested in is the coms traffic." She pointed at Potato, playfully queuing a reaction.

"Where is Sanders?" Potato said.

She made a face, then prompted Wad with a finger.

"Someone stole my shit."

"You're no fun," she poked. "Anyway-" she swiped the screen and a small list of account numbers blipped on, followed by an assortment of time stamps and hash codes. "Seems this guy wasn't the most social of butterflies. Relatively small group of associates."

"Put some faces to those ID's," Gustav said. "I bet we can find the delivery guy in there."

"Put some faces to those ID's" Chelli teased to herself. She tapped a key and the screen flashed with a series of portraits. The girl peered over her shoulder and popped an eyebrow.

"Big deal, baby girl," Gustav said, oozing what he meant to be sex appeal. "So you got a Talkman to show up on a screen. Anybody with a rudimentary understanding of electronics can do that. As long as the thing is connected to-"

Chelli let out a false groan and stood from the chair. She dropped her shoulders and approached the Human with pouting lips. She drew close, nearly bumping into the man, stopping within inches of his face. Gustav was eye-height to her chin. He looked deep into her jet-black eyes, the pores of her skin, the subtle shift in tone of her cheeks, the soft pallet that would have been a nose if she were anything close to Human. She leaned down and let a breath escape across his face, then blew a raspberry in his ear. Gustav nearly melted.

Chelli dropped the routine and resumed the flow of information in his face. "Metanet emulations aren't the easiest things to maintain. It takes the equivalent of a gigawatt tap-routine to stabilize, which isn't something I would assume just *anybody* could pull off, I mean am I right? How many oscillation stabilizers are just laying around willy-nilly? I mean really, what's the tap-rate of an Aerie substation repeater? These aren't scrub toys for little boys. Am I right, little boy? Is that an oscillation stabilizer in your pocket or are you just that unfortunate?"

Chelli left him with a wink and returned to the console. Gustav very much needed to sit down. She went back to work, smacking the keys of the console. Images flipped through the screen like mugshots.

"That's him," Potato said. "Sanders. Right there." He pointed at the screen from the back of the room.

"Wait," Wad said. "You pulled this from Carbon Dale's Talkman? What does Dale have to do with Sanders?"

Gustav snapped his fingers. "Hah, I told you. He's the ringleader. Head of the snake! Bet ya a hundred bucks he's running the whole thing. Find Sanders and we find Wad's money."

Wad nodded. "That's it. So, what do we know about him?"

Chelli feigned wonder, then went back to work. "Looks like the guy's name isn't really Don Sanders. He bumped his block ID a few years ago, which is quite a feat. I didn't know you could do that." She turned to Gustav who popped to attention. "Did *you* know you could do that?" Without allowing a response she was back to it. "I'll have to go back through the logs and see if there was a gap in the updates. Otherwise, I just don't see how it's possible."

"Where is he?" Potato grunted.

Chelli turned around. "I have no idea."

"Can you find him?"

Chelli seemed to search the room in her thoughts. "Ping-triangulation," she said with a nod. "We need a second Talkman and a shitload of processing power. We input the location of the second Talkman, followed by the location of my amazing rig, then let the process run until it pings everywhere he isn't."

"How long would that take?" Wad said.

"About eight years," Chelli frowned. "I mean, you could just go the cheap route and get him to accept a dual account."

Wad stepped in. "What's the tap-rate of Aerie's Metanet?"

Chelli's eyes widened. She yanked the next words from Wad's mind and spun around, pounding away at the keys. "The Tap Sub-routine of Aerie's own repeaters have more than enough processing power to run a scan on itself. There's no latency, which is what would get in the way of a mass ping-triangulation. We could-"

"I worked on Aerie repeaters," Wad interrupted. "We don't need a mass-"

"I know," Chelli said, turning around. "I just went off on my own – for my own fun later on when all of you are gone. What is it you wanted to do again?"

"Wad wants you to run a Metanet diagnostic on a single account," Hesh said. He left his seat and joined Wad at the console. "We can't access an account unless a diagnostic is run on it, and even then, we only get a snapshot. But you leave a ticket in the account for external access and you can jump in there at any time with a master account. We just need another active Talkman."

"Mine!" Gustav said, jumping up.

"Give," Chelli said, not turning around. She held her hand out as Gustav unstrapped the band, then lovingly placed it in her palm. "We're going to have to join your Talkman with Mr. *Walinski's*, if that doesn't bother you too much. My mirror of his Talkman will act as the main connection, and yours will be running the routines to mask the mirror. In order to mask the dual-bands, I'll have to split the connection with your Talkman so we can share the database and find commonalities and erase them. It would be a dead giveaway." Chelli didn't wait for confirmation, nabbing a cable splitter and going right to work. Sparks flew and she recoiled with burnt fingertips. The screen turned to green fuz. She turned in her chair. "Believe it or not, that's two com readouts," she said, pointing at the gibberish.

"You can read that shit?" Gustav said.

"You can't read it but I'm better than you, so does that answer your question?" Chelli pouted, wagging her hips in the chair. She added a smile at the end. Gustav bit his finger.

"Split the readout," Wad said. "Your jamming the signal."

Chelli turned to wad with a look. "I didn't know you knew anything about frequency jamming. Hold on, let me in your head." She closed her eyes and Wad winced a bit.

"You can get in my head anytime you want, honey," Gustav schmoozed.

Chelli looked up. "I'm already in your head, silly. But enough of that. Wad needs me to re-tune the frequency of the Talkmans repeaters to functionally opposite wavelengths and reassign their broadcasting to different IDs so they don't override each-other, all the while maintaining a small enough gap in the feed to still communicate. Congratulations, sunstruck. You just invented dual-frequency banding of multiple connections through a single output."

Wad blushed.

The screen became clear again, showing readouts of both Talkmans. "And there we go," Chelli beamed. Her face then drooped. "Do you know what this means?" She said.

The Old Guard of Zerth

Everyone but Hesh shook their heads. "It means we can gain access to any Talkman that has granted permissions to either of the two in our possession," Hesh said.

"And by extension, any Talkman that we can gain access to remotely," Wad said. "All we have to do is emulate whatever Talkman made the call to MªFuggin Delivery Service and we can ping the guy. Find out exactly where he is. I gotta call Amelia." He poked at his Talkman, then remembered he only had one contact number. "Shit, who's got Amelia's number?"

"Hold on there, cowboy. We would need a reaaaaly big repeater," Chelli said.

"And an unscrambler," Wad said, nodding at his feet. "Otherwise you're just repeating a bunch of raw data."

"Well boy oh boy, I thought you'd never ask!" Chelli smiled. Gustav started to get jittery as she pushed from the pilot seat and leaned over the desk. She spun around and eyeballed the Human. "No staring at my ass," then turned and wiggled her behind. Gustav nearly died.

Chelli pulled a steel box from a graveyard of electronics behind the desk. "Unscrambler," She said, tapping the box, then held it in Gustav's face. "Smell it," she said.

Gustav gave it a confused sniff.

"What's it smell like?" She said.

Gustav couldn't say a damned thing.

"Smells like an unscrambler," Chelli said with a wink.

She ripped a cable from the console and jabbed it in the side of the box, then hucked it to the desk. "Mighty powerful stuff. Thankfully, we've got friends in high places. Really high places." She laughed at herself. Hesh chuckled along with a knowing grin. "Now, we find any commonalities between boner-man and Mister Walinski's Talkman and eradicate them!" She cackled maniacally as the screen scrolled through thousands of portraits, resting on a single one. It was a familiar face. A rough looking Morouni with a distended jaw, deep set eyes and dangly jowls. It was Roldolph.

The room went quiet.

"Why does Carbon Dale have Roldolph in his list of contacts?" Gustav said with a low voice.

Chelli spun around with a smile. "He's the guy that blew up the Whiskey Waffle Emporium," she said without hesitation.

"Preposterous," Mary boomed.

"Bull – shit," Gustav said. "I've known Roldolph for years. He would never... why would you say that?"

"I have sources," Chelli said with a confused look.

"Who is your source?" Wad said.

Chelli poked at her temple with a tight smirk. "We Sectoids see all."

"I'm beginning to see cracks in this myth," Meri said, standing. He took a breath and made sure his shirt was straight before he continued. "Madam, is it possible your clairvoyance is mistaken?"

Chelli shook her head with a blank look.

Meri licked his lips. He held a claw in the air, asking for a moment of silence which he punctuated with a quick breath. "My lady, what did you see in my mind?"

"Clearly, a flower growing very quickly," Chelli said.

Meri turned to Hesh, who was giving the Morouni a skeptical eye. "And you, my man. What did you see?"

The Old Guard of Zerth

"A fast-growing plant of some kind. Munda, I presume," Hesh said.

"You are both incorrect," Meri said with a smile. "What you saw was my own interpretation of something I have never witnessed myself. It is a moss native to the Morouni Homeship called Hardigrave. I'm told it was quite a miraculous organism. It would grow very quickly, and was instrumental in the health of our species due to its medicinal properties. High in vitamin D, I'm told. When we arrived on this planet, the air pressure was too low for the moss to survive, and so it died out quickly in the ruins of the ship. Do you see where I'm going with this?"

Hesh sat back and crossed his arms. He threw a leg over his knee and rocked a bit, thinking it over. Chelli was still. "But it's a real plant, isn't it?" she said.

"Indeed," Meri replied. "One that I have never had the pleasure of seeing myself. I hear it was quite lovely, but who would know? My point is, I'm quite certain you would get a more accurate viewing of it from someone who has seen it first-hand. So tell me, did your source see Roldolph commit these crimes first-hand, or are you seeing what they themselves believe to have happened?"

Chelli turned away in thought but came back empty handed. She couldn't say anything.

"Allow me to continue," Meri said. "I ask you both, what are the odds of a man who has clearly suffered greatly at the hands of the elders, assisting in their campaign of terror? In context, I ask you the same question once more. What are the odds of the two of you returning to the days of Aerie subjugation? What are the odds of Wadley and Potato return to their slavery under your own iron fist?"

"Fucking Zero," Potato said. Wad agreed with a serious look.

Meri continued. "It is not my intent to deflate you, but it is my duty as a skeptic to point out the inconsistencies in your methods. Indeed, your clairvoyance is a gift. No doubt about that, but infallible it is not. Nor is anything in this world. It would do you both good to remember that." The Morouni ended with a stern posture and a tight frown.

Chelli and Hesh exchanged looks. The girl turned to Meri with a smile. "Ya got me there, big guy." She wiggled in her chair and spun back around, typing furiously at her keyboard. The room stayed quiet, save for the hum of electronics and fingers dancing across keys.

"Roldolph Rimbaud," Chelli said, aping Meri's voice. She poked the picture on the screen and it vanished. "Duplicates eradicated!" She broke into laughter again. "Okay, were ready. Now we just need a scammer or something. Something to break into Aerie's systems and convince it that we are *also* Aerie's systems."

"A tap-booster," Wad said. "Or tap-repeater? I don't know."

"Tap-both," Chelli said. "Nevermind. Got it. Tap-thingamabobber. That's what we'll call it. And guess what, it works."

"Whadya mean it works?" Potato said.

"I mean I made it work. I'm in," Chelli said. She turned around with a wide smile.

Wad ran to the console and glared at the screen from a distance of three inches. "She's in," he said. "-with a condenser?"

"I needed an antenna, so I used the condenser on the roof," Chelli said, squirming with delight. "I'm sure I could find something better, but then that would mean I would have to leave this chair and hook something up myself and I really don't like doing that. I'm much better off right where I am, so I figured I would use the first thing in range that was made of metal. Condenser go!" She pointed to the ceiling with gusto.

"So, where's this delivery guy at?" Wad said.

"Get me the Talkman that made the order and I'll find him."

Wad fizzled.

"Where's Sanders?" Potato said.

"That I can do," She said with a thumbs-up. "Coordinates are -472.8/+99.2. He's right outside Ortega. Less than 100 miles from here."

"Well shit, I guess that's where we go," Wad said.

"Good timing," Hesh said. The bus should be here momentarily."

Gustav leaned over Chelli's chair. "You coming with? I got room on my lap."

She turned with a frown. "I don't go outside," she said. "I think I'd catch fire."

"Hehe, so would my pants," Gustav said.

"Careful you don't spring a leak," Chelli smiled, pointing at his crotch. She turned back to the screen and tapped at the keypad. "Looks like three more ID's at his location. They haven't moved either – I'm guessing it's his posse or something. Strange, there's really nothing in the immediate vicinity besides a water pipeline. Coms don't show any electrical disturbance – none at all. No EMF dampeners or frequency scrubbers or anything. It looks like they're roughing it.

"Can we get a visual for those ID's?" Wad said, pulling up alongside Chelli.

"Condenser go!" Chelli pointed at the roof, then slapped her keyboard. Three Humans appeared on the screen. Gustav did a spit take with nothing in his mouth.

"You know them?" Chelli said.

"Bull-goddamned-shit," Gustav cried. He threw his hands up and stomped away from the console. The two Sectoids eagerly searched his thoughts, but couldn't make sense of it. The Human was quite familiar with a face on the screen, but somehow had no contact whatsoever with it. The concept of fame escaped them.

"Luke fucking Skywalker is not a fucking mobster," Gustav grumbled.

"Who?"

"He's my fuckin' hero, goddamit. I fucking grew up with that guy."

Wad looked to Hesh for answers but the bugman didn't have any. He was equally confused, and his telepathy was only making things worse. Somehow, Gustav both did and didn't grow up with the man on the screen. It's name was and wasn't Luke Skywalker, and somehow, Gustav both did and didn't know him at all.

Chelli held her head. "I need a drink."

"What's the big deal?" Wad said. "You told me anyone from Earth could show up here, right? Why not that guy?"

Gustav grumbled. "Wreck my goddamned childhood. The dude still looks like a teenager. You'd think that if he was here in the 70's, he would have said *something* about it in an interview or something. But no, he went on like nothing happened. Luke Skywalkers' a goddamned mobster... no, I refuse to believe it. Unless-" Gustav paused for a moment. "Unless this is just like the movie. Those bastards captured

Luke Skywalker. We gotta rescue that fucker. I refused to believe Luke was complicit in this jibberjab. He must be in trouble. Unless he's turned... to the dark side."

"Don't care if you don't believe it," Potato said from the corner. He flicked his cigarette to the floor. "We're gonna go pound that Sanders guy right now. Go ahead, put some music on. Get pumped up. We're doing this for Wad, whether you like it or not."

"I'm gonna need some really sad music," Gustav said. "I can't describe how depressing this is."

"No sad shit," Potato said. "People hate that stuff."

The sound of spinning gears echoed from down the hall, followed by a mechanical shuffle. Wad's Talkman chirped. "Bus is here," he said.

"The bus!" Gustav cried.

"Into the bus!" Meri howled.

"Bus!" Potato yelled, and with that, the crew piled out the door and into the hallway.

Chapter 16

la cos'ha nostra

Northwest – 115Mph.

Destination: -572.8/+44.2.

Arrival:38 minutes.

Disappears – Magics buzzed through the speakers. A warm breeze danced around the cabin as the bus raced through the foothills of Traderoute 7, and Meri popped a beer. Wad popped a beer and sucked down a sip, then let it dangle in his fingers with his wrist hung over the steering wheel. Potato kicked a foot up to the dashboard and settled in. He popped a beer, then handed another to Gustav, who popped it and threw his elbow out the window, letting the wind blast his hair. Hobby trees flashed by as the road curled around the tail-end of Rusted Bluff.

To the right was a sharp drop into a staircase of redrock pillars. A cloud of sandsquid billowed across the sky with a northeastern wind bringing a smile to Wadley's face. He rattled his thumb across the steering wheel to the beat of the music, watching the formation of creatures chase the next thermal pocket that would carry them across the basin. Before there were roads, he traveled across the same terrain on foot. It was a desperate journey fueled by an ugly passion, but it payed off in the end. Now, as he glared into the shine of seven suns, the same topography shrank beneath him like a tamed beast.

"Samuel Tuber. Who woulda' thought?" Gustav laughed, downing a chug of beer.

"That ain't my name," Potato said. "You call me Potato or nuthin' at all. That name is reserved for people who knew me before."

"Fair enough. If it makes you feel any better, my middle name isn't 'D'.

Meri laughed. "My man, what exactly does the 'D' stand for, pray tell?"

"Dee," Gustav said. "I don't actually have a middle name, so I gave myself one. Everyone else here does it, so I figured, what the hell."

Meri leaned to his knee. "Do you recall the first thing you said to me? What was it, eight, maybe nine years ago? I was just a little dot-of-a-lad. You didn't know what to think of me."

Gustav shook his head.

"You said 'what the hell are you', and I replied. Do you remember what I told you?"

"Not really," Gustav replied.

"I said 'I'm a Merinall', and you immediately called me Meri. Don't you remember that?"

"Are you telling me yer name isn't Meri?" Gustav laughed. Potato pushed his face into the conversation with a worried look.

"No," Meri said. "It's Pershival. Pershival Mung."

Potato blinked and looked away. "I like Meri better."

"As do I," Meri said. He turned to the window with a smile.

"What about you, Wad? What's yer real name?"

"Just Wad," he replied. "Wadley Saxo. Nuthin special." His Talkman chirped and he set his beer in the caddy along the window, then paused. "Wait, someone's calling me?"

"Holy shit," Gustav laughed. "Did you activate that new Talkman? Why did you do that?"

"You must be joking," Meri said. "You've erased everything? Are you mad?"

Wad leaned around with a scowl. "It's fine. Everything is okay. We're gonna get my money back. I did it for good reason." Meri conceded with open palms and Wad turned back to the road. "Now, who the hell got my number after everything was erased?" He held his arm out to Potato in the passenger seat. "What's it say?"

Potato nabbed Wad's wrist and squinted into the screen. "It's Amelia. She wants you to accept her contact request." He poked the button and the Talkman chirped. "Now she's saying a bunch of shit."

"What?" Wad yanked his arm back and stared into the Talkman. He dropped his hands from the wheel, poking and swiping the screen. The music turned to blaring static, blasting everyone's eardrums. Potato went for the volume as Wad corrected the drifting bus.

A voice came over the speakers. "Wad? Did you get your Talkman back? What's going on?"

Gustav shouted. "Tell her we're getting your money back."

"I can hear you, you idiot."

"Oh, hi Amelia!" Gustav said, waving at the speakers. "We've got a positive location on Don Sanders so we're gonna go fuck him up."

"You're sure he has Wad's money?"

"I don't care, but he's holding Luke Skywalker hostage and were gonna go rescue him. This is a good deed we're doing for the good of humanity."

"Wad, are you there?" Amelia said.

"Yeah."

"Slap Gustav for me."

Wad looked around the seat to find the Human wasn't in striking distance. "He's too far away, I can't reach him. Anyway, Don Sanders is just down the hill. We're gonna go take his head off – but hey, just in case he didn't steal my money, you should send your Talkman data to Hesh. He can hack your Talkman to track down the delivery guy."

"I don't want anyone hacking my Talkman," Amelia whined.

"Just do it. No complaining," Wad said. Amelia erupted in a fit of unintelligible nagging. It sounded like a bird was caught in the speakers. He quickly poked the receiver in the dash and Amelia was drowned out by the music. "Goodbye, Amelia," Wad said.

Gustav leaned forward. "I don't know why she's freaking out. We got this in the bag. You know what? Let me handle your girlie when we get back. I'll calm her down with the power of charm."

Wad chuckled. "Sure thing, Guz. We'll be waiting for you in Azura."

Meri went for another beer.

Minutes passed. The bus dipped into the Perna Kebrada river valley where a barrier of wheatgrass rose over the roadside like a wave. A sweet air blew in from the west, carrying the scent of dew and flowering vegetation. Islands of green dotted the landscape, each with a single warpwood tree as a centerpiece. Up ahead, a tuft of clouds clung to the foothills of the Braskey Mounds like a clump of lint. A line appeared in the valley floor. It began as a shimmer, snaking across the plains, but widened to reveal a great plasteel pipeline set high off the ground on forked pillars. It dominated the landscape, stretching from one horizon to the other. Farther below, in the shadows of the pipe was a sparkling dot nestled in the rocks of the foothills.

"That must be the place," Wad said, spotting the readout on the navigation screen. "There's nothing else here."

Gustav's head peaked over the back of Wad's seat. He squinted through the windshield. "It looks like another bus."

"Best to keep our distance," Potato said. He looked around, observing the open terrain. "If that's possible."

"They have most certainly seen us coming over the hill," Meri spoke up. "There isn't a place to hide out here. We should make our intentions known and be on the alert." The crew agreed. They readied their weapons, checking batteries and ammunition, storing them close at hand.

The bus plowed through the field toward the clearing in the shadow of the enormous pipeline. There, a ragged van was tilted atop a rock slab, half ruined by the suns. It was tan and brown in color and the runner was crumbled with rust. All four tires were busted flat. In the shade of the machine were two burly Humans kicking around in the dirt. One wore a sweat-stained Boston Red Sox hoodie and the other, a shredded Lacoste polo. They were armed with Thompson submachine guns and magnetic glares.

"Holy shit, is that a Chevy G20?" Gustav said, as the bus pulled around. "My dad had one of those when I was a kid. How the hell did they get that thing here?"

"Yer familiar with the model?" Potato said. "Weaponry? Gun pods? What are we looking at?"

"It's got a chess board," Gustav said. He leaning out the window and waved as the bus lurched to a halt. Gustav bumped the gullwing open and hopped to the dirt.

The air was dead still. The surrounding area was stamped down with foot traffic around a sickly looking barbecue grill. Something long expired was crumbling on the rack. Several stones were arranged in a sitting area around the grill where stale ashes mixed with the natural soil, making the whole clearing feel like a blight on the landscape. Every subtle noise echoed off the nearby rocks. One of the oafs stepped forward and lifted his chin, examining Gustav. He raised his Tommy-gun and spoke with a heavy lisp. "You boys passin' through? We don't want no trouble."

Mighty Rahiem

Gustav turned to the crew. "See, they're friendly. No worries." He lifted his palms and smiled, "No problems, we're here to see Don Sanders. Might he be at home?"

"Why you wanna see the Don for?" The man said, wiping dribble from his nose. "He don't normally take visitors."

Potato jumped to the dirt with his beer tight in his fist. The rest of the crew followed. "Show me the Don," he said, approaching the bus with a dead look.

"I don't like the way you talk," The man replied, nodding to his partner. "Me and Joey here might have to change that. "Waddya think, Joey. Should we let these turkeys see the Don?"

"Wait a minute. This one looks like a big potato," Joey said. He tugged on Tommy's shirt and the two spun around. They whispered back and forth for a moment, occasionally flashing a look over their shoulders. A moment later, Joey spun around holding a wanted poster for a balding Human with one eye. He pointed at Potato. "This ain't you, is it?"

"Yeah."

Joey gave Tommy a confused look. "What's he doin' here? We're supposed to be lookin' for him. Not him comin' to us."

Tommy leaned into Joey's ear. "I don't think the Don is gonna want this guy. He don't look right."

Potato stepped forward with his hand on Paulina. "Why you gotta price on my head?"

Tommy wiped his nose with his sleeve, then begged for a moment with a finger. "Excuse me, gentlemen." He pounded on the door of the van. It slid open and he vanished inside.

The group shuffled across the clearing to join Potato. Joey gave them all a sneer, keeping them at arm's length

231

with the barrel of his Tommy-gun. The door of the van slammed shut and all was quiet. A dead wind tinkered a spatula against the side of the grill. There was a muffled sneeze from inside the van.

A moment passed and the van bumped. The door slid open and Tommy hopped out, taking his place at the flank of the opening. Through the darkness, a figure emerged, clad in a damaged white suit and split shoes. He shuffled through the door and hit the ground, steadying his posture with a PVC cane. It was rated 450 psi.

He was an aging Human with a bushy white goatee and eyebrows that spun out of control. His hair was equally unruly, mimicking a bad toupee. He had a pair of thick-rimmed Persol Ratti Havanas with one lens missing, and an unidentifiable crust living in the strands below his lip. His gut burst through the front of a formal button-down, yellowed with a pungent residue. In his hand, he held a life-sized cardboard cutout of Luke Skywalker, equally crusted with filth. He shoved Luke's feet into the dirt and twisted him around to stand freely.

"What in the ever-loving fuck..." Gustav mumbled.

Sanders examined the crew and spoke slowly through a punchy Brooklyn accent. "My esqupant has informed me that you wish to converse with my presence. This is admirable. I have great respect for you and your people."

Wad stepped forward with a reserved posture. "We wish to speak with you, Don Sanders. We understand you have connections to a delivery service called MᵃFuggin. Is that true?"

"Ah!" Sanders popped. "I see you speak the king's Italiano. I think that's language of the old country. I have great respect for your tongue and everything it can do for our people. You have my gratitude."

Mighty Rahiem

Wad went to confer with Gustav, but the man just stood with a slack jaw. A moment later, he pulled himself out of shock and turned to Wad. "We gotta rescue Luke Skywalker."

Sanders continued, "Who might be the leader of your little party? I wish to convene with you in my office and discuss our principals and potential future together."

Everyone pointed at Wad.

Don Sanders bowed with his hands together, then performed a stiff curtsy, nearly stumbling. Tommy ran to his aid and straightened the old man's posture. Sanders ripped a great fart and loosened up. He turned to nobody and spoke. "Come, Quentin, we have much to discuss." He lingered for a second and turned to Wad. "Quentin didn't make it, I'm sorry to say. He was a good man. He will be missed. Let us honor his memory with a cannoli and Chanel #5."

"The guy is fucking batty," Gustav said. "But hey, if he's got cannoli, I can't complain."

Sanders nodded to Gustav. "You have admirable taste, Quentin. You're a good man. Let us speak together in my office." He shuffled around and dropped his cane, then plopped down Indian-style on the ground. "Sit," he said. "I beg of thee." He grabbed Luke Skywalker and dragged him close, holding him tightly under his arm.

Everyone took a seat in the dirt. Sanders rested a hand on his belly and moaned. "I'm a very hungry man," he said. "And a poor man. I don't got any money. They call me The Broker – broke alotta' legs, broke alotta' bank accounts. I gotta beautiful collection of decorative plates. Now, how may I help you boys and your little dog?" He spun his finger at Meri, then began to mumble. "If ya mow my lawn, I'll give everyone a dollar."

"Is there someone else we can talk to?" Wad said.

"Who are you again?" Sanders said with a suspicious eye.

"He's Carbon Dale," Gustav said with a wink to Wadley.

"Dale? My son! Come give grandpa a hug." He leaned in with open arms. Wad pulled back in a panic. "He don't wanna hug, he don't have'ta hug. That's okay. He's a man now." Sanders bumbled to himself.

"Dale is your son?" Wad said?

Sanders scoffed, turning to Joey. "Dale is my son? Of course Dale is my son. As my son, Dale should know this. Everyone knows this. My son doesn't know this."

"Did you put a price on my head?" Potato spoke up.

Sanders snapped backward with a finger at the Legomi. "Holy Toledo, what is that?"

"I'm Potato."

"Jesus and Mary Joseph, it talks. It looks delicious. Tommy, Joey, Mark Hamill, get his legs. We'll have dinner!"

Tommy and Joey approached the Legomi who rose to his feet with a deep glare. As the duo continued forward, Paulina sprung from her holster. A great crack rang out and Joey exploded, painting the bus with gore. The crowd recovered with ringing ears as Potato coolly emptied the shells from his gun, replacing them without haste. He slapped the cylinder in place and let the cannon linger at his hip, then aimed his eye at Sanders. "Why ya gotta price on my head?" He asked again.

Sanders looked at the remains of Joey. "You killed my father," he said calmly. "This is admirable. You got guts." He pulled Luke Skywalker from his under his pit and stood him in the ground. "Mark Hamill, shoot this turkey."

Mark Hamill had a .38 special duct-taped to its hand.

"No, you don't wanna shoot?" Sanders said to the cardboard. "He doesn't wanna shoot – that's okay. He has spared your life. I don't blame him. In many ways, he's a wiser man than I."

Gustav pointed with a frown. "You know that's not really Luke Skywalker, don't you?"

"Of course it's not Luke Skywalker," Sanders popped. "Luke Skywalker isn't real, he's just a character in a made-up movie. But behind the character is a very real person. He's a real man and his name is Mark Hamill. Most people don't know this. He's a good man and he gives me all his food. For as long as I've been here, I haven't seen him eat a thing. Look how thin he has become. I suspect he's a vegan."

Meri leaned into Wad's ear. "He appears to be suffering from a stroke."

Wad waved him away, then turned back to Sanders. "Why *are* you here?"

Sanders looked up with a sorry face. "We're stuck," he said. "We ran outa gas. Mark Hamill was supposed to fill up the tank like I told him, but he refused. He has his reasons. I suspect he's working for the tax man."

"Tax man?" Meri said. "The bomber. My good sir, are you being extorted as well?"

"Look at this dog trying to speak," Sanders snickered at Meri. "He thinks he's a person. I had a dog like you when I was your age. Quentin was his name-o. Of course I know the tax man. He robs me blind every Twosday. He says he's got the goods on me and hes gonna make me pay or else he's gonna haul me in to the head hunters. They got a price on my head cos' I'm the Don. Ain't that right, Joey?"

Joey was still dead.

The Old Guard of Zerth

"So how do you pay him?" Gustav said. "I thought you didn't have any money."

"I don't have any money," Sanders said, hanging his head. "I'm a bad Don."

Wad stood up. "So, to be clear, you have no connection to MᵃFuggin Delivery Service?"

"Look at this thing, now. It thinks its lettuce. Good thing I don't eat greens, I'd put a price on your head. I'm a meat and potatoes guy." He turned to Potato. "I think I'll hire a delivery service to bring me your legs. What's the number of the delivery service?"

Wad let out a sigh. He turned to Potato who was looking at dirt and scratching his temple. His aggression had vanished entirely. In fact, he seemed slightly embarrassed.

Gustav stepped forward. He approached the Don who didn't seem aware of anything. Gustav waved his hand in front of the old man's face. "Look here, mighty Don. It's clear to see you're in need of some help. May I?" He reached down and grabbed Sanders' wrist, doing his best to hold his nose from the stench. He held the Talkman to Sanders' face. "Look here, the next time the Tax man comes, you can show him your Talkman, like this. Okay?

"Okay," Sanders said.

"You can swipe his card right here," Gustav said.

"Yeah," Sanders said.

"Now, you can either push the button that says *'pay'* or *'receive'*. Which one do you push?"

"I don't know," Sanders said, shaking his head. "The kids these days with their Game Boys and their Justin Beaver."

"It's okay, we're here to help." Gustav said, nodding.

Sanders looked up to Gustav with a helpless gaze. He turned back to the Talkman and stared at it. Gustav quietly reached into his holster. He pulled his .44 free and gripped the barrel. Without warning, he pounded the grip into Sanders' skull. The old man went down. Gustav snatched Mark Hamill from the dirt and took off running towards the bus. "We got Luke Skywalker – run!" He shouted. The crew leaped to their feet and scrambled after him. They threw themselves into the bus and Wad hit the gas, tearing away from the clearing in a cloud of dust, leaving Tommy to scratch his head.

999 – Nasty Nasty. 125Mph – north-east down Traderoute 7. The wind blew across Mark Hamill's face and bent his head backwards as Gustav went for another beer. "Well, that was fun," he said, popping the top and downing a sip.

"Pointless," Potato grunted. "Wad's still got no money and we've just wasted half the day."

"It was a long-shot anyway," Wad said. "We've still got leads to chase. I'm not too worried."

"...so, to Ortega, then?" Meri said.

"I don't care," Gustav replied. He sucked down his beer.

Meri chuckled. "Care is poison to men without direction–"

"–for sour destiny is unmet by men who seek no end." Gustav replied.

"Arguthaerie. Five and Six," Meri hummed.

"What's that poem, anyway?" Wad said. "I hear it all the time."

"Its Arguthaerie: The High Watcher," Gustav said.

"An Ode to Man," Meri added. "They say the suns sang it to the first Human."

"I doubt that," Potato pushed in.

"And what would you know about it, Sam?" Gustav teased.

"Never mind, and don't call me Sam," Potato grunted. He turned to Wad who was gazing down the road with a comfortable grin. "Whadya think, Wad? Ya think the suns can sing?"

Wad returned with a smile. He looked out across the plains, holding on to a distant moment. Somewhere in his mind a gentile melody sang. He was reminded of days long gone and a journey satisfied. Electric lights and gentile wanderings of a million footsteps passed through his thoughts. "I wouldn't put it passed them," he said.

Potato sighed and sat back. "Ya know what, maybe they can sing," he said, gazing out the window.

"That's what was missing," Gustav spoke up. "Music. There's no music out here."

"But we got speakers in the bus," Wad replied.

"I believe he means *outside* the bus," Meri chided, nodding at the passing scenery. "Out there."

"Yeah, it was pretty creepy quiet," Wad said.

The music cut out with the blip of Gustav's Talkman receiving a call. He jumped at the sound, dropping his beer to the floor. "It's Roldolph," he said.

The crew went quiet. They exchanged nervous looks before Meri spoke up. "This is ridiculous. Put him on."

The speakers hissed and Roldolph's voice came through. "Guz, old buddy. It's Roldolph. You boys survive the drinks?"

"Barely," Gustav said. He meant it to come across like a joke but the humor was absent.

"That's good to hear," The Morouni said. "Say, is Meri there? I don't have his contact number but I figured he would be with you."

"Right here, my man," Meri chimed. "What can I do for you?"

"Hello, Merri. You remember we talked about getting you a spot to speak at the Southtown anniversary of the Great Arrival? Well, our guy just arrived. If he thinks you're up to it, he'll get you spot. How close are you to Ortega?"

Wad checked the nav-readout on the control panel. "About an hour away," he said. He turned in his seat to gauge Meri's reaction.

Meri smiled and spoke proudly into the speakers. "We're already on our way."

"Great," Roldolph said. "Don't forget, Fairaday's Faith on the east side. There, you'll meet a Fendrall. Tell him my name and he'll let you in. I'll be right behind you. And while we're at it, we can share what we know about Sanders."

"No need," Gustav said. "We killed him already."

"Oh my."

"It's no big deal. I think he was half-way there already."

"Understood," Roldolph chuckled. His breathy snorting came through the speakers like static. "Well, I'll be seeing you soon."

The call ended abruptly and the music flooded back in. Wad had to turn it down. He hit the brake and pulled off to the side of the road, carving a path of depressed grass in the wake of the head-fans. He cut the engine and everything went still. As he sat for a moment in thought, he didn't' even notice how quiet everything had become. Nobody was complaining, in fact, the only sound to hear was the subtle brush of grass in the wind. The silence made Wad fidgety so he took a hearty gulp of beer before leaning out of his seat. He found the look on his face was shared across each of the men, save for Meri, who was giving him the stink-eye.

"I can't tell if that was weird or not," Gustav said. "Like, I've known Roldolph for a while, right? But not that long. I don't shower with the guy. Never seen his balls, or anything. Maybe he might-"

"-Good lord, man," Meri said with his hands on his hips. "I fail to see the cause for concern. Don't tell me you are seriously entertaining the words of that ridiculously voluptuous bug-woman? Am I wrong? Was the issue not sufficiently quashed in the moment? If not, I will be delighted to put it to rest a second time."

"Meri's right," Wad said. "Sanders was a bust, but maybe these guys can help." He turned to Potato for a vote of confidence. The big eye was busy in thought.

"Fuck it," Gustav said. "We'll make a day of it. You know, they got those tree farms in Ortega. I can build some more speakers and spread the love. This place needs it. It's fuckin' creepy out here."

Wad turned to Potato again, who seemed to be struggling with the lack of tunes. He was slid down in his seat looking at nothing, but came to attention as he caught Wadley's eye. "Yeah, okay," he said.

"Many thanks," Meri chimed in with a smile of victory. "Now, let us get this beast rolling once again. I've got an interview to prepare for.

Mighty Rahiem

Wad shrugged and turned the key. The bus sprang to life and the music popped on. Everything was right with the world as he cranked the wheel, righting the bus back to the road, then dug his heel into the accelerator.

Destination:-422.2/+121.1. Arrival:48 Minutes.

Ortega
circa 114

Chapter 17

Ortega

In the eastern foothills of the Braskey Mounds, just off a beat-down bifurcation of Traderoute 7, was a lake of rolling red sails. Half obscured in a shallow crater, the City of Ortega fit snug within the contours of the circular depression. The Traderoute struggled to exist beyond that, with the only sign of civilization being the elevated pipeline that curved off into the horizon. Ortega was a last-chance oasis for many a weary traveler, as the next settlement wouldn't be for another two-hundred and fifty bumpy miles north through the downlands of Redrock.

As the sails appeared over the horizon, Wad could see a large terraced structure rising on the northern outskirts of town. It looked like a giant wedding cake with a dish on top. Circling the dish were what appeared to be large aircraft. That must be flight tower, Wad thought to himself. He had heard about Ortega's newest technological marvel, but this was his first time seeing it in person. As the bus dipped into the path of the western gate, his view of the enormous dish became obscured behind the rolling tarps above the city. Between breaks in the red shade, he could catch glimpses of the structure passing by. He nearly plowed into a retaining wall trying to follow it.

The streets of Ortega were meant for walking, leaving Wadley with the difficult task of maintaining foot-speed down the cobblestone through a sea of pedestrians. The subdued keys of **Air – La Femme d'Argent** drifted from a distant speaker somewhere beyond the bustle of midtown traffic.

The Old Guard of Zerth

Gustav made frequent appearances between the pilot seats offering a litany of instructions on how best to navigate. The best attractions in town, the best spot for a quick massage, the best place to be killed in a terrorist attack.

Wad found a spot in the north end and cranked lever of the landing gear. The crew piled out the door, entering into the red glow of tarp-shaded sandstone where they were nearly swept away by a slow-moving crowd. Just up the way was a little alcove of shops and a blackened pile of debris. Not a thought on the minds of the townsfolk regarding the recent devastation. The only thing of note was a directional sign pointing the location of the Whiskey Waffle Emporium. Stamped across it was some sloppy blue graffiti of a fist with the paint still fresh.

The four walked on, entering into the ruined square where Gustav excitedly pointed out the spot where his body was smeared across the ground. The twisted bricks and steel of the diner were left as they fell, jutting from the ground in a pile, untouched as if the townsfolk had accepted the destruction as an addition to the scenery.

Incorporated into the scrap was a shoddy wooden stand, and a sandwich board reading *'Whiskey Rubble Tavern'*. Behind the counter was a smiling Legomi slinging dirty booze. He caught sight of the crew and called out. "Hey, it's the miracle man himself!" He scrambled out of the debris, dragging some bent carbon fiber around his ankle.

The plant-man ambled up to the crew with too much excitement. He wore a gold lame vest with bare threads spinning out of the shoulders, as if he had ripped the sleeves off by hand. Around his neck was a lose-knotted leather necktie with greasy fingerprints all down the side. His shoes were painted some kind of sparkly nonsense and he had an equally gaudy sash over his shoulder that read *'Teh Man'*. The leaves atop his head were slicked back with what looked like motor oil. "Yo, Human-man!" The Legomi waved. He met the crew with vigorous handshakes, never taking his eyes off Gustav.

"Oh hey, it's Bingus, right?" Gustav said, consciously trying to escape the handshake of the vegetable.

"That's so awesome," Bingus spit. "He remembers my name! This guy is is amazing. He said he was gonna give me money and die, then he gave me money and died! It was a fuckin' miracle. That was so awesome, man. You should do it again!"

"Yeah, you should do it again." Potato elbowed the Human with a smile.

"Holy shit! Yer Sam Tuber," Bingus said. "I remember you from the pit. Remember me? I'm Bingus! My cousin was one of your under-sheriffs. That's so crazy."

"Sam Tuber," Gustav laughed and received another, less friendly elbow.

"Goddam," The giddy Legomi continued. "It's like Celebrity day or something. Who are you?" He said pointing at Meri.

Meri took a bow and tipped his hat to the star-struck Legomi. "My name is Meriwether Black."

"That's not your name," Gustav said, slapping the Morouni's chest.

"Oh?" Meri shot back. "Forgive me, my lord. I had forgotten your power to deny me my free will. Allow me to relinquish it back to your capable hands. Besides, if I am going to be making appearances to larger crowds, a catchy pseudonym seems in order." He turned to Bingus. "That is quite the impressive establishment you've got for yourself, my man," He said, nodding towards the booth.

The Old Guard of Zerth

"Yeah, Human guy gave me a hundred bucks and I used it to start a business. Awesome, right?" Bingus said. "Now I got all the money I could ever need! I give people beer and then they give me even more money! Isn't that crazy? I got like, four-hundred bucks now!"

Wadley didn't recognize the guy at all. No big surprise. There were thousands of Legomi in the pit of Aerie Tower that he had never met, but the lack of recognition didn't sit well. He stepped forward with his hand out to shake. "I'm Wad," he said. "Wadley Saxo." He made sure to emphasize the last bit.

Bingus stared with a smile.

"Nevermind."

Meri pushed in. "Well, my brothers, I must be moving on to my destination. Shall we meet back in an hour? Two hours it is." The Morouni tipped his hat to Bingus, then made his way into the street traffic.

Bingus waved with his whole arm. Gustav had to retreat or be caught in the neck. "Well," Gustav said, "I'm thinking I'm gonna find me some wood and build me some speakers. Who's with me? Sam, I need your muscle."

"Goddamit, Guz."

"Awesome!" Bingus cried. "Come on, Sam. Lets go get wood!" He nabbed the brute's wrist.

Potato didn't move an inch. He carefully peeled the fingers off of his arm, then deposited them around Wad's hand. "You take over. I don't wanna have to kill anybody today." He then gave Gustav an eye-full and the two vanished into the crowd.

Wad was left attached to a beaming Bingus.

"Hey buddy, wanna buy a beer?"

Mighty Rahiem

Wadley didn't want a beer. He looked around for some way to ditch the fucker but nothing came to mind. "So, Bingus, is it?"

"Hey, that's awesome. You know my name too!"

Wad rolled his eyes. "So, I see Ortega has a flight tower. How's that effecting the economy?"

"It's great!" Bingus exploded. "Ya got all these people from out of town that show up and wanna sell me things. I like, buy their beer and sell it for more than I paid for it. I think it might be robbery! I hope nobody catches on. It's great business. Lemme show ya!"

Bingus yanked Wads wrist, leading him to a brick wall behind the pile of scraps. He scrambled up the side of the masonry and vanished over the top. Wad followed, somewhat hesitant, but eager to catch a view of the tower. He pulled himself atop the brickwork, finding the surrounding area completely barren. The red shade ended abruptly there, forcing Wad to take a moment to adjust to the suns. From the edge of the brickwork, he could see the whole north end of Ortega was nestled a good ten feet below ground. A garden-level city. The sight of it caught him off guard, as it seemed wholly unnatural. There was no gradual shift between deep city and barren wasteland. Just a hard line of a wall.

"Come on, this way," Bingus hollered. He took off trotting around the edge of the town.

The two made their way up a rocky crag as the bellow of something large sounded above them. It was a deep horn, loud enough for Wad to feel it in his bones. From below, all he could see was a great cloud of mist pushing through the rainbelt. Only momentarily did he catch a glimpse of rusted iron scaffolding before it was once again swallowed by jets of fog. The shape descended and the cloud enveloped the two Legomi. For a brief

247

moment, the chilled air was like heaven. Wad closed his eyes and let it pass over him, taking up as much sweet moisture as his skin could hold. His leaves unfurled with a shiver.

The fog lifted, leaving the two doused in dew. Through the breaking light, the ship emerged. A Morouni Steamer, looking like a burned out warehouse in the sky. It must have been over a hundred feet long. The lumbering giant drifted well overhead before another jet of steam shot from the port quarter – then another jet from the starboard bow. The hulking craft was coming about. The two Legomi shared an exited look. They chased the iron beast over the top of a hill where the great concrete dish rose above the barrier dunes. As they made their way closer, the rest of the tower came into view.

It was seven or eight layers stacked like a ziggurat. The base of the tower seemed to be about a hundred feet in diameter, with the uppermost layer only twenty or so. Then, an enormous concrete dish that shrouded the area in shadow. Around each layer's perimeter were docking bays, all of which occupied by light aircraft. Suspended around each bay were smaller crafts seemingly stuck in a holding pattern. There were dozens of them. Two-fan carriers and single-jet pods. Pubbers and mod-wasps. All ringing the structure in stasis until a bay was left vacant. When one departed, another took its place without any sense of order or courtesy.

From the base of the tower, an open service elevator cranked upward along a rickety channel in the side of the structure. The platform was doubled-up with pallets and barrels while a single operator struggled to find room for himself. As it rose, it vanished into a gap in the underside of the concrete, which appeared to be held in place by a series of steel catwalks that hung in the shadow. All around the edge of the dish were moored aircraft of great size, as well as their steamer, pulling up to dock.

Mighty Rahiem

The base of the tower looked like some kind of festival. There must have been hundreds of pedestrians milling about in the shade of the enormous thing, hocking their wares from behind ruddy-looking merchant stands. As they made their way around to the front, they found themselves dodging bodies on all sides. Waves of people entered and exited through a single entrance at the bottom tier. It was marked with a bronze plaque above double-wide doors.

FLIGHT TOWER 1

EST:113.

Thoughtfully and selflessly donated to the fair city of Ortega.

"The freedom to materialize is the blood of Zerth. The freedom to innovate is her heart."

-Murphy LeBlanc

Wadley had heard about the flight tower but he had never seen it himself. It was a new concept that had taken him by surprise, especially due to its stunning simplicity. All it took was one guy to get angry at the lack of parking, and viola – a place to park. It was just one of hundreds of incredible inventions that had eluded his imagination. Southtown didn't have an issue with aircraft parking so the idea never came up, and that irked him. As the sight of the structure overtook him, so did a bit of jealousy. If *he* hated parking so much, that tower would have been *his* invention. He was sure of it.

Bingus again had Wad by the wrist. He pulled him through the curtains of the double-wide door and into darkness. A brief corridor opened up to a great, round room littered with tables mashed tight with patrons. Dim orblights flickered yellow in the walls, illuminating the cloud of tobacco smoke hanging from the ceiling. The smell of fried rice filled the air, leaving a slick residue across Wad's pores. At the rear were two eateries handing out food by the tray. It was standing room only. Wad had to fight to walk. "This is the first floor," Bingus said. "And over there is bathroom. I really like it in there. It's really nice!"

The excited Legomi yanked Wad through the tables to the center of the room. Down a couple of wide stairs was a large elevator shaft rising through the ceiling. "This is how you go up!" Bingus nodded. You go in there and it takes you to the next place! I don't know how it works, but it puts you up there."

The door chimed open and a mass of people poured out. They swarmed around the two Legomi like water, nearing bowling them over – then the tide shifted and they found themselves pushed from behind, heaved into the elevator car against their will. The car was packed with so much meat that Wad could barely move. The doors shut and all was quiet for a moment, save for the coughs, sniffling, farting and throat-clearing of two-dozen people sharing his personal space. He couldn't see Bingus, but he presumed he was smiling.

Suddenly, Wad felt himself rising – then his stomach was in his throat as the car came to a swift stop. The doors opened and the bodies removed themselves. Wad was able to breathe, but only for a moment before the empty space was again packed with more. The ride lasted until the two Legomi managed to push their way through the living barrier, arriving at an unknown tier. Wad felt seasick. He tumbled through the door, avoiding another wave of patrons, then found himself a wooden bench alongside the elevator. It took a moment to gather his wits to survey the surroundings.

The tier was much smaller and quieter than the first. By the size of it, he figured he must be on the fourth or fifth tier. The outer walls were a series up UPP-15 docking ports, each with a blinking light above. There were five of them in succession. Some filled with miniature storefronts, others with tiny taverns. Some were occupied by hauling craft dumping crates of much needed bullshit to the local economy. All were connected via standardized UPP ports, which doubled as coupling connections to the craft.

A group of Sectoids hurried around one of the docks, pulling large boxes through the door on a dolly. It took four of them to move it – or maybe they all just wanted to share in the responsibility? It seemed like a waste of manpower to Wad. One could easily move it alone, but four had their hands on it.

The bugmen wheeled the dolly to the back of the room where they neatly unloaded the boxes against the wall. Some information and pay was exchanged with a small Morouni there, then the Sectoids rushed back through the dock, hunkering down inside the ship. A wide set of horizontal doors closed, then the blinking light above the portal went green. It quickly shifted to red. The doors again slid open and there was a silly looking woman selling shoes from behind a counter.

The chaos of it all had Wad's head swimming. It was stimulus overload. All he could do was watch and wish it were his. He could only imagine how busy the lower floors were. It was like a whole town down there. He sat back to take it all in, sliding down in the seat and getting comfortable with the sound of movement all around. It took him a moment to notice Bingus was still there next to him.

"You can fly anywhere from here," Bingus said. He stood from the bench and pointed above Wad's head. Wad leaned craned his neck to find a large electronic display on the wall above him. He had to leave the seat to see it fully. It looked like a flight log.

The Old Guard of Zerth

ARRIVAL: TARQUS – 28:18 – FID:T-BLUNDERBUSS

DEPARTURE: AGORA POINT – 15:78 FID:C-HALSEY

ARRIVAL: +198.15/-000.25 – 17:33 FID:(unscheduled)

DEPARTURE: CALIBUR – 15:12 FID:C-ALPO

ARRIVAL: SLUGGPORT – 22:11 FID:T-KIKX

DEPARTURE: GHONG – 18:37 FID:T-BEAGLE

DEPARTURE: -00.02/-400.10 – 33:00 FID:(unscheduled)

"Just scroll through it and see if anybody is going where you wanna go," Bingus said. "Ya poke the one you want and it'll show you who ya need to talk to. The pilots mostly hang out on the first floor, so ya gotta go down there to find em. They get so drunk down there."

Wad was impressed. He pulled his finger across the display. Some were random coordinates of far off places, but most were names of larger settlements. He scrolled through looking for the name of his home, but Southtown was nowhere on the list. He kept scrolling. Surely, the town he built was important enough for people to travel to. No luck. After a few minutes of searching, he started feeling empty.

"Anyone going to Southtown?" Wad said.

"Where's that?"

"It's Southtown," Wad repeated. "Everyone knows Southtown."

Bingus shrugged.

Wad sank back into the bench, desperately trying to convince himself Bingus was more of an idiot than he appeared. Was it true? Was Southtown just a blip on the map? A blip on the map *he* charted? The world *he* discovered? The world *he* set free?

Mighty Rahiem

Wad drooped. It wasn't anger he felt. It wasn't depression. More shock and disbelief. Was somebody fucking with him? He couldn't tell.

The dock in front of him slid shut. The light went green, then then red. The portal slid open and another Sectoid was standing there with an envelope in his hand. He was wearing a stupid goddamned hat. His face was ugly. Wad was pretty sure he smelled like piss. Blue and yellow piss jacket. Blue and yellow piss pants. Piss shoes. Piss vest. MᵃFuggin logo on his piss vest. MᵃFuggin logo? Wad shot to his feet. The bugman was a courier for MᵃFuggin Delivery Service. He had the hat and everything!

P:9 - G4
COMPACT PLASMA PISTOL
Semi-Automatic, High-Profile
Bolt Projectile Launcher

Effective Range: 150ft.
Capacity: 1,200 - 1,500 bolt

Chapter 18

Todo Yasodo

Todo Yasodo was the perfect Sectoid for the job. Someone needed something delivered and Todo was a delivery boy. At least, he was now. Two weeks prior, he had thrown his name into the registry of eligible staffers with access to a pubber. As fortune would have it, a small courier service picked him up without much questioning. Todo preferred it that way as his pubber wasn't entirely his. It was on loan from his father who had made a living flying the thing, but had recently taken up retirement. As a hand-me-down to his next of kin, Todo's father wrote up a rent-to-own agreement with his son at the cost of five bucks a day. After a year, the pubber would be his.

Unable to register his ship under the Aerie Tower Busing and Universal Transportation Treaty, he was mostly stuck running small hauls. Nothing to or from the tower. He wasn't certified for that. ATBUTT only allowed fully-owned crafts, but outside of the tower's influence, the sky was the limit – literally. Todo made it his motto. *The Sky is the Limit, Literally.* After the craft was his, he would paint it across the side in bright red letters. But until then, it would keep his father's given moniker, Marduuk.

The courier service in question was a dubious little operation based in the south of Tarqus. Two guys, one ship. There were a few other contractors on the job but they were clearly just criminals looking for quick work. Nothing permanent. They'd swoop in for a one-off and keep the uniform for nefarious purposes down the road. As for the owners, Marty MᵃFuggin was one of them. The other was his

The Old Guard of Zerth

brother, Clarence. Clarence Danby. Marty changed his name for reasons that made no sense to the Sectoid. What Todo could understand is that the two men were in somewhat of a pickle financially. They were desperate for cash but the lack of reliable personnel made things tight. People kept walking off the job, often times in the middle of a delivery. The Sectoid quickly picked up on the reason for the shortage. The men were assholes. One of them was a really big asshole. Either way, it was Todo's first real job and he was eager to earn the big bucks to pay off his father's ride.

He took the job as it was offered and received a uniform, log book and was swiftly pushed out the door. His pay was decided to be ten percent collected off the top of COD payments, as well as a scaling percentage of whatever the other two men earned – which was nothing. They said they would cover the fuel for the pubber too, but they were lying. Todo could tell. Todo was a Sectoid. Todo could read their minds. He never understood how easily Humans could forget that fact. Regardless, he was determined to zip around the planet delivering as many COD deliveries he could. On average, twenty a day would fetch him forty bucks. That's more than his dad pulled in.

The day came for his first delivery. A crate of wiring harnesses to some little place down river called Halstaff. Barely fifty miles out. Lots of Sluggs there. Not a whole lot going on, but there was free beer and one of the little green guys gave him a bag of tobacco. As for the cargo, it was fully paid. No COD. He didn't take another delivery that day.

His second day was a bit more fortunate. Delivery to Bask's Landing. Box of chocolate. Just one box. It wasn't COD either but there had apparently been some kind of violent revolt moments before he landed. Lots of dead bodies laying around with nobody to claim their bank accounts. He managed to loot up a cool thirteen bucks and a pistol that looked like a knife – or was it a knife that looked like a pistol? Didn't matter. He turned around and sold it for another ten. Things were starting to look up for the young delivery boy.

The week flew by and before he knew it, Todo had seen more of Zerth than he had in his 14 years prior. To top it off, he counted a whopping eighty-five bucks in his Talkman. Strangely, only four of which came from actually being paid. He started to realize the side-hustle of just being somewhere was more of a benefit than his actual job. Stuff was everywhere and everyone wanted stuff. Stuff from somewhere else was even more valuable, and he, by virtue of his profession, always came from somewhere else. The spiffy uniform didn't hurt either.

The thought occurred to Todo that he didn't really need the job in order to just show up somewhere, but there was a growing sense of familiarity with Marty and Clarence. That and the brothers were up to some sneaky bullshit and Todo knew it. It provided him with enough leverage to hold over their heads if he ever felt the need to bring it up. He loved working with Humans.

The next Onesday came and went, then Twosday morning when he revived an order to deliver a fist-sized bundle to Southtown. A four-hundred and fifty buck COD. That was forty-five bucks in his pocket! The recipient, a mister Wadley Saxo. *The* Wadley Saxo? Todo was intrigued. The legendary Legomi who brought the Aerie Empire to its knees, then went on to map the entire planet. The man must have been a millionaire. What could he possibly need delivered that was so important? Maybe he would take a peak – unseal just a little corner of the brown paper wrapping for a look-see. The thought had crossed Todo's mind more than once as he took to the air and headed south.

The Old Guard of Zerth

Upon arrival to the quiet little burg of Southtown, Todo was met with the overwhelming smell of fish. They were all over the street. Loose fish everywhere. Like a bomb went off and the debris was seafood. The townsfolk seemed okay with it so he tried to put it out of his mind. On the other hand, he had a bit of trouble pinning down the exact address. Nothing was marked well in Southtown. Addresses were posted on plaques, roughly eyeball height on dobistone walls with arrows pointing in every goddamned direction. 212-1/2 South Saxo Street was his destination. 212 proper was some fugly little nub of a boutique who's proprietor was a horrible bitch-Morouni that didn't help him at all. Only then did he discover 212-1/2 was the building *above* the boutique, which required him to tip-toe through the most fucked up, dilapidated tavern he had ever seen. There was a hole in the wall and blood all over the floor. It looked like a place for people to come and die, but in the back of the mess was a thin staircase leading to the roof which took him directly to his destination via a suspended catwalk over an alley.

Arriving at the drop point, Todo had no luck finding his contact. His Talkman would usually bleep with a proximity notification, but the lofty Mr. Saxo was nowhere to be found. It was a bruise to both his hopes meeting the man, as well as to his pocket book. If he couldn't make the delivery, he'd be missing out on all that dough. With no hope of either, Todo was left to consult the delivery procedure. He scanned the code on the package into his Talkman and the secondary delivery options appeared.

IF IN THE EVENT OF NON-CONTACT, DELIVER PACKAGE TO NEXT AVAILABLE CONTACT.

From the looks of it, Wadley Saxo had uploaded his contact list to the MᵃFuggin network. That wasn't unusual, but for someone of high status, it was a bit strange. He clicked the link and his Talkman lit up with a thousand scrolling names, then addresses, then property titles... bank account? Holy Shit. Everything was there. Saxo hadn't just uploaded his contact list, he uploaded his entire identity. And none of it was encrypted. All Todo had to do was copy over the data to his own Talkman and he'd be a millionaire. Todo Yasodo was stunned. He didn't say a word. He didn't mention it to anybody as he returned to his ship with the package in hand, then went about his day as if nothing had happened.

Threesday came and went, then Foursday. Todo arrived at the dispatch office to receive a single delivery. An envelope, manila in color with the little poky aluminum bits to keep it secure. It didn't weigh anything. Just a single sheet of printed paper within. The kicker? COD was over a thousand bucks. That would be more than a hundred smackers in his Talkman for just one delivery. Todo suspected money laundering, as a massive transaction like that for a piece of paper just wasn't realistic. His clairvoyance didn't help much, only revealing that the M^aFuggin Delivery Service had been approached earlier in the day by what was perceived to be some high-status Sectoid wishing to do business outside the influence of Aerie Tower.

The package's recipient was a Morouni by the name of Mason Jarr. He was to be met at Flight Tower 1 in Ortega at precisely 18:15 – Dock 3 – Top Shelf. He recognized the terminology to mean the main dish of the tower. He figured that out by screwing up a few days prior, attempting to deliver a casket to a tavern at Flight Tower 3. How was he to know the tavern was called the same thing? His pubber was small enough for the UPP-15's, so he never needed clearance to land on the Top Shelf, so the phrase never came up.

It was around that time he started to understand the lingo of the pilots a bit better. They all hung out in bars with names they understood. The Top Shelf Lounge, The Two-fan Tango,

The Old Guard of Zerth

The Public Pubber. Limited people with a limited mindset – but he was one of them now and he was determined to take it seriously. That big chunk of change would make a serious dent in the debt to his father.

The time came for Todo to load up his cargo. All eight grams of it. He did his routine post-flight check from the day before, which was a habit he was starting to develop. Then he did his pre-flight check so as not to break regulation, noting the battery housing to the port-side head-fan could use some sprucing up. Had some wear on it. He made sure to decouple the empty gaylord containers as there was no use for them, and dead weight eats fuel. Afterwards, Todo realized how naked his pubber looked. Positively anorexic. It had been so long since he had seen an empty pubber that he forgot what it looked like. A cockpit, a manifold and a rail with four empty UPP-ports. Big, fifteen foot holes with nothing attached. If 'pubber' was short for UPP-HUB, he felt more like a NOPE-HUB. Todo laughed to himself. Maybe when he retired, he'd paint that on the side. Fly around in an empty rig like some kind of clown.

With that revelation, he decided to decouple his cockpit entirely from the rail that would otherwise be hauling a dozen gaylords. More dead weight that didn't need to be there. And besides, how was he supposed to dock with a giant, empty bone sticking out of his ass? With the help of Clarence, the two managed to hoist the forty-five foot mast off the butt of his cockpit with the use of a borrowed crane. Now his ship looked like a butt-plug, but it was presumably really fast. All that thrust for what amounted to an enclosed chair. 144,000 lbs of hauling capacity under his ass, all for an envelope. It was time to hit the clouds.

Todo hit the ignition switch. The Bumhauzer 30/30s fired up, free from encumbrance. He eased the altirator and Marduuk fired into the sky like a bottle rocket. The oppressive G-force put his head in his neck until he managed to stabilize around 3,500 feet, a good 2,000 feet higher than the average ceiling for a pubber. Upon reshuffling the deck that was his scrambled brain, he found himself well above the glide-lane for his descent. He could cut the fans and drift to his destination. Just level the nose and point it in the right direction. Let gravity do the rest.

As Todo glided groundward, he felt like he was looking down at a toy model of Zerth. From the Muscan ridge to the Braskey Mounds, all of it was clear in his sight. Erebo Peak looked like a toy that someone plopped down and forgot about. At the base, the Pereggi River seemed like nothing more than a hairline crack in the dirt. The curvature of the world was almost embarrassing. Like a little pearl marble below him. He took it all in while settling down for a quiet descent.

ALTITUDE WARNING: 615ft.

Todo snapped awake. About two miles out, the flight tower emerged through the mist of the rainbelt below. High moisture. He hurried to drop the supports and open the resistance louvers of the landing fans to mitigate turbulence, anticipating a bumpy slide through the belt. Just outside the canopy, the wind whistled through the wide open heads. As he entered the cloud, the whole ship began to rattle as a mist formed over the cockpit.

ALTITUDE WARNING: 220ft.

A moment later, he was free. The ground opened up below him like an ocean of sand and the tower was directly below. Docked at the east end of the Top Shelf was an enormous steamer. It was almost bigger than the tower itself! All around the concentric layers of the tower proper were a flurry of light craft, buzzing and bobbing. Todo counted no less than thirty restless ships, all vying for a chance to score a dock, if just for a moment.

Just then, his com blipped. Todo hit the receiver.

"TOWER ONE CONTROL TO INBOUND, OPEN TO RECEIVE CALL-SIGN AND PURPOSE."

"MARDUUK TO TOWER ONE CONTROL, PURPOSE IS NEGLIGIBLE. FIVE OR TEN MINUTES. JUST DROPPING OFF."

The com crackled and went quiet. Todo found himself forced into a holding pattern while he waited, just like everyone else. He dropped his nose and fell into an open spot behind a two-fan and began circling the giant structure while he waited for instructions. Passing into the shadow of the top shelf, he noticed some kind of vehicular ruckus below. Some asshat in a Boyo was trying to forcefully remove a pubber from a dock. The little scooter was full-reverse thrust against the port-side of the hauler. Blasting hot air all over the place. Todo could see the smoke of the burning paint starting to form. The com blipped again.

"TOWER ONE CONTROL TO MARDUK. YOU HAVE CLEARANCE TO DOCK IN RING FIVE, DOCK FOUR. THE TIME IS 18:03. YOU HAVE UNTIL 18:23. HAVE A NICE DAY."

Ring five. Just a jump up, Todo thought. He craned his neck to see what was above him. Through the canopy, he saw a solid line of traffic. Carbon fiber hulls and rippling hot air passing overhead. But there, an open spot! Todo didn't wait. He jerked the alterator and slapped his foot on the brake, rocketing his ass out of his seat and his head into the canopy. He recovered gracefully with a mental reminder to buckle-up while landing. The sting of parking, he knew it too well.

As Todo came around the north side of the ring, he spotted his dock, as indicated by a big white '4' painted above the UPP-15 sleeve. Someone was parked in his spot. Todo squinted his eyes through the glare of the canopy. In the rival cockpit was some horrible woman. A Human woman. Her hair was all fucked up. She looked terrible. Her rig was a crunchy little two-fan all done up with hearts and flowers painted across the plasteel plating. She wasn't even docked right.

Across the windy expanse, the two met eyes. She smiled in an innocent kind of way, but Todo knew better. He could see what she was thinking. He knew that that smile really meant. *"I'm going to pretend I parked here by accident. Woopsie! Oh well, I might as well stay. If you complain, I'm going to act like a victim. I might roll around on the floor and make a scene."* Silly Humans. A moment later, the woman stood from the pilot seat and disappeared into the rear of her ship, presumably to open shop. From the thoughts Todo was able to glean from the woman's vacuous mind, he knew she had no intention of leaving any time soon, so he took it upon himself to motivate her.

While the Marduuk was equipped with a perfectly capable 20mm burst-fire cannon, Todo wasn't about to make a scene. He checked the time. 18:08. Well, maybe he would make a scene. He flicked the thumb-covers on the flight yoke, revealing big red buttons. The motion triggered the auto-targeting system, which scrolled into view from the left side in the form of a green overlay featuring a brilliant white reticle display. He lined up his shot through the display, Zeroed over the horrible woman's intake manifold. He popped off a shot.

It was a hollow PUK sound, like the clang of a dropped bucket or a ball-peen hammer going to work. The woman's manifold erupted with a hiss of pressurized air. Todo then waited patiently as the rival ship's canopy began to fog up. A moment later, a shadow appeared, wiping the condensation aside with an open palm. The ugly Human bobbed her head around in the window looking for the problem, then presumably gave up. Not a minute later and she disembarked, face full of steam and a plume of hot air spitting out her ass.

The Old Guard of Zerth

Todo checked his Talkman for the time. 18:11. Yikes, four minutes. At least he could finally land. He pushed forward, aligning his nose to the dock, then cut the port-side fan, coming about in a tight circle. He extended his docking probe and let the stiff wire fish out the perfect angle of approach. It found its tag, allowing for Todo to engage the auto-docking sequence. A few seconds later, he heard the hiss of UPP-Sleeves mating and the docking light flashed green. Todo jumped from his seat, slapping the cockpit door control, envelope in hand.

The interior of tier-5 wasn't too busy. Just a few warm bodies milling around in the dusty air. He checked his Talkman. 18:13. Two minutes. The elevator was directly ahead. Just a few skips and jumps and he'd be on the Top Shelf delivering his package, and receiving his pay. As Todo made his way to the center of the ring, a shiver ran up his spine. It felt like someone was breathing down his neck. He didn't mean to look, but some ancient instinct triggered a prey-response in his brain. There, standing between him and the elevator was a set of glaring eyes and balled fists. It was a Legomi. Short, leafy and full of rage. The only thought Todo could read was one of pure spite. The Legomi was going to kill him.

Slowly, Todo tucked the envelope into the liner pocket of his vest. He did what he could to fish through the man's thoughts for an explanation. Revenge. Violence. Righteous murder. The Legomi must have him mistaken for someone else, but the thoughts were so clear they clouded any sense of reason or detail. Had he somehow wronged this man? He couldn't tell. The rage was too loud in the man's mind.

Without warning, the Legomi's finger shot forward. "MªFuggin Courier Boy!"

Mighty Rahiem

Todo panicked. His eyes darted around the circular room for some kind of escape that didn't involve engaging with the frothing menace. There, in the east-side of the ring, the service access to the Top Shelf. He made his move, feigning to the left to catch the Legomi off guard, then darting to the right at full speed. The Legomi was tripped up and stumbled to the floor, but was back on his feet sprinting after him. Todo shot through the service door, into a darkened stairwell dense with exposed wiring and vents. He flew up the grated iron stairway with the sound of clanking boots directly behind him. He continued, zig-zagging upward, spotting a ray of sunlight blasting through the walkway above. His pursuer was just below, pressing the assault, snarling with rage.

Todo rounded the final staircase and darted into the blinding light, not slowing until his eyes adjusted. He wasn't on the Top Shelf, he was under it. The stairwell had taken him to the service catwalk that hung beneath the dish. Below him was a dizzying drop of a hundred feet or more, with nothing to support him but a rickety iron walkway suspended from the underside of the concrete slab.

Todo steadied himself, struck by vertigo. He wobbled, gripping the railing with both hands. Down below, dozens of craft circled the tower like buzzing insects. His pubber was down there somewhere, docked awaiting his return. Lord, how he wished to be back in that cockpit, safely bugging the fuck out. Up ahead, he could see the catwalk rounding the circumference of the dish, but about seventy feet ahead was a ladder leading upward. That must be the way out.

Just then, Todo felt a tremor in the walkway. He spun around to see the Legomi staggering around blindly in the light of the day. It was muttering something about alcohol, and the thoughts running through its mind were a nonsensical mish-mash of memories involving fish, bullets and bitter jealousy. Todo used the opportunity to overcome his rubber legs. He took off running, feet clanging against the iron with one hand sliding over the railing. A moment later, he could feel the pounding of feet close behind. With no time to spare, he reached the ladder, yanking himself up the rungs. Above him was a small square opening with blue sky shining through – but something snagged his boot. It was the Legomi. It had his foot! Todo howled, jerking his legs wildly. His left heel made a solid connection with flesh and the beast let go, dropping to the catwalk with a hard clang. The terrified Sectoid clamored up the rungs as fast as his arms could carry him.

As Todo pulled himself through the floor, his eyes were once again overcome by the light. The relative brightness in the shadow of the dish was outdone by the clear blue sky. He looked around, finding he had arrived on the Top Shelf; a giant, circular slab of concrete, busy with dock workers rushing to and fro with hoverjacks and dollies. In the center of the ring was the doorway to the main elevator, and above that, the pimple of a control tower with unconcerned faces peering out a thick, glass window.

The wind was harsh that high up. It whistled across the surface like a freight train. There was a distinct moisture in the air. Silty with a bit of grease. The workers skipped across the concrete in organized fashion, moving from the rear of the hulking iron steamer that had had seen as he arrived. There were large crates of something unidentified, but bore the markings of Bumhauzer. Some kind of machinery being transported. His Talkman blipped.

18:18. PROXIMITY TO DESTINATION ALERT. YOU HAVE ARRIVED AT YOUR DESTINATION. PLEASE AWAIT YOUR CONTACT.

Todo had made it. His contact must be on the steamer at the edge of the dock. Finding his balance, he made his way across the concrete towards the massive ship. He struggled against the wind as he approached the iron hulk, spotting a raggedy looking fellow with fuzz for a face tapping his foot impatiently at the docking ramp. "Mason Jarr?" Todo called out.

"You're late," The Morouni shouted.

"I have a package for you."

"You're late," The Morouni barked again.

Todo approached Mason, pulling the envelope from his vest. "My apologies, sir. Your COD is one thous-"

"MªFuggin Delivery Boy!"

Todo spun around to see the Legomi standing in the center of the shelf. The wind was blasting the leaves across its top, giving the appearance of a wild animal. Its eyes were bulging as it started moving forward. Todo nabbed Mason and flung him between himself and the charging horror. Mason tried to calm the beast with open palms, but the Legomi socked the fucker in the lip, then swung again, connecting with the Morouni's forehead and sending a greasy hat spinning into the wind.

Mason went down as a heavy grip clamped around Todo's wrist. It yanked him backward and pulled him to the ground, then engulfed him in a leafy mass of muscle. It began to shake him left to right, then a blow to the back of the head sent the world spinning. Todo could hear shouting and cursing from several mouths, but he couldn't place any of it. The world was wobbling as pain throbbed in his head. His adrenaline spiked as he found solid ground, allowing him to squirm free. He rolled to the side but the Legomi still had his wrist, spinning him onto his back. There, he could see four or five Morouni were wailing on the brute with pipes and bats. It was howling in pain and babbling about its bank account.

The Old Guard of Zerth

The Morouni crewmen yanked the Legomi to its feet, dragging Todo with it. Out of nowhere, music erupted from the bowls of the ship. **Loverboy – Working for the Weekend.** It came through clearly and the Legomi menace was suddenly bursting with rage. It yanked Todo closer, wrapping its arm around the Sectoid's torso, then began bending his arm in unnatural directions. In an instant, Todo could see a flash of the Legomi desire. It didn't want the envelope, it wanted his Talkman. Todo heaved backwards and the Morouni workers responded by nabbing Todo around the waist, pulling him into the steamer. It was a tug-of-war and Todo was the rope.

A handful of workers rushed in to help. They began pounding on the Legomi from behind. The brute dropped to the ground, but still held tightly to Todo's wrist. With a burst of energy, the Legomi lunged forward, snagging both hands around Todo's wrist. The force was too much to handle. He let lose his grip on the envelope and it slipped into the wind, fluttering wildly into the sky, then skidding across the concrete. Several workers broke off diving after it, but it was no use. A gust of wind sent it sailing over the edge.

The loss sent the Morouni into a frenzy. One pushed through and sank a pipe deep into the Legomi's stomach. Bits of spittle hit Todo in the face as the beast doubled over, then a bat struck it across the back of the head. The enemy was belly-down while boots and bats thrashed its body. Brown sap began to pool from the wounds, then splash across the concrete with each strike, but the fingers still held firm around Todo's wrist. The angry hollering of the Morouni drowned out the cries of pain from the battered Legomi.

The men continued pulling Todo into the steamer, dragging the struggling Legomi with him. As they pulled him across the threshold and into the shadow of iron grates, Todo met eyes with his attacker. Squinting with each blow, it stared through him with a determination he didn't understand. Through the agony of violence, the animal wasn't going to give up. It would die before it let go.

At that moment, Todo didn't know if it was empathy or defeat that drove him to concede. He squirreled his hand around the latch of his Talkman and popped it free, sending the Legomi tumbling backwards into the hands of the workers. Todo struggled to his feet as he watched the mob of angry dockmen smash away at the intruder. They pounded him from every angle, but the beast didn't have any fight left in him. They gathered around, hoisting the brute to its feet, then dragging it to the edge of the dish. On the count of three, they hucked the bloody pile over the edge.

Todo caught a brief glimpse of the animal's eyes before it vanished below the dish, the only feeling in its mind was resignation. A well fought victory – and the desire for a beer.

The Old Guard of Zerth

Chapter 19

Old Town

Meri shuffled against the crowd as he made his way through the streets of the north-east quadrant. By the looks of it, he was entering into the older part of town. The building materials were entirely different from the stucco-style dobie walls he was used to seeing. Iron lattice took its place, along with riveted sheets that rattled in the desert wind. In the crimson shade, the whole neighborhood looked like an open-air sewer. It was clear the materials were repurposed wreckage from something off-world, something very dirty. On top of all that, there were very few cross streets, meaning he had to follow the damned road all the way around, or do the stupid thing and try to pass through an alley. It was clear the town plan was set up to promote the Elder's ways of Kaerpo-ma.

Prior to the great arrival, space was quite limited aboard the homeship, leading to rampant overcrowding. Thus, the practice of Kaerpo-ma was established. It allowed each individual about three feet of personal space. Anyone entering an individual's privacy would submit to shame, berating or even assault by the stationary individual. After all, you were treading on their ground, why wouldn't they have the right to defend themselves?

The practice promoted the survival of the biggest dick. From what he was told, it wasn't uncommon for more aggressive folks to stand in doorways all day long, waiting for someone to come by and be blocked, lest they forefit their dignity. It was the Morouni way. Judging by the layout of the city it was clear the same practice was in effect. If you wanted to get anywhere quickly, you would have to be treading on someone's ground. If Meri needed any further evidence to confirm his theory, it seemed the older folks of Ortega spent a lot of time eyeballing passersby from just outside their front stoop.

As Meri rounded the corner, the buildings fell away and he found himself walking across a swath of empty cobblestone. Like a park, but unfinished. It must have stretched eight-hundred feet or more. Nothing but brickwork. Folks were gathered across the bare space as if it were soft grass. They picnicked and strolled and rolled around in the open, making it clear they were enjoying the grit and heat of it all. It was such a strange sight to see. No decoration, no trickling pools of water, no plant life, just cobblestone. He wasn't sure, but there may have been a statue at the opposite end. If so, it was the only one. He felt compelled to rush through, as if he had stumbled upon something embarrassing.

Reaching the relative comfort of the other side of the park, he found himself moving through what was undoubtedly the oldest part of town. It was a rebar jungle. No discernible walls or boundaries, and certainly no privacy. He wasn't even sure they were homes, yet the attitudes reserved for seclusion were on full display. An elder matron bathed atop corrugated sheet roof and an old Bendo was pleasuring himself behind a thin post. All too naked and too old for Meri to find any kind of amusement.

He wasn't sure what he had just walked into, but he began to get the feeling that whole area of town was a fairly accurate recreation of what life must have been like aboard the homeship. It was an odd feeling. Those were his people, yet he couldn't feel more out of place. From that moment on, he kept mental blinders up with his eyes stuck forward. It must have been how the older generation got along all those years, but all it did was leave a sour feeling in his gut.

Mighty Rahiem

Up ahead, Meri found a clearing. More than a clearing, it was another 'park', somehow larger than the first by a factor of four. It was an enormous circular gap. Fully blanketed in cobblestone just like the first, and equally as barren. There, the great tarps receded, bathing the whole space in raw sunlight. At the center was something huge and rotting, jutting from the ground like a monument. He shielded his eyes as he approached the shape, only able to see clearly as he entered into one of its multiple shadows cast by so many suns. It was a ragged chunk of debris, or so it seemed. Gray and tan with bits of blackened carbon streaks. Exposed wires and ripped steel. It must have been a hundred feet tall. A chunk of the worldship, he assumed.

It then occurred to Meri that the whole city was built in a crater. This wreckage must have been the cause. The centerpiece of the city. He found it odd that nobody was around. No sunbathers or picnickers, no playing children or lovers walking hand-in-hand. No merchant carts or anything of the like. Strange for the center of town – such a giant open space to be so desolate. As he walked along, the smell of decay filled his nose, like rotting plants or vegetables. Nearing the wreckage, it became clear. The whole underside of the debris was covered in smashed garbage, as if the entire town made a habit of hucking their waste at the thing. The base of the structure was piled with all kinds of refuse. Everything from broken electronics to feces, and everything in between.

As Meri passed the pillar of shit, he found the city spring up once again on the other side. Familiar dobistone. It must have been a newer addition. Strangely, the shade of the rolling red tarps began only as the multiple shadows of the wreckage ended. It was clearly purposeful, and the irony struck Meri hard. They hated the thing. That was the point. They made it their duty to avoid the memory of the past, only to uphold the backwards bullshit it preached. All around were relics of an ugly history, one that clearly deserved to be abandoned and one that was obviously despised. The elders recognized it, yet still they were unable to escape it, regardless of how far from its shadow they built their homes.

As he hit the street, the crowd picked up. Meri found comfort reentering the pile of bodies. Up ahead was a solid line of cargo trucks moving slowly against the traffic. He must have been near the industrial quarter which is where he was to meet his contact. Despite the slow travel, he at least felt a sense of familiarity among the wash of pedestrians. If Southtown were more populated, he imagined that is what he was to expect. If all went well, it would be. Despite the inconvenience, he forced himself to wish for it.

Pushing between two idle truck bumpers, he found his destination. A rooftop sign reading *Fairaday's Faith*. It stood atop a corner market bar and eatery that catered to outsiders. A haven for MERCS, as he was told. No worries, he had his sidearm if his size didn't deter aggression. And besides, he much preferred no allegiance to bad allegiance. Easier to calm amorality than to deflate a lifetime of indoctrination.

As he made his way across the street, he noticed a Legomi sprout standing at the mouth of the alleyway he needed to pass through. His mind quickly switched to Kaerpo-ma, but then realized the tyke probably didn't know a thing about it. The little weed was holding an armful of paperwork under his arm. As Meri approached, the little runt jumped in his path and waved a crumpled paper. He couldn't have been taller than Meri's knee. "Hey, motherfucker," The sprout yelled. "Do yer duty! Take this and do what I say," The little twerp shoved the paper into Meri's crotch with a balled fist.

Mighty Rahiem

Meri guarded himself, but gave the little bastard the benefit of the doubt. Legomi weren't exactly the most intelligent beings, let alone their sprout offspring. He let the runt do his spiel.

"Take the paper!" the sprout cried. Meri held the kid off and took the pamphlet with a bit of difficulty. The runt didn't seem to want to let go. He gave Meri an aggressive eye as it was wrenched from his hand. "Fine," he said. "Have it your way."

Meri chuckled a bit before turning his attention to the pamphlet. There was a familiar emblem stamped center-top, and below, a list of demands:

Koplin's Chosen

-The rightful heirs-

It is the duty of all of pure blood to maintain that purity. Corrosion of your identity is the stated goal of the legion of Billion and his ilk, so do your part and report dissident activity to your local chapter house.

Do not speak with the enemy.

Do not dine with the enemy.

Do no associate with the enemy.

Those who choose to do so are the enemy.

The flame of Koplin's fist will consume the enemy and burn all impurity with righteous fire.

So says Koplin.

"Propagandist filth," Meri spit. He turned his attention to the sprout who seemed to have forgotten what he was doing. Meri let his anger dissipate through a breath and knelt down to the little Legomi. "Who gave you these?" he asked gently.

The Old Guard of Zerth

The sprout seemed to regain his composure. "Bossman said so. He give me a buck to do it. Last time I got a buck but I ate all the paper but this time he says I can't have a buck if I eat em all."

Meri forced a smile. "That's wonderful, my little man. Who is bossman? Do you know where he is? I would very much like to speak with him."

The sprout shook his head. "Bossman flew away. He went up in the sky and went fwoooosh!"

"Do you know his name?"

"Bossman!" the sprout smiled.

"What does he look like? Can you describe him to me?"

"Um, he looks like a cigarette." The kid dropped his head. He seemed quite upset about it.

"Enjoying the local entertainment?" a voice croaked.

Meri looked up to see a Fendrall smiling at him from the far end of the alley. It was a rugged looking louse of a Morouni with ears like kites and teeth like a bear trap. His eyes were set close, flanking a pair of flared nostrils that rose up to the man's forehead. A receded mohawk feathered over his head and vanished somewhere down the back of his vest. He wore a tweed bandoleer of heavy-caliber bullets over his chest, and clawed feet punched through a tattered pair of someone else's boots. From his ass, a stiff, waving tail dragged across the ground. He leaned against the wall of the alley and lit up a cigar. "You must be Meri."

Meri turned back to the sprout. "Is that bossman?"

The sprout gave the Fendrall a good look, then hesitated. He scratched his chin and seemed to lose interest.

Mighty Rahiem

The man blew a trail of smoke, then locked his giant teeth around the cigar as he approached. He leaned over the sprout then nabbed a pamphlet from the pile. "What do we have here?" he said to himself.

The sprout retaliated, swinging around to retrieve the paper, but the Fendrall's hand was planted on the kid's face. After a moment of reading, the man let go and the sprout fell forward. "Who gave you this?" He snagged the sprout by the stalks and yanked him around. "Get outta here, you little twerp." He swung the kid aside, sending him tumbling across the alley. Pamphlets scattered to the wind as the sprout jumped to his feet, thumbed an angry gesture and took off running.

The man turned to Meri. "If it wasn't bad enough to be a mutt, we got these paid stooges doing the enemies work." He held out a bony hand. "I'm Hackler. You must be Meri."

Meri gave Hackler a suspicious squint. "Indeed. I've come at the request of Roldolph Rimbaud. Might he be available?"

Not right yet," Hackler said, waving his hands, "but he'll be here soon. Those are some pipes you got on ya. Roldolph was right to pick you. I bet you don't even need a microphone. Why don't ya come inside? I Got a both set up for us here at Fairaday's Faith. Best bole stew in town."

Hackler turned and Meri followed. As the two made their way through the alley, Meri noted the emblem tattooed across Hackler's scaly shoulder. A black cross-hair with a slash through it. "That mark," Meri said. "You're a wanderer?"

Hackler responded with a smile over his shoulder. "They call us MERCS these days."

The Old Guard of Zerth

The decor of Fairaday's Faith was a drab, lime-lit miasma across badly upholstered seating. Everything was badly upholstered, even the tables. It felt more like a place to nap in shame. All around the walls were curtained alcoves, between which were buzzing electric sconces. The fans in the ceiling did nothing but keep the smoke at eye-level.

The place was packed with thirty or so patrons, each with an aggressive demeanor, but everyone seemed in good spirits. Judging by the apparel, Meri was certain the establishment was free from the influence of the Elders. All around he saw relics of Human and Aerie culture. Pauldrons made of tin cans and plasteel headgear. Most, if not all of the guests were marked in some way with the same symbol. MERCs, every one. Not all Morouni, but by far the majority. There were a small hand-full of Legomi who kept to themselves and a scattering of Humans who intermingled with all.

Hackler led Meri to a curtained-off corner of the room concealing a large booth where the two took a seat in privacy. As Meri slid in, the Fendrall shuffled the curtain shut. The alcove was illuminated with a single glow-orb set within the table, giving the space a cool blue glow. The heat of the lamp fizzled away at a cube of cider oil resting on top. It wafted with a strong scent of mulled fruit.

Hackler leaned across the table with a jagged smile. "So, ya got the voice. No doubt. Ya got the charisma. I wanna know about yer message. I'm going out of my pocket to get you in the mix. I wanna be sure its worth the effort."

"What exactly are you expecting, pray tell?" Meri said. "I'll go on stage, deliver my remarks and hope to not get shot."

"That's not unreasonable," Hackler said. "But I want to guarantee the message gets across. I wanna set a good example for the people. If I'm sticking my neck out to put you up there, I don't want to waste the opportunity."

Meri smiled, but just for a moment. He leaned forward, studying the Fendrall. "Not to seem discourteous, but you don't exactly strike me as a man of high moral values." He let the point stew.

Hackler brushed his fingers through his mohawk. "Hey, you can't argue with the situation. We're both in the same boat, you and I. Anybody can see it's a lose-lose to go down this road, so I'm doing my part to put an end to it. So, I may not be the most... principled man, but even I can't deny the benefits of moving society out of the gutter and into the light. There's money to be made in the suns."

Meri didn't answer. He maintained eye-contact with Hackler who started getting restless. Hackler could see he wasn't dealing with an imbecile, so he thought for a moment before stomping his cigar out on the table. "Okay, big guy. I can see you got something on your mind. What do you want to know?"

"I want to know where Roldolph is."

A bell jingled from the opposite side of the curtain.

"Enter," Hackler said.

The curtain opened and a Human girl leaned in with a notepad. "Two beers?" she said.

"Two beers," Hackler replied.

"Three," Meri said, sternly. "We're expecting another."

The girl nodded and vanished through the curtain. Meri turned back to Hackler. "Aren't we."

Hackler smiled with his palms up. He leaned back in the booth and nabbed his trashed cigar, plugging his face with it. "I get it, you don't trust me. No problem, I don't trust me either. Yer a sharp one, but that's why I think you're the best man for the job. You got a name for yourself around the parts that matter."

"MERCs," Meri said, loudly. His tone carried passed the curtain, quieting the discussion of the patrons on the other side. "Men without conscience dabbling in social politics. And you expect me to take your side?"

Hackler's smile became forced. He hesitated before replying. "Roldolph was right about you. You certainly are the genuine article. I suppose we may have been wrong to think you would stoop to working with MERCs. I mean, even though we've got the same goal in mind. Even though we both want the same thing." He snapped a lighter and lit the exploded end of his cigar, then puffed away, waiting for Meri's retort.

"I'll ask you a second time, and if I must ask a third, I may as well shoot you where you sit," Meri said plainly. "Where is Roldolph?"

Hackler's smile shrank. His eyes narrowed and his tone lowered. "He'll come when I call him. Now, go ahead, ask another question."

Meri didn't have a chance to pick the words apart before the curtain flung open. A big fuzzy head plowed into the alcove. "Meri buddy!" Roldolph howled.

"Roldolph, my man!" Meri hollered, pushing from his seat.

The two locked hands and Meri helped the great oaf into the booth. Roldolph squeezed in, squirming around to get comfortable.

Roldolph turned to Meri with a smile. "So have the two of you worked something out for the festival? I'd love to see you up on the stage. It's where you belong – believe me. And I'm not just saying that because I'm a fan."

"I believe we've come to an agreement," Hackler said, rubbing his knuckles.

"We've done nothing of the sort," Meri spit. "I've got myriad questions that must be answered before I do deals with MERCs."

Roldolph broke out into a chortle, jabbing Hackler. "I told you he was a sharp one, didn't I?"

"Sharp indeed," Hackler smiled, puffing away at his cigar. "Sharp as a spearhead."

"Ho ho," Roldolph bellowed. He nudged Hackler again.

Meri began to realize the two MERCs were closer than he thought. He started to feel like the butt of a joke he wasn't around to hear. Still, Roldolphs presence put him a bit more at ease. "So, you want me to be this 'spearhead' for your clandestine cause? Tell me what you have to gain, and I won't be tolerating any of this shallow, altruistic tripe about *doing the right thing*. At least do me the courtesy of speaking openly."

Roldolph turned to Hackler with a smile. "Should we tell him?"

"I think we can tell him," Hackler replied. The Fendrall leaned forward with his elbows on the table, smile wider than his ears. "My father is a man of great wealth and stature. You know him. Everyone knows him. His name is Ammison Kagg. I'm Kagg's son."

"Kagg?" Meri said, sitting back. He tumbled the thought around in his mind before the music shifted dramatically to something silly. It took him off guard as there was some shuffling and loud noises going on behind the curtain.

The bell rang and the waitress poked through, unprompted. She was gripping a tray of drinks tightly. Behind her, there was a scuffle between two tables. "Your drinks, boys. Sorry about the noise. The music went wrong." She leaned in to set the tray down but was bumped violently

281

from behind. Meri managed to save the tray with only minor damage to the beer.

"Nice catch, champ," Hackler said, tonguing his teeth. He snuffed his cigar out in the spilled beer, then sat back, awaiting Meri's prodding.

Meri passed the beers around. "So, you're Kagg's son. Mind revealing what that has to do with me?"

"Spearhead," Roldolph snickered. The oaf drank deeply.

Meri was starting to get the idea that he may have been wrong about Roldolph. The man didn't seem to have a mind of his own while in the presents of the Fendrall. All he seemed to care about was laughing.

Hackler downed a sip, then wiped his teeth. "Spearhead. It's the name of something very special that my father is building. He thinks it's his ticket off this planet. He thinks he's going to round up every pure-heart Morouni and skip town. Take off into the sky where he and his backwards-ass friends can live free from the influence of us mongrels. The old man wants to break away, and so I'm going to help him do just that."

Meri huffed and crossed his arms. "You want to help him 'go away'. Is that all?"

"Well, we wouldn't be proper, respectable MERCs if we didn't have an angle, would we? You see, this Spearhead naturally requires a whole lot of something I happen to have a stake in. Polerite, to be specific. Tons of it."

Meri gave Hackler the stink-eye. "While I appreciate what you *intend* to be honesty, you'll have to forgive me for calling maximum bullshit. You'd be rich enough to position yourself far above any of this nonsense."

Mighty Rahiem

"Well, you're not wrong there, big guy," Hackler said. "While it's not *immediately* available, I do happen to hold the keys to the kingdom, so to speak. The land out east, other side of Agnay. It's teeming with the stuff. And yes, I can extract it... for a price."

"So, you get rich while your father flies away, never to return. Am I getting the gist of it, my man? Seems a bit too simple."

Hackler leaned forward with a finger raised. "You're right, it's never that simple. That's where you come in. The more the rabble cries out, the more my father is motivated to leave, which translates into quicker business, quicker money and quicker happiness for me. You get it? You get your weird little utopia, I get my money, and the pain in both of our asses gets to fly away. All good in the hood, understand?"

Meri grumbled. He let out a hesitant breath, turning to Roldolph who didn't seem too engaged in the conversation. He looked down to his beer. The suds had cleared and the top of the table was smeared with dry booze under his sleeve. Hackler wanted a rabble-rouser. Meri didn't like it, but he couldn't deny that he was made for the job. In fact, on occasion, he would say it was his calling. Not for the reasons Hackler wanted, but for reasons he at least deemed honorable.

Meri cleared his throat and went for a sip, after which he straightened his collar, then shot an open hand forward. "You've got yourself a deal, my man. I speak for you and you benefit however you feel is in your interests. As long as the message isn't corrupted, I suppose I have no qualms."

"Wonderful," Hackler said, jumping out of his seat. He grabbed Meri's hand, shaking it vigorously. "Now, sit back and listen to the plan." He slapped the table and downed a gulp before starting. "So, you go up on stage. You do your little talk. There's gonna be a shitload of angry people. No problem, we got your back. Don't worry about it."

283

The Old Guard of Zerth

"Oh, I'm most certainly going to worry about it," Meri interrupted. "Explain to me *exactly* how you plan to keep me protected."

"No problem," Hackler said. "Just look for the guys in the crowd with the Blue Fist on their shoulders." Roldolph broke into a laugh.

"Blue fist? You can't be serious," Meri said. "They're fanatics. They're the reason all of this-"

"Relax, it's just a cover. We got guys on the inside. Gonna take care of you. Keep you safe, right?" Hackler said, his smile calming down. "They got a part to play and they're gonna play it real convincing-like, okay? Just let it happen. I promise you, they are no danger to your speech."

Meri sat back with a scowl. He went for his beer. "I must say, I'm having a few reservations about these actors of yours. What guarantees do you have that I won't be staring down the real thing."

Hackler laughed. "I promise you this, we own the crowd. Go get me a bugman if you don't believe me. Honest-to-Koplin, the crowd belongs to us."

Meri set his beer down with a deep breath. He looked deep into Hackler's eyes, hoping to find some glimmer of honesty there. To his dismay, he realized he wouldn't recognize it if it were there to begin with. He tapped his finger on the table, thinking it over. "Fine," he said. "I'm in."

Chapter 20

Consolidation

Wad wasn't feeling too well. He stumbled through the alley, dripping sap down his pant leg. His metabolism was in overdrive, coalescing the moisture in his veins around the various wounds across his body. His lips were drying out and his vision was blurry. The leaves atop his head were going gray and brittle. He needed liquid. He needed a beer. Despite the pain he felt in every inch of his battered form, he had his prize. The delivery boy's Talkman was jealously guarded in a clenched fist, held tight against his aching chest. He wanted to tell the world about it. He wanted to shout it from the rooftops. He wanted to beat someone over the head with it... but only after he got a drink.

The weary Legomi moved gingerly around the bend where his plant-man senses started to tingle. There was moisture nearby. Somewhere to the west. The platelets in his skin were going wild, dragging him closer to the source. There, over a shitty little garden wall was someone's back yard, and in that back yard was a barrel of water collecting a steady stream of munda dew. He painfully lifted a leg over the foot-high wall, then staggered across some neatly kept cobblestone. An interloper crossed his path, but he waved them off with his gun while doing his best to explain the situation in short, to-the-point sentences. He even pointed to his blood in case they didn't believe him. They thanked him for his courtesy by running in the opposite direction with their hands in the air.

The Old Guard of Zerth

With labored breath, he hoisted himself head-first into the barrel, displacing a wad-sized amount across the cobblestone. He stayed there for time unknown with his feet poking skyward and face pressed comfortably at the bottom. He took deep breaths, pulling the sweet nectar into his lungs. He could feel it rushing through his veins, pulping up his muscles and filling his belly. It felt too good to move, but as Wad knew, all good things must come to violence. It wasn't long before someone was banging on the side of his barrel. Presumably the owner. In his current position, he didn't think he was nimble enough to engage in combat. Not in that tight space, but he was pretty sure he could pull off a middle-finger. He tried and succeeded. By the time the integrity of the barrel was compromised, Wad was filled with enough life-giving water to pull off several additional fingers as he hobbled away towards his bus.

An hour earlier on the other side of town, Gustav flicked his finger across his Talkman. He found something suitable for a working man. Loverboy. Hell yeah. He wagged about comically while feeding a 2x4 through a circular saw.

Harvin Hobbart's Woodworking Wonderland was a ton of fun. 23,000 square feet of sawdust, buzz-saws and bloody fingers. It was a hanger-sized tent with huge fans in the walls that kept a steady cloud of musky chips swirling. At the back end were racks of lumber three stories high. Mostly bohboh wood but with smaller piles for hobby, warp and alcai. From there, row upon row of machinery of all kinds. Everything from saws and lathes to mills and drills. The place was a handyman's heaven.

It was one of several communal workshops in the city. All Gustav had to do was drop a buck an hour for use of the machines and an additional ten bucks per pallet of raw bohboh wood. It was imported directly from the lumber

286

farms in Halstaff. There were no guards on the machines, no safety, no regulations and no lawsuits. Gustav loved it that way. If you cut your arm off, there was a first-aid kit by the front door with some aspirin and band-aids, but you had to pay extra for the morphine. Harvin kept that in a locked box behind the front counter.

As Gustav bounced to the beat, Potato sat quietly atop a pallet of speaker parts, not sure how to feel about the music. He munched away at the scrap pieces of wood occasionally discarded by the Human.

"Must be nice being half-plant," Gustav said, looking up.

Potato gulped down the pulp. "I'm pretty sure it's edible for you," He said. "It's got water in it."

"And fiber for days," Gustav joked to himself. The 2x4 popped loose and he held up both ends. "Looks about an inch, I think." He notched both ends with a quick dip into the blade. "We just need a hundred and twenty more of these bad boys and we can get on to assembly."

With wood in hand, Gustav made his way to the front counter where he nabbed the PA microphone and cleared his throat. "Attention motherfuckers-" His shrill voice echoed through the building. "Putting out an order for a hundred and twenty notched corner supports. Bohboh. None of that expensive shit. Thirty-six by one by one. Eighth-inch notch, one inch deep, typical – centered on both ends. Coordinate that shit because I don't want extra. Payment is twenty bucks split however many ways you weirdos want. Delivery to station 9. Also putting in an order for assembly of three-dozen cabinets. See the ugly brown fucker with one eye at station nine for component schedule and print. Paying a buck a piece for completed units. Come get it."

The Old Guard of Zerth

Gustav tossed the microphone to the cradle and looked down the aisle to where Potato was sitting atop the pallet. The Legomi only had a moment of eye-contact before the station was swarmed with volunteers from all direction. The cyclops made a tiny yelping sound as he fell off the pallet and was swallowed by bodies. Gustav chuckled to himself. He pulled his cred-card from his wallet, swiping it through the reader on the counter and depositing sixty bucks to his workstation, and an additional two bucks for a couple of beers. Two Bubblin' Browns rolled out of the beer dispenser. He set one aside for mister Samuel Tuber and he popped the other without hesitation. A sip and a lean, he congratulated himself for a job well done. This must be how the president of LINTECH feels every day, he thought. What a life. What a life indeed.

Potato ambled to the front desk. The left side of his face was smudged with sawdust and dirt. He nabbed the second brown and popped the top, offering only a dirty look as thanks. "Must be nice having *all the money*," he said, downing a sip.

"It's not that much," Gustav said. "Lotsa people could do this. What did we pay for the parts, forty bucks? Another ten for the lumber and sixty for labor. A Hundred and change for thirty six cabinets. Sell em for four bucks and you got yerself a profit. Sell em for ten bucks and you got a nice markup. It ain't hard."

"Yeah, but you don't sell anything," Potato said. "All you do is buy things. It's weird."

Gustav had a great comeback prepared but the chirp of his Talkman preempted it. "It's Meri. He says he's all done. Wants us to bring the bus around."

"Where is the bus?" Potato said, sucking down a sip.

Mighty Rahiem

"I dunno. I think Wad has it. Lemme text him." Gustav poked at his Talkman, only to find a blank registry. "Oh shit, I forgot Wad got his shit stolen. What's his new ID?"

Potato shrugged, then finished off his beer. "No idea. We'll have to get that from him when he shows up.

A turd-looking Legomi scampered up the aisle holding a fucked speaker cabinet. Gustav took one look and exploded, chasing the little runt into the sea of machinery, hollering obscenities.

Wad moved the bus through the streets at a staggering Two miles per hour. His Talkman reminded him of that fact. Caught behind a confused elderly woman and a guy doing donuts on the back of a Macromite, he wasn't getting anywhere soon. Foot-traffic pushed passed him like he was standing still. Most times, he *was* standing still. His ribs ached and the dried sap around his pant-ankle scraped painfully against his leg. He had his prized Talkman but he couldn't do anything with it. Not until he got it back to Chelli. The excitement of retrieving his stolen identity had shifted to nervous anticipation. Everything in his body hurt and everything outside his body was annoying. The dashboard was beeping at him. He wanted out of Ortega as soon as possible but the old woman had apparently manged to wreck her cart. It lay in the road, sideways and on fire. Wad's head throbbed. He was having trouble staying awake.

As he stared into oblivion there was a knock at the door. Wad turned to see Meri waving at him from the other side of the gull-wing. It took him a hard minute to register what he was seeing. After coming to his senses, he popped the hatch and let the Morouni in.

The Old Guard of Zerth

"Gridlock is the way of things," Meri said with too much enthusiasm. He then saw the state of the Legomi and recoiled. "You seem a bit worse for wear, my man. You look as if someone has tried to eat you and succeeded in spirit."

Wad did his best to buck up.

Meri took shotgun and went for a beer below the seat, then handed another to the driver. Wad didn't pop the top whatsoever. He swallowed the bottle whole.

"Bad day, my man?" Meri said with a bit of worry.

"Good day," Wad replied through a distorted smile. He didn't know how to continue so he left it at that. He wasn't prepared to declare victory just yet, and besides, the last thing he wanted to do was repeat himself. He would wait until everyone was there to break the good news. He shifted the conversation back on the Morouni. "What about you? You seem upbeat."

"Most certainly," Meri replied, unsure of how to pussyfoot around the mood. "The deal is done. I'll be speaking tomorrow." He left it with a pregnant pause, hoping to spur conversation.

"What do you suppose it all means? Why do they hate you?"

Meri had to find the mental space before he could reply. He thought for a moment to allow himself the illusion of introspection. "I'm a traitor," He said. "They think I'm betraying my kind."

"How so?"

"It's not so," Meri replied with a stiff lip, "They see me as an abomination. Poison in the well. I fly in the face of their tradition. If you ask me, some traditions are not worth saving. Take yourself, for example. The Legomi people as a whole. If one were to inquire about the history of your people, what could you tell them?"

"Slaves," Wad said.

"Precisely," Meri said. "Would you ever wish to preserve your heritage by returning to slavery?"

Wad was getting agitated.

"I did not think so," Meri smiled. "And that is the point. The Elders mean to return me and my kind to the same. Madness." He said. "Pure madness... are you sure you're feeling well?"

"The Morouni were slaves too?" Wad asked, waving off the concern.

"To an ideology, yes," Meri replied. "A bitter retreat from sense and reason, we were taught elevate men to godhood then follow them without question."

"So that's why you give your speeches," Wad said.

"Indeed it is," Meri agreed. "But enough of that. Let us leave these ancient memories to the back-end where they can rot away."

"I just don't see it," Wad said. "I mean, not that I don't believe you. I'm just... removed from it, I guess. No Morouni ever bugged me about purity or anything."

"Nor would they," Meri said. "It is a subtle thing. Bigotry, that is. It exists in the shadows of conversation. In the subtext. The under-current that guides the collective consciousness without notice. You do not see it because they do not wish for you to take part in the argument. You are irrelevant to the scheme. If anything, you, my man, are the audience. The one to applaud their success when they feel their duty is done. In a sick way, they do it for your approval. Not that they have the mental inclination to realize it. It is a fear that drives their thinking. They fear they will not stack up evenly when compared to others, therefore they must improve. The Elders see your kind as successful in ways they wish to attain for themselves."

The Old Guard of Zerth

"They're wrong," Wad said.

"Undoubtedly."

"No, I mean they're wrong about all of it."

Meri let Wad's words sink in. He dropped it and tried to change the subject. "Are we running low on batteries?"

"I dunno, maybe. Why do you ask?"

"That light there on the dashboard. It appears to be blinking."

"What light?"

"Nevermind, my man. Just focus on the road."

Pulling the bus though the lumberyard gave Wad a boost of jealous inspiration. Through a permanent cloud of sawdust, dozens of laborers scurried around with their own projects at hand. Tables, chairs, door frames and pillars, and that ripe bite of fresh-cut wood on the taste buds. Wad was struck with the urge to slap something together and be proud of it. He didn't care what it was, as long as it had his name on it.

Up ahead, Gustav stood atop a concrete loading block waving for the bus to back up. His voice vanished behind the whine of saw blades as he called out. Next to him was an over-sized wheelbarrow filled with six or seven wooden speakers. "Put the seats down!" Gustav yelled out. "We got more coming!"

Wad threw the bus in reverse and slung himself out the window for a better view. The bumper nudged the concrete and he threw it in neutral, then popped the rear hatch as Potato climbed in, bouncing the back end like a wobbling canoe.

"Jesus," Wad said, eyeing the wheelbarrow. "How many of these things did you make?"

"About forty!" Gustav yelled as he dumped the speakers to the floor. "I got a really good deal."

"They all gonna fit?"

"We'll make it work."

Wad reached for the console to lower the seats, noticing the blinking light on his dashboard. The indicator was unfamiliar, a new addition it seemed. A flashing series of wavy lines, blipping for his attention. "Hey guys," he called out, "what's this mean?"

Gustav dropped his wheelbarrow and poked his head between the seats. "Holy shit, dude. You get run over or something? You look like hammered ass!"

"Don't worry about it. Tell me about the light."

Gustav shook his head with a frown. "That's the thing Hesh installed. It's part of the fetch system. We're being pinged."

"Pinged? Like Talkman pinged?" Wad said, unnerved. "Is he trying to call us or something?"

"Probably just trying to figure out where we are. Not sure why he would care. Give him a call and see." Gustav nodded.

Wad tapped the contact list on his Talkman. Hesh's number was the only one there. He poked it, then switched the audio to the speakers of the bus. A moment later, a crackle, followed by Hesh's voice. "What's up buddy? What can I do for you?"

"Hesh? Are you pinging us?" Wad said, turning to Gustav to confirm he used the correct terminology. Gustav gave a thumbs up.

The Old Guard of Zerth

"No. No, why would I do that?" Hesh said.

"Cause' someone's pinging us, I think," Wad continued. "Should we be worried?"

"Who knows," Hesh replied. "Could be a glitch. I'll take a look at it when you get back. In the mean time, keep yer eyes on your tail. Potato still has a price on his head so it could be bounty hunters. No need to worry, unless they've got some kind of world-class hacker on the job."

"In theory, what if they did?" Wad said.

"Well, you saw what Chelli could do. If they managed to ping you and unscramble the feedback, they would know where you came from, where you are and probably figure out where you are going. I wouldn't worry too much about it, unless you have reason to believe the Aerie Nation is on your back. Outside of Aerie com-stations, I don't know how anyone could have that kind of tech. We just happened to get lucky with ours."

"Aerie put a price on my head?" Potato said, butting in. "I shoulda' known."

"No, you big oaf," Hesh laughed. "Why would they do that?"

"Plenty of reasons," Potato growled.

"I'm sure you'll be fine," Wad said. "Either way, We're heading back to Ender. I've got something for Chelli."

"I got something for Chellie, too," Gustav hollered. He was wagging around, humping a speaker cabinet. "Let's get back to her moist, underground lair where we can engage in some more 'hacking'."

"If we're getting pinged, the last place we wanna go is back to Hesh's place," Potato said. "They'll know we're coming."

"You worry too much, big guy." Gustav poked the Legomi.

Mighty Rahiem

"You got a price on your head?" Potato said.

"No."

"Well, when the Aerie Nation wants you dead, we'll let you decide what's important. Right now, we need-"

"-oh for fuck's sake, Sam," Wad interrupted. "We have no way of knowing that it's the Aerie Nation."

"You heard Hesh," Potato said leaning in. "They're the only ones with that tech. You tell me who else it could be."

"I bet it's Chelli," Gustav said, rubbing his chin. "She's going in deep, pinging my privates. Looking for my golden rod. I think we need to interrogate the girl's privates... I mean – privately. Er..."

"She can hear you," Hesh said. She says *'come and try it'.*"

"That's all the invitation I need," Gustav whooped.

Meri chucked the remainder of the speakers into the rear hatch, squishing Luke Skywalker against the window. The crew piled in the empty spaces, crowded around wooden cabinets. The load was substantial. It weighed down the back of the bus, pushing the front-end skyward. Wad was forced to cut the forward head-fan RPM to 30% just to balance the thing out. The rear view mirror was strictly a no-go unless he was interested in staring at speakers. They chugged down the road at half speed to the tune of **Beak – Yatton**, drawing a sophomoric snicker from Gustav as he feigned ignorance. Enderbound – Southwest–62Mph. Destination:-565.1/+26.4. Arrival:137 minutes.

Chapter 21

Bills to Pay

The mood was upbeat as the bus lumbered southbound traderoute 7. A pleasant breeze bounced around the crowed cabin carrying the all the musk of fresh-cut lumber and quick-stain oil. Speaker cabinets filled every possible space. Gustav had followed through with his promise of minimalist-neo-postrock, as he called it. **Brad Sucks – Making Me Nervous.** Nobody argued. Nobody was sober. The team had found their way into the whiskey reserves which required a bit more than a wave of Wad's hand to keep them on the narrow. That is, until the ache of his ribs made a strong enough case for him to join in. Wad didn't know how fast he was going, nor did he care. He had a feeling he could go faster but he didn't consider it too important. He had his prize and there was nothing in the way of making himself whole again.

As they made their way towards Junction 2/7, pink sandstone crept up like a wave over the west side of the road, morphing into the rocky incline of Rusted Bluff. An hour of pounding baselines later, they were well in the shadow of the northern shears. Traffic had picked up at that point. Wad kept to the right to allow his drunken swerving to not impede too much on passing haulers. He had eased in to the alcohol naturally, enough to be cognizant of his handicap. His relative awareness gave him a feeling of modest altruism, so he rewarded himself with his own bottle that he kept safe between the seat cushion. That and he was pretty sure he would tip the bus over if he tried sharing the other bottle that was being passed around. Good, clean vibes.

The Old Guard of Zerth

As they approached the mouth of Georgio Gorge, Wad felt a rush of triumph. He had entered the lion's den, done battle with the evil delivery boy, fended off his minions and made it out the other end with the spoils. The cost was only a few broken ribs. Maybe a broken leg, too. He wasn't sure. He couldn't feel his right foot but that could have been the booze. Either way, he had made it back to home base without fucking anything else up. With that thought, he felt it was safe to share the good news. He eased back on the thrusters, letting the bus come to a halt on a dusty turn-off near the junction of trade-route 2.

Meri poked his head between the pilot seats. "Everything on the up-and-up, my man?" He burped a bit, which seemed to surprise him.

Wad waved off the intrusion. "Everybody, I have an announcement to make. It's a good one, too."

"A good one-two!" Meri echoed.

Potato nabbed the bottle and plugged it into his face.

"Two-Two!" Gustav yelled.

"Three-"

"Stop," Wad said, hiding his amusement. "Okay, so you know how I lost my Talkman, right?"

"We should give you our numbers," Potato said. "That way we can talk to you when you're not here."

"Not right yet. I want to tell you what happened in Ortega."

"Interesting place, indeed," Meri said, rocking with his hands on his knees. "Interesting place filled with interesting people. Myself included, for a time."

Wad found himself about to fall into conversation with the Morouni. "Okay, hold on-"

298

Potato shoved his Talkman into Wad's face. "Put your number in there. I can't see the buttons."

Wad stared into the glowing green screen. Thankfully, it was one thing that actually made sense at the moment. He poked his code into the keypad.

"Thanks."

"Okay, I wanna tell you guys what happened to me in Ort-"

Wad's Talkman blipped causing him to trip over his words. He looked at Potato who wasn't calling him. It could only be one other person. He scratched his forehead, thinking for a moment. It blipped again so he poked the receiver in the dashboard. Hesh came through the speakers.

"Hey Wad, you guys expecting company?" The Sectoid said.

"No. Should we be?"

"There's someone here. They're parked outside the garage. Looks to be about thirty or forty guys in uniform.

"Sounds like trouble," Potato said, reaching for Paulina. "Best to be ready."

"What do they want?" Wad said.

"I don't have the slightest idea," Hesh replied. "I can't read them at all. No brain signals whatsoever. It's like they're dead or something."

"We're on our way. We'll get it all sorted it out. But after this, I gotta tell you what happened to me in Ort-"

"Okay, they've got guns," Hesh said. "Big, stupid guns."

"Bloody confrontation," Meri said with a smile. "The spice of grand folly! Where is my gun?"

The Old Guard of Zerth

"I say we go in shooting," Potato snarled. He turned to Wad who sighed.

"Who's Mark?" Hesh said.

"What?"

"Who is Mark? They say they're looking for Mark." I think they've got the wrong house. Ooh, they're pointing their guns at me. Gotta go."

"Hang on, Hesh, we're coming!" Gustav cried, "Fuckin' Battle Music. Lets go!" He slapped his Talkman and cranked the volume. **Golden-Frost by the Brian Jonestown Massacre.**

Wad didn't know how to react but he had the feeling he had just been buckled in for a ride. A good rumble might make his broken bones feel better. The thought amped him up, which killed any motivation to be angry – but vengeance worked. Gleeful vengeance. Sure, he could do that. All he knew was that his blood was beginning to boil to the tune of exploding guitar riffs. That was good enough. He cranked the headfans in gear and pounded his foot into the accelerator. The bus bucked and spun off into the canyon.

The electric jam of the music made it easy for everyone to drink. Wad's double-vision gave him the satisfaction of swerving between even more vehicles. Potato anxiously tapped Paulina to the beat while Meri hunkered down in the rear, ready to spring from his cover. Gustav took a heavy gulp of whiskey, swaying his head with his .44 at the ready. The tension was starting to eat away at parts that Wad needed to function, but at that point, even smashing into a rock would be an acceptable gain. He held his breath as he pulled north, peeling around around the sandstone pillars that marked the hidden entry to Ender. With tightened knuckles, they careened up Veres Avenue – and there it was.

Mighty Rahiem

All at once, the tension deflated. Wad slammed the breaks, causing the bus to drift perpendicular in the road.

Parked lazily outside Hesh's garage was the rusted out 86' Chevy G20 surrounded by three-dozen Dollar Bills. They brandished carbon-copy Thomson sub-machine guns and dead, mustachioed grins behind mirrored Oakley Shields. They smiled like they didn't have a choice.

"The fuck is this?" Wad said, tossing up his hands. He popped the hatch and jumped to the ground leaving the bus to wobble freely. The sting in his ribs returned as he stood up straight. Potato leaped out after him with his eye on the flanks.

Gustav leaned out the window and waved. "Hey Bill!"

At once the Bills dropped their weapons to the dirt and threw their hands up in greeting. In unison, they fumbled to pick up their guns in a choreographed lean. Some even returned empty-handed, though still with hands in position to fire.

A crackle came over a speaker atop the van. It was a sloppy Brooklyn accent. "I see you are familiar with my esqupant. You have my thanks."

"What the hell is an esqupant?" Potato said. Wad shook his head.

Sanders' voice echoed. "Now, you have someone very valuable to me. If you would be so bold as to hand him over, I will gladly give thanks without bullets."

Wad turned to Potato and shrugged. "The fuck is he talking about?"

Gustav poked out the window with stiff middle finger. "Skywalker belongs to me! If you want him, come and take him!"

"Very well," Sanders burped. "You have forced my hand. Gimme a second."

The Old Guard of Zerth

The door of the van slid open with Tommy emerging from the side. He grabbed an awkward-facing Bill by the shoulders and twisted him to aim at the bus. He moved to another, retrieving the machine gun from the ground. He placed it in the hands of a second Bill, then shifted the body to face forward. He gave the crew a threatening gesture, then dove back into the van.

"This is pathetic," Potato said. "Are they serious?"

"Not as serious as I am," Sanders said. "You should never let your food talk back to you." The van bumped and rocked a bit. "Gimme another second, here."

Hesh called out from above, leaning over the balcony. "Hey, you guys know this person?"

"It's okay, we got this," Wad yelled.

"You sure?" Hesh said. "I swear, if you make a mess of the place..."

"I got this, everybody," Gustav yelled, leaning out the window. He mashed his Talkman. "I'm gonna start the music over."

"Oh no you don't," Sanders called out. "I'm not gonna listen to that crap. Joey, play the music of my people."

The music stopped. Gustav shrieked. A moment of silence, then the pop and scratch of a needle on vinyl. Then, **Bobby Darin – Mack the Knife**. The van bucked sideways, lifting off the ground as a pair of metallic feet sprouted from the underside. The machine rose high up on a set of mechanized steel legs. The quarter-panels flipped open revealing a pair of high-caliber Gatling guns at the ready.

Wad's mouth hung open. "Guz, what's going on?"

"Holy Jesus," Gustav shouted. "They aren't bums, they're Technobillies!"

"The fuck is a technobilly?" Wad yelled.

Mighty Rahiem

"Homeless Hackers. Transient Technophiles," Gustav shouted, as he fumbled around in the bus. He yanked Luke Skywalker free from the speaker cabinets and held him out the window. "Don't shoot, we're coming out." Gustav inched out the door with the cardboard cutout under his arm. "You shoot me, you kill Luke Skywalker."

"Luke Skywalker isn't real, you dumb turkey," Sanders coughed. "Now, gimme back Mark Hamill or you all taste lead."

"It's a fair trade," Meri yelled from the cover of the speakers. "Give them what they want and we can all go home."

Gustav stepped out to the road. He eyed the mechanical beast with an army of Bills at its feet. An ugly smile crept across his face as he slowly pulled his .44 from the holster. Drawing it upwards, he planted the barrel at Luke Skywalker's forehead. "Walk away or the cardboard gets it."

"You wouldn't dare," Sanders choked.

"Oh I most certainly wo-"

Like a crash of thunder, the Dollar Bills let loose, pounding holes through Gustav's chest. He shook with each burst of flesh as the lead tore through him a thousand times over. The two Legomi dove behind a rock, bracing against the sound as a cloud of dust erupted from the scene. The cardboard turned to pulp in Gustav's arms while his body was forced against the bus. Bullets pinged against the plasteel plating pushing Meri to duck for cover beneath the spray of blood across the windows.

The Bills rested. Gustav's body lay in pieces across the street. Bits of Mark Hamill fluttered to the ground with the settling dust. The machine recoiled. "Mark Hamill, no!" Sanders cried. The legs of the beast spun around in the dirt. A foot lifted, tilting the van off-kilter. "You killed my father! I shoulda' known you was no friend of the Don." The foot came down atop a Bill, mashing him into the dirt, and like that, the rest of the Bills turned on a dime. They took off up the street, trotting like a marching band. The van followed, kicking bodies aside with its massive feet.

Wad emerged from his cover to see the mechanical beast plodding through the canyon, chasing a gaggle of Dollar Bills. It smashed through a catwalk then turned a corner, drawing aim at the flock. It opened fire with a deafening series of cracks.

"Dammit, Wad. You've got to stop that thing before it wrecks the whole town," Hesh yelled from the balcony.

"I'm on it," Potato said. He leaped up and sprinted down the street with his hand on his holster.

Wad crawled out from behind the rock to see Meri picking apart the remains of Gustav. "I suppose this means the music situation has once again gone sideways," Meri said. The Morouni snatched the Talkman from a disembodied wrist, then pocketed it.

"Wad, what are you doing?" Hesh yelled. "It's heading for the market square."

"What am I supposed to do?" Wad yelled.

"He's chasing the clones," Meri said, hopping over the smashed Bill. It was still kicking its feet in a running motion. "We need to find the original and stop him."

"How the hell are we supposed to-" A crash of stones halted Wad mid-sentence as a pillar of rocks came loose from the canyon walls. They dashed across the ground, knocking Meri on his ass.

"That's it, I'm finished," Hesh shouted. He turned from the balcony and vanished inside.

Mighty Rahiem

Wad coughed through the dust. As it lifted, he found the road was blocked by the rubble. "Guess we gotta climb over."

"Merinall aren't made for climbing, my man," Meri choked. "Best go around unless you care to see gravity do me in. Tell you what, I will go around and you find Bill. If I had to hazard a guess, I would say he's perched somewhere high." He pointed up the canyon walls.

Farther down the canyon, they could here the sound of grinding steel and more gunfire. Wad let out a huff, then nodded. Meri gave him a confident slap on the shoulder, then took off lumbering down the south alley with his sidearm at the ready.

Wad gazed up at the rock. He found a strong seem and dug his knuckles into the cold stone. Drawing in a deep breath, he braced against the pain in his chest. One hand after another, he began to pull himself up the wall. About twenty feet off the ground he could see the path of destruction carved out by the van. A string of wrecked catwalks following a trail of munched Bills, still writhing around in the dirt. He pushed upward. Another twenty feet. Looking over his shoulder, Hesh was glaring at him from the balcony of his home. No words were spoken.

-Krakoom-

Paulina went off. A 30mm slug slammed into the side of the van with a dull clap. It seemed to bounce right off. No damage. Potato ducked down behind his rock, spinning the cylinder open, loading two fresh slugs. He peered over to plan his next shot, finding the town square was quickly turning into a war zone. The townsfolk were taking up arms from the cover of sandwitch boards and park benches. They blasted at the machine with hot plasma as it veered around in circles, firing on anything resembling Bill. The clones were scattered in every direction, chugging through the square in flocks while others were stuck running in place against walls.

A formation of Bills trotted by causing the van to spin around, letting loose on Potato's position. The Legomi dropped to the ground as a hail of bullets swept across, pelting his stone to pulp. He heaved himself blindly through an open window as hot metal sprayed at his feet, coming down atop a wooden table that splintered under his weight. He found himself in a well furnished boutique of some kind, laying in a pile of wool socks.

No time to react as a massive foot crashed through the wall, followed by a brigade of fleeing Bills. They scurried throughout the aisles, dragging bits of clothing off the shelves. The van opened fire, mowing down display racks and exploding mannequins. Potato squeezed tight against the wall as the beast spun around, heading back into the square.

Peering over the debris, Potato spotted a shadow moving through the smoke. It looked like a jiggling barrel with a necktie. "Meri, over here!" He shouted. The portly figure wobbled across the square as a flood of Bills engulfed him, drawing the fire of the van. The Legomi snapped to his feet and dashed into the chaos, flattening Meri to the ground as a foot crunched down inches from where they lay. It continued on, leaving the two fully exposed. Potato watched as the monstrosity barreled into another wall, hurling a pile of Bills through the air.

"I'm here to help," Meri grunted, waving his pistol.

Potato wrapped his knuckles around Meri's collar, dragging him to his feet. He spun around and heaved the Morouni into the blown-out wreckage of the boutique. "Stay there and stay down!" He slapped his Talkman and began dialing Wad's number.

Mighty Rahiem

Wad pulled himself over the lip of the canyon and staggered to his feet. He took a moment to catch his breath and dust off his knees. The heat of the shears scorched his skin and he had to shielded the sun with his hand for a look around. It wasn't difficult to spot. In a sea of dried grass was a bright red tent with a hyperbike parked at the side. Back a ways was a hastily crafted fifth-wheel, presumably to haul the clones. He whipped out his P:9 before his Talkman beeped.

"Wad, the Bills are making a mess of the place. Ya gotta get em away from the town." Potato's voice echoed through the microscopic speaker.

"I was just gonna kill him," Wad said, "that's a lot easier."

"No, that's not good enough. He's going after the dead ones, too. You gotta get em out of town."

Wad sighed, holstering his P:9. He made his way through the wheatgrass, kicking stones aside. Reaching the tent, he noticed a dozen or more power cables snaking out the back, and there was a whizzing sound coming from inside. He threw open the flap to find an awkward sight. There were fans everywhere and it stank to high-heaven. There was Bill, sweating his balls off on a treadmill with a look of concern on his face. On his head was a little steel beanie with a tiny whirling satellite dish. His lazy eyes were focused on a display screen with what looked like a real-time feed of the carnage down below.

"Oh shit," Wad said. The startled Human popped and seized-up, clutching his chest, then keeled over. The treadmill carried the lump of a man to the door, depositing it at Wad's feet. "Fuck!" He knelled over, smacking Bill's face around in a panic. "Wake up, wake up."

The Talkman beeped again. *"I told you not to kill him, retard!"*

The Old Guard of Zerth

"I didn't kill him, he just passed out!"

"Well wake him the fuck up, and don't scare him – he dies when you scare him. Be quick, we're getting slaughtered out here."

Wad grabbed Bill's head. He didn't know what to do with it. He looked around the tent for a clue, but settled on grinding the Human's face into the belt of the treadmill. It made a terrible noise. Bill spat awake, flailing around causing Wad to jump back. He drew his P:9 and aimed it at the reeling Human. Bill pushed to his knees, squinting at the Legomi. "Oh, it's you," he said.

"Get yer ass on that treadmill and start running, you weird bastard." Wad ordered.

"But I'm so tired. I need to take a break," Bill said. "I can always get more bodies. I don't care if they die."

"It ain't about you, jackass. Look what your friend is doing to the town." Wad yelled, pointing at the screen.

"Fine," Bill wheezed. He climbed onto the treadmill and began jogging lazily with his arms to his side, all the while glaring at Wad like a scolded teenager.

"Now you gotta make em run out of town," Wad said.

"That's really hard to do," Bill moaned. "They all get facing different directions and you can't control them."

"Look, I don't give a damn how hard it is," Wad spat, "You gotta get em out of town."

"What if I don't wanna?" Bill sneered. "What are you gonna do, kill me? I don't care, go ahead and kill me. I'd rather be dead than put up with this crap."

"Fine, I'll just blow out your kneecaps and take your bike," Wad said with a devilish grin.

Mighty Rahiem

Potato threw his arms up as all the Bill's collapsed a second time. "Guess I'm doin' this shit myself," he muttered. He turned to Meri who was picking out a necktie from the rubble of the boutique. Fuck it. The van seemed to be doing a jig atop a pile of bodies as the townsfolk wailed on it with sticks. The thing was a tank and there was no stopping it from the outside. "Guess I'm goin' in." The Legomi worked himself up, slapping his biceps. He bounced in place, breathing deep, then took off towards the hulking machine.

Potato studied the exterior as he approached, searching for the best way in. Fuck it, go through a window. He took a running leap, latching his fingers around the steel plate of a foot, then yanked himself up the struts of the leg, mindful of pumping pistons and bursts of steam. He clawed up the side of the machine until he found a firm grasp on the runner, then hoisted himself to stand on the rusted-out plank.

Hugging the side of the van, he balled his fist and pounded it into a window. It didn't budge. There was some kind of coating forming a skin over the glass. It seemed to turn glossy with the strike, then fade back to a dull luster. Without warning, the door slid open throwing Potato off balance. He snagged the top of the sliding door as it dangled him off the ground. Joey poked his head out from the darkness. "Hey boss, dinner is here." Potato didn't hesitate. He swung his boots into Joey's chest, following him in as the Human fell backwards, recovering atop the man's gut.

The interior of the van was a mess of tattered upholstery and dried offal. It had the smell of unspeakable deeds throughout. In the back was a lopsided credenza stacked with decorative plates. There were blinking monitors and ticking readouts in every wall, giving Potato flashbacks to Chelli's cave. Sanders was a lot more tech-savvy than he appeared. But there, in the front of the van. The controls appeared to be unmanned.

The Old Guard of Zerth

A series of shots lit up the cabin, pelting Potato's body with hot pain. He spun around, raising his forearm to soak up the last of the clip as Joey unloaded. The Legomi lunged forward, backhanding the man and nabbing the pistol in the same motion. He ripped the steel from the oaf's grip, nearly pulling the man's arm off with it. Joey lumped backwards into the aisle as Potato pounced onto his chest, digging his knee into the man's throat. He went to work, clutching Joey's ear, ripping it clean off his head, then hammered his fist into Joey's mouth again and again. Broken teeth stuck in his knuckles as Potato foamed with a primal rage. Then, a cold shock to the back of his head. His vision blurred.

Potato staggered for a moment pawing at his skull. He grabbed hold of a shredded curtain to keep straight. Finding his bearings just made him more angry. He pivoted quickly, discovering the old man standing over him with a thick wooden chessboard in his hands. They met eyes. Sanders shrank, stammering back, clutching the board to his chest. Potato rose up, approaching his attacker with his heart pounding fire. His wounds were dripping and his hands were wet with blood. The old man backed into the cab, bumping against the dashboard with terror in his eyes. The Legomi could taste the fear. It was palpable. Sanders dropped the board and fell to his knees. "I... I just wanted my friend back," he pleaded. He clutched his hands together, "I just want my friend."

The man's words stopped Potato in his tracks. His fists dropped open as the rage deflated, leaving him drained. He squinted at what the man had said, trying to make sense of everything. There was a mangled body on the floor and a town reduced to rubble, all because he wanted his friend back. He looked Sanders up and down, finding a man without any sense of stability or support. An old man without anyone to point him in the right direction. No one to keep him from hurting himself or others. He found no guilt in the old codger. Turning a town to rubble to protect the ones he loved. He might do that himself. In fact, he was damned sure he would.

Potato let out a huff, trying to think of the least threatening way to open a dialogue. Nothing sprang to mind so he sat down on the floor and thought for a moment, occasionally trading a guilty glace with Sanders, who replied with nervous blinking. "Sorry," Potato said. "Lets go find yer friend."

Wad found himself in the same spot he stood just a day prior when he and his friends had discovered the body of Carbon Dale. Sand squid had made quick work of it in his absence, leaving little more than a Human-shaped depression of shredded clothing in the wheatgrass. About twenty yards back, Bill was fanning himself in the shade of his tent. When the bullets stopped flying, Bill gave up as well, opting to use the last of his energy to complain about the heat.

Down below, Ender was in shambles. The town square had been reduced to a smoldering crater. The bite of gunpowder lingered in the air, joining with the dust of pulverized cobblestone. The Gregor's Gall Bar and Grill had collapsed completely, while the Amber Hollow's snug ambiance was now fully open to the elements, albeit half buried beneath a pile of stone. Pipelines were exposed like compound fractures, leaking water down the walls of the city. It gathered in burnt depressions throughout the square, blending with blood to form black pools. All in all, eighteen storefronts and six homes were beyond repair, with untold damage to the city's infrastructure.

The townsfolk had emerged from the wreckage to survey the waste. They shuffled around, not quite able to process what had happened. They wandered from ruin to ruin, just looking at it. It was all the same. Each scene was a catastrophe, and in the center of it, a Chevy G20 on mechanical legs playing Dean Martin records. The reality of it all hit Wad in the gut. Despite not being the aggressor, he couldn't help but feel wholly responsible. He wasn't alone in the sentiment.

From behind, he could hear the footsteps of someone moving through the grass in his direction. "I suppose you've got something to say," Hesh said.

Wad didn't feel like turning around. He didn't feel like talking either, but there was nowhere to escape to. "I don't know what I did, but I know this is my fault."

Hesh didn't bother with encouraging words. His tone was clear. "I know you found the delivery boy. Give me the Talkman. Once we restore your bank account, the cost of the damages will be charged."

Wad felt a bit of relief. He turned to Hesh with a light smile. It wasn't shared. The Sectoid looked through him like a stranger. "Look," Wad said, "this is all going to blow over. Once I get my money back, we can rebuild. We can fix it all up and go back to-"

"Normal isn't good enough, Wadley. For you, normal is drinking yourself into oblivion. For you, normal is you wrecking people's lives and I'm not going to be taking part in it any longer. I will not be having a beer with you. I will not be nursing you back to sobriety. I will not be repairing your bus when you destroy it after yet another daily rampage. I've had enough of your normal and I won't be entertaining it any more. Now, give me the Talkman and get out of my city."

Wad felt a shock up his spine. A pump of cold adrenaline that seemed to be distorting reality. The Sectoid's words didn't make sense. "You're banning me from Ender?"

Mighty Rahiem

"I'm protecting my friends and family from a clear threat," Hesh replied. "And I'm protecting myself from a one-sided relationship. Do as you will, but do it away from me and mine."

Wad took a step back with his hand to his temple. The jolt of the words settled in leaving him with an unbearable sinking feeling. "Okay," he said with his head down, "I understand. I'm not in a good place. I've not been in a good place for a while now. But you can't just leave me like this. You can't just abandon me."

Hesh held up a stony face before letting out a breath. He could see the Legomi wasn't lying. He could feel the bite of regret and the sting of apprehension. The weight of true guilt. "I certainly will abandon you, Wadley. I'll do it in the blink of an eye... but only when you've abandoned yourself. You're not quite there yet, but-" Hesh's face then contorted. His cheeks went flush pink. "-but I'm telling you right this moment, you son of a bitch – you useless, shiftless, trash-heap of a man – I will put you down if I have to."

Wad wasn't sure if Hesh was threatening violence or being metaphorical. Either way, the point was well made. He nodded with pursed lips. "So, what now?"

"Now, you make things right," Hesh replied.

The Old Guard of Zerth

Lorem ipsum dolor sit amet, consectetur adipiscing elit, sed do eiusmod tempor incididunt ut labore et dolore magna aliqua. Quis ipsum suspendisse ultrices gravida. Risus commodo viverra maecenas accumsan lacus vel facilisis.

Chapter 22

Making it Right

Gustav's eyes fluttered open. His head was all floaty and fun. His divorce attorney had a silly voice. Lunesta. His eyes drifted through the darkened living room until he noticed he had a gun in his hand. He briefly entertained shooting his lawyer, but realized that would take effort. His eyes drew down. Back to sleep. Warm, comfy darkness.

A flash and release, then all was bright as Gustav gazed into the infinite blue with nothing under him but air. It was the usual greeting of chest-in-throat with a tickle up his spine as his equilibrium flipped. He began to fall. The air rushed through his hair and his bathrobe drew upwa-

-Fhuh-

The usual greeting of air forced from lungs as he slammed into bricks. It was all so routine that he found it annoying that his body would overreact, seizing and convulsing for breath. What a damned chore. His lungs finally got with the program and began to function normally. Wiping the tears from his eyes, Gustav propped himself up to sit. Same spot as usual, just a bit lower to the ground this time. He stood up and dusted off his bathrobe.

The ruins were especially inviting this time around. Great blue brickwork stacked for reasons unknown by hands unremembered in a time lost to memory. They say even the Aerie Nation didn't know who built it. It was before their time. A haunting, ancient vestibule to the world he called home, nestled snug in a basin of sand at the foot of an impossibly tall cliff. There were times when he wondered if the cliff was put there just so people would have something to look at as they fell. As he wandered around, the earthy croon of **Tom Waits – Alice** swayed through the Azura spawn point. Meri must have his Talkman.

Up a small brick stairway was the spot the fishers picked to linger. Two Sectoids hunkered in the shade of parasols. Lawn chair aficionados with beer to spare, drunk and not too worried about respawns clogging up their agenda. The container of Morton's salt in Gustav's hand gave him away so the Fishers didn't hassle him. He handed over his salt for a new Talkman, which they pulled from a crate of thousands. He found some shade to keep the suns off the screen, then entered his number. It blooped and bleeped, followed by his account balance. 416,478,598,729,849 bucks. Meri had been spending his money.

Gustav pressed his thumb to the top-right of the screen until the debug menu appeared. It was a trick not many people knew about. First things first, decouple from the metanet. The screen went green, then flashed a warning.

'NO SOURCE FOUND – CONNECT TO LOCAL SOURCE'.

A list of a thousand off-wrist storage banks appeared. He scrolled through until coming to an unassuming folder with the name *NEDM*. A password prompt appeared and he began to type. *I-D-D-Q-D*. The folder opened with a single file present. *GODSOUND.EXE*. He double-poked the file and his screen went black, then lit up again with a string of coordinates.

'STREAMING DATA: CONNECTED – LAG_TIME: 4hr – 32min – BUFFERING: ON – GODMODE PLAYLIST'

There it is. **Aerosmith – Back in the Saddle Again.** Of all the secrets he kept, that was his most coveted. He relished in the fact that only he knew what planet he was really on. Everybody else could suck his dick. Gustav sauntered up the stairs to make small talk with the fishers until his friends came to pick him up.

Mighty Rahiem

An hour or so passed. Gustav and the fishers chortled over beer at the contorted bodies that occasionally fell from the sky. He did his civic duty to pass on advise to the newcomers while welcoming the respawns with a haughty middle finger. It wasn't too long before the bus came buzzing up the dune, riddled with dings and dents. It looked like it survived a sideways hailstorm. His blood was still splashed across the passenger side windows. Nifty. It drifted to a stop and the gullwing opened to a whole slew of ugly stares.

Gustav jumped to his feet to greet the crew with open arms and open bathrobe. "Hey boys, what took ya so-" He paused at the sight of Don Sanders limping out from the bus, then Dollar Bill. Potato followed behind, meeting Gustav with a look reserved for victims of impending violence. Gustav panicked as the Legomi marched forward. He waved his hands, not understanding how to react. The eye was on him. It was like being stabbed with a brick. Potato didn't blink as popped Gustav with the force of a speeding Buick. The man hit the floor, inertia carrying his legs over his head.

As the initial shock faded, Gustav's brain was swimming in every direction. He gasped for breath as he tried to right his vision. One eye was stuck looking the wrong way. The next second, he was dragged upward by a hot fist around his neck and forcefully stood on his feet.

"You did this," Potato spat. "Now you fix this."

The force rattled his brain. Gustav couldn't understand why Wad was glaring at him from the driver's seat. He turned to Potato, asking him to repeat the question. Potato answered with another Buick to the gut. Gustav was finished having fun. He lay curled up in the sand as the fist came back again, preventing him from cradling a collapsed lung. It pulled his head around to face the eye.

The Old Guard of Zerth

"We brought Mr. Sanders here because this is where Humans show up. We're gonna wait here until Mark Hamill comes back. You got that?" Potato snarled.

"Buh... but he could show up at any of the spawn points," Gustav eeked.

"No," Potato said, "He's gonna show up here."

"But he's not even rea-" The eye popped and Gustav winced. He looked at Sanders who was ambling about in the sand, blissfully unaware of anything of consequence. The old man was squinting in the sunlight.

Bill approached, speaking deliberately. "We think you need to go back to *Earth* and *find Mark Hamill*. Bring him *home* so he can be with his *friend Don Sanders*." He nodded with wide eyes.

"How the hell am I supposed to-"

Paulina whipped from her holster and everything went black.

"Gustav, why don't I come back another time," Devin said. Gustav stared at himself in the bathroom mirror. The lights were off. He poked at the darkened reflection with the barrel of his .44.

"Potato?" Gustav mumbled, turning to his lawyer. "When did you get more eyes? You look... terrible."

The Lunesta was making things difficult.

"Gustav, I really think you should sleep now," Devin said, never taking his eyes off the glinting chrome in his client's hand. "You said you wanted to sleep. That's probably what you need right now."

Gustav scoffed. "Pfft. That was like, three days or something... ago. I need to do things right now. I'm super busy.

Why is the salt?" He dropped the carton of Morton's salt in the sink. "Where am I?"

Devon eased his hands to Gustav's shoulders. He steered him out of the bathroom and down the hall, then into the living room. Gustav was in awe. "I told you I wanna buy this place," he said. "I'll give you Five Billion!"

"Gustav, you already own the house, but you won't if your wife takes it. You don't wanna see that happen, do you?"

"I have a wife?" Gustav snapped. "Ohh, is it that super hot chick? Does she have a nose? She's a super hacker. She doesn't have a nose." He giggled, then heaved himself onto the couch and squeezed a pillow into his face. "Hmmm, boobies."

Devin nodded slowly, reaching for his things, "That's right, Gustav, take a nap. You need sleep right now."

"No!" Gustav shouted, hoisting the gun over his head. "I'm on the mission. I need to rescue Luke Skywalker." He squeezed the trigger and made a face. "I'm... I'm gonna shoot the ceiling." He fumbled with the piece and found the safety.

"Gustav, don't shoot the ceil-"

-PAK-

The lawyer dove behind the ottoman as chucks of stucco landed in Gustav's afro. "Jesus, Gustav. You need to give me the gun right now!"

Gustav gave Devin a look. "You shot me," he said, waving the loaded pistol at his lawyer. "Potato have to shoot me because I killed Luke Skywalker. Why'd you kill me? We have to save Luke Skywalker."

"Dammit, Gustav. If you don't drop the pistol right now, I'm going to call the cops. The neighbors are probably calling already."

The Old Guard of Zerth

Gustav let out a chortle. "There are no cops here. How do you even know about cops. That's a Human thing. Let's go save Luke Skywalker!" He leaped from his chair, thrusting the pistol into Devin's face, gangsta style. He lifted his chin and widened his eyes. "I have to be responsible now. I'm in no condition to drive. You need to drive or I'll kill you."

Eastbound State St. Rockford Illinois – 3am. Gustav had no idea how fast his lawyer was driving. "Where's my Talkman," He mumbled.

Despite it being mid November, his lawyer made sure to put the top down before driving his client's 2002 Chrysler Sebring in public. He hoped someone would see the crazed man in a bathrobe waving a gun around and call for help. As luck would have it, they seemed to be the only one's on the road. Gustav was leaned over the passenger side door, transfixed by all the lights shooting by. "Are we in a cave? Why is it so dark?"

"It's night time, Gustav."

"It does that here? Wow, I never knew that. Since when?"

"Since always, Gustav."

"Sheesh, you learn something new every day... or should I say, every *night*!" He laughed into the wind, then sat down and fumbled under his seat. "I need so much beer right now."

"There's no beer in here, Guz."

"Since when?"

"Since always."

Gustav threw his arms up, "Why does everything have to change? Why are you driving and not Wadley?"

"Who is Wadley, Gustav?"

"Wadley is made of lettuce! He's a Brussels sprout."

Mighty Rahiem

Devin pulled up to the left turn lane at the intersection of State Street and Buckley Drive. In the opposite turn lane was an old Chevy conversion van, waiting patiently for the light. Gustav freaked. "It's the Don!" he yelled, waving the gun at the van. "He needs Luke Skywalker. Lets go get him!"

"No, Gustav. We aren't going to-"

-Pak- -Pak-

Devin decided he wasn't going to wait for the light. He slammed his foot to the gas and tore through the intersection, tires squealing, missing the median entirely. He floored it down Buckley Drive in the wrong lane, forgoing the left turn onto Walton Street, opting instead to plow through the greenery surrounding the Walmart parking lot. Gustav's head missed an electrical box by inches as the car bumped across patches of grass and slammed over the curb. They tore across empty asphalt, squealing to a stop at the entrance. Devin was in full-on survival mode. He didn't say a word.

Gustav couldn't wrap his mind around it. He was genuinely perplexed. "What is this place?" he said, as if it were an existential question. He turned to Devin. "What's going on? Is Luke Skywalker in there? Why aren't you answering me?"

Devin shook his head with squinted eyes.

"Ahh," Gustav said. "Yer doing the smart thing and staying quiet. I get it. Okay, lets get out of the bus. Where's the door?"

Again, Devin shook his head with his eyes clamped shut.

"Get out of the bus or I shoot you," Gustav said, jabbing the gun in the air. "Or maybe... maybe I'll just shoot myself." He turned the gun and pressed it against his forehead.

The Old Guard of Zerth

For a moment, Devin thought the nightmare could come to an end. He wanted so badly for the nutcase to off himself but he couldn't bear the thought of standing idly by. It would look pretty bad for the firm if one of their partners was found in a convertible with a dead client... at Walmart. If he was going to get of this unscathed, he was going to have to play along. "No, Gustav," he said, stammering. "Please don't do that."

"Why not," Gustav said, lowering the barrel. He placed it between his teeth. "It's not bad, I do it a lot. I feel so much better when I do it. I promise."

"No, Gustav," Devin said, psyching himself up. "We have to do this. We cant shoot you – we need you to live. I think we can find Luke Skywalker in there and than we can all go home. Deal?"

Gustav dropped the gun in his lap and gave Devin a heartfelt smile. "You're a good guy, Potato. Yer a brother to me."

"That's right, Gustav, I'm a potato. And do you know what? The cave people don't like it when you bring guns into their home, so you're going to have to put the gun away or we'll all get in big trouble."

"Cave people?"

"Yeah, the cave people, remember? We're in a cave. That's why it's so dark."

Gustav gave Devin the stink-eye. "What the hell are you talking about?" he said, then leaped out of the car with a wobble.

Devin thought to ask Gustav if he wanted the top up, but stopped himself. That might make things worse. Gustav jammed the gun into his boxers, then spun around with his arms out. "Are the *cave people* happy now?"

"Very happy," Devin said, "And if you could tie up your robe. The cave people aren't used to seeing bare skin. They might attack." Devin cringed. He scolded himself under his breath, then tried to back-track. "I mean, they wont give us Luke Skywalker."

"Are you confused right now? I'm confused right now. You should get some sleep!" Gustav laughed. "Whatever, I'm the brains anyway. Lets go get Luke Skywalker for the Don." He did up his robe and moved to the entrance where the doors slid open automatically. Gustav remarked with a novel nod of the head. "This is new."

The two men passed through the foyer where a large woman on a scooter was too eager to say hello. Devin waved her off with a heavy smile, pulling Gustav down the aisle by his wrist. "Luke Skywalker is just over-"

"Wait," Gustav said, stopping dead in his tracks. "There's something wrong here. Whats with this shit music? It's soooo bad."

"Gustav, it's always bad."

"Like hell it is!" Gustav howled. He yanked his wrist free staggering away in a fury. His attention darted to the speakers in the ceiling. "Someone's hacked my playlist!" He turned to Devin with a look of death in his eyes. "Ya know what? I bet it was the Don. He's done it before. Screw this mission, he can get his own Luke Skywalker."

Devin ran to Gustav, shushing him. "So – so we don't need to rescue Luke Skywalker?"

Gustav gave Devin a mournful look. "No... no, we *do* have to."

"Why?"

"Because," Gustav said. "If we don't, you'll shoot me."

"No, I promise I wont. I super promise!"

"Come on," Gustav said, grabbing Devin by the wrist. "Lets get this over with."

Gustav dragged Devin down the aisle, passing by the men's clothing racks and a display for Dubblestuff Oreo's. The place was dead but for the occasional Hispanic driving a floor buffer. Night stockers mulled around in royal blue vests doing as little as possible. "There!" Devin said, pointing to a colorful display.

Star Wars: Episode 7

Coming December 18, 2015

Devin spotted a cardboard display for 'life-sized cutouts'. "Look, It's Luke Skywalker. Here he is, we found him!"

"No, we need the younger one," Gustav said.

"Well, okay," Devin said, scratching his head. "There's a whole bunch of em in here. I'm sure we can find a younger one." Devin dug around in the display, pulling out 'Jedi Knight Luke', in all black with a green lightsaber.

"Yeah, that works," Gustav nodded. "Grab a couple of em."

"See," Devin said excitedly, "We did it. We rescued Luke Skywalker! Now let's get outta here quick before the cave people show up." He grabbed the cutout by the shoulders and shouted into its face. "You hear that, Luke, we've rescued you. Isn't that great!"

Gustav scoffed. "Jeez, man. It's not *really* Luke Skywalker. It's just cardboard."

Devin panicked. "No, no. It's not cardboard at all. It's really him, I promise!"

Mighty Rahiem

"Look, asshole," Gustav shouted. "We've been over this a thousand times. It's just – fucking – cardboard."

"No!" Devin cried. It's really him, I swear!"

As the two men hollered at each other in the middle of the aisle, a portly sales rep approached from the rear. "Excuse me, gentlemen. Can I help you?"

Gustav swung around, finding an elderly Morouni woman getting in the way. "Look at this shit," he said. This nutball thinks this is *actually* Luke Skywalker. I know you don't know what that is, but it's a big deal where I come from."

Devin peaked over Gustav's shoulder, winking furiously. "No, it *really is* the *real* Luke Skywalker. It's not cardboard, it's really him!"

The woman gave them both a look. "You boys are too old to be out drinking."

Gustav huffed. He threw open his bath robe. The woman's eyes popped as he drew his .44 and plowed the barrel into the cardboard's face. "Fucking – cardboard," he yelled while blasting the face off the thing. The shots echoed through the open space. Shrieks were heard from the electronics aisle. The woman dove for cover behind a rack of baby clothes, flat on her face. Devin flew off the handle and bolted, screeching away with his hands in the air. Gustav was done with all the silliness. He dug through the display, nabbing two or three cutouts, then jammed them under his arm and did up his bathrobe. Nine minutes after shots were fired, the police arrived to find Gustav curled up in a stall in the men's bathroom, sucking his thumb and hugging a bundle of cardboard.

The Old Guard of Zerth

-Fugh-

Gustav came down in the fetal position. A cannon ball into solid brick. He sat up, shielding his eyes from the sunlight while rubbing his tailbone. The crew was waiting patiently by the bus, welcoming him back with with crossed arms and stone faces. Gustav stood to clear his mind, trying his best to piece together the last few hours of his existence. Not much of it made any sense. He looked at the cardboard under his arms. They were wrapped neatly in polyurethane bags that were starting to fog up in the heat. He tore the tag off one, removing the folded cutout, then shook it open and stood it in the ground. He took a step back to see it clearly.

"Mark Hamill, my friend!" Don Sanders cried. The old man pushed through the angry mob, hobbling up the hill to meed his compatriot. Forgoing formalities, he went in for a bear-hug. Gustav gave a half-hearted shrug and ambled to the van. The crowd parted enough for him to crawl through the gullwing and plop down in a seat where he stewed for a moment before scrapping around the floor for a beer. The journey back to Southtown was a quiet four hours of joyless drinking.

Chapter 23

No Fun

Fivesday morning was indistinguishable from Foursday evening, save for two additional rising suns. Wad's office was mired in the heat of the morning. The broken ceiling fan wubbled, having no effect on the climate of the room.

Meri was doing himself up in a standing mirror in the back. He straightened his tie then mugged for himself, wagging his lips and practicing exaggerated vowels. Potato nursed a bottle of whiskey on the couch while Gustav kept his mood in place with **Sneaker Pimps – Small Town Witch**. A beer dangled between his fingers.

Wadley pushed through the curtain with Amelia on his heels; her demeanor, not so bright. She followed him through the office with a wagging finger. "I don't care if Hesh can get your money back. That doesn't mean it's okay to go around blowing up people's houses."

"I never said it was okay," Wad said. He motioning for a swig from Potato's whiskey, downed a gulp, then resumed pacing throughout the room. "It's not like we meant to blow anything up. We were trying to stop the dumb bastard. If you wanna yell at someone, why aren't you yelling at him?"

"It's not about yelling at someone, Wad. It's about your reckless behavior. Everywhere you go, something goes wrong. That's not coincidence, Wad. You have to think for once."

"We're taking care of it," Wad said, crossing his arms.

Amelia threw her hands up. "Oh sure, you're taking care of it. Tell that to the families in Ender. Tell them how it's okay that you blew up their homes because you might have some money coming in soon."

"That was actually-" Potato thumbed at Gustav.

"Fuck off, prick," Gustav grumbled. "I fixed my mistakes."

Amelia shot a finger at Gustav. "You don't get to talk. I don't even know who you are or why anyone likes you, but you are clearly a danger to everyone around you."

"Lay off the guy," Wad pushed in.

"No," Amelia barked, "I want to know what you think your deal is, mister. Who the heck are you and why the heck are you such a nuisance? Wad seems to think your a great guy, but we can all see Wad is a drunk who doesn't know a darn thing. From the minute I met you, things have gone wrong. Why is that? You tell me, why is that?"

Gustav gave Amelia a glance of spite.

"Oh is that it? Nothing to say for yourself?"

Meri's voice cut through. "To the travelers far from home, I whisper to thee -"

"-this world is yours and here you are free," Gustav replied, then resumed his angry drinking.

"Arguthaerie: Ten," Meri finished.

Amelia scowled. "What the blazes is that supposed to mean?"

"It means you don't know where you are," Gustav replied, setting his beer down. He leaned forward. "Lemme ask *you* something, girlie. Why are *you* here?"

"I'm the Mayor's aid." Amelia fired back, as if it were obvious.

"Oh, is that right?" Gustav said with an aggressive smile. "Has it ever occurred to you that the Mayors might not *need* an aid. Look at them. Do you even know who they are? Where they come from? They kill each other daily and you help them do it. Ever think of that? Do you even know the names of the people you work for? Does it even matter? Would the town collapse without your *vital* input, or maybe, just maybe, you're doing all this because deep down, the thought of freedom terrifies you and you're desperate to find some kind of order to make sense of it all. The same misguided order that has evaded you all your life. You think you can make it all right by putting your foot down on all the things you could never understand. No, girlie, *you* are the one that doesn't belong. This ain't Earth, stop pretending it is."

Amelia struggled for words. She turned to Wad for support but he looked to Meri instead. "How did that last line go, Meri?"

"To the travelers far from home, I whisper to thee. This world is yours and here you are free," Meri smiled, doing up the last button in his collar.

Wad turned to Amelia. He made sure to hold her attention with his eyes. "What have you fought for?"

"What do you mean, fight? I shouldn't have to fight for anything?"

The Old Guard of Zerth

Wad's fist slammed to the table. "What did you fight for? Because I fought for this. For everything you see. How many beatings did *you* endure at the hands of the AATF? How many years did *you* spend rotting in a prison, mind blown to hell with no hope of escape, only to throw your wretched life in a blender because you'd rather die in the sand than face another minute of hell. I ripped my life apart to find freedom and I learned to hate my own people because they didn't even care to look for it. Just like you. You don't know what to do with yourself. But you know what? We fixed all that and we built this world. We built this world for people like *you*. For people that didn't know they had a choice. And I don't give a damn if they wreck it – if we wreck it. It's ours to break. Then you show up and wanna turn it all upside down. Where I come from, people didn't have the chance to live their lives. Where I come from, people like you are called tyrants."

"We don't like tyrants," Potato said, wiping his lips.

Amelia recoiled. She looked around the room, holding back tears. "If that's how you feel..." She turned and hurried through the door flap.

"Well, that's that, I guess," Gustav burped.

"She ain't wrong," Potato muttered, turning to Wad.

"I don't wanna hear it. I'm done with this shit," Wad spit.

"So, will you still be working with the Mayor's office?" Meri asked.

"No," Wad said. "I'm done with that, too. Doesn't do any good either way. Why do you wanna know?

"Well," Meri said, stroking his chin, "I thought It would give my speech a bit more credibility if I were to say I was working with the Mayor's adviser. Might you hold off on your resignation for another day?"

Mighty Rahiem

"Fuck it, I'll just keep advising the Mayor's office from this window." Wad moved to the bay window, then swiped Gustav's beer and took a chug. The beer dribbled down his lip as he kicked open the shudders. "Hey Mayors," he yelled, heaving the bottle out the window. "Quit fuckin' around!" The glass shattered at the steps of town hall to the applause of the protesters below.

"Wadley Saxo!" A voice cried out from the street. It was Dingus Mackey with a hell of a look on his face. "You owe me two barrels of fish!"

"Oh shit." Wad pulled the shudders closed and turned to his crew, expecting some kind of rowdy approval but nobody reacted. No one gave a shit. No one seemed to care about him throwing glass into a crowd of people, nor did they care that Mackey had no more fish to sell because they turned his supply into ammunition. He was starting to understand why Amelia was angry. Wad sighed. He took a seat next to Potato, motioning for a swig of whiskey. Potato obliged. "Maybe she is right," Wad said, wiping his lips.

"Maybe *you* are right," Meri said, moving to the easy chair. He tugged the knees of his blunderhose and settled in.

Wad nodded solemnly.

"My man, I believe you misunderstand me," Meri said. "I said you were right. Not so much in agreeing with Amelia, but rather, what you said when you told the girl off. In my relatively few years of life, I've learned a thing or two about responsibility. I know how easy it is to make a mess of things. I also know how much it can hurt to fix them. We all know this yet we continue the same behavior that led to those mistakes."

Wad buried his head. "Dammit, Now you're starting to sound like her."

"Quite the contrary," Meri said, reaching for a beer. He popped the top with his thumb. "I suggest we maintain our heading." He raised his beer with a smile, then downed a hefty gulp.

The two Legomi responded with blank stares. Wad's posture begged for an explanation.

Meri took a wild swig, dribbling foam all over his new shirt. "Ahh, that right there. The essence of folly!" he said, poking at the wet spot.

"The big guys' lost it," Gustav mumbled, standing up. "I'm leaving."

"Hold for a moment, Human. You've got more to hear," Meri said, raising his voice. "You say you come from a world of law. A world of strict guidelines and boundaries, yet here you are a god, of sorts."

Gustav paused. "Okay, I'm listening."

Meri smirked. "In all the time we've shared together, I have not once seen you lord that power over another."

"What are you talking about?" Wad said, "Guz is the biggest asshole I know."

Gustav toasted his beer to the Legomi.

"An asshole does not a tyrant make," Meri added. "It most certainly is within his ability to dominate, yet he chooses not to. Pray-tell, my man. Why do you restrain yourself? Why not use that vast pocketbook of yours to plant your thumb upon this world? Remake it in your own image, so to speak?"

Gustav found himself thinking too hard. Everyone was looking at him. He felt a bit awkward so he took a seat.

"Nothing to say? Meri pressed.

Gustav hesitated. He sipped his beer, then sat forward. "What are you *supposed* to do with all this money?" he said. "Whatever the hell you want."

Meri leaned forward, encouraging the Human to elaborate. Gustav didn't say anything else. "Well, I suppose that should illustrate my point, though I had hoped for a bit more depth."

"I don't know," Gustav said, getting defensive. "I guess I'm just not an evil person?"

"That's debatable," Potato mumbled.

"I don't think it is," Meri said, wagging a finger. "The man has had ample opportunity to do much, much worse."

"So he's only a little bit evil," Potato said.

Meri nodded. "Possibly, but the question is, who is stopping him?"

"*I am*," Gustav barked. "Yer talking about me like I'm not even here."

Meri smiled, poking his claw into Gustav's face. "And what are you going to do about it?"

Gustav caught himself. He snatched his beer and sank into the couch. "I'm gonna have a drink."

Meri burst into laughter "Hah, you see that? The man clearly has a moral compass."

The two Legomi recoiled, preparing for Gustav to retaliate.

Gustav shrugged. "What? So what if I have a moral compass?"

Potato rubbed his chin. "This isn't how I pictured this conversation going."

"Me neither," Wad said.

Meri laughed. "The point is Gustav's compass clearly-"

The Old Guard of Zerth

Wad's Talkman blipped, pausing the room. He could see the majority were looking to exit the conversation gracefully, so he took the call. Scrolling through the screen on his wrist, a familiar name appeared. "Oh shit. It's Chelli. How'd she get my number?"

"Woah, woah. Let me set the mood," Gustav said, sitting up. He flipped the song. **Oh Yeah – Yellow.** He mimicked the tune, dancing to his feet, then yanked the view screen from the ceiling. "Make it so, captain!"

Meri sat back, blinking. "Another time, then." He returned to his chair and nabbed his drink.

"Wad, for the love of all that is holy, pick up the phone," Gustav yelled.

The irritated Legomi unlatched his Talkman and set it on the back of the couch, then tapped it. The view screen flickered before coming through. It was something blurry and super-saturated.

"Shades," Gustav shouted. "Close the shades!"

Potato ran to the window to draw the shades for a better view. In the darkness, all became clear. It was a fantastic pair of teal breasts forced through a taut cotton beater. Potato downed a swig of approval.

"Hey boys," the disembodied voice said. The things wobbled.

"Hi Chelli," The men replied.

"Uhh – my eyes are up here," Chelli teased.

"Don't you dare move that camera," Gustav said.

"Is Wad there?" said the boobs.

"Ya."

"You find my bike yet?"

Wad threw his hands up and walked away.

"Is he angry? I cant see anything with the camera down here."

"Yes Chelli, he's very angry," Meri said.

"Good!" Chelli jiggled. "Hey listen, I've got news for Wad."

Wad spun around. "Get on with it!"

Chelli took a deep breath to the delight of everyone but Wad. "So, I was able to crack the MᵃFuggin delivery boy's Talkman. Fun times were had. Many lines of code were laid to waste but in the end, I overcame the encryption – and lo, there was singing throughout the land. Funny story, it was just a kid named Todo Ya-"

"We don't care," Wad shouted.

"-Yasodo," Chelli continued. "Can someone turn Wadley's volume down, he's cramping my style. Anyway, irony strikes again. The kid actually had a charter to follow you. He was supposed to track you down to deliver a package. We rerouted it for you. I can't say why he didn't do that to begin with, but I suspect it has something to do with his lack of professionalism. He was just a kid. I don't know if I mentioned that yet."

"Go on," Gustav said, resting his chin on his hand.

"Is that Gustav?"

"Yes it is."

"Hi Gustav. Tell Sam to punch you in the neck."

Gustav caught himself before following the boobs orders. The look on Potato's face gave him the impression that he was prepared to do it. He sat back and stayed quiet.

"Anyway," Chelli said, "we were able to crack the Talkman and recover everything that was taken from you."

"Thank god," Wad said. "Tell Hesh he can use whatever he needs for repairs. I owe the people of Ender that much."

"They didn't take any money."

"..."

"Wad, are you there?"

"Wait, what?"

"They didn't take any money. They just copied the hash of your account. And technically, they didn't take that either. You gave it to them so they could track you."

"...what?"

A great blue face invaded the camera. It was Hesh. "Wad, the M^{a}Fuggin delivery service didn't steal your money. They didn't steal your property, Wad. They didn't steal anything. Any possibility of recovery vanished the moment you transferred your ID to the new Talkman. My condolences, though I must admit a modicum of satisfaction in your loss. One can only hope you learn something from this disaster. Speaking of which, the damages to the town clock in at a whopping twelve and a half thousand bucks."

"Bring the boobs back!" Gustav yelled, hurling his beer at the screen.

"Is that Gustav?" Hesh said. "Under the current circumstances, I think your considerable fortune-"

"Stop. I know what you're going to say. Don't say it. I don't wanna hear it." Gustav twisted around with a scowl. He poked at his Talkman, transferring a hefty sum of cash to the Sectoid.

Hesh's Talkman blipped. He looked off screen. "Money received. Thank you, you miserable asshole. I'll be sure the funds are distributed properly."

Gustav sank back into the couch, searching for his beer.

Mighty Rahiem

"As for you, Wadley... Wadley? Wad, are you still there?"

Wad wasn't paying attention. He sat quietly, half-buried in couch cushions, running his fingers through the leaves on his head. The jolt had sent him into a semi-catatonic state.

"I suppose that's enough bad news for one day. I'll call back later. Hesh out." The Sectoid's face retreated leaving only boobs, but nobody was looking at the screen. Wad stared at nothing, rubbing his scalp.

"Wad?" said the boobs. Chelli leaned her face into the camera. "Hey Wad, I have your old contact list. Sending it now. 'Till next time..."

The screen blacked out leaving the room in darkness. It stayed that way until Potato tugged the curtains open. Everyone was staring at Wad. Wad wasn't looking at anything at all. His Talkman bleeped but he didn't care. He turned to Potato who was leaning against the windowsill. "You okay, buddy?"

Wad looked his friend in the eye. "So, everything is gone?"

Not everything, "Potato said."

"Yeah, I got my contact list back. Whoopie."

The curtain flew open and a small man entered the office. Blue hat, blue shirt. M^aFuggin Delivery. In his hands was a small, gray box. He spoke with a thick, jersey accent. "Delivery for Mr. Wadley Saxo? Gotta delivery here."

Everyone looked at Wad.

"Put it on the table," Wad said.

Everyone looked at the Delivery man.

The Old Guard of Zerth

The man was shaken by all the stares, but swallowed the lump in his throat and began to recite a scripted spiel. "On behalf of MᵃFuggin Delivery Service, I want to apologize for the incident involving loss involving this particular package. It is the policy of MᵃFuggin Delivery Service to reimburse those inconvenienced by errors caused by MᵃFuggin Delivery Service- um... their full compensation."

"What?"

The man had seemingly exhausted his vocabulary. His eyes darted around the ceiling as he continued. "A previous Service Specialist who is no longer employed by the MᵃFuggin Delivery Service- um... not only failed to deliver your package, but has allowed fraud to be committed at your account. I have relieved the previous associate of his duty and delivered the package in question" He patted the gray box.

"MᵃFuggin Delivery Service would like to reimburse you for the fraud committed at you because-um, cause the previous associate mishandled his Talkman, and therefore mishandled your account information. Um. Our insurance policy covers all costs related to your loss. You're welcome."

"You have insurance here?" Gustav said.

"What are you saying?" Wad said.

The delivery man wiped the sweat from his neck. "MᵃFuggin Delivery Service protects your account security by insurance provided by Henley and Henly Fraud Insurance. You are covered in case of loss, which has happened. We need your signature to verify your account." The man produced a bio-metric signature tablet and approached the couch. Wad snatched it, then walked it into the light for better reading.

Mighty Rahiem

Henley and Henly Fraud Protection and Insurance

Incident Report #: 216

Name: Wadley Saxo

MF Account#: 007783

Payee TM Account#: 001x212

INCIDENT REPORT: Service Specialist T.Yosodo failed to keep the customer's account secure when he allowed his Talkman (containing the customer's account information) to be compromised through theft. Below is a snapshot of the customer's account balance before and after the incident.

Balance prior to incident: 1,389,023

Balance after incident: 0,000,000

Proof of ownership of assets:

101-213 Saxo St. Southtown – MEAPOS

102-104 Saxo St. Southtown – MEAPOS

306-312 Bermont St. Southtown – MEAPOS

414 Bermont St. Southtown – MEAPOS

112 ExHaddok Blvd. Southtown – MEAPOS

200 ExHaddok Blvd. Southtown – MEAPOS

501-508 ExHaddok Blvd. Southtown – MEAPOS

406 – 410 Koplin St. Southtown – MEAPOS

(swipe screen for assets: pg2)

The Old Guard of Zerth

A full value assessment of property cannot be determined. Therefore, an estimate of 2.2m is proposed to cover these losses. It is clear to Henley and Henly Fraud Protection and Insurance that fraud has been committed against Mr. Wadley Saxo, and therefore a payout of 3,500,000 has been approved. By providing a bio-metric signature, Mr. Wadley Saxo verifies his account information and agrees to accept the above settlement.

Wad scratched his head. "So, all my stuff *was* stolen?"

Gustav jumped up to join Wad at the window. He nabbed the tablet and adjusted his glasses. "Goddam. Fuckin' amateur hour up in this bitch. People really need to work on their legalese."

Wad peeked over Gustav's arm. "But Hesh said-"

Gustav pounded the top of Wad's skull with his fist. "Shut up and sign the damned thing."

"But I thought-"

"Doesn't matter. Sign the fucking thing. Argue later."

Wad rubbed his scalp, giving Gustav a dirty look. He reached over Gustav's arm and pressed his thumb into the signature block. He felt a tingle on his skin, then the sides of the tablet light up in green. His head was swimming with questions.

The delivery man retrieved the tablet, storing it in a fannypack around his waist. "MᵃFuggin Delivery Service thanks you for doing business with- um. With Mᵃfuggin Delivery Service. Thank you for- uh. Okay. There's your package. Good day." He bowed a half-dozen times as he backed out of the room.

"Okay," Gustav said. "Now you can argue."

"Okay, what the fuck just happened?" Wad said. His Talkman Blipped.

"I'll tell you what happened," Gustav said, laughing. "Some dumbasses thought it would be a good idea to bring insurance to Zerth. See how long that lasts. But yeah, some idiot insurance company just handed you three million bucks."

"But I thought my account wasn't stolen. And I didn't lose three million bucks. I only lost a million."

"The report didn't say it was stolen. Just said they *concluded* it was. That fuck up is on them. Too bad there aren't any lawsuits here, we'd win that defense a hundred times over. I'm just amazed it happened so quick. Shit hasn't even been a week. Fuck yeah, I like my insurance settlements like I like my women. Fast, sloppy and staggeringly inept."

Meri butted in. "Mind if I attempt to wrap my head around this? Could you please explain."

"Wad's money wasn't stolen, but he got it back, plus a butt-ton more. On the other hand he no longer owns anything, including this office... but now that I think about it, I guess nobody does. As far as the insurance people are concerned, they assume the property was taken by thieves, but since there aren't any thieves, the property is owned by nobody."

"I don't get it," Potato said.

"There's nothing to get," Gustav said, "unless you're Wad, in which case, you get three million bucks. Congrats, buddy. How do you feel?"

Wad did his best to work through the situation in his head. None of it matched up. He tapped his Talkman to find a new balance pending. 3.480.000 lit up in green. He didn't like it. He couldn't understand it and he wanted to put it out of his mind. It was too easy and nobody learned a damned thing.

The Old Guard of Zerth

None of it was earned. In fact, much the opposite. While his friends congratulated him for his success in doing nothing, Wad found himself cursing the situation for invalidating the last four days of his life. Four days of frustration, injury and high emotion, all boiled down to a sickeningly large consolation prize that he would have gotten either way. It was a prize he didn't sign up for, a prize he didn't want. He wanted *his* money, and that wasn't it. The glowing digits on his wrist felt like another man's stash, dirty in his possession and shameful to hold. But that was it, the fight was over. He lost and gained everything.

In that moment, Wad became sick of everything in his immediate field of view. Too much noise. Too many people who thought he should feel good about himself. There was some shit spilled on the rug. The ceiling fan needed some work, but not right then. With that thought he found a moment of solace. The idea of grounding himself in a task that made sense. Spend some time doing something meaningful that can't be scrutinized by an overactive sense of justice. Something to make up for the massive embarrassment on his wrist. More than anything, he needed some time away.

Wad turned to his friends, rubbing the back of his neck. "I've got some stuff to do. I – I gotta go."

Meri perked up. "My man, won't you be attending the celebration – if only for my speech?"

Wad raised his hand. No one questioned the look on his face. He left the office in silence, dreading any possible interruption as he brushed through the curtain and into the light of the day. He made his way across the catwalk, then down into the darkness of the Leaf. It was empty. No surprise there. Who would want to hang out in a bombed-out hole? On top of that, most of the booze was gone from behind the bar. No surprise there, either. The place was as dead as the feeling in his chest. But now he had the means to fix it up, however dirty those means were. He thought about making quick work of it himself, but the proximity to potential interruption was too great. The looming threat of questions he couldn't answer were just above him in the form of three rowdy men with no concept of shame. And so he continued on, through the hole in the wall and out to the street where the bus was parked along the sidewalk.

Wad couldn't think. His life didn't compute. He looked around the street for an answer to his problems but there was nothing there. The one thing that did make sense was a fast ride and a few cold beers. Wad slapped the gullwing door and it lifted with a hydraulic hiss. He threw himself into the drivers seat, shuffled the key into the ignition and twisted. The headfans buzzed to life as he reached between the seats for a beer. The coolant had gone bad in the stash so he had to fish through a foul-smelling pool of liquid for a warm beer. No problem. Wad was long gone, rocketing up the street that shared his name.

The Old Guard of Zerth

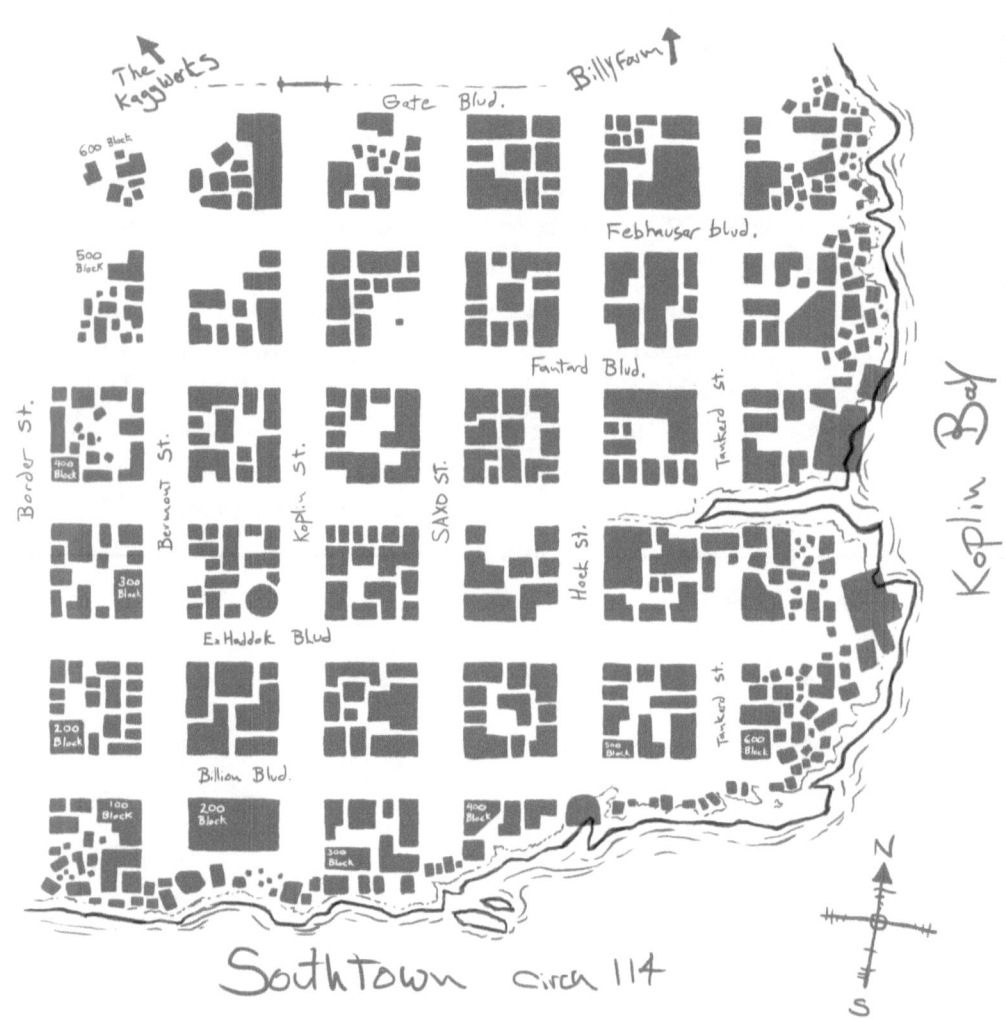

Southtown circa 114

344

Chapter 24

Speech!

Saxo Square was packed with all kinds. Half the town showed up, all mulling around in the shade of munda vines stretched over the square like a canopy. In the center of the crowd was a modest hobbywood stage assembled over the top of the fountain. The water was rerouted to a handful of pumps which supplied dozens of temporary marketeers. They ringed the park in tents, adding a deep red shade to the mix of colors. They were mostly confectionery in nature, catering to the sweet-tooth in everyone. Sugared celery and caramel-dipped sardines were free of charge. Caramel-dipped twigs and gravel for the Legomi in the crowd – all courtesy of the festival sponsors. Stagehands rushed to and fro, managing audio cables and power lines. The 17th anniversary of the Great Arrival was kicking off to a lively start.

Potato and Gustav stayed in the outskirts of the crowd near the corner of the street where personal space was easier to maintain. They had secured a spot near a planter housing some rustic potted vegetation, along with a large, trimmed hobby tree. It was ten years earlier that Gustav had helped Wad plant the same tree, and the sight of it so healthy brought a tickle to the Human's chest. Potato noted the clear segregation of the crowd. Of the Morouni, there were the Cambrio breed, lizard-like and bony; the Darlin breed, rodent-like with bushy tails and hairy cheeks; The Bendos, barely tall enough to spot in the crowd; the Fendralls with their ratlike tails and enormous ears; the Merinall, round and happy; and the Corbinall, timid brick walls. Each group seemed to associate together and not much intermingling went on. Peppered throughout the mass were dozens of Humans and Legomi, with the odd Sectoid for added flavor, but there was no mistaking the core demographic.

A young Morouni took the stage to adjust the microphone stand. He twisted the lock and lowered it to about two feet, then fled into the crowd. A moment later, the announcer appeared. It was a large Legomi, well rooted with more mouth than head. When he spoke, it was clear the mic was not adjusted for him.

"Fellow citizens of Southtown. It is my great pleasure to welcome you all to the 17th annual Southtown celebration of the Great Arrival. We've got fun and games for the whole family, and coming up, we've got a metric fuck-ton of wisdom delivered via verbal vocalization. A myriad of merriment. An inundation of inspiration, a slew of socialization from our speakers here today. Join us in this, the 17th anniversary of the Great Arrival!"

The crowd applauded and the first speaker took the stage. A Bendo by the name of Bert Beriwater. He carried with him a toolbox for no clear reason but to distinguish himself from those who didn't carry a toolbox. Though upon closer inspection, Potato was able to make out a smudged mark across the side. A stamped blue fist.

"Greetings and Salyertations to my fellow brethren," he began. *"Seventeen years ago this day, somethin' extraordn'ary happened. I don't think I need to remind y'all about t'wat it was. But for those of you who ain't with us, or two young or too stupid to figure it out, seventeen years ago, we found our home here. They said t'wasn't possible. They said t'wasn't true. From their lips to your ears, 'twas a fable. And as we stand here on this glorious morning, in the light of eleven suns made to shine their light upon our future, we now know of their lies. It couldn't be more obvious.*

Mighty Rahiem

We came to this promised land pilgrims of a dying world. Refugees from a wicked land, long since having strayed from his almighty grace. And what did they get? Y'all know what they got. Judgment, pure and simple. Ain't no two ways to see it. Yes, Koplin, in his infinite wisdom, smote the heretics from their pedestal. He laid the wicked low and fulfilled his promise to his chosen people. And here we stand.

Now, you might be thinkin' that all was rich and clean in this new world of ours, as it should be. But as we all know, the influence of the evil Billion stretches far beyond the fiery grave. He put roadblocks in our way. He doesn't wanna see us succeed, for he is the enemy of Koplin.

Now I ain't gonna go point'n fingers, but the evidence is all around you. Billion even got his name on a road here in town. You can't tell me his evil ain't felt right here in our beloved city. And that's how he gets ya. Creep in, all slow-like. Tells ya he can make a deal with ya, if you give up a bit of yourself. But we all know, Koplin made us whole, and Billion just wants a piece for himself. Now, we ain't gonna let that happen, are we? No, we are not.

Ya see this here toolbox. This is who we are. This is why the Kaggworks is the blessed friend of the Morouni people. Koplin made him rich so he could give us a place to labor. And so we labor. Ya wanna know why we labor so well? Cause' the Kaggworks is for the Morouni and by the Morouni. It's ours and we are in abundance. And what happens when we are in abundance? That's right, Billion shows up for a piece. He says he wants some. He'll come to you in various forms, under the guise of a friend. A Human, or a Legomi, or a Bugman. But worst of all, he comes under the guise of a fellow Morouni. A Morouni who has lost his way.

These lost brothers wear the clothes of the bugman and the Human. He eats the food of the Legomi and cares not for the history of his ancestors. Now, no offense to y'all Human Logomi Bugmen, but this place is ours, and it was given t'us by Koplin. We're glad to share, but never at the cost of losin' who we are."

The Old Guard of Zerth

Meri pushed through the crowd, making his way to his comrade's holdout. He wasn't hard to spot, maneuvering through a sea of midgets. He greeted the two with a sweaty palm. "Well," Meri said. "I've made myself available. Looks like I'm going on after the keynote speaker. And guess who that is."

"Who's that," Gustav said, picking his teeth.

"Ammison Kagg himself," Meri said, with wide eyes. "Quite the tough act to follow. If I didn't know any better, I'd say they were trying to stonewall me. But never mind that, I'm on the hunt for my benefactors. Be on the lookout for our man Roldolph, if you would be so kind. We've got business to discuss before I take the stage." Meri adjusted his tie to accommodate the heat as the speaker continued.

"-and if it twernt' fer the words of Koplin himself, in the great book of Memwar, we would be lost and hopeless in a world of outsiders. But we have so much evidence that this world t'was meant for us. The simple fact that we all speak the same language. If this world twernt' meant for the Morouni people, why does we all speak Moroush?"

"Pfhh, Rubbish." Meri said, shaking his head. "What in the blazes does that mean?"

"It's the language of your people," Gustav said, swatting the Morouni. "How do you not know the language of your own people."

"Nonsense! Moroush my rear end. Esperanto is our language."

"Esperanto? You kidding? Who told you that?" Gustav said.

"Zsofia, the old hag in the market. The universal language, she says. It's how we all understand each other."

Gustav gave Meri a look. "For a man so eager to rap about culture, it might do you some good to actually know about it."

Mighty Rahiem

"I know enough to know that I don't care to know any more," Meri said, then dropped the conversation – then picked it back up, "If this speech wasn't evidence enough."

"*-and so I make it clear to y'all. Morouni places of business is for and by Morouni. We don't need Morouni business sellin' Human artifacts. We don't need Morouni business sellin' Legomi food. They got their own businesses, let em do it themselves. T'ain't right to give up yer heritage to make a quick buck. That's how Billion gets what he wants. The end.*"

The audience applauded as Bert waddled off the stage, toolbox firmly in hand. As he slipped back into the crowd, Meri caught sight of the symbol on the box. "Blue fist," Meri said.

"Sons of bitches," Potato grumbled.

Meri turned to Potato. "Under normal circumstances, I would be inclined to agree with you, but in this case, I'm not so sure."

"How do you figure," Gustav said.

"My benefactor clued me in, my man. He claims there are actors sporting the icon for the purposes of securing my safety. To fit in with the rabble, so to speak."

Potato scanned the crowd, taking note of dozens of Blue Fist tattoos, patches and buttons. Too many for his one eye to track. "You sure about that?" he said.

"Not entirely," Meri replied, running his claws over his scalp. "But that is exactly why you are here. Isn't that right? Always good to have a backup plan."

Potato nodded.

Moments passed and the crowd was starting to liven up in anticipation of the keynote speaker. Meri wasn't sure who to watch for as nobody knew what he looked like. Word was, he rarely left the confines of the Kaggworks at all, but his influence on the town was undeniable. Three quarters of all the aircraft in the region were meticulously crafted in the bowels of the factory, and jealously guarded by the Morouni people. It wasn't an accident that Carton's Famous Flightpad was the target of so much hostility. A Morouni incorporating Aerian tech? Billion would be proud. Regardless, Meri was interested in seeing the man speak. Anyone that influential must have developed quite a gift for oration.

The crowd hushed as a black hovercar lumbered into the square from the north end. The crowd parted to let it come to a stop near the stage. The driver's door popped open as a large Merinall emerged, swiftly rounding the front of the vehicle to the rear door. He unlatched it, then stood at attention.

From the back of the car, a figure emerged. He was an older man, a Fendrall with his tail crimped and ears tucked under a massive gambler hat. His face looked like a hasty construction of pebbles and chipped bricks. His mustache was on Viagra. He wore all black tweed, which seemed to be painted on. A Black button-up work shirt with buckles instead of buttons, all strained and tight under the stress of a body too far gone to fit neatly. The pants were the same, buckled and braced against age and self-awareness.

Meri watched as the old codger worked his way up to the stage. With a bit of beer, maybe he could see the resemblance to Hackler. Same loping gate, same deep eyes, same over-sized ears. As Kagg reached the microphone, Meri realized the man had no interest in speaking. Not once did he address the crowd with his eyes, instead wavering his attention between the sky and his feet. He took the microphone from its stand and held it jealously, as if to guard it from the mob. Then, he spoke with a voice that could shake the fillings from your teeth.

"Morouni own this world-"

"Hah!" Gustav belted.

The town paused as all eyes turned on the Human.

Mighty Rahiem

Potato jabbed Gustav in the ribs. "The fuck are you doing?"

"Sorry," Gustav mumbled.

"Get the fuck outta here."

Gustav ducked his head as he backed away from the crowd. He gave his friends a timid peace sign as he slinked away towards Meapos Avenue.

The street was quiet, but for the occasional group of townsfolk making their way to the festival. Gustav found a shaded archway with a set of stairs leading to the rooftop seating of 'The Black Swan Lounge'. The place was closed on account of the owners being heavily involved in the festival, leaving Gustav a buffet of seating options. He found a spot near the ledge and slumped down in a cool, carbon-fiber chair beneath a bright red umbrella. From there, he could see the west end of the festivities over the rooftops, along with the leaves of the hobby tree he had just run away from.

As he sat and watched, he noticed some voices coming from street level. Down below, there were a couple of figures lingering across the street in the shade of the alley between Harry's Pillage and the Fodroy's. One big and one small, obscured in the shadows. It was no surprise when Gustav heard the familiar, breathy snicker echoing into the street. It was Roldolph and Hackler.

Gustav felt the urge to say hello, but the voyeur in him forbade it. Not until he was sure there was nothing to gain from his stealthy perch. He shrank down behind the ledge for better listening.

"So, our guys are in place?" Hackler said.

"Got three of em. Fourth one said he wouldn't do it," Roldolph said.

"They all got patches?" Hackler said.

The Old Guard of Zerth

"Yeah, I gave em all the patches. Got one left, though."

"Get rid of it. You don't wanna be caught with that."

Curious, Gustav thought. That must be what Meri was talking about. Plants in the crowd to keep Meri safe, but why? Plenty of folks in the crowd didn't sport the logo at all. He kept listening.

"You sure your pops is gonna do the deal?" Roldolph said.

"After bein' in the center of the shitstorm that's about to go down, he'll sign anything. You wouldn't believe the shit I had to pull just to get him out of his office. Trust me, when the bullets start flying around him, he'll melt like butter. All's I gotta do is give the signal and our lives change forever. The Spearhead will go forward. I guarantee you that."

Gustav's heart began to race. The plants, they weren't to keep Meri safe, they were assassins. And what the fuck is a spearhead? He paused in thought. Despite how neat it would be to watch a shootout from a safe spot, that was his friend they were trying to kill. Not much thought needed. He poked his Talkman, scrolling through the list of contacts until he reached Meri, then began to type.

GUZ: Yo Meri!

GUZ: Found roddolf and hakder.

MERI: yo

GUZ: Yo gotta watchout they gonnda kill yo

MERI: lolwut

MERI: Bzy. Talk to Pottot

Mighty Rahiem

Gustav burred his face in his palm, then scrolled down the list to find Potato's name, marked Samuel Tuber. Gustav couldn't help but chuckle, but quickly brought himself back to panic.

GUZ: Yo Potot

Potato: Yo

GUZ: They donna kill Meri. Wathout for guys with blue fist

Potato: lolwut

GUZ: Blu Fsts got asssins in teh crowd gonna kill meri

Potato: ther to many like hundreds

GUZ: no ther like only 4

Potato: there more than that like a lot more

"Fuck!" Gustav yelled, then covered his mouth. He poked his head over the ledge to meet eyes with Roldolph, who was staring directly at him.

"Guz, old buddy, is that you?"

Shit, Gustav thought. Oh well. If he couldn't prevent the assassins, maybe he could stop Hackler from giving the signal. Just keep em occupied. He poked his head over the ledge. "Heyo, Roldolph. Got a great view up here. Come on up, but be careful, these chairs aren't too sturdy. Mine just busted and I hurt my butt! That's why I yelled because I landed on my butt!"

"We'll be right up!"

Good job, Gustav thought. Way to cover your ass. Now you've just got to break a chair before the two men arrive, otherwise they might get suspicious. He got to work, kicking a chair over and yanking at it with both hands. No dice, the weld wouldn't budge. The chair was just too quality. Across the street, he could hear applause. Kagg's speech must have ended. Not much time. He gave the carbon fiber one last yank as he could hear voices coming up the stairs. Fuck it, Gustav thought, just make a scene. He hoisted the chair over his head and let out a primal scream just as Roldolph poked his head into view. "Substandard junk!" He flung the chair over the ledge and into the road, then turned to greet the MERCs with a smile.

Potato was having trouble keeping track of all the Blue Fists. There were just too many of them, but at some point, he was going to have to let go of Meri's shirt.

"It's okay, my man. I trust you'll do the job," Meri said, removing Potato's fist from his sleeve. The crowd was getting antsy and he still had a job to do, despite the danger. He mustered his courage and made his way towards the steps. Along the way, he could feel the eyes of the crowd poking at him, some friendly, others not so much. As he took the stage, the crowd settled down. A veritable eye of the storm, as far as Meri could tell. It can only go downhill from here. Nonetheless, he was going to speak his mind to all that wished to hear. It's all he had.

Meri grasped the mic stand, twisting the lock and extending it to accommodate his height. He grunted deliberately, searching for his voice in the monitors. The rumble echoed over the crowd. He scanned his memory for the opening of his speech, which he only half memorized. In times like this, he preferred to wing it. Only keep the key points in mind and let the rest slide out naturally. After all, he was only speaking his mind. As long as that were true, he couldn't say anything wrong. All eyes were on him as he began:

Mighty Rahiem

"There are those among us who, despite all evidence of the contrary, believe that unity cannot in any way benefit our flowering society. Sticklers and try-hards for chaos slide through the cracks and emerge in our presence with heads full of fuel to ignite the flames of discord. This behavior cannot stand if we, as a unified people, wish to thrive. And so I tell you now, lovers of hate, history will not lie on your behalf!"

Meri felt electric in every way. The Morouni's words sent shocks through the crowd, eliciting yelps and hollers from his supporters and galvanizing his detractors into huddles, no doubt whispering violent thoughts.

"And while it's true that I myself had not yet been birthed at the time of the great arrival, I assure you that my heart beats the same Morouni blood as the rest. Brethren we are, and brethren we will forever be, for in the years since the great arrival, I myself have harbored nothing but love and gratitude for my family ties."

The roil of the crowd fueled Meri's speech and elevated his energy to unnatural levels. In those rare situations, when all ears hung on his every punctuation, his words flowed like water, spilling across hot rocks and giving off a steam of appreciation that super-charged his ego. He paid close attention to not let the excitement cloud his speech as it would be too easy to start barking orders.

Gustav was uneasy, despite his behavior. On one side was Roldolph Rimbaud, snickering through his breath. Hackler on the other, rested against the dobistone with arms crossed, laughing it up as the Human held their attention with his stories of conquest. The mood was jovial.

"-and so I tell the girl, that's not your bike, this is your bike!" Gustav cupped his hand around his crotch and wiggled. Roldolph doubled over.

The Old Guard of Zerth

Hackler cleared his throat, letting the laughter die down naturally. "That's a good one, Hu-man. Roldo wasn't wrong about you. Anyway, I got some business I gotta attend to. If you'll excuse me." He turned to look out over the rooftops to the festival below.

Gustav knew he needed to act quickly. He could hear the boom of Meri's voice over the speakers. It was just a matter of time before the shit hit the fan. He needed something to hold the MERC's attention permanently. He thought hard, trying to recall anything from what he had overheard.

"Spearhead," Gustav spat.

Hackler swung around.

"Yeah, that's right. Operation Spearhead."

"The fuck are you talking about?" Hackler said. His lips drew back, revealing a bear-trap of teeth.

"I'm in on it. Hell, I'm with you guys all the way. Take a look." Gustav rolled up his sleeve, revealing the tattoo on his shoulder. A circular cross-hair with a slash through it. No aim. The universal sign of the wanderer.

Roldolph lumbered over, throwing a huge arm over Gustav's shoulder. "Holy shit, Guz, I had no idea you were a MERC."

"Bullshit," Hackler barked. "MERC my scaly ass. That ink is new. Look at it." He poked at Gustav's shoulder with a claw.

"That's cause I got it on Earth," Gustav said. "Every time I die, it's like new again. Just like everything else. Trust me, I've been a MERC for years. Now, I wanna let you know, Spearhead is safe and sound. All quiet on the western front, as we Humans say."

"Is it, now?" Hackler said. "That's good to know. Now tell me, what's your position with *Spearhead*. Where do you 'sit' so to speak?"

Gustav let out a chuckle. "Well, I'd be lying if I said I wasn't a big influence on the whole thing. I mean, someone had to come up with it."

"Guz," Roldolph said. "What are you-"

"-Don't," Hackler interrupted. He calmly produced a large knife from his knickers, then waved it casually. The pregnant pause caused a lump in Gustav's throat. He couldn't respond if he wanted to. Hackler scowled. "I see what you're doing, Human. It ain't gonna work. So, the way I see it, you got two choices. You either leave this roof on your own, or you stay here with a hole in your belly where you'll get to watch your friend become Swiss cheese. The choice is yours. But I'm telling you now, there's no way your friend gets outta this alive."

Gustav turned to Roldolph, who shrugged with a dumb smile.

Hackler followed with a shrug of his own before tapping his Talkman. "Go ahead, boys." He sheathed his knife and rested on the ledge, smiling at Gustav, who took off running down the stairs.

"We cannot lean on our own small minded assessments of the world to judge for the rest, as one would look backwards through a telescope. It is in our collective best interest to toss aside our personal views and remain open to, not only all things new, but all things old that remain worthy of mass consumption, and toss aside out personal gripes; for history is the god of impartial judgment."

A bottle hit the stage and a segment of the crowd dog-piled the attacker, signaling other dissidents to follow suit. Meri continued speaking over the ruckus of his audience as the disturbance began to grow outward. Potato saw it all from his stage-side vantage. He worked himself up, never taking his eye off the action. Meri plowed forward, hiding a crazed smile. He was in the moment and he wasn't going to let a little violence change that.

"-and if our challenge cannot be met, the doom of us all is surely in the cards. Can we not see our faults and rush to repair what has been done, or will we forever be known as 'the ones who almost made it'. No, my friends, my brethren, I believe in a brighter future. A future that includes us all. A future without segregation."

A fuzzy fist raised with a pistol in its grip. It was an assassin. Potato was on the move. He heaved himself into the sea of bodies, watching the weapon take aim. He moved on, plowing the crowd aside with the strength of his arms. The gun came down and the crowd had now seen it as well. Hands grasped for the weapon, dragging the attacker sideways and throwing off his aim. Potato continued, charging through the mass. There was a scuffle as more Blue Fists tried to free the assassin from the grip of the crowd.

Potato broke through and the attacker was in sight. He quickened his pace and readied himself for a full on tackle, but a glint of chrome flashed in the corner of his eye.

"Gotcha, Spud."

Potato spun around to find himself staring down the barrel of a revolver. The moment went silent as the gun clicked... then shook and clicked again. The chrome of the pistol lowered to reveal a terribly frustrated Carbon Dale, wiggling his gun side to side. "Goddam Chinese junk!" Potato's eye sharpened and he dove after the cowboy. A shot rang out, but not from Dale. It came from behind! Meri grunted through the microphone as Potato turned to see his friend reeling from the shock of a bullet to the chest. The assassins were in all directions.

Mighty Rahiem

Gustav barged into the crowd, hollering for Meri to get off the stage. The second gunman was dragged to the ground by livid supporters, beaten into the cobblestone. Then, a third gunman appeared – west end of the crowd. The man took aim as Gustav called out. "Meri, get down!"

Meri growled in pain, squeezing his wound with his claws. It burned deeper. He let lose a gut-twisting howl into the microphone' his pain echoed through the speakers, announcing the havoc of the park to the whole town. He was finished with his speech, now he wanted blood. He reeled as the pain stabbed through his body like a hundred knives. He reached into his vest and yanked his sidearm from a blood soaked holster, flinging it around and letting loose in the direction of the third attacker. The crowd scattered, screaming in every direction as the man on stage blasted away at random. Meri let up and fell to his knees in biting agony. Then, the third shot came. All Meri heard was a zip and pop. Hot blood poured down his cheek and he fell to his side. His ear was on fire.

It was a stampede. A bomb-blast of bodies emanating from the stage, scattering like a shock wave. Gustav braced against the force as he tried to weather the onslaught, but was dragged under. He felt the kick and stomp of a thousand feet across his body. He curled up, covering his head as feet struck and tripped over him. It was the loudest thing he had ever heard.

Potato stood with Dale's face in his hands. The Human was out cold, dangling limp from a meaty fist. The Legomi didn't know what was going on. He scanned the storm of bodies as they pounded against him and bounced. What was he supposed to be doing? He moved against the wave, splitting it down the middle and making his way to the stage where Meri lay in a pool of blood. He dropped Dale's unconscious body and knelt over the Morouni, rustling his shoulder. The Morouni turned with clenched teeth. "First day on the job, my man?" Meri eeked.

Potato didn't know how to respond.

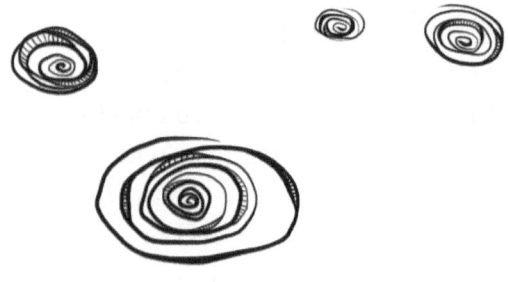

Chapter 25

Hazy Afternoon of the Soul

The city he built was far behind but Wad kept his foot on the accelerator. Northbound, Traderoute 1, speeding through the shadows of Meaposian peaks as they rolled across the farmlands. It wasn't long before the last of the greenery was behind him, sinking beneath a shallow hillside. All that lie ahead was a parched highway and two-hundred miles of wheatgrass before the next settlement, a chicken shack with a few dozen permanent residents. It didn't have a name. At least, it wasn't marked on any map. That far out, name's weren't too important. To the east, a little hutch-town called Bostoe was geographically closer but it was off the main road. An unwelcome deviation to those who valued a smooth ride and the shade of the highlands. And besides, nobody liked Bostoe.

As the sunlight peeled over the asphalt, Wad recalled the events of the last few days. He rolled them over in his head, examining every misstep, every flaw and every choice of word, only to conclude the sum of his repulsive behavior, without an ounce of rectification, somehow equated to a net neutral standing with karma. The math didn't add up. The consequence for his bad behavior was a cosmic shrug. The thought gnawed at his chest as he felt he had stumbled across something deeply wrong. Did others know about this? Was he the first to make the discovery? If there truly were no repercussion for acting like a monster, why bother keeping up appearances? Could he just drop the act and give in to base urges of violence and depravity? Was it an act at all? It was a dirty thought, but one he was willing to work on. After all, he was pretty good at wrecking things.

The Old Guard of Zerth

At a point, Wad drove without a thought of where he would end up. Something would surely block his path, at which time he might just plow into it. See what damage that might cause. Every rock formation and dry creek bed was a potential target for his bus, if only he could dredge up the nerve to twist the wheel at just the right moment. Make a bus-sized landmark of destruction, peppered with bits of leaves and guts. Call it Wad's End. Put a sign up. No doubt he'd survive to charge admission. The humor of it brought him back to his senses and he realized that no amount of anger could bring him to off himself that marvelously. He wasn't the type to go out with a bang in a spectacular, fiery crescendo, he was the type to wither away quietly without fanfare. At least, he hoped so. He then thought about driving into the water, until deciding that he'd probably end up having a decent life at the bottom of the bay. That isn't what he wanted. He wanted someone to slap him.

-785.8/-95.8. The dashboard lit up with a warning. A little red indicator light above the speedometer. It blinked in the shape of a lightning bolt and made a nasally blippy noise. It was the battery cell for the forward-left head fan loosing steam. The alternator must be shot. He could manually swap the cables to the reserve battery, but that would only take him so far. A healthy head fan battery could carry you a thousand miles before it petered-out, but the reserve wasn't meant for longevity. His Talkman chirped, but he ignored it.

Wad pull the bus to a halt in a patch of wheatgrass where he popped the gullwing and took a stroll around, stopping at the rear for his toolbox which he kept secure in the aft weapon pod. Upon reaching the passenger side, he was reminded that it was riddled with bullet holes. Hundreds of them. No doubt a few shots managed to breach the armor and connect with some core components, but there was no way to know unless he had a look at the undercarriage. Under normal circumstances, he could lift the bus by throwing it into hover, but if one fan went out, he

362

would be mashed into pie. He opted for the more invasive, yet safer method of cutting the driver-side fans and just letting the bus tip over onto its side.

From there, Wad wrenched around, removing the inner head-fan housing, which came apart in his hands along with chunks of blackened metal with that distinct, acid smell. He found the battery cables and followed them to the voltage regulator, then the alternator. It was half dust. Shot in the literal sense. He could swing a bypass to the reserve which would take him a little farther. A hundred miles, maybe.

Wad pushed to his feet and looked around. To the east, nothing but wheatgrass curling over a crude horizon. To the west, the imposing silhouette of Mt. Jumbie with its characteristic salute, towering over the Meaposian range like knife. Without consulting his Talkman, Wad knew his only stop could be Bostoe. Due east from the peak of Mt. Jumbie by a hundred and twenty miles. Maybe he could make it. No use in dawdling. Wad wrenched the battery cables off the terminals and uncoiled them to reach the reserve. He tied them down tight, then checked the amperage. All was clean. He then scrambled up the side of the bus and lowered himself through the open gullwing, where he was able to squirm into the driver's seat to reach the ignition switch somewhere around his ankles.

Strapping himself in sideways, Wad engaged the driver's side head-fans and the bus began to shift across the ground, then slowly right itself. The under-cage bounced hard against the dirt as Wad could hear the sound of dozens of bottles of beer breaking inside the coolers. He checked the beer between the pilot seats, finding two or three that were unharmed, so he popped one and let it fizz before gulping it down. The indicator in the dash seemed to recognize a connection to a reserve battery, with the lightning bolt indicator glowing blue. If he could make it to Bostoe, they'd surely have a replacement battery. He bet his life on it.

The Old Guard of Zerth

About forty miles out, Wad began to entertain into the technicals of procuring a new battery. What if they didn't have one? What if they sold him a bunk battery? What if he didn't have enough money to pay for... scratch that. Wad's swollen bank account brought him back to the same feelings of rage that put him in the bus to begin with. He didn't want to use that money. He didn't want to touch it. It was tainted, dirty. Maybe he didn't need it. Maybe he would entertain the life of a bandit. Maybe he could roll into town, demanding negligible electronic equipment at gunpoint. Then maybe he'd rob a parking lot. Maybe he'd throw rocks at old people. What did a battery cost? Two bucks? Maybe they'd just let him have one. That thought made him even more angry. Of course they'd let him have one. Nothing ever goes wrong, does it? Nobody ever calls him out for his bullshit – except Amelia, but she doesn't count. Would he end up killing a bunch of people in Bostoe? How many would die? How many people lived in Bostoe? Six? Twelve? Thirty? Didn't matter, they'd be mulch before dinner. He'd do them in by accident with a rogue fart and everyone would be cool with it. Hell, they'd like him for it. He'd probably end up with more money. That's it, fuck Bostoe. Wad slammed on the break. Nobody likes Bostoe anyway.

Wad took a deep breath and looked around. The peaks were out of sight. Everything was out of sight. Wheatgrass on every horizon. His Talkman blipped a second time, encouraging him to dig his heels in. He cut the controls to every secondary power hog he could think of; climate control, interior lighting, radio, refrigeration, and lastly, navigation. He cranked the wheel and did a few doughnuts until he was certain he had no idea which direction he was facing, then gunned the fans into oblivion. Care to the wind, determined to make a mess of himself. Wherever he ended up is where he would be.

Mighty Rahiem

About a half hour later, Wad found himself regretting his decision. Not due to the recklessness of it, but for the mind-numbing bore. He thought it would be more exciting, but the endless blanket of beige and copy-paste hills did nothing to stimulate his desire for self-destruction. It just made him tired. He went for another beer, popping the lid of the cooler to meet a wafting, skunky smell that filled the cabin. He wallowed his hand around in lukewarm juice, nabbing the last unbroken bottle that left his hand sticky on the steering wheel. Wad's journey into the abyss was turning out to be more like a leap into mild annoyance than anything profound. The sentiment was compounded as he made his way over a hill, only to find himself entering the outskirts of Bostoe.

There it sat, quiet and peaceful in the cool breeze rolling off the bay. A dozen or so chunky buildings flanking the coastline. There were some people sweeping their front porches, others were mulling around in the shade of a thicket in the middle of town. Some boats floated around in the fucking water. Wad threw his hands up. It was a hell of a middle finger. Come get rescued, Wad. We're here to make everything fine again, like we always do. They even had a sign up. It said "Welcome to Bostoe." Wad was certain that if he got closer, he would read the words "Free batteries for anyone running away from their problems." Fuck Bostoe. And with that, the reserve battery cut out with a whine. The front end of the bus slumped to the ground, spilling Wad's beer into a puddle in his lap.

With a renewed appreciation for irony, Wad took the wheel. Without power to the forward head-fan, he wasn't going anywhere properly, so he might as well go improperly. No need to conserve power any more. He cranked the AC to max and threw the bus into hover. The horizon sank below the windshield as the bus lifted off the ground in a wide spin. He couldn't drive straight, but that didn't mean he couldn't drive at all. As the bus spiraled out of control, Wad could see the tops of buildings whir by. Maybe he could manage enough control to dive-bomb Bostoe. Fuck that place. As he came around again, he could see some of the townsfolk emerging from their homes. They were gathering into groups and pointing at him. If he could get the bus spinning the other direction, maybe he could roll down the window to yell something profane, but alas, the counter-clockwise nature of his plight wouldn't allow for it.

After about ten minutes of flying in an angry circle, Wad started to question his motivation. The AC suite was making his wet lap uncomfortably cold, and the whole town of Bostoe was watching him throw a fit in a flying bus. They were taking pictures and laughing. He couldn't help but think back a few days to the last time his bus was stuck in a circular motion. He was still going in circles. No more, Wadley, just let it go. He cut the engine and let the bus glide safely to the ground. It bumped to a soft patch where he burred his face against the steering wheel.

Wad let a mad chuckle escape. There was no fighting it. Getting angry would undoubtedly result in more good things coming his way. Something in the air made it so. He let out a sigh. From the sticky driver's seat of his bus, he looked out across the bay. Somewhere over the horizon were the cliffs of the northern shear, and beyond, the staircase of red stone descending into a sea of sand. The Burning Basin, home of Aerie Tower. The same tower he fled from seventeen years prior. He had weathered the scorching sands, climbed the staircase and eventually ended up in the care of Hesh of Ender. What a strange journey it was. But once again, he found himself running. Not from the chains of slavery, but of the excesses of freedom. If it weren't so real, it would be laughable – and if it weren't so ridiculous, he might be taking it more seriously. His first escape was so harrowing, so close to the heart. The kind of story people tell their kids. It truly meant something. And what was this? This was just sad. Nobody would be telling their kids about this. Wad was interrupted by a pounding on the window. It was a well dressed man with wild gray hair under a floppy hat. He was holding a backup battery. He pointed at it as if Wad didn't know what it was. Fuck Bostoe.

The bus rocketed southbound along the coast. It wasn't a smooth ride, but Wad felt the lumps and shudders were a fitting compliment to his mood. His Talkman peeped for the third time without his attention. He didn't want to hear it. He was still trying to beat himself up but was so far unsuccessful, and the thought of leaving the task unfinished weighed a bit too heavy. He hadn't bothered to thank the old man from Bostoe. Not verbally. He didn't have the energy to fake sincerity so he paid the man a hundred-thousand bucks. It was the only way he know how to properly dispose of his cursed stack. Just get rid of it. It felt good in the moment, like he had managed to dump a bit of the weight on his back, but there was so much left.

As Wad was lost in thought, he hadn't noticed the gain in altitude over the last half-hour. It was a gradual climb, easy to miss but for the sinking coastline a few miles out. It wasn't until he found a break in his wanderings that he realized the shore was out of sight completely, replaced by dots of shrubbery and white boulders in grassy nests, scattered as if they were placed deliberately. With a lump, the bus passed over what must have been a northern tributary of Billycreek. The south end marked the boundaries of Billyfarm on the outskirts of town, so he figured he must be getting close to home. The thought should have caused concern, as there was still much to dwell on, but the scenery took president. Mounds of green rose and fell around him until he felt the urge to ease off the gas, so as to not let it pass by so quickly.

The Old Guard of Zerth

A light dew began to form across the windshield, rolling off the glass in beads, and once fog was evident, Wad decided to pull over and roll down the window for a taste. Immediately, the leaves on his head reacted to the sweet air, fluffing up and giving him a jolt of energy. It must have been someone's private garden. There were flowers and bushes sprouting against great ivory veins of stone that extended into the mist like hedgerows. It was too uniform to be incidental, but at the same time, too natural to have been planned. It occupied an uncanny middle ground that Wad had never seen, as if nature itself was attempting to imitate the structure of civilization. It couldn't have been the farmlands, as the Traderoute was easily twenty miles to the west, so what was it?

As Wad stepped to the ground, his foot sank into a blanket of clover. It was wet, almost saturated, leaving him with a feeling that he was disturbing something pristine. It was cooler there, and the mist hung in place as if time had stopped. As he moved eastward through the fog, he soon found himself at the edge of a sharp drop into the bay below. To the south, he could see a swirl of clouds forming in the rainbelt. They curled around the end of the bluff like a tail, dispersing as they reached the shore. Wad figured the mesa must be some kind of dead-zone for wind. The Meapotian mountains funneled wind southward, which was the cause of most of the arid nature of the peninsula, but this spot was just the right height to touch the rainbelt. It was like a ceiling for wind that the air currents avoided.

Despite only living fifty miles south, Wad was amazed that he had missed the place in all his travels. Surely, someone had claimed it by that point, but there was no evidence of development. He approached a vein of the white rock that seemed to burst from the ground like exposed bone. He ran his fingers across it, finding it to be quite rough. No weathering, and certainly no tool marks, yet somehow so uniform. Perfect rows of stone, spaced evenly about thirty feet apart. There must have been a dozen of them, trailing off into the mist. Clumps of white flowers lined each span, but only on the north side. The south were what looked like pygmy Hobbytrees, no more than a foot tall. Natural bonsai. They were quite stocky in the trunk, as well, leading Wad to believe the roots grew deeper than usual. Easy to believe in such a place, but nowhere else. Odd to think with all of the air travel in the area, nobody thought to dip down to plant a flag of ownership. Or maybe they did? He consulted his Talkman for an explanation.

PROX/GEO SEARCH: CURRENT LOCATION (-649.1/-199.4) 78°F – RELATIVE HUMIDITY: 72% - WIND SPEED: 0mph S/SE. TRAVEL SPEED: 0mph.

DESIGNATION: WILDERNESS – NEAREST SETTLEMENT: BILLYFARM(-640.3/-238.8)

The bluff must be at the northern edge of the farmlands, Wad thought. It's possible the ring of clouds concealed it well enough that nobody thought to look there. From above, It might have just looked like an extension of the fields. Hard to say, Wad wasn't a pilot, but he was an explorer – at least he was in another life. Back then, he wouldn't hesitate to register the land in his name. Slap a tag on it and upload his conquest to the mapnet. Saxo Bluffs, perhaps, or maybe Wad's Shelf? He thought back to the readout on the contract he signed. Big words spelling out each and every piece of the world he had ever laid claim to. But they were all lost now. The pain dug deeper than any he had felt in recent memory. The realization that his entire history had been erased. Sure, he could meticulously sort through each of his properties, one by one, re-registering plots and acres, then contesting their ownership against an absent defendant, but he couldn't muster the thought. He made those things with his own two hands, built them up. He did it for a purpose, and the purpose has been served. There was no joy in it, only aggravation, and the act of doing it all over again only made him feel sick to his stomach. Like a greedy old man hoarding his spoils. But maybe he could plant his flag in one last place. Somewhere that wouldn't be occupied by others. Somewhere a final purpose could never be realized. Somewhere that was all his.

Wad got to work on his Talkman, doing his best to avert his eyes from the shameful account balance. He skipped right over it, accessing the mapnet and connecting to the property registry. With the tap of his finger, the deed was done. The bluff was his... then it asked him for a name. Ah hell, Wad thought. Where the fuck am I? What is this place called? He looked around for some kind of inspiration. There was almost too much to take in. It was everything he could ever hope to enjoy, all in one perfect spot, far away from the rest of the world. Wad's mind drifted to his friends back in Southtown. What would they call it? Meri might say something wordy and overly complicated, whereas Potato would probably just call it green. Then Wad thought back to Gustav in Ender. The way his face lit up when he walked into Hesh's house. The man was in heaven. No, that's not what he would call it, but it did give him an idea. Gustav may have all the money in the world, but Wad would own Everything Else. He chuckled to himself as he typed.

Once the name was secure, Wad found himself staring at the landing screen of his Talkman. His account balance was there, as were the q-links to various networks. At the top was a notification.

4x) MISSED CONTACTS

Wad let out a huff. He made a quick mental scan to assess his mood, finding that his aggression had been stripped away by the surroundings. He had managed to quiet the dumb beast in his heart, at least for the time being. Any further aggravation could be dealt with in the company of his friends. In fact, he was almost excited to get back to town to share his discovery. With a bit more confidence, he poked the notifications button. The screen flashed. It was Potato. Three calls in two hours, then another message that didn't seem to register. Either way, no need to panic. He'd be home soon enough. He made his way back to the bus, satisfied to return when he felt it was necessary. Before climbing through the gullwing, he took a final look around with the intent of committing as much to memory as he could. Not that he was afraid of loosing it, rather, he wanted to make it permanent in his mind. It was a gold nugget in his heart, and he hadn't even left yet.

As Wad was settling into the pilot seat, he thought about the best method of exiting the mesa. He didn't want to leave a trail of blasted clover in his wake, so with caution in the forefront, he turned the key. The headfans buzzed to life and the bus found balance. He scaled up the clearance between the bus and the ground with a deliberate cranking of the altitude shiftier, hoping an additional foot or so would allow for a less invasive blast of air beneath him. Without warning, there was a spitting sound, then a whine. The blue indicator light popped on once again, and with no time to react, the front end slammed to the ground, throwing Wad violently out of his seat as the bus began to up-end. He regained his senses to find himself crammed between the windshield and the dashboard. The bus was digging itself into wet soil!

Wad panicked. He spun himself around on his belly, desperately reaching for the break with one hand and the fan shifter with the other. The sound of plasteel scraping against stone terrified him even further. The bus had dug itself to bedrock! Wad shrieked, cursing his luck as he twisted at the fan shifter from his backwards vantage, hoping to cut the power to the rear fans, only to hear the sound of ramping tension to the back end. He had pushed it into overdrive!

The Old Guard of Zerth

There was no stopping the forward motion at that point. He could only grab hold of something as the bus flipped over, ripping his hands from the shiftier and tossing him swiftly against the glass.

Wad recovered from the shock to his cranium. There was a deep vibration moving through his whole body, and he seemed to be laying in a pool of warm liquid. The smell was overwhelming. Beerwater. He couldn't make sense of his surroundings, but could clearly hear what sounded like crackling earth in all directions. The cabin was dark, save for the occasional break of sunlight from above. He was on his back, head pushed harshly into the overhead AC unit which was blasting cold air into his scalp. The bus was upside-down and moving. He craned his neck against the windshield to see waves of dirt-clods and clover rolling under the glass. He calmed himself, doing his best to replace his rapid heartbeat with a more manageable impotence. No amount of flailing was going to do any good. He was making a mess of things once again.

As he struggled to right himself, Wad was reduced to sloshing through beerwater on all fours. All that wasted booze. He moved across the roof until he could reach the headrest of the pilot seat, doing his best to avoid jagged bits of broken bottles that floated around the cabin like caltrops. Brown goop dripped abundantly from the open cooler between the seats, and he could see that all of the coolers had dumped their contents into the mix. Beer, whiskey, bourbon, scotch – every drink with a pulse was blended into a foul, quivering pool around his knees. The upholstery was fucked.

He found a good enough spot, at which point he kicked his feet out to lay on his back for a better view of the controls. The vibration was stronger there, feeling like it was pulsing directly into his skin. He had always wanted to swim in a pool of liquor, but the circumstances made the idea a bit less appealing. Either way, he had a clear view of the fan shiftier, confirming his suspicion. He had thrown it into overdrive. Figures. He leaned up to grab the shifter, bumping it into idle. The fans murmured and the shaking stopped. A moment later, the only sound was that of the sloshing of dangerbooze.

With a bit of effort, Wad was able to pop the latch of the gullwing, which could only open so far against a wall of dirt. He squeezed through the gap, pulling himself out of the darkness and onto the greasy undercarriage of the bus. As his eyes adjusted to the light, the devastation became clear. The bus had carved a gash through the clover field. Plowed right through it. Two, maybe three-hundred feet of maimed earth. Possibly more, as he couldn't see where it started through the fog. As Wad surveyed the carnage, he didn't know what to think. He was stuck between emotions. Flattened by a sense of deserved irony, while at the same time, traumatized by the sight of blasted tranquility. Of all the things he felt, the only feeling he recognized clearly was shame.

Wad plopped down on the transmission block, not feeling too keen about sharing the discovery with his pals anymore. As he stared into the dirt, a sense of outrage took over. If this was karma kicking back, why did it have to take its revenge on such an undeserving target? The mesa was an innocent in all this. Its only crime was welcoming him with open arms. Letting him partake of its beauty. Smelling its sweet mist and breathing its loving air, and this is what happens. The thought then occurred to him that if he had never claimed the land, it may have escaped his fuckery. He settled on that being the truth, then kicked himself mentally for the crime. It was his fault, and no, he wasn't going back to town a changed man. At least, not changed for the better. Maybe a bit more resentful. A bit more estranged. It was then that he was reminded of the fact that he was sitting on an upside-down bus with a busted headfan. He wasn't going anywhere at all.

The Old Guard of Zerth

Wad's Talkman blipped again. Potato, once more. He didn't want to talk to Potato. He didn't want to have to muddle through an explanation as to why the bus was fucked and he had to walk home, sour from an embarrassing journey where he managed to not only worsen his mood, but also wreck a pristine gift of nature in the process. No, he wasn't going to talk to Potato... but what about the other message? The mystery ID? Wad tapped the notification.

MISSED MESSAGE: 1 – SENDER: 004231

Who the fuck was that? And how the hell did they get their hands on such an old Talkman? It only had six digits. And why didn't they change the name from the default? The anomaly mucked up his brain enough that he almost forgot that a message had been sent at all. He tapped the text, opening the file.

HELLO SUNSTRUCK HOW ARE YOU BEEN IM BEEN FINE IM IN TEMPEG FOR THE END OF THE WEEK FOR BUILDING A PUMP FOR WATER THATS ACROSS THE WATER FROM YOU NOW DO YOU WANT TO MEET WE CAN CATCH UP ITS BEEN ALONG TOME

Sunstruck? The only person that called him that was Chelli, and she had better diction than that garbage. Unless... it was someone he hadn't seen in a very long time. Was it possible? When was the message sent? Threesday? Today was the last day to meet. All sense of self-pitty went out the window as Wad realized who the message was from.

Chapter 26

Resolute

Gustav had Meri in stitches. The coffee table rumbled with every joke the Human told, followed by a wince of pain. Gustav tied off the fishing line in Meri's sagging pectoral, then cut the thread with his teeth. He stepped back to admire his work, bobbing his head to the tune of **The Model – Kraftwerk** on low. "Well, you've still got a bullet in there, cos I'm a shit doctor. But it's okay because Potato is a shit bodyguard, you're a shit speaker and Wad's shit at answering calls."

Potato was still deep in thought about the whole ordeal. He hid behind a bottle on the couch, focused on nothing out the window.

Meri hopped from the table and started to roll his shoulder but quickly decided against it. "Feels like a bug inside me," He said, laughing, then took a man-sized swig of scotch. He nabbed his beater from the couch and wriggled into it, poking at the pinky-sized hole in the shoulder ringed in dry blood. He then gestured for Gustav to help him with his suspenders. The bandage over his ear popped loose but he failed to give a shit.

"Well, that's that," Gustav said, "As your personal physician, I recommend you don't do jack shit for about two weeks."

"As a shit patient of your admittedly shit healing skills, I'll opt for a second opinion. Potato, my man, what do you think?"

"Huh?"

"Lucky for me, I don't take medical advice from bodyguards. I think I'll just get back to work." Meri snapped his suspenders and regretted it.

"Wounded or not," Gustav said, dropping his doctor act, "I suggest we take a moment to reflect. Roldolph tried to have you killed, which doesn't seem very friendly to me. Whatever hair-brained scheme they cooked up, you stepped right in it. I don't know what it was all about, but I caught them talking about something called the Spearhead plan. When I repeated it, the little one got all bent out of shape."

Meri rubbed his shoulder gingerly. "Ammison Kagg's son. Hackler, he's called, and the Spearhead is their goal. Ammison's goal, I should say. The two of them only mean to coax the old man into building it."

"What is it, some kind of super weapon, or something?" Gustav chuckled.

"It's an escape method," Meri said. "A ship large enough to transport a million Morouni off-world, at which point, they can resume the old ways of living. I must say, I am all for it. Best to be rid of them for good."

Potato entered the conversation without saying a word.

Gustav took a seat, scratching his head. "I don't get it. Why would they have to convince the old man into building it in the first place? Sounds to me like that's exactly what a guy like him would want."

"Uncertain," Meri said, shaking his head. "Though I do know Hackler and Roldolph stand to gain much from the plan. They claim to sit on a large deposit of Polerite far to the east, along with the ability to extract it."

"So, the MERCs get rich by selling all that Polerite and dear old dad gets to fly away. It's a win-win, as far as I can tell."

"And you see why I was so easily duped," Meri said with a raised eyebrow. "The only angle of the plot that evades me is my death. I cannot see the reason."

"The old man don't wanna go," Potato said.

"Why wouldn't he want to go?" Gustav scoffed. "He clearly hates everyone. He's built an entire industry around excluding everyone but the people who agree directly with him. He's got the Blue Fist bombing stuff for him. He's a goddamned super villain."

"Didn't used to be like that," Potato said.

Gustav shrugged, waiting for the Legomi to expand on his statement but nothing was said. "Nothing? Okay, then. I say Fuck the subtle approach. If Kagg is hiring MERCs to blow up buildings, I say we flip the script on the old fart. Let's blow up the Kaggworks."

"No," Meri grumbled. "We will not be taking that approach."

"Why the hell not?" Gustav said, waving his arms. "You can't ignore the facts. The guy is a menace. We need to take him out before he hurts anyone else."

Meri took a swig, then took a deep breath. "Is it the man you hate or his actions?"

"Both, fuck it," Gustav replied.

"So, you know Kagg well enough to have determined his character? Tell me, my man, how long have the two of you been acquainted."

"Oh, fuck you, Meri," Gustav groaned. He slumped to the couch with crossed arms.

"You miss the point. We are blind to Kagg's motivations. All we are witness to is the results of his actions, which we find reprehensible. That being said, to entertain the same actions would make us equally reprehensible, would it not? Are we nothing more than dumb beasts engaged in a shit-slinging contest? I certainly hope not. I, for one, would prefer to take the high road."

"And what would that be?" Gustav said.

"I'm going to the Kaggworks to speak with Ammison Kagg."

"Sounds like a plan," Potato grunted. "Go hang out with all those guys who just shot you. Be sure to bring me a souvenir."

"I feel I should do this," Meri replied with a stone face. "I cannot in good conscience let this slide without first attempting to open a dialogue. If they want me dead, let them explain themselves."

"Dude, we know why they want you dead. At this point, you're like, the face of the opposition," Gustav said.

"I want to hear it from their mouths," Meri announced. "Let them tell me why I'm wrong. And as you are well aware, the Kaggworks is strictly Morouni only. I will be doing this alone."

Gustav struggled for words. He looked to Potato for help but the Legomi just shrugged. "Well, I suppose I can't stop you-"

"Nor would you want to try," Meri said, coldly. "This is something I feel needs to be done. All problems can be solved with words, if all are willing to listen. I need to exhaust that option before I can allow myself to entertain a more violent solution."

"Well, shit man. If you think that's what needs to be done. You don't seem to worried about getting yourself killed," Gustav said, rubbing the back of his neck.

"Oh, I'm not afraid of that, that shouldn't concern you. What *should* concern you is what might happen if they convince me that I am wrong."

Mighty Rahiem

"I don't think that's possible," Potato said.

"Nonsense," Meri said. "I will not be approaching this with a closed mind. If I did, I could not blame them for doing the same. You should both keep that in mind, always." Meri stood from the chair and set the bottle down on the end table. He brushed his hands clean and headed for the door. Before ducking under the flap, he turned with a slight grin. "If I'm not back in twenty-four hours, you have my permission to sling your shit, so to speak." And with that, he vanished through the curtain.

Gustav and Potato sat in silence for a moment, somewhat frazzled by the Morouni's determination. Meri had always been a vocal proponent of moral conviction, but never once had they seen the man actually do anything about it. Gustav didn't know how to take it at all. Potato shrugged, "Can't fault a guy for doing what he says he's gonna do."

Gustav popped a beer with a grave look on his face. "I gotta feeling we should probably go after him. Dude's a walking target out there."

"So was I, but that didn't bother me." Potato said.

"That's different," Gustav laughed. "Doesn't count if you're bullet-proof."

"Bullets still hurt," Potato said, clearly rustled by the comment.

The conversation was interrupted by a clanging from the back room, followed by curses in a southern drawl. Gustav spit his beer into his lap. "Shit, I forgot Dale was back there." He wiped his lips with his arm.

Potato replied with a look of mild annoyance.

"We should probably tell him that there isn't a price on your head anymore... either that or we can finally stuff him. Lemme call the taxidermist!" He poked at his Talkman for a moment. "Shit, he's still booked solid. Why are taxidermists so popular?"

The Old Guard of Zerth

The noise continued, irritating the Legomi further. He couldn't take it any more. Potato jumped to his feet and stomped towards the back room. "I'm gonna fuckin' kill him."

"Well, I guess that settles it," Gustav said, clapping his hands. "We're back to square one. Let's take turns kicking the shit out of Dale until he dies." He pushed from the couch with beer in hand, following the Legomi into the storage room.

As Gustav ducked through the curtain, he found Potato had already yanked the cage open and was approaching the captive with a determined scowl. Dale was chirping half-words, darting around like a trapped rat. With a swift motion, the Legomi pounded his palms into the man's chest, bouncing him off the wall and to the floor where he curled up in a ball, wheezing.

"Get up, jackass!" Potato snarled. He grabbed hold of Dale's boot and yanked him backwards through the door, leaving a trail of dry straw behind him. The man struggled, kicking his leg wildly while making a yodeling sound. Potato pushed passed Gustav, dragging the struggling cowboy into the office where, with a violent thrust, he swung the man upright. Dale rag-dolled through the air in a cartwheel motion, landing hard on the coffee table with a crack. He sat up, rubbing the back of his head. "The Fuck is wrong with you?"

"The fuck you keep trin' to kill me?" Potato growled. "I ain't got no price on my head anymore."

"You can't lie to me," Dale said, spitting. "Check it yourself. Someone wants to zero you. You and your friends ain't long for this world. It may not be me, but somebody's gonna do you in. I promise you that."

"Bullshit!" Potato snarled. "Yer gonna tell me who put that price on my head."

"No way," Dale laughed. "That's cowboy code. A cowboy never reveals his sources."

Potato turned to Gustav.

"That's not a thing at all," Gustav said. "Where did you come up with that?"

"Fuck you, pervert," Dale hissed. "You don't know jack about bein' a cowboy. Go neck yerself. You guys wanna kill me again, go ahead. I don't care, I'll come right back anyway."

Potato wrapped his fist around Dale's ankle and squeezed. "What if we just pull your legs off and let you scramble around. How's that sound?"

"I'll call the taxidermist!" Gustav cried, then ran off, tapping at his Talkman. "Wait, nevermind."

Dale sneered, "You guys really are a bunch of fuck ups, you know that? You can't do nuthin' right. Y'all can't even interrogate a pris- eagh!" Potato snapped Dale's shin at a 45° angle. The Human shot up in pain and the Legomi moved on to the other shin without missing a beat. Dale flapped his hands around in a fury. "No!" he cried, "No! I'll talk. I'll talk! Jesus Christ, I'll talk!"

Gustav knelt down, resting his hand on Dale's oily haircut. "So, how does the cowboy deal with a broken leg?"

"I'm not a cowboy. I'm not a cowboy," Dale pleaded through clenched teeth. "I swear, I'm not a cowboy. Please!"

Gustav gave Potato a quick nod. Without concern, the cyclops snapped the bone back in place. Dale made some gulping sounds while his eyes rolled back into his head, then promptly passed out. "What the fuck, man?" Gustav cried, swatting the Legomi.

Potato pulled back with a shrug. "What, I thought you wanted me to fix him. He gave up, right? I fixed him!"

The Old Guard of Zerth

"Humans don't work like that," Gustav shouted. "You can't just put em back together. They're not made of plants like you. They heal really slow. Why do you think I kill myself every time I break a bone? For a break like that, he's gonna be out for, like, six months. You really fucked him up."

"Okay, well. What do we do?" Potato said, starting to panic. "How do I fix him?"

"Don't fix him, just kill him!"

"We'll never find him again," Potato cried.

"Fine, get a splint," Gustav said, pointing nowhere. "Find something sturdy to hold his leg together, then tie it up."

Potato hopped to his feet and clamored around the office for something of use. He jumped behind the couch and scurried around behind the file cabinet. The hollering of his comrade did nothing for his state of mind. He gave up and threw himself atop Dale's body, grabbing the man's head and tucking it into his armpit.

"What are you doing?" Gustav yelled.

"You're right, I'm just gonna kill him. But you gotta promise me we'll go find him after this." Potato said, determined to remove Dale's head for the second time. In an instant, Dale's eyes snapped open and he gasped for breath. "He's awake, I gotta put him down."

"Hold on, don't kill him yet. We gotta find out where he respawns first. Otherwise, we'll be looking for him forever." Gustav protested.

"So do I kill him or not?" Potato said in a panic.

"No!"

Mighty Rahiem

Dale slapped at the meaty arm around his neck, gasping for breath as his face went purple. "Fuck it, I'm out." Potato relaxed his grip and let Dale's skull crack against the table. The Legomi pushed to his feet and backed up, lighting a cigarette and crossing his arms. He blinked uncomfortably between puffs. "Ya got me all flustered."

Gustav looked Dale over while shaking his head. The cowboy was going pale. "Okay, so here's what we do. The dude's going into shock. That makes it harder for him to lie. We should be able to extract some info." He knelt down and glared into Dale's eyes. They were heavy and dim. He snapped his fingers in front of the man's face. Dale leaned his eyes over. "Where do you respawn?" Gustav said slowly.

"Huh?"

Potato gave Gustav a look. "Is he stupid now?"

"No, he's in shock. We just gotta keep talking to him." Gustav leaned down again and spoke into the Man's face. "Dale, when you die, where do you respawn?"

"What?"

Potato pressed his fingers to his temple. "This isn't working at all." He flicked his cigarette and approached Dale, grabbing his collar and lifting him up. "Hey, Buttface. Who's gonna pay you to kill me?"

Dale choked for breath, peering through squinted eyes at the Legomi. "I don't know."

Potato dropped the man to the floor and leaned into his face. "How were you supposed to collect the bounty if you don't know who's paying?"

Dale looked up at his aggressor with drooping eyes. "I'm gonna take you to the headhunter's guild. They're gonna pay me five-thousand bucks."

"That's not how it works," Gustav laughed. "You don't just show up at the headhunter's guild with a dangerous criminal and collect cash. You're supposed to contact the source of the bounty, *through the headhunters guild,* and bring the target to them. Did you even talk to the source?"

Dale shook his head with a desire for more information. Gustav face-palmed and walked away.

"Goddam you son of a bitch," Potato said through his teeth. "Your pops told me to my face that he'd drop the bounty. He told me he was sorry. So, if it ain't your father, who else wants me dead?"

"How do you know my dad?" Dale said. "My dad is sick. He's a sick man. I don't even know why he's here. He's in a coma in Loveland in 1998. He dies in 2002."

Gustav gave Potato an awkward look. He held off the Legomi with a hand, then knelt down. He spoke softly. "Dale, when are you from?"

"2014."

Gustav cocked his head and attempted the math with his fingers. "Wow, so your dad went into a coma in 1998 and showed up here. Sixteen years later, you pop in, 12 years after the death of your father, and you get to see him again? That's actually kind of touching."

"He doesn't recognize me," Dale said with a dumb smile. He leaned back to the floor. "He thinks I'm Luke Skywalker... or his dog from when he was a kid."

"Quentin?" Gustav said.

"No," Dale said with a sickly laugh. "Quentin was my brother. He's dead too. He doesn't come here though. My dad's dog was named Shark."

"Christ," Potato said. "Now I feel bad about fucking him up. What should we do?"

"The humane thing, I guess?"

"What's that mean?"

"It means you should kill him, like, fast. Don't let him feel pain, and shit like that."

Potato nodded and shuffled over to the broken man. "Hey Dale," Potato said quietly. "Where do you respawn? We'll come get you."

"Bonzo Beach."

"Okay." Potato bent over and wrapped his arm around Dales neck, then rested his knee on his shoulder. A quick jerk backward and Dale went still. The Legomi stood up and dusted his knees, then looked to Gustav. "We're gonna help Carbon Dale get his dad back."

Gustav rubbed his chin with his eyes to the floor. "I mean, we're all kinds of spread out right now. We should probably tell someone we're leaving. Try calling Wad again. We gotta let him know that we're helping Carbon Dale and that Meri is trying to kill himself. It's been what, three hours since you called him last?"

Potato checked his Talkman. "It's been five hours."

"What the hell could he be doing?"

Chapter 27

Sluggish Philanthropy

The town of Tempeg was a quiet little burg of fisherman and retirees. It was generally seen as a satellite of Southtown, but it had it's own charm. Mainly an export economy, with the standard Zertian style marketplaces, and Dobi-style homes on stilts for when the river overflowed. It lay just across Koplin bay, at the mouth of the Seguero River, a quick sixty mile jump for Southtownies looking to get away to a quiet afternoon in the shade of the cliffs. You could catch Salmon there, a Human import that saw the shallow rapids as an ideal spot for the species. They did well, and so the fishing business boomed. At most, the town hosted a modest population of about four-hundred souls. Morouni mostly, with Sectoids making up a good chunk as well. Space was plentiful, and there wasn't much going on to disrupt the general peace. That is, until a visitor arrived on a hot day.

Sluggs weren't too common around Tempeg, until Gill showed up. Before that, they were rare enough to draw a crowd whenever one came through. In fact, outside of the forests of Shishir, one could go a lifetime without getting the chance to meet one face to face. It was akin to crossing paths with a mythical woodland nymph, or maybe a leprechaun. A sign of good fortune for everyone around. When a battalion of the little guys showed up with cranes and pallets of plasteel, the townsfolk were beside themselves. After all, if an encounter with one Slugg was good luck, what about three-hundred of them? The Tempeggians were eager to find out.

The Old Guard of Zerth

As for their appearance, not one Slugg was any different than the other. Each had the same green, rubbery skin in the approximate shape of a sack of grain. Their legs were stumpy pipes, capped with floppy, clown-like feet. The bulk of their form curved into a soft, amphibian belly, with the other end trailing backward into a chubby tail that was prone to being dragged. The doughy midsection drew upward and outward like a curled finger, or maybe a soggy pickle. That was their head. No face, no mouth, no ears or hair. Just two blinking dots on either side of a nub. A mockery of the humanoid form.

Their arms, in total contrast, were slender and muscular. Long enough to scrape the ground as they hobbled along. They dangled at their sides, giving the whole package an obtuse form. From a distance, they appeared as fat geckos walking on their hind legs, or maybe a small, bottom-heavy man lost in a pillowcase. It got stranger when when they chose to wear clothing. For Gill, the look was his trademark. A man-sized, button-up, white collar shirt was his choice of attire. It covered him from head to toe like a fine robe. Atop each shoulder were equally oversized PISS packs offering plenty of moisture for long days in the sun. Gill wasn't the only Slugg to wear clothes, though he may have been the only one to wear them properly.

On top of the intrigue that the average Slugg inspired was the inevitable confusion over their attire. They wore anything, and they almost always wore it incorrectly. Wrecked electronics around their wrists, ripped pant-legs as girdles, shoes as hats. Some even wore body parts of the dead in equally random fashion. Everything was acceptable, and every Slugg found each other's choice of accouterments to be wildly entertaining. Nobody could tell if the little guys were making fun of the practice, or if they legitimately thought they were being stylish.

Mighty Rahiem

That being said, the Slugg's demeanor was always bright. *Always.* In fact, no one had ever seen a Slugg get angry, or even argumentative. No amount of abuse could pierce the overwhelmingly cheerful aura that a Slugg projected at all times, and all criticism was waved off with an agreeable nod and promise to do better next time, that is, if one were blessed with the gift of understanding the little things. Having no mouth, they communicated through grunts and clicks that reverberated from their chest area. For those able to decipher, it was less a language of vocabulary and more an emotive burst of common thoughts. In fact, save for proper nouns, vocabulary wasn't a thing at all. This lead to many arguments over the precise verbiage used. Each interpreter would hear the message differently, depending on their own background and personality. To speak with a Slugg was to understand metaphor, and those rigid in the ways of expression were doomed to stare blankly.

Some Sluggs took to learning the common language for the purposes of communicating via text. It worked in theory, but still relied on the Slugg's own interpretation. In short, it read like slop. Punctuation wasn't a thing, as there was no punctuation in verbal communication. They had a habit of rambling in never-ending blobs of exposition, inserting opinionated commentary in the middle of sentences, and so on. Often times, Sluggish texts would descend into mood-ending tangents musing over the silliness of the verbiage itself. For this reason, they had a penchant for puns, as well as a propensity to crack themselves up. Not that the people of Tempeg minded. They didn't need words to show their gratitude, and it's not as if there was a danger of an argument breaking out. All they knew is that the stubby green army was doing something that would bring their humble little town even more prosperity. No words needed.

The Old Guard of Zerth

Just across the river from Tempeg was the Sluggish worksite. The Sluggs found a suitable chunk of land on the northern riverbank, just under the base of the cliff, and figured it would be a perfect spot for a pump station. For a good week, the beach was littered with bright green midgets, shuffling one direction or the other. It was a workforce of nearly 300. Gill had great difficulty procuring enough PISS packs for his brethren, but he wasn't about to let one of his own wither in the western sun. Luckily, the people of Tempeg were more than accommodating. The townsfolk welcomed the onslaught of cheerful Sluggs with free room and board, as well as plenty of PISS packs. The workers nearly doubled the population of the town for the duration of the project, but the locals took them in eagerly. They happily ferried the workers across the river to the worksite whenever it was needed.

From their vantage, the people of Tempeg watched as an entire pumping facility sprang up over the course of a week. From enormous plasteel tubes, to the great cylindrical pumphouse, to the filtering and processing turbines, all of it rising out of the shoreline like steel fingers reaching for an enormous hockey puck. But when it was finished, it would supply the entire western coast, Meapos included, with clean, refreshing water. That was Gill's gift to the world and he was more than anxious to share.

Of course, sharing meant trade deals, if not in name only. Most of the larger settlements of Zerth claimed to be lawful, regulated establishments. Whatever that meant, Gill wasn't sure. To him, the whole thing seemed like a poorly choreographed dance. Each town with different rules, none of which were ever followed by the ones who made them. Luckily, neither did the townsfolk. Ignored by the commoners and broken by the elite. Regardless, he wanted to keep up appearances if only to show solidarity with their endeavors. Live by example, that was Gill's motto. One of his mottos, at least. One of many. And it was that Motto that reminded him to call on an old friend. One that he hadn't seen in quite some time.

Mighty Rahiem

When the cabbie arrived on the beach, he wasn't sure what to think. He pulled up to the riverbank in an old pickup, bobbing atop some worn Blinkbottom 4s. He was expecting a group of tourists, or maybe a fisherman, perhaps, making their way back to Southtown after a lucrative catch. The last thing he expected to see was a horde of green things that seemed to be barking at him from across the river. Then, one jumped in his cab and wouldn't stop waving at him.

Gill raised a friendly hand to his cabbie and chirped, "~*Lovely to meet you, honest cabbie. I very much appreciate you taking the time out of your day to assist in my travels. Tell me, how is the weather in grand old South Town? Much like the weather in grand old this-town?~*" Gill broke down, laughing.

The cabbie rubbed his chin nervously as the frog thing squeaked at him. It sounded like a duck-call. It was poking its Talkman with a really weird looking finger.

"~*I admire your stoicism, dear cabbie. Would you kindly drive me to the coordinates on my Talkman? The place has a silly name, don't you think? The one who named it must be a dim wit! Who names a place Everything Else? Would you join me in mocking this person if we ever meet them face-to-face? It'll be a spectacular time, I'm sure.~*"

The man scratched his head, reading the coordinates off the lizard thing's wrist. He poked them into the nav panel on the dash, then turned to Gill for confirmation.

"~*Ah, you must be waiting for payment. No worries, I intend to pay my fare, fair and square!~*" Gill giggled, then reached into his oversized shirt, producing a credcard. That much the cabbie understood. Gill pondered for a moment, wondering how much he should pay the man. He checked his Talkman for his account balance. 3,034 bucks. Sounds like a good tip, Gill thought. He was never too good at math, and it was much easier to hit the *'pay all'* button on the tiny screen, so he swiped the card and dumped every last buck into the cabbie's Talkman. The man's eyes popped. Gill never understood why everyone reacted that way, but he loved seeing the excitement. It was like a free hug!

Gill turned to the buzzing worksite and waved to his comrades, who all found a way to stop what they were doing to wave back. He then hurled himself into the flatbed of the cab and slapped the side panel a few times, signaling that he was ready to go. The cabbie obliged, revving the fans to point westward, and off they went, sailing across the rolling waters of Koplin Bay.

Wad sat atop the undercarriage of his fucked bus. He puffed away at a cigarette, nervously awaiting Gill's arrival. It had been nearly ten years since he had seen the little green bastard and his mind was swimming with questions. Back then, Gill and his crew were building a Pump Station way up in Muscan. At the time, Wad couldn't see the logistical benefit of pumping water into an area with zero population, until he saw the pipes. It was then that the scope of the job became clear. The little guy wasn't irrigating a field of cracked mud, he was bringing water to the whole planet.

It was that kind of thing that really got Wad's gears spinning. The thought of big projects with mass benefit humbled the hell out of him, especially when they were done for free. After his last meeting with Gill, he was inspired to smooth all the roads of Southtown and put up traffic lights. The latter was a suggestion by Gustav, who insisted it was a necessity. It didn't seem to help much with traffic accidents, but the Human assured him it would be weird if they didn't exist. Wad agreed, then went on to build Saxo Square in the middle of town.

Mighty Rahiem

The more Wad waited, the more anxious he became. His thoughts drifted to the first time he met the Slugg. Aerie Tower. A lifetime ago. Back then, Gill was called the Scribe of the Gregors. Wad wasn't entirely sure what the Slugg's job was, but he certainly had the respect of some very powerful people. After the exodus, they spent a good deal of time together, traveling around and naming things. In retrospect, the two of them must have named half the planet. Potato was with them in those days, but Gustav had yet to make an appearance, and Meri hadn't even been born yet. A lifetime ago indeed.

As Wad stared off into the fog, the sound of struggling head-fans broke his concentration. Rolling through the mist was a blue pickup, bouncing across the clover like weary animal. He could tell the fans were struggling with the moisture. Blinkbottom 3, maybe 4, Wad thought to himself. It came to a stop alongside the upturned bus. From above, all he could see was a shuffling lump under white cotton rummaging around in the bed. A moment later, the featureless nub of a face turned to greet him with a wave.

"~Greetings, Sunstruck. It's been too long!~"

Wad took a puff of his cigarette through a grin, then reached over the ledge of the bus to give the Slugg a hand up. "Holy shit, it's good to see you," Wad said, unable to hide his smile.

"~All shit is holy when friends reunite!~" Gill gibbered, *"~though I must let you in on some terrible news. Your bus is upside-down.~"*

Wad rubbed his neck, thinking the reunion would have kicked off a bit differently.

The Old Guard of Zerth

"~And did you know the name of this place is Something Else? What kind of dim wit would come up with that name? My cabbie and I have decided the giver of that name is a dim wit.~"

"Hey now," Wad said, standing up. "I think it's a great name."

Gill made a croaking sound. "~Never in a hundred years would I have a reason to accuse you of being a dim wit, until now. Brother, you have committed a great offense in the naming of this place. Future generations will laugh at your deeds, but until then, I will laugh at your deeds!~" The Slugg went after Wad with playful slaps.

Wad fought back with his palms, remembering how easy it was to set the little bugger off on a giggle-fit. It was an annoyance that he was quickly being reminded of. "Cut it out!" he cried, shielding his cigarette. He managed to get hold of an arm and reluctantly pulled it close, tucking it against his ribs, at which point he realized he was committed to the struggle. He rolled to the ground, bringing the little green thing with him.

Gill squirmed free, chirping with excitement. He hopped to his feet, then danced around with his dukes up. Wad followed suit, kicking up with his cigarette firmly in his lips, prepared for a scuffle.

"~That lovely tobacco,~" Gill grunted, "~You mock my inability to inhale with your lovely tobacco.~"

"So what if I do? What are you gonna do about it?"

With incredible speed, the Slugg dove for Wad's midsection. Wad reacted, attempting to shield himself, but the arms were already around him. It was then that he noticed he was being hugged. He looked down to see Gill's snout pressed into his belly. Wad looked around nervously to make sure nobody was watching, then came to terms with the absurdity of the thought. He let Gill finish, then shook his head with a laugh. "It has been too long," He said.

Mighty Rahiem

"*~Too long is always too long,~*" Gill said, seemingly drifting in thought. "*But your timing is impeccable. Without me, you'd be stuck here with an upside-down bus! Now, you're stuck here with me with an upside-down bus! The tables have turned! Tell me, Stunstruck, how did your bus become upside-down? Did you have another one of your fits of self destruction?~*"

Wad tried to answer, but realized he didn't have to. He made the point by flicking his cigarette out.

"*~Do you remember my book, Sunstruck?~*"

Wad was caught off guard by the sudden change of subject. He had forgotten how flighty his friend could be. "I do," he said. "Why do you ask?"

"*~My book is finished. Dictation is finished. You should read it. Especially the parts about you. Their words are very, very close to the heart. If you had the chance, it may have averted the disaster of the upside-down bus. You should read it!~*" Before Wad could answer, Gill yanked a little black notebook from his shirt pocket and shoved it into Wad's hands. "*~I asked them about you. They know you very well. They wrote a part in there all about you. I don't know what part it is, but they said it's in there.~*"

Wad peeled Gill's fingers away from the notebook to reveal a faded, cardstock cover. It wasn't more than a few inches wide. Scratched into the face were the words 'Reclimation of Nod' in a Slugg's handwriting. "I remember this," Wad said. "I can't believe you still have this thing. You were always going off alone and scribbling things in here."

"*~Not alone. Never alone. This was dictated.~*"

Wad flipped through the pages, noting the difference in penmanship from the start to the finish. "It's not very big. This really took you seventeen years to write?"

The Old Guard of Zerth

"~*Seventeen years to record,*~" Gill said. "~*And now it's ready to share with the world. Like the water I dig up, the wisdom will flow across the land like a wave, and before long, our thirst will be quenched and we will be free.*~"

Wad laughed, looking the book over front to back. "Free from what?"

"~*It's not for me to understand. Only for me to share.*~"

Wad flipped through the pages again, looking for something to justify Gill's exuberance. There must have been three hundred pages of gibberish. Some pages were crammed with scribbles, while others were neatly formatted. He found one that caught his interest.

MUNDA FINE (round, blue seeds):

Poke holes in ground every two yards.

Put seeds in holes.

Cover holes with wet soil.

Keep soil wet every two days.

Bohboh tree (white acorns):

Pokes holes in ground every four yards.

Put seeds in holes.

Cover holes with dry soil.

Keep soil wet every six days.

Mighty Rahiem

"These look like instructions for farming," Wad said. "Maybe this is worth spreading."

"*~Instructions, warnings and prophecy,~*" Gill replied. He clapped his rubbery hands together.

"Prophecy? Like, you know the future?"

"*~Not me, they. And not the future, only what happens in order of succession.~*"

Wad rubbed his chin. "And you say I'm in here?"

"*~Indeed!~*"

"What's it say about me?"

"*~I don't know. I'm just the messenger. But trust me, they say you're in there, so you're in there.~*" Gill began to hop around excitedly. "*~Oh, maybe you're one of the nine figureheads of prophecy! Let's find out.~*" Gill snatched the notebook and flipped through the pages. He scrolled through with a curved claw. "*Here we are. The Construct... no. Stranger? No... Tyrant? The Savior? Tell me, Sunstruck, do you feel like a savior?~*"

Wad chuckled, feeling it necessary to humor the Slugg. "I don't know, maybe. What's it say about the savior?"

Gill flipped a page with a bony finger. Wad watched as the little black eyes darted across the page. "*~It says the following:*

The Savior: He comes to you in darkness, casting out the light, though his hair is gold and shines as we shine. He comes to bring an end to all suffering, promising peace, though he knows no peace himself. His crown is broken and his journey is long. His coming will signal the end of all ignorance, though you will not recognize him for who he is, for he dwells with us in the light. His coming is the end of the Construct.~" Gill punctuated the reading with a lengthened stare. "*~No, I don't think that's you.~*"

The Old Guard of Zerth

Wad found himself thinking too hard about what he had just heard. Despite being deliberately nebulous, the words struck a nerve. There was something strange about them. Something not quite stable. Not quite tangible. He couldn't put his finger on it, but he was starting to believe they weren't merely scribbles from the mind of Gill. They were a bit too lofty for that. He decided to give his friend the benefit of the doubt. "So, you think there's anything in there that would help me not be such a fuck up?"

"~Undoubtedly,~" Gill said. He flipped through more pages, landing on one towards the middle of the notebook. "~How about a poem? Here we go.~" Gill began to read, but interrupted himself to show Wad the writing. "~This one is written in a circle. See?~" He pushed the page into Wad's face, showing him the circular shape of the text, then went back to reading.

I've watched you, dead man.

Bitter and harnessed by burdensome time.

What sense in suffering when the goal proves sour?

What better reprieve than to escape from laborious care?

For care is poison to men without direction, and sour objective is unmet by those who seek no end.

So, no end will you find, dead man. No bitter fruit and no cold.

For you – Everlight. For you – Forever Morning.

To the travelers far from home, I sing to thee.

This world is yours and here you are free.

Mighty Rahiem

Wad perked up. "Hold on," he said, "I've heard that before. That's Argutherie: the High Watcher, right?"

Gill dropped the notebook, clasping his hands over his head. *"~You've heard the voice of the balls, too?~"*

Wad recoiled. "Balls? What?"

"~The balls! The big balls!~" Gill grabbed Wad and spun him around, aiming his face into the sky. He pointed a bony finger at the light streaming through the mist. *"~The balls. The bright balls! You've heard their voice?~"*

"It's a poem," Wad said. "Lots of people know it. My friends talk about it all the time. They say the suns sang it to the first Human that showed up."

Gill clung to Wad's chest. *"~Not all of them, only one sings that song. Argutherie sings it to Humans, but mostly they don't want to hear it. The others sing too. Some sing to you, even. Can you hear it?~"*

Wad stood still, doing his best to stay in the moment. There wasn't much to hear. Only the light sprinkle of mist across his leaves and the low idle of the fans of the pickup below. He turned to Gill with a shake of the head.

Gill seemed to get upset. He made a growling sound and walked to the far side of the bus, waving his arms. *"~Too loud with fog, here. Not enough light, I think.~"* He turned to Wad. *"~Go somewhere high. Somewhere quiet. Somewhere that isn't hiding in a cloud. They'll speak to you, if you let them. Will you promise to listen? They have so much to say, and they love you so much, Sunstruck. You've touched them deeply and they only want to return the favor.~"*

Wad started to feel like he was being recruited into a cult. He nodded to keep the peace. "Well, at least you're here now. Maybe we can head back to town. Meri was supposed to give a speech, but I guess I missed it."

"~Ah, the one who speaks,~" Gill squawked, "I've heard much about him as well. They say he is growing fast!~"

"Really. The suns talk about Meri? Is he in your book, too?"

"~No, Sunstruck. Not that I know, but his people are and he is a voice for them. Much of what I have heard was not meant for dictation, but she has spoken about his deeds.~"

"And who is she? Another Sun?"

"~Therepherie is her name. She sings to the hairy ones. They need her wisdom badly. She sings to your friend but he doesn't recognize her voice, though he often mistakes her guidance for his own thoughts. That is how they sing, Sunstruck. Do you understand?~"

Wad thought for a moment. "I guess maybe I-" His Talkman chirped, granting him an easy exit from the topic. He paused the conversation with a finger while he glanced down at the screen to see who was calling. It was a text message.

POTATO: Yo – Guz and me going to Bonzo spawn. Gonna get Carbondale. Meri got shot but hes ok. He went nuts and went off to kaggwers. Where are u? Can you make sure Meri is ok?

"Oh shit," Wad said aloud. "Meri got shot?"

Gill reacted as if he had been beat over the head. He cried out with a nasal squeal, clasping his hands over his head. "~Calamity Dark times are ahead!~" He shoved the notebook in his pocket and leapt over the edge of the bus, scampering on all fours to the driver's side of the truck. He scaled the door and scurried through the open window to the screeching protest of the cabbie.

Wad didn't hesitate. He went right to typing.

Mighty Rahiem

WAD: Yo Mer – Potot says you gt shot. U okay? Need helf?

Wad hit the 'send' button and waited, tapping his foot against the carbon-fiber undercarriage. Down below, the sound of Human and Slugg squawking at each-other just made him more anxious. A moment later, his wrist bleeped.

MERI: OJAY. All is well. Not DeadYEt. Waiting to meet. Mite need a ride after. Longer walk than I rember.

Wad caught his breath. He stood with his hand over his chest, waiting for his blood pressure to drop. Then, a terrified yelp broke trough the air, followed by a thump. Wad looked over the side of the bus to see the cabbie running off into the mist, screaming bloody murder. Gill poked his face out the window of the truck. *"~He doesn't want to drive anymore. Come, Sunstruck, we must find your friend.~"*

The Old Guard of Zerth

Chapter 28

Coming Down

7:22 – Onesday morning. The start of a new week. Too much had happened in the previous week for Wad to have much recollection of the passage of time. Two suns peaked over Gate's Bluff in tandem, making the factory appear as a silhouette of smokestacks against a stoic wave of red earth. He puffed away at a Cigarette while pacing across the front gate of the Kaggwerks. His energy had run down in the last half-hour and the caution that drove him there in the first place had been abandoned in favor of counting paces.

Gill poked around in the gravel lot surrounding the fence. He followed Wad's lead, secure in the feeling of calm anticipation, as long as he wasn't alone in doing so. From time to time, his tedium would be interrupted by something in the air. He would perk up and listen, as if a voice were calling to him from over the hills, then return to examining pebbles at his feet without much urgency.

The Slugg's impatience had him trying to start a conversation with his friend shortly after arriving, but the situation proved too dire for casual dialogue. He had known Wad a long time. Long enough to know when he should keep quiet, despite the prolonged absence. It wasn't the pleasant outing he had envisioned, but few things rattled him more than seeing Wad in trouble, and by extension, anyone Wad cared about.

The Old Guard of Zerth

The factory was enormous. Its smoke stacks rose high above the tilted bluffs that dotted the north-western boundary of Southtown. Every minute or so, a great plume of steam jetted out from the foundry on the western side of the building. The two had become accustom to the echoes of the factory to the point of ignoring them entirely. The gate itself was a ways from the Kaggworks proper. Probably a hundred yards. There was a great field of dirt between the chain link and the rusted orange facade of the building. In different times, it could have been a staging area for some of the larger projects to be assembled in the open air. A steamer or two would fill up the space pretty easily, Wad thought.

Aside from the occasional delivery, there wasn't a soul in sight. Fully loaded pubbers approached from the south-east, always circling once, then settling down to dock on the western side of the building in the steelyard. Only then could Wad see the mass of workers flood out through bay doors with all kinds of buzzing equipment. Their efficiency was staggering, stripping a full load in under a minute with coordinated hoverjacks. The Morouni were a punctual people who didn't seem to do much of anything alone. If Wad was to be confronted, he was prepared for a mob. Fortunately, none of them ever seemed to have a problem with him. In fact, he had never even heard a sour word spoke in his direction. At least not one that he didn't rightfully deserve.

The whole situation had Wad wondering what he had missed. Was he blind to the Morouni's plight, or was it all just a big misunderstanding? The only thing that kept him wondering was Meri's words. The length his friend had gone to in the name of justice forced him to believe it. Who would speak so deliberately so as to instigate violence against themselves unless they truly felt they had something to prove. That didn't come from nowhere, and Wad knew it. He only wished he could see the wound that effected his friend so deeply. Meri had been shot, then went off to confront his attacker, unarmed, using only his speech as a defense. He didn't know what to call it, but that act of courage was leaving an impression. It was a painful impression, but one that he was sure would last longer than any wound. It was deeper, too. Deep enough to keep Wad nailed to his spot until his friend returned.

Forty-seven minutes. Gill was off somewhere whistling into the wind. Wad couldn't help but feel a bit guilty dragging his friend into the situation. If he had his way, the two would be soaking in alcohol, recounting past triumphs in the shade of a parasol atop Mackey's, but that guilt would quickly be replaced by growing anticipation with each pubber that flew overhead. Three more had departed and each one brought Wad closer to anxiety. What if they had Meri on one of those things? What if they cracked the big guy over the head and dragged him into a crate – flown him off to some deep part of the ocean and chucked him in. It wasn't out of the realm of possibility. Was he just going to mull around and feign ignorance if he heard that Meri was dead? How long was he going to wait around until he was convinced of it? Potato and Gustav's absence wasn't helping, either. Wad typed into his Talkman.

"STILL WAITING..."

His Talkman blipped back.

"LOL – LOL OUR PILOT IS DURNK"

Wad shoved his hand into his pocket. He kicked around irritably, building up the nerve to settle on failure so he could be indignant about it somewhere else. He gave the factory another look. Still bare. Still shimmering in the heat of the suns. Far in the distance, the buzz of Southtown made him antsy. The echo of civilization left him feeling out of place among the dust and quiet wind. He felt stuck between two points, and neither of them were where he wanted to be. Strangely, the sound of the same music could be heard from both locals. Despite being overt xenophobes, the Morouni of the Kaggwerks still enjoyed Gustav's tunes.

- *blip* – Wad pulled his wrist from his pocket.

"LOL WE ALMOST CRASHED"

He wanted to rip his arm out of his socket and smash the Talkman to bits. Calm down, Wadley. He took a breath and shut his eyes. Gill appeared out of nowhere, lumbering through the dust like an animal in search of a meal. He rested at Wad's feet with his tail curled around the Legomi's boot. *"~Soon, Sunstruck. He is coming.~"*

Wad looked down to his feet. The Slugg was staring up at him with eyes he couldn't read. "How do you-"

His query was interrupted by the kicking of rocks in the distance. Wad turned to see a large barrel of a silhouette emerging from the shadow of the factory. It walked intently across the gap, coalescing into the form of a stern Morouni. It was Meri. He wasn't dead, but he didn't seem very happy at all.

Meri stopped at the gate with a look in his eye. He gave it to Wad with pursed lips and Wad knew not to ask. After a pause, he swung the gate open and plowed through. Meri didn't let Wad speak. His demeanor shut down any questions the Legomi had. Wad wasn't about to argue. At the last minute, he opened up. "My man, where is your bus? Did you walk?"

Wad was nearly appalled by the question. "That's what you have to say? You've just-"

"It's still my turn to speak," Meri said, making clear that he wasn't finished with his silent rant. He then took one look at the junker of a pickup and deflated. He turned to Wad with a smile. "My man, you certainly have a way of killing the mood."

"I'm just borrowing it," Wad said.

Mighty Rahiem

"I most certainly hope so," Meri replied. "But despite the drop in tension, I do have a point to make. This building behind me, the one shrouded in shadow. I most adamantly desire to- my word, what is this?" Meri stopped himself, eyeballing the Slugg at his feet.

Gill waved with a squeak. He turned to Wad. "~*Will you tell him my name? Tell him I am happy he is well, and that we were very worried for his safety.~*"

Meri gave Gill a tired look. "My man, in the scant few seconds we've been acquainted, are we no longer on speaking terms?"

Wad gave Gill a sheepish smirk.

"~*My apologies, fellow traveler. By default, I assume none can hear my words. My name is Gill and I've been told of your struggles. I'm very happy to see you safe and untampered-with. Word of your deeds have spread wide, and so I find it agreeable to assist you in your goals, whatever they may be.~*"

"He's quite the gentleman," Meri said with a laugh, "and positively verbose!" With a grunt, He knelt down to the Slugg's level. "My little man, your devotion to the cause is admirable, though I fear it may be blind. What I intend to do is not befitting of a slugg, nor would it be appropriate of me to encourage any *sane* man to follow my lead. You see, I will be demolishing this building and I do not intend to spare the lives of any who refuse to leave. I have thought long and hard about this decision and it wouldn't be fair of me to hoist such a soul-burden upon an innocent such as yourself."

"So you're going to blow it up?" Wad said.

"Indeed, and you're going to help me."

"Hold on, I thought you just said it wouldn't be appropriate to ask-"

Meri balked. "If I thought of you as sane man, I would have omitted your participation. Lucky for me, I surround myself with lunatics. No, my man, a change in the natural order is required and we will be its harbinger. The shadow of this monstrosity will be erased and I cannot do it alone. Call the others. We are going to war."

East–508Mph. Destination:-000.2/-200.0. Arrival:16 minutes.

Placebo – Pure Morning. The pilot was out like a light and Gustav couldn't figure out how to do a barrel roll. Potato was trying to show him, but the Human just didn't want to listen. All the booze in the cockpit was gone but there were a few more cases of the good stuff in the cabin. Off and Away indeed.

Down below, the April Hills shimmered a suede green in waves. The tobacco silos were close enough to tempt Gustav further. He wanted to dive-bomb the tobacco. A brief skip across the Esconder Sea and the off-kilter Mike's Hard Mountain Range rose above the horizon like a broken window. Four minutes later, Potato had to rouse Carton from his slumber as they had overshot their destination. Neither of the two knew how to slow the thing down.

The cockpit was a mass of pullies, valves and ropes tied to things that looked like they would fall off if you tugged too hard. No big deal for Carton, who hopped to it without taking a first breath. It was as if being startled awake was his primary mode of operation. But not before a swig of whiskey. Gustav was instructed to refuel the pilot as often as he could manage.

The craft slowed to a crawl through a corkscrew landing with Carton's foot on the brake. They came to a stop at an impressive 12ft above the surface of the water. The dashboard said so in flashing red. Carton loved the music. Everyone loved the music. Down below, a dozen sauced fishers bobbed about in the shallows with bright yellow dingies in the shade of parasols. The occasional Human broke the surface of the water, crying for help as beach-goers laughed and cheered them on from afar. New Humans. They always brought a smile to Gustav's face.

Carton cranked a lever as the cockpit took on wind. Potato slapped the leather of the seat with a determined smile and made his way through the cabin to the open hatch in the rear. He stood out on the plank, scanning the shoreline, giving a subtle salute to the fishers below as they acknowledged his altitude. Potato shielded his eyes from the sheen of the suns off the leisurely waves, looking for a familiar face. There, on the beach, sitting alone in the sand was a scrawny looking fucker in a wet suit and a cowboy hat. Potato pounded on the plasteel frame of the ship and shouted for Carton to pull around.

Dale watched nervously as the painted character of a Morouni drifted closer. The hull of the ship he had so eagerly chased was now upon him. He chose not to fight it. He wasn't spent, he just didn't have a reason. Not any more. It was lost and his head was swimming with emotions. Anger was no longer one of them. It had been replaced by the same apathy that he used to drop out of collage. Sitting alone in his wet suit and cowboy hat, he started to question the purchase. Not the wet suit, that was actually useful. Fifty bucks for a Stetson. What a goddamned waste.

The ship came closer and the blast of hot air from the repulsers kicked too much sand in Dale's face. Men and women ran screaming. Dale slapped his googles around his eyes and held his lips tight. He sat still, resigned to his fate, whatever it may be. As the craft came about, he expected the barrel of a gun to be pointed roughly in his direction, but what he got was a big brown palm inviting him aboard. The great eye wasn't angry, it was offering help. Through the kicking sand and rushing air, Dale stood up and grabbed the meaty hand, and was hoisted inside.

The Old Guard of Zerth

Filter – Take My Picture. Gustav thought it was appropriate for the world to hear. Dale didn't mind. Memories of skipping High school poked at his thoughts while a blurred green horizon darted passed the porthole. He didn't hesitate to accept a flask of good stuff from the potato across the aisle. It was a generous release. Like the whole crazy planet was begging him to take a breath and he finally gave in. It smelled like oil and sand and tobacco. Blown capacitors and sweet whiskey. Nothing bad.

Potato leaned across the aisle and gave Dale a look. Dale didn't hold back with a smile. It was rough, with bad teeth that he didn't mind hiding. He didn't have to. Not here. If it wasn't bad teeth, it was blue skin, or bug-eyes, or the smell of cabbage – or cabbage for hair.

"Yer pops is a good guy," Potato said. "He's kinda fucked, but he ain't bad. He's gonna be happy to see you."

"Yeah, maybe," Dale said. "If he remembers me."

The cockpit door slid open and Gustav bumbled his way down the aisle, plopping down in the seat ahead of Dale. He swung his arm around the headrest, beaming at his fellow Human. "So, Dale! Sorry we keep killing you. Your dad is psychotic."

"Yeah, I know," Dale said, somewhat embarrassed.

"He put legs on a van and made it walk!"

"Bill did that," Dale said. "Bills' a real techie guy. My dad is just an old hacker. He used to hang out with Kevin Mitnick and stuff. They used to get in all kinds of trouble."

Gustav laughed. "I remember that shit. I still have my 'Free Kevin' t-shirt. Good stuff. Fuckin' technobillies. Who woulda' thought, right?"

"Yeah, Bill came up with the name," Dale said timidly. "I never got into it. After he built his brain-cage, he kinda got sucked into the whole lifestyle. He met my dad and they just clicked. They both just wanted to hang out in the desert and build stuff. Then I come along and try to turn him into a cowboy. See what good that did."

"Small fuckin' world," Gustav laughed. "I knew Bill back home. He's a fuckin' looser."

"He's a god here," Dale said without hesitation.

Potato spit. "That doesn't mean anything. He's just a guy doin' what he likes to do. If he's good at it, you think he's a god?"

Dale sat back in his chair and looked out the window, somewhat hurt by the comment. "It works for him," he said under his breath.

Gustav came away with a thought. For some reason, his mind was drawn to the giant number in his bank account and he realized he couldn't argue. He shifted in his seat, kicking his boots into the next one over with his back on the porthole. "Maybe we are gods here," he said.

Potato gave him the stink-eye.

"No, seriously, think about it. I mean, you don't have any frame of reference, Sam-"

"You don't call me that."

"You don't have any frame of reference, *Potato*. Where we come from, bullets kill people. Permanently. People live and die in total captivity to a system of abject authoritarianism. They don't even know what freedom is. You couldn't show it to them, you couldn't teach them about it. It's not even a glimmer in their thoughts. And then they come here-"

"And they're happy," Dale added.

Potato sat for a moment before granting a nod. The Humans were starting to sound a lot like Wadley. He knew what they were talking about, he knew all about it, but it wouldn't do any good to push the point so he let it slide as if he were ignorant of the whole thing.

"And I'm sure you're happy too," Dale said, poking at Potato's arm. "Mister invincible. Mister impervious to bullets."

"I'm only impervious to dumb people with bad aim and bad luck," Potato countered, attempting to sound profound.

Dale threw his hands up. "Ya got me. I'm a dumb guy with bad aim. You are invulnerable to me. I give up. Gimme another drink."

Potato scoffed, then handed the kid the bottle. His Talkman beeped with a message as he reached across the aisle.

WAD: GONNA FUCK UP THE KAGGWORPS

"Shit," Potato said, jumping from his seat. Gustav perked up as the Legomi rushed to the front of the cabin and pounded on the cockpit hatch. It slid open with a hiss and he poked his head inside. "Switch my shit to the speaker. Do it now!"

The music crackled and Wad's voice came through. "Hey, yo. You there?"

"Is Meri okay," Potato said loudly. His eye bounced between the speakers above. The pause before the answer nearly stopped the Legomi's heart.

"Yeah. Yeah, he's okay. He's pissed."

"What did they do to him?" Gustav said, standing up.

"Nothing, he's fine. Kagg is playing dumb. He says he doesn't know anything about the Blue Fist, and the whole town is on his side. Will of the people, he says."

Meri's voice cracked through. "He claims he had nothing to do with me being shot. I showed him the wound. *'Don't stand in the way of progress'*, he says, before apologizing for my misfortune."

"What did you say after that?" Gustav said.

"I asked him how many dead men will he apologize to when he's finished. He said very few. I stormed out."

"We're gonna blow up the Kaggwerks," Wad said.

"We're gonna blow up the Kaggwerks!" Gustav cried.

"Fuck yeah!" Dale cried. He flew out of his seat and pumped his fist.

The cabin went quiet.

"Who is that?" Meri said. "Is that Carbon Dale?"

"No," Dale said. "It's just Dale. I'm just Dale now."

"Bullshit," Potato growled. He ran down the aisle and crammed a bottle of liquor into Dale's hand. "You're Carbon Dale – always." He grabbed the stetson hat from the chair and slapped it over Dale's greasy haircut. "You wanna be a god, you go be a god. Fuckin' be a god."

Dale guarded himself against the window.

"What's going on?" Wad said.

Potato eyed Dale.

"We're gonna blow up the Kaggworks?" Dale said, sheepishly.

"Fuck yeah, we are," Potato howled. Gustav joined in. Carton screeched out a war cry from the cockpit.

"We'll sic my dad on the place!" Dale said, getting pumped. "He'll fuck it all up. Send his vanwalker in there and open fire. That thing is a tank. We can get Bill to help too. I bet he's got a hundred bodies by now. My Posse is back!"

"Significantly less, actually," Gustav said through his teeth. "Maybe we can have a kill-bill party... hah! Give him a call. Tell him we're all ready to *rumble*!"

The next hour was a litany of motivational grunting and pep-drinks from three drunks and fake cowboy. Outside, a flock of sandsquid rode the rainbelt across the basin, and the gleam of a great tower shimmered in the distant sands.

West–482Mph. Destination:+599.4/-261.0. Arrival:37 minutes.

Chapter 29

Doctor Plz

Herb Alpert – A Taste of Honey. Meri insisted on it. He sat in a beam of dust overlooking Saxo Street with a chewed pencil in his hand, studying a loose sheet of paper covered in scribbles. Within a ring of eraser gunk was was a crude floor plan of the Kaggworks, drawn up from memory. He had dispatched the crew around town to load up on supplies. Gustav and Potato hit up Fodroy's for ammunition and a couple of barrels of incendiary jelly. Wadley was across the street to meet with Herman Wibble about some boner inducing mortars and a very large gun for the back of the truck he had stolen. Gill had gone off on his own to 'work some magic', whatever that meant. Meri sent a message to Carton for air support but had yet to hear back. And then there was Carbon Dale. It was assumed that the ground assault would be an easy task to organize as the Dollar Bill's were in tight with the Cowboy, and Don Sanders had no problem plowing his van through walls. Nobody even gave it a second thought.

The group's entire mode of operation terrified Dale. There was never a plan-B, just a string of half-assed plan-A's that were cooked up at random, sometimes even before the original plan-A had failed. Nobody asked him what to do if he couldn't get the Technobilies on board. It was just his job to make it happen. The spontaneity was infuriating. Dale couldn't help but wonder how the most of them managed to survive this long.

As Meri waited for a reply from the pilot, he paced through the office. Dale stared at his Talkman, thinking of how to open a dialogue with his estranged father. The anxiety brought him back to middle school, waiting in the principal's office for his old man to take him home. Two weeks of detention. He was accused of setting fire to an old shoe on the playground. He wasn't even the one that did it, but he did cheer on the flames. The actual perpetrator's only punishment was a one-day suspension. A day off for being a better liar. The worst part was, his dad didn't even ask the principal what his son did – certainly never asked his son if it were true. And now the old man didn't even know who he was.

What made it all worse was the reality of his Father's eventual death, remembering the porcelain look of his dad's face lying in the casket. For three years, his father was in and out of a coma. He spent his time awake mumbling about things that made no sense. The first time Dale ran into him on Zerth, it didn't take a great feat of mental gymnastics to realize that his father had been trying to recant his adventures in the sand in a world outside of time. For a brief moment, there was a glimmer of hope in Dale's mind, until realizing that his Father had no idea who he was, or the fact that he never really cared much for him.

It was like a fairy-tale gone sideways. Like some otherworldly force was trying to right a cosmic wrong by jamming a square peg into a round hole just because the colors happened to match. Dale felt as if he was being forced into making nice for the sake of some grand narrative for the appeasement of an idealistic simpleton who, by an ugly twist of fate, was pulling all the strings. And now the same force was telling him to call his dad.

"Are your compatriot's on board?" Meri asked, turning to Dale.

Dale just nodded. He didn't know how else to respond.

Meri turned in his chair. "Say what you will, but that nod didn't inspire much confidence," he said with an upturned eyebrow. Dale tried to go on the defensive but was preempted by a warm smile from the Morouni. Meri pushed himself from the chair and moved across the office, taking a mindful seat on the couch. He reached for the scotch, then leaned his feet to the coffee table.

Dale was shocked by Meri's patience. The Morouni was entirely too forgiving for his taste. He allowed Meri to pour himself a drink before making excuses. As he began to open his mouth, a furry hand hand cut him off, then poured a second glass and handed it to the Human. "Take your time," Meri said, enjoying his drink.

Dale swallowed a gulp like a cowboy would, strictly out of habit. "So, how come you guys hate this Kaggwerks place so much?"

Meri calmly set his drink to the table and lifted his shirt, showing the bullet wound hidden within many rolls of fat. "This is why," Meri growled.

Dale wasn't sure what he was looking at, but he got an eye-full of manboob and gut. He said nothing.

"I know you don't like me," Meri said, tucking his shirt back into his pants, "and I don't particularly like you-"

Dale tried to interject, but Meri was on top of it, steadying Dale's expectations with a raised hand.

"-and none of that matters. It's been decided that we're going to stop killing you as long as you can hold up your end of the bargain. Now, I have no idea what you Humans go through each time you meet an untimely end. No doubt it must be quite traumatic. At least I prefer to believe it is. That being said, I would appreciate it if you were to take this seriously. You claimed you can get Sanders to help. Can you make that happen or not?"

"Yes," Dale said, in spite of his better judgment. He raised his chin to better illustrate his resolve.

"Good," Meri said. "I'm counting on at least twenty to twenty-five Dollar Bills and a large walking van capable of knocking down concrete walls."

"You got it."

Meri rose from his seat and lumbered to the desk by the window. He snatched his plans and poked at them with a claw. "The Technobillies enter the wall at the north end. The Bills will push through and form a Human net on the other side moving southward. Nothing passes that net. Do you understand?"

"Yes I do." Dale was starting to get amped up.

"Sanders' job is to shoot anything that tries to leave through the hole in the wall. You'll be there to keep him straight, as I'm quite certain the man isn't all there on his own. My condolences."

"None taken," Dale said with a nod.

"You and your team need to be prepared to attack at noon. That doesn't leave you much time. Can you do that?" Meri said.

"Yes, sir," Dale nodded.

Meri turned his back and gave a thumbing motion towards the door. Dale turned to the door but didn't notice anything unusual. Meri looked over his shoulder to see Dale's slacked jaw. "My man, must I dismiss you by force or are you capable of finding the exit without my help?"

Dale popped out of his stupor and scrambled for his hat. He paused at the door, "How do I-" then changed his mind.

"Noon," Meri hollered, as Dale vanished through the curtain.

Roughly ten minutes passed. The door flap lifted and Wad entered, ruffling an invoice in the air. "We got a gun for the bus," he smiled. "Wibble says it's not the best, but it'll do the job. And here's a bit of irony. Kaggwerk's own Sandhill 2/80. We're gonna use their own gun against em."

Meri moved to the window and rubbed his hands. "Plenty of ammunition?" he said.

Wad was surprised at Meri's lack of appreciation for what he considered to be poetic justice. He almost forgot to answer. "Seven hundred round. It's gonna fill up the whole back seat. You're really taking this seriously, aren't you?"

"I am, indeed," Meri nodded with confidence. "Just waiting on Carton to confirm his roll. We're going to need him at his best so I took the initiative and raided the whiskey reserves. Gustav and Potato are out gathering the explosives." Wad nodded and started to move away before Meri caught him. "Wadley..."

Wad spun around. "Yeah?"

Meri gave a genuine smile. "Sandhill 2/20. The irony isn't lost. Thank you for doing this for me."

"It's the least I can do," Wad said, returning the smile.

Just then, Gustav entered. Under each arm was a load of plasteel trench-helmets. "Let the games commence!" he announced. Potato followed, looking perfectly casual + bandoleer. Gustav tumbled into the couch, dumping the helmets roughly on the coffee table. "Everyone grab a helmet, in case it gets messy." Nobody took him up on the offer.

"Good," Meri said. "Now that we're all here, I suggest we go over the plan as it stands."

"Plan time!" Gustav hollered. He fiddled with his Talkman to set the mood. **Clinic – Evil Bill.** He politely placed his hands in his lap and prepared to listen.

The Old Guard of Zerth

Meri started. "As you all well know, It is not in my nature to resort to violence. In fact, under normal circumstances, I would much rather take our usual approach of accidental detonation. Less soul-searching in the aftermath. Messy business, tarnishing the soul, you know. A healthier option would be to allow lady luck guide our vengeance as we drink until the Kaggwerks explodes itself."

"Ya know, that's not out of the realm of possibility," Gustav laughed. "We could just get blitzed and hang out near the place. I'd say that's a reliable strategy.

"I had hoped it would be," Meri replied. "until I realized we've been quite sauced for a while now and nothing of the sort has happened. It is for this reason that I've asked you all to help me in this task." He waved his hands, inviting the group to gather around the coffee table. He placed the paper down and poked at it with his pencil. "This is the Kaggwerks. By my estimation at least two-thousand men, women and children make their living in the belly of this beast, presumably half of that present at all times. To be clear, it is my primary concern that the workers escape with their lives. This is about making a statement, not taking lives." His pencil ripped the paper as he circled key locations. "The attack will begin with Gustav and Carton aboard the Often Away. They will the drop barrels of incendiary jelly into the forge through the smokestacks in the roof. Step two: the Technobillies will come in through the north wall with Don Sanders' walking bus. The Bills' will run a Human net to push the workers southward as they flee from the fire out the front door. Step Three: Carton and Gustav will take up the western position, setting up a small blockade of the docks with steady fire into the bay to deter escape from that exit. Wadley and Potato will hold the southern line. They will weld up the gate and hold back the workers. It is your job to keep them passive under the threat of very large gun. You will keep them corralled behind the fence until the show is over. En mass, they will witness the fall of the Kaggworks."

"This is a good plan," Potato said, reaching for the scotch. He thumbed the cork and threw back a swig, then passed it to Gustav.

Gustav took a swig and offered an agreeable nod, then turned to Wad. Everyone turned to Wad. "We gotta time this just right," Wad said. "Pubbers bring deliveries every 30 minutes or so. We don't want to get in the way of that. How long do we think this is gonna take?"

"I expect to use their efficiency to our benefit in this regard. Despite my limited time on the inside, I did take note of the flow of things. There are 'tributaries' of movement throughout the facility, leading into main thoroughfares. From there, they split into 'estuaries', or exit-hubs. It's quite mechanical, I must admit. That being said, I believe we can count on full evacuation in under twenty minutes," Meri said.

"Good," Wad said. "We start as soon as we see a Pubber leave. Guz, I'll give you the signal to drop the barrels. Then, you get Carton to take you to the docks."

"Got it," Gustav said happily, then dumped more booze down his gullet.

"After that, I'll give Dale the sig-" Wad turned to Dale who wasn't there. "Where's Dale?"

"I sent him to do his part of the bargain," Meri said. "He was dawdling and I didn't have the patience to watch him give up. He's going to talk to Sanders in person."

"Didn't we drop them all off at Tempeg?" Wad said. "How are we going to get everyone across the bay in time?"

"Fuck it," Gustav said, interrupting his own drink. "We'll just get Carton to drag them over here. He's got clamps, right?" No sooner than he finished, his Talkman blipped. "Speak of the devil, I just got a message from Carton."

The room paused in anticipation.

The Old Guard of Zerth

"-and"

"He's a father!" Gustav shouted.

The room remained paused, but the anticipation fizzled.

"Carton is out," Gustav continued reading. "His wife just had a shitload of kids. Twelve Kids. He says they're all assholes. He wants us to call a doctor because one of em is fucked."

"The hell are we supposed to do about it?" Wad said. "Why doesn't *he* call a doctor?"

"He said he tried but he's drunk and doesn't remember the number," Gustav said, reading the screen. "Besides, he's got his hands full."

"What is the Midwife doing?" Meri shouted.

"How should I know," Gustav replied, throwing his hands up.

"No, you dolt," Meri cried. "Ask Carton what the Midwife is doing. She's supposed to be overseeing the situation."

"How the fuck do you know so much about Carton's wife's pregnancy?" Gustav shot back.

"All Morouni birth's require a midwife," Meri snapped. "When they come ten at a time and hungover, one man can not do it alone."

"The fuck do you mean, hungover?" Potato said holding back a snicker.

"It's tradition!" Meri hollered, then spun around and poked at his Talkman.

Gustav's Talkman bleeped. "Carton says forget about any more rides unless we call a doctor for him."

Potato burst into laughter.

Mighty Rahiem

"What the shit! He's got the only flight pad in town." Wad started to panic.

All at once, every Talkman lit up with a photocapture. The air was sucked out of the room. It was an image of a newborn Morouni with an inside-out head. The scrolling text below stated *"call doctor plz"*. The office buzzed to a panic as each tapped away furiously at their wrists, all except Potato who was content to watch from the safety of his drink.

"I got the doctor," Wad said. "He's at the bonehouse across the street. Where is Carton?"

"The flightpad, man. He's at the flightpad!" Meri replied, with eyes glued to his wrist.

"Good," Wad said. He ran to the window and flung the shudders open. Up Saxo street he could see the doctor emerging from the local bonehouse. He had his bag under his arm as he casually strolled southbound without much urgency. Wad cupped his hands around his mouth and made angry noises, urging the man to hurry the fuck up. The man did not comply.

As the doctor passed in front of city hall, there was a great crash from above. Smoke poured out of the second floor window as bodies were hurled through, all wearing mayors outfits. They rained down atop the doctor like burning meteors. They slapped against the street in piles. Denizens emerged from alleyways to applaud the grizzly scene. Dingus Mackey even put out a sandwich board advertising free beer to celebrate the occasion. Then, the doors of city hall burst open and a dozen mayors flooded into the street, firing weapons into the air and howling.

Just up the road, Wad spotted another group of rowdy-looking fellows. They marched down the street waving signs, each with a monocle, top hat and sash. Leading the pack was

The Old Guard of Zerth

Mayor Studdwanker brandishing a coroplast yard sign reading *"Down with Me – You Down With Me?"* Signs in the rear appeared to be emblazoned with the logo of the Wanderer, though some quite ironically had the symbol 'X'd out. They were clearly intent on violence.

"What on Zerth is going on out there?" Meri said, joining Wad at the window. He said nothing after seeing for himself.

Gustav pushed through and poked his head out the window. "Holy shit. Mayor fight! Wait, who's on what team?"

Potato's laughter was causing him to tear up. He pushed from the couch and ambled to the door. "I'll be downstairs drinking. Wake me up when it's over." He vanished through the curtain.

Down below, the street went quiet as the second group of Mayors approached city hall. They formed a defensive line, grunting calls to order. The defending Mayors squared up as well, thumbing gestures of intolerance and mumbling for a recess. A slight breeze kicked a tumbleweed through. Nobody said a word. Then, a rogue voice echoed through the dust. "Fifty bucks on the mayor. Who's in!"

"I'll take that bet," Gustav shouted through the window. He started toward the door before Wad wrapped his knuckles around the Man's collar and dragged him back.

Then it started. From the steps of city hall, Mayor Crawdog let out a cry. "You fucked my wife!" He drew his baton and swiftly cracked it over Mayor Brubek's skull. Brubek was presumably all for it, as he let out a cheer on his way to the dirt.

"I fucked your wife!" Mayor Steve wailed, and popped Mayor Crawdog in the knee with a .22. Crawdog went down. Mayor Steve let out a whoop, which was cut short by a baseball bat to the face from Mayor Locus.

Mighty Rahiem

There was no time to gloat as the opposing Mayors took flight. They rallied together and rushed the steps with the fury of a cavalry charge. "I fucked my wife!" Mayor Studdwanker yelped, as he led his men into the fray. Canes were swung and bullets flew, shattered monocles and coroplast sailed through the air. Townsfolk rushed to the scene, snapping pictures with their Talkmans and whooping it up.

-Blip- *"Docter plz"*

"We've got to get that doctor to the flight pad," Wad cried.

"You mean the mess smeared across the pavement? I don't think he'll be much help." Gustav said.

"I believe he may still be moving," Meri said. "That doctor needs a doctor. Might be best to call for another one?"

"I've got an idea," Gustav said, dashing to the door. He turned back with a finger in the air. "Wait for me."

Wad and Meri returned their eyes to the ruckus below. They watched as Mayor Digby entered the melee with a stick of dynamite, but it detonated in his hands. His armless body skid across the cobblestone. Mayor Steve ran to the mess waiving his .22, but was cut short with another baseball bat to the face. Mayor Locus was cutting everyone short with a baseball bat to the face, before he was cut short with a baseball bat to the face from Mayor Meecrob – who was cut short with a chainsaw to the groin.

Without warning, the music cut out. The chaos paused. Then, a strange sound. It twitched and shrank, then popped rhythmically. A guitar riff born of a plastic candy store and a beat too inane for mortal ears. It was like the sound of a happy aneurysm. **Len – Steal My Sunshine.**

The Old Guard of Zerth

Gustav came rushing down the street, hoisting a speaker by the post in the base. He brought it down, brandishing it like a battle ax. The music popped on as he waved it at the horde of frothing Mayors. They gazed back like a pack of hungry animals. "I regret nothing!" Gustav wailed. It took a moment for the mob to piece together what was happening. Gustav didn't linger. He cranked the volume to max and with widened eyes shouted, "I fucked *all* of your wives!" He turned on his heel and sprinted down the street. The mob of Mayors unpaused and took off after him like a school of piranhas.

From above, Wad spotted the Doctor in the debris below. He wasn't moving. "Guz did it! We gotta get that doctor!" He turned to see Meri popping another bottle of scotch. "Meri!"

The Morouni gave Wad an awkward look. "My man, what do you expect me to do, dive out the window?"

Not ten seconds later, Gustav came rushing in through the door flap, breathing heavy. He dropped the speaker cabinet to the floor and rested his hands on his knees. The volume was intense.

"Gustav, what the fuck?" Wad yelled.

"It's okay," Gustav yelled with a raised palm. "I lost em." He took one more breath before a barrage of bodies plowed through the door, filling the office with angry harrumphing and wild declarations of no confidence. They swung blindly at each-other with all kinds of weapons. Wad took a coroplast gash to the cheek and shot sideways as Meri dove for the window, but was nabbed by the ankle and dangled. Multiple pencil-jabs pierced the Morouni's calf as he shrieked and scrambled. He kicked his assailant away, tumbling out the window to the street below. Gustav was lifted by a dozen hands and pushed towards the ceiling fan – balls first. The blade found its mark and punted his nads to one side. He shriveled and fell to the floor, surrounded by shuffling loafers.

Mighty Rahiem

Wad recovered in time to accept a bat to the eyebrow, snapping his head back with a flash. He grabbed at the air, falling backward into the couch. The stars faded just in time for him to see Mayor Digby entering through the door flap. His skin was charred black and he had no arms. In his teeth was another stick of dynamite, and he was determined to make it work this time. The look in his blazed eyes said everything. All Wad could do was shield his face.

The noise went dead. It didn't seem to reach Wad's senses. Time turned down to a crawl. For a moment, all he could see was a wave of rag-doll bodies, wreathed in flame, spiraling around him. The walls gave way to sunlight, briefly disorienting his vision. Heat and bits of grain flecked into his skin as he fell back with the wall. The couch came, too. Inside the wave, he could swear he saw Gustav's twirling form spin by with a smile. The big coke-bottle glasses had departed from his face and Wad was treated to a rare view of the man without his second eyes. They looked really tiny. Then, a sick thump, followed by a shocking surge of debris, then all went black.

As the air cleared, Wad swatted at the dust in his eyes. He was sitting on the couch, and the couch was in the alley, and the alley was much bigger than he remembered. All around him were chunks of furniture, but the heat of the suns assured him that he had exited the building. Meri was there, too. The lump of a Morouni was laying in the road, not looking at anything in particular. He popped his broken pipe between his lips and tried to get it started, but it seems his lighter was dead.

-Blip- *"Docter plz"*

427

Chapter 30

The Song of my People

Wad's leaves were singed black. He stayed on the couch in the alley while Gustav shuffled around, examining the damage. Meri sat beside him with a low brow and limp posture. His calf wound was done up in the ripped leg of his own pants where the blood had started seeping through. The pea-green stripes were turning a crusty brown and he wasn't happy about it. Potato stood by with nothing to say. Though unscathed, he was clearly effected. He gazed up at the wreckage like a hurt puppy.

Above, there was no longer an office, just a wall and a doorway. The flap fluttered in the wind while a trickle of water ran down the remaining structure from what used to be the bathroom. A chunk of dobiestone bounced down the shell of the building, landing next to Wad. He followed it as it rolled into the street, joining with a thousand more crumbled bits of his home. Everything was covered in a fine layer of dobi-dust, and Strudel's Closet now had a sunroof.

Scattered in all directions were bodies sporting the mayoral sash. Some not quite dead, but surely on their way. There were monocles everywhere. A few managed to walk away from the blast, while others opted to remain to be counted among the dead, but not before being recognized as present. They heaved and groaned, calling for order, but it was swiftly overruled by the majority vote. Abstaining on account of detonation.

The Old Guard of Zerth

About ten minutes earlier, Wad caught a glimpse of Amelia leaving the town hall with packed bags. She hailed a cab and headed off for greener pastures, if such a thing existed. No words were exchanged, no eyes met. A fitting end to a relationship he didn't deserve.

As he scanned the bodies and debris, Wadley realized he was too sober. It made him testy. What was next? What else could go wrong? Crumpled beneath one of a hundred lifeless mayors was a blood-smeared yard sign with the symbol of the Blue Fist plastered across it. He followed it down to the handle, which was clutched tightly in the gaunt hands of Mayor Kiff. Kiff wasn't even a Morouni. What the hell did a Sectoid care about Morouni Supremacy? And a young Sectoid at that. By the look of it, the guy couldn't have been any more than fourteen or fifteen years old.

Wad found himself unable to look away from the body as it drained its fluid into the gutter. Mouth cracked open and seeping, neck snapped back at a stupid angle, eyes faded to a lusterless gray. The teal mark of the Aerie Nation endured beneath a crumbled top hat. The dumb bastard had it strapped to his head with a rubber band. Hiding the shame of the past, no doubt. But the way the corpse guarded the yard sign was off-putting.

As Wad had lost himself in thought, Gill emerged from the alley behind Mackey's. He was carrying an armload of vegetables and an electric blender with the cord dragging behind. He waddled through the bodies in the road, nodding with piqued approval at each one, as if they were decoration. Upon reaching the couch in the alley, he dumped his haul at Wad's feet. *"~Nutrients for the attack!~"* he gibbered.

Wad didn't have the emotional energy to react. "You're a bit late, don't you think?"

Gill craned his neck towards the ruins of the office, then down to the street where mayors were scattered. *"~Sunstruck, did you explode your office?~"* He continued before Wad could reply. *"~I must congratulate you on such a drastic decorative decision. Many would not have the courage to take such steps. I have to say, I approve! Much more roomy up there, I would imagine. Were all these men casualties of the renovation?~"* The Slugg poked at the face of a mangled mayor.

"Yep." That's all Wad could say. His Talkman blipped and he was drawn to it by the pure compulsion of grief. It was Carton.

-Blip- **"LOL DID YOU ExploDE?"**

He wanted to reply that all was well and that he hoped Carton's kid died a painful death, but the spite didn't jive. He couldn't find it. He leaned forward and rubbed his eye with a finger, thinking of how to respond. Gustav joined in with a cheerful demeanor. The man didn't seem to care too much that his adopted home just fell apart. He was more excited by the rush of surviving it. "Goddam, that's a hell of a thing," he said, gazing up at the bombed-out structure. He shielded his eyes from the sun with a dumb smile on his face. He was in awe.

Gill offered Gustav a carrot. *"~Manman, take this sustenance. Sunstruck isn't in the mood to eat and I'd hate for it to go to waste.~"*

"Oh, shit, it's a Slugg. Where did you come from?" Gustav said, kneeling down.

"~I come from the light, Manman, as do we all, though not evenly, and some without direction. It is a great pleasure to meet more friends of friends! I urge you to take this carrot. It will sustain you.~"

Gustav belted out a laugh. "Hah, what did he say?"

"He said take the carrot," Wad mumbled through his hand.

Gustav knelt down to the knee-high Slugg. He talked as if he were addressing a toddler. "You see that building there? That building just blew up. It went boom! I was in there and I didn't die. Not a scratch on me. Can you believe it?"

"~It's not advisable to be in such close proximity to this type of renovation. Sunstruck isn't known for his subtly when making changes, though I am so very glad you weren't hurt. In the future, you should be more careful. Perhaps you could coordinate your schedules to avoid harm.~"

"Hah! I'm just gonna pretend I know what you're saying, okay?"

"~Okay!~"

Gustav plopped down in the dirt next to the Slugg. He spread his legs and pointed to his crotch. "You know what did it? I probably would have bit the dust if I wasn't laying on the ground holding my balls," he said, beaming. "That's like, one in a million, ya know? Providence. It pays to protect the balls."

"~Most certainly, the balls must be protected at all costs! Tell me, Manman, do they speak to you as they do to me?~"

Gustav continued. "-and like, my glasses flew off, but when I hit the ground, I could swear they landed right back on my face! This has got to be some divine shit."

"Indeed, your *god* must have a plan for you after all," Meri scoffed, dripping sarcasm.

"Hey, come on. It's not like that," Gustav said. "Ya gotta realize, I just survived a bomb!"

"You all did," Potato grunted, attempting to put a stop to all the talking.

"Yeah, but like, I didn't *have* to survive, right? But I totally did. It's a fuckin' rush. It feels great!"

"Yeah, real nice," Wad said, cradling his forehead.

Gustav turned to Gill. "You know what, screw these sadsacks. You understand, don't you? This wasn't luck, this was fucking magical. You know what magic is, right?"

Gill clapped excitedly. *"~I don't understand the source of your excitement, but I applaud your positive energy!"*

Gustav turned to Wad with a toothy smile. "See, he said he agrees. Just look at him. He's clapping."

"He said you're delusional," Wad said. "He's just happy you're happy about it."

Gustav scolded Wad with his eyes. He leaned over and fell into the couch, bouncing the Legomi aside with his weight. He settled in, throwing his arms over the back. "Delusional or not, you know what I say? I say it's all about perspective, boys. For a million years you could live underground, then suddenly emerge! The sunlight would never be brighter than the first time you saw it. You could be a slave for your whole life, and you'd never be more free than the moment you remove the chains. It ain't about the state of being, it's about the state of change. And I gotta tell ya, I can feel it!"

Wad sat for a second to think. Despite being aggravatingly optimistic, Gustav was making some sense.

"~Manman isn't as stupid as he acts. He is a Manman of many secrets, I believe.~"

"What did he say?" Gustav said, excitedly.

A hundred jabs ran through Wad's head, but he opted to hold back. The Human's words had struck a cord. "He said he agrees with you."

The Old Guard of Zerth

"See," Gustav said with his hands, "When I'm right, I'm right." He leaned into Gill's nub of a face. "Now, let me play for you the song of my people." He fucked with his Talkman. **Doves – Catch the Sun.** With the strumming of the guitar, Gustav leapt from the couch and started dancing in the road. Less coordinated and more of a wild flailing. He twisted through the bodies and debris, singing along to the tune as it echoed through the street. Gill didn't hesitate. He scampered into the street to join the Human in his gyrating. The two went wild, trading steps to the beat as the townsfolk looked on with curiosity.

Wad was confounded by the sight, but couldn't help but see the absurd humor in it. A pink giant and a green midget going in circles among a pile of bodies. Before he knew it, the couch shifted again as Potato plopped down next to him. "So, when do we tell him he's dancing with a god?" Potato said.

Wad was taken off guard by the question. He genuinely didn't know which one Potato was referring to. Before he could finish his thought, the brute popped a beer and offered it up. "Where did you get that?" Wad said.

"Bars' still got beer," Potato replied.

"My oh my," Meri whistled. With a limp in his step, he propped himself up and hobbled down the sidewalk, vanishing around the corner of the Leaf. He returned a moment later with a few more cold ones, then planted the bottles in a pile of rubble to keep them cool. With a tremendous grunt, he heaved his girth into the couch, nearly bouncing the two Legomi off the cushions. The three sipped beers in the shade of the wreckage, watching the Human and Slugg rope around each other in the sun.

As the song came to a close, Wad noticed something else on the wind. It could have been the music, but it sounded more distant. A bright wail from far to the north, heavily muffled and slow to build. It reached a high whine, then descended again. It wasn't music, it was an air raid siren. Wad perked up, thinking the town might be under attack, but he quickly calmed himself. There was no budget for a siren. The town didn't have one... but the Kaggworks did.

Shuffling feet scurried down Saxo Street, causing Wad to rise from the couch. A Morouni darted by, heading south. He paused in the road, shouting something unintelligible, then resumed his escape. Wad and Potato exchanged a blank look. Then more came. Some were black with soot, while others were clearly cradling wounds. Soon, a dozen Morouni were scattered through the street. Wad gave Potato a look of dread before jumping from the couch. He rushed around the corner and into the Leaf, then scampered up the staircase and onto the roof. Potato joined him, hurrying up the steps close behind.

As the two gazed across the skyline, they discovered a great column of smoke rising over the horizon. There were wild curls of exhaust pouring up from just out of view. Up Saxo Street, a steady stream of workers were filtering into the city calling for reinforcements. There were casualties. Hundreds of casualties. The Kaggworks was under attack.

Carbon Dale lay prone among piles of twisted rebar and failing machinery. The ground was drenched in cutting oil where he lay. The heat of the fire had deadened the nerves in his legs, but he had given up long ago. His six-shooter was spent and his stetson showed signs of structural failure. All around were bits of Bill. So many bits of Bill in every direction. Some still kicking awkwardly. Stupid Bill. The silly bastard had sworn off guns, opting to storm the factory with a hundred-man squad of knife-wielding maniacs. Sure as hell did the trick, though. He just hoped Wadley had kept up his side of the bargain.

The Old Guard of Zerth

It was half-passed noon when Dale figured the signal had been sent and he just missed it. No big deal, he got the job done. *They* got the job done. The look on his Father's face when that great machine plowed through the concrete was awe inspiring. Never before had he seen that crazed smirk on his old man. It was something entirely new to him. In that moment, when he thought he could finally introduce himself, his dad remembered his name. Sanders remembered his son, and he called out his name in triumph. A war cry. A battle shout that shook the walls of the Kaggworks. Let's get this job done, Dale.

Dale cracked a broken smile. He couldn't hear the stamping of metal feet any longer. They stopped around the same time that the forge went up. His old man must have done it. What a goddamned party that was. After making it through the machine shop and into the loading bay, they found the forge was still entirely functional. It wasn't on fire in any way. Got to git er' done. That was right around the time they were swarmed with workers. The great stabbing Bill-net did a decent job at running interference, but even then, those shifty bastards were disassembling the van from the outside. Someone with a six-shooter had to put a stop to it.

Dale must have gunned down six of them before running out of bullets. At least five maybe, before getting thrown off the runner and tossed into a barrel of steel shavings. He got cut up pretty good, but cowboys don't care about blood loss. Scars make for good stories, and what a great story this was.

As the flames crept up his jeans, Dale's eyes were filled with stars. Chin raised high and a smile as wide as a boat. He brushed his hand across the ground to try to stand, but the sting in his cuts asked that he just lay low and let it happen. Dale obliged. He pulled in a hot breath of aerisolized grease and gave in. Yes sir, that was a good go-around. Gotta do that again some day.

Mighty Rahiem

Dale didn't wake up in Greely. He didn't wake up at all. The paramedics had a good laugh that night about the Overdose they bagged. Some dumbass hick dropout with a kink for scuba gear. The kid offed himself trying to hook a car battery to his nipples. That's what the report said. Not all that uncommon. They saw it happen all the time.

The Old Guard of Zerth

Chapter 31

Consequences Have Actions

-KRAKOWWW-

Wad was awakened from his booze-slumber by the sound. It was so sudden that he wasn't sure if it was imagined or not. The rumbling carried like an aircraft passing overhead. With a few deliberate blinks, he propped himself up to sit, finding that he had passed out behind the bar again. How long he was out? Nobody knew, especially not him. It was becoming routine. The days had begun to melt together. Onesday was no different than threesday was no different from fivesday. Every day started with a headache and ended with more drinking. That was the goal, at least. Not much else to do after that.

As Wad staggered through the empty bar he made a mental note of his surroundings. Everything was in pieces. Good thing nobody showed up anymore. If they did, he'd have to buy new furniture. There was nowhere to sit at all.

-KRAKOWWW-

Another crack rang out. The sound felt like it was going to split his head. He tried to swat it away with a feeble hand before stumbling over a busted chair. His momentum sent him shuffling right through the hole in the wall. As the light blasted his eyes, the only thought in his addled brain was to categorize the hole somewhere alongside the chairs. Might need a new wall if people started showing up again. Might need a new bar if people started showing up again.

The Old Guard of Zerth

Outside, the heat surround him. He swayed for a moment, bent over, attempting to clear the stars from his eyes. Standing upright sent him right back down to the ground. It had been three weeks since the attack on the Kaggworks. Saxo Street was silent. The smells of the marketplace had gone, allowing the sea breeze to encroach through the alleyways like a vine growing unchecked. A wanderer's footsteps could be heard for blocks in any direction. They echoed off the dobistone walls like an audible shadow. A bitter reminder of how suddenly everything could change. The last time he remembered seeing anyone on the road was a small caravan of farmers heading north. Everything they owned was packed in the back of a couple of pickups. That was days ago.

-KRAKOWWW-

Wad's body shuddered with the sound. He curled up to protect his head from the next inevitable boom. It was then he noticed he was laying in the street. Not that it mattered. He was pretty sure anybody would be okay with it. He looked through the gap between his elbows to see the open bay doors of Herman Wibble's Exploding Erotica. There was a figure moving around in the shadows.

Koenig wiped the grease from his face, then tossed the rag into a cart where he kept the rest of his tools. At first, he didn't notice the wobbling apparition of a man stumbling across the street. Not until the reflection appeared in his toolbox did he recognize the wreck standing in the doorway. He spun around with a smile. "Yo, bigman. Where you been for so long?"

Wad found a table to lean on, then did so out of breath. "Did Herman come back? What's going on?"

"Nahh," Koenig said. "But I had the keys to the place. Figured I might as well do some work for a change, seein' as how there's nothing else to do around here. Ever since the Kaggwerks went down, business has been kinda slow. But hey, that means I got a lotta free time, right? Good a time as any to get to that old backlog."

"Backlog?" Wad said, puzzled. "What kind of jobs are left?"

"Yours," Koenig said. He nabbed a printout from the cart and shoved it into Wad's chest. "The job is done."

Wad flattened out the print then held it up to the beam of light creeping through the bay door.

Writ of Completion

Purchase Order Number: 0001487

1x) Twin 30mm AP-6260 Anti-Aircraft Cannon – 1860

1x) UPP-9 Swivel-mounting bracket – 140

1x) Conversion package for UPP-9 – 45

1x) Leather easy-chair w/ cup holder – 25

4x) Assembly and Installation Charge – 8,400

Total Charge: 10,470

Completed by: Koenig Loomis

Witnessed by (Government Representative): _____

"The gun on the roof? It's done?" Wad said.

"Correct-o-mundo," Koenig said with a smile. "It's all done. The other three guys walked out last week so It looks like that big chunk-o-change is all mine. They didn't think anybody would be coming back to sign over the payment so I took it upon myself to complete the job all by my lonesome. All's I need is a signature from a government witness."

"Ah, I get it," Wad said. "Well, I got news for you. There is no more government. There are no more officials. Wouldn't do you any good if I signed it either way."

Koenig shook his head. "Oh, I don't want you to sign it. I was gonna bring it to the mayor's office. But seein' how you could probably be heading that way instead of me, I thought you could get the signature instead."

Wad scratched the leaves on his head. "But the mayors are-"

-KRAKOWWW-

The sound reverberated through the shop. Koenig laughed. "There it is, right there. That baby purrs, don't she?" He threw some tools into a shoulder-bag, then zipped it shut. He spun around, slinging it over his shoulder. "Well, that's it for me. On to greener pastures. Be a pal and get that signature, will ya? I don't want it to look like I been stealing from the treasury, you know. Even if it is the treasury of a ghost-town. Looks bad on the resume. Makes future employers ask questions."

"Wait, you're leaving?" Wad said.

"Why would I stay? Place is fucked, right? Half the Kagg-force went north. Said they could do better homesteading the hills. They got the expertise. The other half went West."

"West? There's nothing west. We're on a peninsula," Wad said.

"So far West they end up East, right? They went across the ocean. Calibur, on the coast. They got some good contracts out there. I hear there was some big catastrophe that fucked up their competition and now they're putting out jobs like mad. Infrastructure type stuff. Walls and canals, stuff like that. Maybe you should think about doin' that here, right?"

Wad sighed and hung his head. "Yeah, maybe. Anyway, you leaving without your pay?"

"Nah, I already collected," Koenig said. "Paper's just to make it legit-like. The Mayor cashed me out. I just came back for the PO."

Wad burred his face in his hands. "Oh hell. Who's the mayor now?"

"Don't know the guy's name, but he's some Human dude."

Wad rolled his eyes. "Son of a bitch."

The conference room was trashed. Stacks of paper were strewn around like confetti and there was a feint odor of spent gunpowder in the air. Gustav lay on his back across the conference table, thumbing through a small notebook. He was covered in dust. **Waylon Jennings – Waymore's Blues**. The deep base swayed low through the speakers in the ceiling.

Wad stepped over the door in the hallway and entered the room, shaking the purchase order in his fist. "Guz, you've done a lot of silly shit since I've known you, but I never once thought you'd stoop so low as to try to be the mayor."

Gustav turned his head, confused. He looked like he had been ripped from a dream. "Huh, what?"

Wad stomped across the room, waving the paper. "Don't you play dumb with me. Koenig says you payed out ten-thousand bucks from the city treasury. Says you need to sign this to make it legit."

Gustav stayed on his back. He rested the notebook on his chest. "That doesn't ring a bell."

Wad was about to blow his top.

The Old Guard of Zerth

"I payed him. I'm the Mayor!" A small voice said. The chair at the head of the table spun around to reveal Mayor Steve. He was wearing an eye-patch and a red cape. He had a gavel in his hand.

"Yeah, the kid payed him," Gustav said.

"You will address me as the mayor, slave!" Mayor Steve said, pointing his gavel. He jumped from the chair and charged around the room, making a shwooshy noise.

Gustav returned to the notebook. He flipped through it with magnetic interest. "Have you read this? This thing is amazing. It reads like some kind of alien poetry. It's fantastic."

Wad felt like he had been punched in the face by ten kinds of stupid. He didn't know how to respond.

Gustav continued. "It's like, something from a dream. I don't know how anyone could write like this. It's like, not Human at all... or Legomi, or whatever. Or Slugg. Unless this is just how they talk. You can understand them, right? Is this how they talk?"

Wad looked down to the notebook in Gustav's hands. It was Gill's book of strange dictation. "Where did you get that?" he said, defensively. He approached the table, having to dodge Mayor Steve as the kid zoomed by.

"Calm down, dude. The little guy gave it to me. He pushed it right into my hands and made a noise and stuff. He was nodding at me. The little green guy, not the little mayor guy."

Mayor Steve climbed onto the table, holding his gavel to the ceiling. "I'm the master!" he cried in a grumbly voice, before jumping back into the chair. It teetered sideways and crashed to the ground. Steve rolled across the floor and laid still before crying out. "Man down! Man down!" He made machine-gun noises, then jumped to his feet. "I gotta go pee." He ran out of the room, holding his crotch, then tripped over the door in the hallway. "Man down, man down!"

Gustav chuckled. "Cute kid. Makes a good mayor. You can put that PO in the kid's 'in' box. He's actually pretty good at signing stuff."

Wad held his hand to his temple. "Why are you here?"

"Why not?" Gustav said. "City Hall blew up my favorite hangout spot so I might as well hang out at City Hall. Am I right? Meri and Potato are on the roof checking out the new gun. They got a cooler up there if you want a beer."

-KRAKOWWW-

-KRAKOWWW-

Wad recoiled as the room shook violently. Bits of dobistone rained down on his head. He looked up to see deep cracks forming in the ceiling.

"Yeah, probably not the best idea to put a giant canon right on the other side of the ceiling," Gustav said. "Probably not super safe, but whatever. A little Spackle should fix it up, right?"

"I'm surprised you aren't up there with them," Wad said, brushing the dust from his leaves. "Seems like your kind of mess."

"Nah, I got this new reading material," Gustav said, waiving the notebook. "This shit is great! Like, if Zerth ever needed a bible, this would do the trick. It's got prophecy and everything in here. I don't understand a word of it, but it's really fun to read."

"Neither do I," Wad said, moving to the window. From above, the city looked even more desolate. The ubiquitous crimson sashes that once adorned every nook and cranny were either tattered in place or removed altogether. Their absence left too many buildings looking like hollow shells. He wanted to look away, but the view was just too candid. "Where is Gill, anyway?"

The Old Guard of Zerth

Gustav shuffled off the table and joined Wad at the window. "If I knew, I'd tell you. I mean, he probably said where he was going, but it's not like I can understand the little fucker." He wanted to make another joke but his sense of humor fizzled as he watched the Legomi stare into the empty street. He sighed. "It's pretty dead out there, huh?"

Wad didn't say anything.

-KRAKOWWW-

The room rumbled once again, raining dust. Wad hung his head. "I'm starting to see where Amelia was coming from."

"Yeah, what happened to her, anyway?" Gustav said, turning away. "Didn't she used to have an office in here somewhere?"

Wad looked up at Gustav. "You know this is our fault, right?"

Gustav paused. He turned to the window. "Yeah, it is." He fidgeted for a moment before heading for the door.

Wad raised his voice. "Where are you going?"

"I'm going upstairs," Gustav said. "I need to think."

Potato's head was stuck deep inside the vertical tilt axis of a large, twin-barreled cannon. Tools were scattered around his feet, some black with soot and others drenched in oil. He made loud grunting sound, then reached blindly for a wrench that was nowhere near his hand. Meri watched with amusement, not saying a word as he sipped a beer in the shade of a large parasol. His feet were kicked up on a cooler dripping with sweat. The roof access door swung open and Gustav climbed out, followed closely by Wad, who had a much easier time getting through. "Yo, Meri," Gustav shouted. "You're the literary type. Tell me what you think about-" he paused seeing Potato waist-deep in the machine. "What the hell? You break it already?"

446

Potato wriggled out of the gears, wiping his hands clean. His vest was dotted with blobs of grease. "It's broke."

"It's broke," Meri echoed with a grin. He took a deep swig of his beer.

"Broke already? What did you do to it?" Wad said, shaking his head. He joined Potato at the side of the cannon, taking a quick second to survey the mechanics of the thing.

"The up and down is stuck?" Potato said, tossing a pair of pliers into the pile of tools. "It don't go up and down anymore. Just stays right there."

Wad followed a trail of oil dripping down the side of a piston. The problem was obvious, but the thought of getting into it right that second just made him eager to move on from the subject. He captured Potato's eye and held on for a second, hoping it would be enough to change the subject gracefully. "You know where Gill went?"

"Ya, he went for supplies. Said he'd be back in an hour," Potato said, wiping his hands on his pants. His focus darted to the ground, then around the roof. "Son of a bitch," he said to himself before hurrying to Meri's footrest for a drink. He motioned and Meri obliged.

"That was about an hour ago, I suspect," Meri said, attempting badly to lift the lid of the cooler with his bare foot.

"Good," Gustav said, following Potato's lead. He nabbed a cool beer, then another for Wad. "Once we're all here, I gotta ask the guy some questions. Kinda need an interpreter, if you know what I mean." He chucked the beer to Wad who intentionally let it smash against the ground next to him. Wad held his temple in frustration. Gustav shrugged. "What the hell, man? You gone sober or something?"

The Old Guard of Zerth

Wad approached the cooler with his face in his hand. "Just *hand* me a beer, will you?"

"Touchy, touchy," Gustav said, waging his finger. "Somebody woke up on the wrong side of the wreckage." He popped another beer and handed it off, then sat down in the shade of the parasol. He twisted his beer into the gravel of the rooftop to keep it steady, then went for the notebook. "Anybody else get a chance to read this thing?" he asked.

"Indeed," Meri said with a grumble. "Tripe. Obscure tripe. I've seen that kind of nonsense before. Let me tell you, it's nothing to fawn over. In fact, it should be avoided entirely."

"What are you talking about?" Wad said, joining the group in the shade. "That's Gill's book, he wrote it. He's not a wacko zealot or anything. He's just writing down what he hears in his head."

Meri harrumphed. "My man, if I were to brain you a half-dozen times, then ask for a treaties on general living, I quite suspect your advice would be a bit off."

Gustav pushed in with a finger. "Yeah – *But* – This shit ain't Deuteronomy. This actually makes sense. Listen to this. '*Those among you who wish to attain rest through deviation are drunk on account of blindness.*' That's badass, man. That's like, Dio lyrics or something."

Meri blinked in shock. "At what point did I suddenly find myself surrounded by idiots?"

"We've been here from the start, buddy. Taken you long enough to figure it out," Gustav laughed. He guzzled his beer like lunatic, keeping eye-contact with the Morouni the whole time.

Potato lumbered into the conversation. "I read it," he said flatly. "I read it a long time ago. Gill wrote that book about us.

We're all in there." He pointed at Gustav. "Guz, you're the Man of the West. You're in there. Read it."

Meri grumbled.

Gustav was enthralled. He flipped through the pages of the notebook, then paused. He adjusted his glasses as his eyes scanned the text. "Found it. *'To those in Chaos and Disorder, the Men of the West. They will find peace through order and repetition. Bring to them a message of quiet solitude, for they dwell in fear of collapse.'* Dude, that's totally me. I dwell in fear of collapse all the time!"

"I'm leaving," Meri grunted, attempting to stand.

Potato jumped it, nabbing Meri by the arm. "Just hold on. Think about it. Men of the West. Where does Gustav spawn in?"

Meri thought for a moment. "Agora," he said. "The western spawn point."

Potato nodded. "Okay, now read the one about the men of the South."

Gustav thumbed down to the text. *"To those in doubt and guilt, the Men of the South. They will find peace through confrontation. Bring to them a message of courage and strength, for they dwell in weakness and cowardice."*

"Who does that sound like?" Potato said, gesturing with his hands.

"Shit, sounds like Dale," Wad said. Meri gave him a skeptical eye.

"And where does Dale spawn in?" Potato said.

"Bonzo Beach," Wad said, starting to get excited. "That's the southern spawn."

"This is ludicrous," Meri said, throwing up his hands. "To think, associates of mine could be so easily mystified by nothing more than flowery text. The literature is quite obviously an interpretation of current events. The Slugg gets around, don't you see? He forges poetry from his experiences with the newly-spawned Humans. I promise you, there is nothing hidden in those words."

Potato stomped over to Gustav, nabbing the notebook from his hand. He turned to Meri, waving it in his face. "Gill wrote this before he even met a Human. I was there, I saw it happen."

A jabbering voice came from the far end of the roof. "*~Samuel is correct. The words were dictated before the great fall of Aerie. They were of the first to be recorded.~*"

"Oh shit," Gustav said, perking up. "There's the little guy."

Gill waved from the doorway. At his feet was a bucket filled with some kind of liquid. He gracefully slid his arm through the wire handle and hobbled over to the crew, careful not to splash the contents.

"You got supplies?" Potato said.

Gill sat the bucket down gingerly, then stepped back, motioning to his haul. "*~Supplies for everyone.~*"

"What's he saying?" Gustav said.

Potato stood over the bucket and peered inside. He reached in, pulling out a dripping hammer. "It's a hammer in a bucket o' sea-water."

Meri let out a chuckle. "Hah, this is your mystical scribe, most certainly." He crossed his arms in defiance.

"I actually need this," Potato said. He lifted the pail over to the cannon where he splashed a handful of water across a hydraulic line. Bubbled oil spit from a split in the rubber. He smacked it around with the hammer until the leak subsided. "Fixed it," he announced.

"That's not how you fix things," Wad shouted.

Gustav shuffled closer to the Slugg. He waved, as if he were confronting a child. "Hey there, buddy. I know I can't understand you, but Meri can. He can translate for you. I got a whole lot of questions about your book."

Gill waved back cheerfully, then clasped his hands together. *"~I will do my best to assist in interpreting. Just know that these are not my words. This is dictation.~"*

Gustav turned to Meri, who was caught off guard. "Surely, you don't expect me to indulge your silly fantasies, do you?"

Gustav paused with a finger. He gave Meri a stupid look.

"For the last time, I did *not* address you as Shirley. Will you kindly purge that nonsense from your vapid skull. You do yourself no favors, man." The Morouni stood to leave, but was halted by Gill's innocent black dots staring at him. He fumbled around for a moment before taking his seat again. "Fine, but don't expect me to tumble blindly into your so-called 'holy text'. I have far too much respect for myself to be taken as a fool."

"~Not holy, just helpful.~"

"What did he say?" Gustav said, excitedly.

Meri let out a sigh, then nodded. "My mistake. I apologize. Gustav, my man. Ask away. I am standing by to interpret."

Gustav turned to Gill with a toothy grin. "Wow, you've got a way with words. I've never seen him turn on a dime like that!"

"Gustav!" Meri hollered. "My patience with is hair-thin."

The Old Guard of Zerth

Gustav threw his hands up. "Fine, fine. Okay!" He scooted closer to the slug, opening the notebook. "It says here that a Savior is coming to put an end to all the bullshit. I'm just really wanting to know what you mean by that. Does Zerth really need a savior? What are we being saved from?"

"Fah, nonse-" Meri started, but Gustav shushed him with a look. He put his hands up. "Again, my apologies. Please continue."

Gill made a chirping noise that sounded like laughter. *"~Manman, you must understand that these texts are not my words. They are the words of the light and not to be taken as rigid as concrete fact. It is for an interpretation either now, the past, or far into the future. I cannot interpret that in the way you desire.~"*

Gustav looked to Meri.

"That's quite sensible, I must say," Meri said, rubbing his chin.

"What did he say?" Gustav said.

"He called you Manman," Potato laughed.

"Pff, whatever," Wad chimed in. "He called *you* Samuel."

"Wait, he gets to call him Sam, too?" Gustav said, getting upset. "That's not fair."

Potato stomped in. "I told you, he knew be from before. He gets to call me whatever he wants." He plopped down in the circle, nabbing the book. "Besides, I'm in here somewhere." He flipped the pages around before poking one with a meaty finger. "Look, right there. That's me, right? I'm the Stranger."

Gustav stole the notebook back, then adjusted his glasses. "It says here - '*The Stranger: He comes to you in desperation. He asks only for your company and nothing more. Be kind to the stranger and he will reward you with kindness of his own, but beware his temper, for he is a callous judge. He may lash out because he has lost everything.'* Sounds like Potato to me, right?"

Meri piped in. "My man, if the work is up to interpretation, I'd say that descriptor fits another much more accurately."

"Hold on, let me guess," Wad said, sipping his beer. "You think it's talking about *you*."

"Not me," Meri scoffed. "I wouldn't be so bold. What I'd say is that it refers to my people. The Morouni people as a whole."

"Bull shit," Potato said, condescendingly. "It clearly says *'The Stranger'*. That's me. That's what Potato means in Human language."

"Phah, what?" Gustav tumbled over, laughing.

"That's what it means, right?" Potato said, checking the eyes staring at him."

Gustav propped himself off the gravel. "Sure, buddy. That's absolutely what it means. Please, go on believing that. It totally doesn't mean a brown chunk of starch that we turn into french fries. I am begging you to keep believing that."

"Whatever," Potato said, waiving his hand. "I met other Humans before you and they told me that's what it meant.

Wad scratched his leaves. "You know, I think I remember you telling me that a long time ago." He turned to Gustav for confirmation, but all the Human could do was nod and hold back laughter.

Gill gibbered, clapping his hands. *"~It is just as the light told me. The words in my book offer many interpretations. Just as the Slugg will be heard with different ears, their words have many meanings.~"*

"Holy shit," Gustav said. "I understood him that time." He started poking at his Talkman.

"My ass," Potato spat. "What do you think he said?"

"Dude," Gustav looked up, "He clearly said **Pish, by the Brian Jonestown Massacre**. Greenboi's got kickass taste in music. That's amazing!"

From the street below, the twang of the guitar punched through the speakers. Gill was shaken. The sound of pure love flowed through his body. It was a warbled beat and vibrations he didn't understand. He stared wide-eyed at everything as the tone of it all thumped in his chest, pumping it hard like a righteous fist. It was anger and fire, but so measured and controlled. A flame, cooled to a raw skin, housing molten aggression within. It spit in the face of all things unworthy. It cared nothing for fear. It shunned fear – only love. It was an unstoppable world beyond his own and his willpower was trampled under its might. He couldn't even form his own thoughts. They were dictated to him by a flying guitar and throbbing kick.

"I think we killed him," Wad said, as he watched the Slugg writhe around on the ground.

Gill swung up and wrapped his hands around his knees, swaying to the tune. He waved at his comrades. The little guy was in rapture.

As the music petered out, Gustav was johnny-on-the-spot, keeping the next song from playing. He was more interested in watching the little lizard thing come down from his high.

Nearly a minute passed before Gill spoke. He craned his head away from the sky and looked around. Everyone was staring at him and that made him laugh. Manman had given him such a glorious gift. Something to be treasured, for sure.

Mighty Rahiem

His little Slugg heart couldn't bare the thought of letting the moment pass without repaying Manman for his kindness, but nothing came to mind. In that instant of nearly tangible rapture, he felt a voice in his chest. The words came across softly, but so clear that he could not mistake them for anything else. He turned to Potato. "*~Samuel, take my hand. You have a message for the Manman that he must hear.~*"

Potato recoiled, nervously. The Slugg was reaching for him. Reluctantly, he took the rubbery fingers in his palm. With a sudden shock, he was reliving a memory of a time long gone. It was a vision he experienced so long ago that it had been ground into obscurity, but a light in his mind reshaped it into a clear vision.

"*~Go on, Samuel. Tell the Manman what you have seen. Your thoughts are my gift to him.~*"

"I see-" Potato staggered a bit before continuing. "-greenery. I hear music. I see – I see -" He could no longer speak. The vision was too clear. It was a city in the sky. It moved through the clouds like an arrowhead speeding toward its target. It was then that Potato realized the vision he had experienced so many years prior was somehow the same moment he was experiencing now. Just as it happened then, something else emerged. A golden crown rose from the sand. It blazed with the light of all the suns at once, leaving him unable to maintain his breath. He shuttered violently before being ripped from the images. The next thing he knew, he was lying on his side.

"Holy shit," Gustav cried. "Don't let the Slugg touch you. He's got fuckin' demon powers." The Human laughed while helping Potato to his feet.

Potato's head was swirling. He felt like he had been socked in the face by a truck. As Gustav was pulling away, Potato snatched his wrist. "Spearhead," he said, out of breath. "Spearhead – a city in the sky."

The Old Guard of Zerth

Meri pushed in, grabbing Potato by the shoulder. "Where did you hear that name?"

Potato blinked, clearing the stars from his eyes. "I didn't. I saw it. It's in my head."

Meri pulled away with a dark look in his eyes. He turned to Gill with his mouth agape. "What have you done to him?"

"~A gift. It's a gift for the manman who feels so lost! Manman will know what to do!~"

Meri turned to Gustav to relay the message, but there was no need. Gustav had removed himself from the circle and was staring out over the ledge of the roof. Meri stood to join him. "My man, the Slugg says-"

"Hold on," Gustav said, pausing Meri with a hand. "I have an idea." He turned around with a striking look in his eyes. "We killed Southtown's economy. I feel pretty shitty about that, it's true. But you know what? I've got a few hundred-trillion bucks burning a hole in my wallet." He took a final swig of his beer, then casually dropped it from the roof. He turned and started towards the door.

"Where are you going?" Wad said.

"Got someone to talk to," Gustav said. "I just hope he's still alive."

Chapter 32

All the Money in the World

Those among you who wish to attain rest through deviation are drunk on account of blindness.

Gustav kicked rocks up Saxo Street. The weight of the words hung heavily in his chest as he passed by the shambles of everything he had broken. Families displaced and dreams dashed. Lives upset and spun on end, and for what? Vengeance? Righteous reprisal? It was a feeling that crept in, even in the best of times, but was all too often quashed by the promise of the next high, the next rush of adrenaline to wipe away all introspection. He never wanted those quiet moments, but now, as he shuffled up the dead-end avenue, there was nothing but silence.

Still, an indignant pride lingered. Like he could push it all away in the name of upholding some backwards standard that had allowed him to maintain the roller coaster. The thought faded as he passed by the empty doorway of a familiar location. The Reaver Dove. It was there that he started his journey into godhood so many years ago. The place where he killed a man and inherited divinity. He so badly wanted to regale the story, but there was no one left to share in the fun. They had all run screaming, as they should.

Those among you who wish to attain rest through deviation are drunk on account of blindness.

Was rest the point? Was that the reason for this place? He didn't know. In truth, he had never really sat down to think about why he was brought to Zerth in the first place. Nobody else did, why should he? But those words struck a nerve, and he was watching himself pulled down by them. Rest through deviation? He certainly was a deviant, no question there. He reveled in it. But look where that got him... more appropriately, look where that got everyone else. The more he thought about it, the more it hurt. He was trapped in a world that rewarded folly, a world without consequence... at least without consequence for him. Everyone else was doomed to suffer the recoil of his actions. Like a karmic shield to ward off all repercussions, only the repercussions had to land somewhere nearby.

Gustav was drawn back to the hours of drunken ramblings with Hesh upon meeting for the first time. He was immediately taken by the Sectoid, with his bite-sized esoteric quips and treaties on self-harmony. That was a long time ago. They sat in the corner of the Leaf over a bottle of scotch, trading words of half-wisdom and enduring each other's reply. 'Laws of the Universe' was Hesh's wisdom. He never left it alone. Gustav laughed it off at the time, but was finding it difficult to do so now.

The suns found their way into Gustav's eyes and he realized he had made it to the edge of town. Behind him, the shadows of a city on life support. Ahead, the open wilderness. Just over the hill was the sputtering rubble of the Kaggworks. He spent a moment shading his eyes for a better look. Not once did he ever think of the consequences. It was all gung-ho and fist-pounding. Bring it down, the bastards. He never realized how vital it was to the town he called home. Not much of a town anymore.

The fence had been pushed over and trampled into the dirt. A thousand feet must have passed over it, all in a panic, fleeing the chaos he himself helped orchestrate. There was a brief flash of jealousy. He didn't even get to take part, but the thought was swiftly quashed. If Southtown could speak, it would be wheezing curses in his direction. Nothing to be proud of. Oddly, for once he couldn't be directly blamed. His fingerprints were nowhere near the destruction, but that didn't change the facts he knew to be true. He didn't want to brush them off this time. Besides, he had a plan to make it all right again.

The welcome shade of the factory was undone by the tinge of burnt copper. It was everywhere, hovering around charred machinery and dumped crates of metal shavings. Gustav had to wipe his glasses at regular intervals to combat the gathering grease in the air. As he moved further into the darkness, he discovered large caliber bullet holes trailing up the walls and piercing the roof. The suns shone through, illuminating bits of oil stained concrete in dusky rays of light.

The strangest notion came through Gustav's mind as he passed through the maze of turret punches and vertical lathes. None of the machines had guards. It was like the 70s in there. As Gustav removed his glasses for another rubdown, contemplating the possibility of Zerthian worker's unions, a feint shuffle came through. Just an echo, but not far off. He waited for another to judge the direction of the source, and it came again. He wasn't alone.

Following a lose recollection of where the sound might have come from, Gustav entered into a carpeted hallway off to the rear of the factory. Lights out, but seemingly untouched by the havoc. It seemed to be a reception area for clients to meet with sales reps. Foamcore prints of high end products and future endeavors were proudly displayed in dimmed cubicle walls. Swivel chairs and cluttered desks brought the familiar feeling of office life to Gustav's mind. So Human a concept it was, and so strange to see the same mentality employed by self-avowed Morouni Supremacists. The shuffling came again.

The Old Guard of Zerth

Up ahead, sunlight flooded into a large foyer with floor-to-ceiling glass windows. Regal display cases flanked the doorway with the hottest new advances in Morouni tech, and there the carpet ended, giving way to smooth, redrock tile. In the center of the room was a great round standing desk with holoscreen at the ready. A stunning first impression, for sure.

"Are you here to finish me?" a voice said, causing Gustav to jump. It was coming from his crotch.

Down beneath the standing desk, a figure was huddled in the shadow. The glean of two beady eyes, followed by a glint off barbed whiskers. It was Ammison Kagg, ragged and defeated, cowering in the darkness.

Gustav stepped back and knelt down to meet the man eye to eye. Though misty-eyed and wounded, Kagg's suit was remarkably pressed. It had more life than its wearer. The man's haircut was firmly dapper as well. Completely unscathed and never unprofessional. Gustav couldn't help but be impressed. As their eyes met, Kagg perked up. "You're not him. Who are you?"

The thought occurred to Gustav that he could say anything. The first thing to come to mind was *'I'm your worst nightmare'*, which would have been hilarious, or maybe *'I'm Batman'*, which would be equally hysterical. In between thoughts, he found he wasn't in the mood. Both felt flat in the face of the man who's life was in ruins, and it was all his fault. Not that there was any way to prove it, or that Kagg even knew who he was. He could say anything and it would be believed. But no, it just wasn't right. Where would the karma go for that? Who would be the collateral damage for his cosmic bullshit this time? Gustav didn't have the luxury of working it out then and there, so he did the only thing that came naturally. He reached out his hand and spoke up. "We've got to talk."

Mighty Rahiem

A fuzzy palm wrapped around Gustav's fingers. It was like the hand of a child's. For a moment, Gustav felt a bit embarrassed for his own size. He realized how terrified the old man must feel in his presence. Something five times his size reaching out for him, but the man came willingly, out from under the desk and into the light. Kagg stood for a moment, never taking his eyes off the Human's. He patted himself down, removing the wrinkles of his suit with a stiff upper lip, forcing down all signs of loss. "This is highly unprofessional," he said, before rushing to the light switch and flicking it in vain.

Gustav stopped the man and turned him around. "You have no idea who I am, do you?" Gustav said.

Kagg twisted. "Of course I know who you are. You're with that Meri punk, aren't you?"

Gustav couldn't joke. "Yes I am," he replied.

The Morouni shuffled around a bit, looking at his shoes. His eyes narrowed. "I'm sure this is all just dandy to you," he said. "You come to laugh at a man on his knees? Rub it in my face?"

Gustav was sensing some poorly placed righteousness in Kagg's voice, and couldn't help but intervene. "Maybe I am," Gustav said.

Kagg turned away, rubbing the back of his neck with a sweaty palm. He didn't have much to say.

"Yeah," Gustav continued, "maybe I am. You shot my brother. What do you expect?"

Kagg looked to his feet. "It was not my intention to draw blood. Never my intention to harm another. If I had known, I would have tried to put a stop to it, but it was the will of the people that damaged your friend. I cannot stand in the way of that."

The Old Guard of Zerth

Gustav rose up to his feet. "You think this is the will of the people? You think this is your pride? I'll tell you what it is. Every one of your die-hard foot soldiers are nothing more than common, dirty MERC's. Your son played you. Nobody cares about your message. Nobody wants the great Morouni spirit to rise up and conquer the land. Nobody gives a single shit about it. Your crusade is a sham. Your son played on your fears for his own gain."

Kagg lowered his head. He dropped his shoulders and sat down on the floor. "I know," he said with a small voice.

"You what?" Gustav spit.

"I know," Kagg shuddered. "I know nobody cares. Nobody cares about anything anymore."

"So why did you let it happen?" Gustav said.

"You don't know what it's like," Kagg said, his voice quivering. "To have everything taken from you. Your whole way of life ripped away. Everything you've ever known turns out to be a lie, and you're expected to play along as if you knew from the start. I was sixty-two years old when the great arrival happened. I had lived a full life by then, no reason to think different at all. Then we come here and everything changes. People change. So many of us elders are still around. What are we expected to do, just die off? Die off without a sound? Have we nothing left to offer?

There's so much chaos and violence, and no respect. Nobody believes in anything. I remembered the days before the great arrival. Back when we all believed in something. I found myself in a position to make a change, so I thought I could make it happen again. I didn't care if it was a lie. It worked. We loved each other and we loved morality and goodness. Isn't that true enough?"

Mighty Rahiem

Gustav didn't have to think before his words came out. "It doesn't have to be a lie," he said. "It can't be a lie. You shouldn't have to cheat people into being better. You just end up with hollow people with hollow morality, with nothing but empty laws in their heads. I've seen it all my life. If you want the people to change, you need to let them find themselves. Let them discover it on their own."

Kagg raised scowled. "In this place? I won't happen."

"I don't believe that," Gustav said. He found himself holding back a smile at an incredibly inappropriate time, but something forbade him from keeping it hidden. "I'm sorry," Gustav said, beaming. "I'm sorry I blew up your factory. I'm sorry I killed the town and I'm sorry I ruined your shitty plan. Now you're just gonna have to live like the rest of us. Confused and carefree."

Kagg could swear the Human was loosing his mind in front of him. He wondered if he should turn and run, but Gustav started talking again.

"But I came here for a reason. I have an Idea. It's a good idea. What if I told you I could bring your factory back. What if we could bring the whole town back? Bring it all back and your shit-brained son even gets his cut."

Kagg took a slow step back, beginning to fear for his life.

"What if we could build a new town, but this one will fly! It'll be a flying town!"

Kagg took another step back. "How do you know about that?" he said in a quiet tone.

Gustav gave a sly wink. "Spearhead."

"You've lost your marbles," Kagg said. "I can see you've been cavorting with my dimwitted son. Did he tell you about the polerite, too? Did he tell you how he plans on extracting it?

The Old Guard of Zerth

The cost would be astronomical, not to mention the rest of the materials. Labor, too. It would take thousands of hands and a decade of work to-"

"How much?" Gustav interrupted with a smile.

Kagg shuffled around with a load of foul words stored in his cheeks. He wanted to kick sand in the man's face for daring to mock him. "It would be astronomical. The GDP of an entire region!"

Gustav knelt down to eye-level. "How – Much?"

Kagg scoffed. He turned his back and shuffled across the stone floor to a doorway on the east side of the room, his bare feet squeaking with every step. He pushed through the door with his elbow and vanished inside. A moment later, his raspy voice called out. "Do you want to see it or not?"

Gustav shrugged and followed the man into the office. Upon entering, he found a large conference table ringed with leather chairs. As in the foyer, the entire south wall lit up the room with floor-to-ceiling glass. Scattered across the table were dozens upon dozens of scattered prints and purchase orders. Kagg stood atop the table holding a little black cane which he used to poke at the papers. He began to shout. "This is the cost of the project. Seventy-five million pounds of raw steel, thirty-five million pounds of iron. Five million pounds of plasteel. Do you know where plasteel comes from? And that's not the least of it. There's the matter of the polerite. Fifteen-hundred tons of polerite! Do you have any idea how much polerite that is?"

Gustav rubbed his chin while doing his best to ignore the rant. He scanned the papers, recognizing what looked to be a Zerthly equivalent to his old life at LINTECH. There were elevation plans, electrical layouts, floor plans, even a crude mockup for what might be close to HVAC. All of it made sense. But if he were back at LINTECH, it would be his job to confirm it all. Underwriting, what a bore. But for some reason, a return to the hellish grind seemed so much more inviting when it involved a flying city. He turned to Kagg, nodding his head. "This makes sense. We can do this."

Kagg was starting to lose his cool. "Makes sense, does it? Well here's something else that makes sense. Handing over millions in capitol to what amounts to a band of pirates in the sand. MERC's! That's where the polerite comes from. Can you imagine the long-term ramifications of supplying those beasts with that much money?"

Gustav drew his sleeve upward without a hint of regret, proudly displaying the mark of the wanderer inked across his skin.

Kagg retracted. "So, you're one of them, are you? That answers every one of my questions."

"Wrong," Gustav said. "I'm no MERC, I'm just me. This ink means I am who I am and that's all there is. Whacha' see is whacha' get, and I'm not going anywhere fast. But you know what? I know who I am and I know what I'm capable of." He nabbed a cost-analysis sheet of the table and waved it in Kagg's face. "Now, these numbers don't add up. What's the cost? The *final* cost?"

Kagg spit. "That number only covers materials. Nothing else has been calculated. Why would we bother when no organization could ever possibly afford it? You have to think. Two-thousand workers for ten years. Ten-years. One entire decade of feeding, housing and entertaining. Two-thousand workers and their families!"

"Families that will come back to Southtown," Gustav said, getting agitated. "And none of this Morouni-only bullshit. You hire anyone that can work, you got that? Now stop tap-dancing around the goddamned question and tell me. What's the bottom line?"

"Seventeen and a half billion!" Kagg cried, slamming his fist on the table.

"Double it, motherfucker!" Gustav cried.

Kagg's words stumbled. "What do you mean, double it?"

"Pay em double, you son of a bitch," Gustav yelled, grabbing the Morouni by the shoulder. Years of pent-up white-collar rage bubbled over as he pinned the old man to the table. He jabbed his finger into Kagg's toothy muzzle. "You pay em double, and I swear to god I'll be watching those numbers. I'll be watching every single one, and if I even suspect your employees aren't receiving their fair compensation-"

"Thir-thirty five billion?" Kagg stammered.

"Sold!" Gustav barked. He let Kagg go, then began to strut around the room. "Thirty-five billion it is. So, I have to ask, do you accept checks?" He doubled over, laughing at himself.

"You're mad," Kagg said with disgust. He quietly reached for his cane.

"As a hatter, my friend, I will not lie. But you've just made the deal of a lifetime. Where do I sign? Where's the paper with the big blank spot? Where's the secretary with the champagne? I thought this was a business you were running. Was I wrong?"

"You're serious, aren't you. How can that be?" Kagg said. No one has that kind of capitol.

Gustav sat his ass down on the table and slid to Kagg's side. "Au contraire mon frère." He flipped out his cred-card. "I got all the money in the world."

Mighty Rahiem

THE OLD GUARD OF Zerth

Mighty Rahiem

ABOOT THE AUTHOR

Mighty Rahiem is a huge jerk. Don't let him sleep on your couch or you'll never get rid of him. He's always naked and he smells. He'll steal all your pants and throw them in the garbage, then he'll steal your garbage. He never sleeps.

Other Books
by
Mighty Rahiem

The Zerth Series:

Zerth

The book in your hands right now

Forthcoming Zerth Novel with an uninspired title (coming soon)

Zerth Unwinding:

Zen and the Art of Magenite Suspension

Rubin Walter: Danger to the Max

www.ingramcontent.com/pod-product-compliance
Lightning Source LLC
Chambersburg PA
CBHW030748030726
47497CB00001B/187